TURNING TOWARD EDEN

$\wp$

"This is storytelling at its most atmospheric—brimming
with quirky, well-drawn characters, razor-sharp prose,
and the kind of setting you can almost smell. The writing
is lyrical, grounded, and often laugh-out-loud funny—
even in the midst of deeply poignant moments. With a
cast of endearing misfits and a tone reminiscent of
Southern Gothic charm, this story lures you in from
the very first line and doesn't let go."

—ZENA DELL LOWE
Screenwriter, Story Coach, and
Founder of The Storyteller's Mission

$\wp$

CATE TOURYAN

TURNING TOWARD EDEN

A NOVEL

2025 IAN BOOK OF THE YEAR
FOR CROSS-GENRE FICTION

For Daniel
and our father who loves him

ONE

SHE STOOD AT the far end of the pier, sun-spangled skirts billowing and scarves whipping, raised her arms above the sea—and vanished.

Just as the rumors said.

"Lord a'mighty!" Battling a churn of waves and the stink of rotted kelp, I tightened my grip on Hollis and stared, mouth like a codfish. "Lordy, oh Lord!"

"Will you hurry up, Eden?" Hollis reeled beneath the surge. "How many *oh Lords* you gonna say? Get to the prayer already."

The usual fisherfolk, most slouched against the slatted railing, paid the spectral girl no mind, eyes cocked on slack lines or shuttered in sleep. But I'd seen her, the glint of dawn on her bangles, the summer shimmer of raven hair.

And then I didn't.

Hollis, being partially dunked when she took flight, missed it all.

"The prayer!" He sputtered, but he didn't wait, plunging backward of his own accord and nearly slipping from my grasp. Havin' made it to seventeen on the strength of infant christening, Hollis no more wanted to be baptized than did a perfect heathen, indulging me only out of pity an' resignation. Took to mid-July before he finally hollered uncle.

"You missed it!" I bellowed, a breaker rocking us both.

My rolled-up jeans sagged with salt water as I squinted across the swells, my sinner's prayer having taken flight along with Raven. I was in danger of losing my pants *and* Hollis, but the rapid retreat of frothy waves meant he didn't have far to fall.

Without lettin' go his neck, I scanned the narrow wooden pier, the far ocean, the crimson horizon. Fog clung to the eastern bluffs, hugged the coastline. I could just make out a sailboat mast, the lazy bob of buoys. The bicker of two fishermen caught my ear as they ambled down the weathered deck, their buckets slapping against tattered overalls. A few others stared out to sea, reeled in empty lines, recast.

But I saw no trace of the teenage wraith who, two minutes before, had hovered at the outmost edge, leaning into the wind like the witch on the *Cutty Shark*, or *Cutty Snark*, whatever the clipper ship's name—like a figurehead anyhow. A trick of the sun? The angle of the pier? Or had she done it? Had she jumped? Mercy's sake, I hoped not. She'd been bullied enough, that was a fact. Or were the rumors true? Had she turned into—

"Lord a'mighty!" It bore repeating and allowed Hollis a gulp of air before a second dunk.

Taking the Lord's name in vain was a serious offense, I knew, and now that I meant to be a missionary to the Aucas in Ecuador, I believed it too. Mama used to threaten my mouth with soap when I so much as whispered "geez," saying to my alarmed face, "Comes from the Son of God's name, just like gee, Jehoshaphat, and jiminy." And so did—as I learned later through further threats of scented lather—*golly* and *gosh* come from God and *darn* and *dang* from damnation.

That was during our Texas heyday, before my father shanghaied us to the Golden State—all but Dex, that is—and then ditched us. The start of a new life, he'd said—or a return to his old one, as it turned out—back to his stompin' grounds and the home of Tricky Dick, our newly elected United States president. Didn't take but six months on the sun-kissed coast till my father packed up, making good on his promise—*Dex comes, I go.*

Even though Mama no longer bothered with my mouth, no longer bothered with me, now that Dex had come home from the institution, the nights filled with screams and sobs and lullabies, I'd sworn off swearing. Only in the direst circumstances did I utter irreverence, and then only with the word *condemnation*, the second syllable said with gusto and a slight vowel shift—a word straight from the Good Book. These outbursts often met with a peculiar look, but never a mouth-washin'. On occasion, a heartfelt imploration to the Almighty might likewise cross my lips. Anyway, Reverend Travers had cleansed my soul more than any bar of soap could do.

If Hollis hadn't been flailing under my grasp, he'd have cussed too—at me for nearly drowning him. Most like, he *was* cussing, right there under the waves, if the frenzied eruption of bubbles was any indication. Rev. Travers hadn't gotten to him yet, but I was working on it.

He righted himself. "You done yet?"

"For Pete's sake, you can't baptize yourself. Now I gotta do it again—proper this time."

"When you said you'd get me through the pearly gates, I didn't think you meant today."

"Just lemme pray. Oh, Lord," I began, a rogue wave near toppling me, "I baptize this sinner, Hollis Sweet, who, pricked mightily in conscience, pitifully invokes your divine mercy and grace and who does, on pain of death, swear to reform his wicked ways—you do, don'tcha?" I had to assume a burbled assent. "Cleanse him of his many grievous sins and lead him not into temptation." I dunked him a final time.

"Holy smokes, Scoot. That sure beats sprinkling." He shook free of my grip, salt water streaming from his matted hair, rubbed his nose ferociously, and grinned. "Those alpacas don't know what they've got comin'."

Hollis Sweet never got mad, even when he swore. That infuriated me to no end, but I was too distracted to chide him or, for that matter, to inform him that alpacas were Armenian sheep, not an Ecuadorean tribe.

"It's true!" I squinted at the pier.

"Yep, you told me already. Infant baptism by sprinkling can't wash away sins. They've got to be drowned." He plodded through the water toward shore, shaking his head and poking a finger in his ear.

Yanking up my pants, I splashed noisily after him. A white bird circled above us, its cry brassy. "Hollis, look! A goose!"

"Well, bless my drenched soul! Must be a sign from heaven." He tossed a windblown Snickers wrapper into the trash. "And it's an egret."

Even when he tried to be sarcastic, Hollis beamed sweet as a saint on a cathedral window—fittin', considering his last name and his Roman Catholic roots. As good-natured as he was, I wondered if he really had all that many sins to drown.

"Well, I'll be tar-nated!"

"You were expecting a dove?"

I kicked sand over his foot. "S'pose not all of it's true, then."

"You mean I almost died for nothing? Without salvation?"

"It's *her* I'm talking 'bout, Hollis. We reckoned she turned into a raven. But maybe she can take on any shape, even a goose."

"Snowy egret."

I stared with wonder and new appreciation as the white bird flapped toward a clanging buoy. "Well, bird or human, she's behind the mayhem. I bet those rumors are true."

"Aren't rumors a sin?"

"Sure they are, 'less they're true."

We reached our beach towels and set about mopping ourselves dry, Hollis wringing water from his cutoffs. Tucking his towel 'round his waist, he grabbed his fishing rod and empty bait bucket. "Listen here, Eden. I gave up the best fishing of the day for my salvation. It'd better all be true. Besides, there's rumors about you too."

"What rumors?" My breath caught.

"Can't say what I don't hear." With that, he let loose a funky whistle sounding suspiciously like "I Heard It Through the Grapevine." Aggravatin' me with Marvin Gaye, he headed across the beach, his low-top Chucks sloshing. I scrambled after him, my own shoes tracking his, my jacket flapping with wings of its own.

Not much for hearing folks talk, Hollis wasn't much for talking 'bout folks either, so I kept my musings to myself, swatting at a cloud of flies. And what I was musing was that maybe she *was* a witch, just like they said. Better a witch than the sister of a half-wit, even if it wasn't charitable to listen to rumor.

And rumor was that we had Soviet spies in our midst.

For starters, no one had lived in the old gabled house 'cross the ravine for years—a ravine that cut and twisted through the north canyon—what with its peeling paint and broken shingles, the porch a near collapse of rotting timbers, the yard a snarl of weeds and brambles, and best of all, ghost stories aplenty. Not that I'd seen it myself—or even knew about it—until weeks after the girl and her uncle had taken up residence, the house as unseen from the road as they were, not until their strange ways became fodder for town talk. Rumor was that she stayed boarded up like the windows, pacing the dark, dank attic, setting up clandestine meetings, conjurin' Soviet mischief. Never mind she roamed the coast all hours of the night or that no one had ever seen the uncle, not even Joe over at Lucky's—Lucky Liquors & Sundries, to be exact—and Joe didn't miss a sand flea.

The crimes began in February, shortly after she entered school midyear, petty thefts at first—an ice chest of live crabs off a truck bed, Revlon nail polish from the Rexall drugstore, spray paint, rope, and a crowbar from the hardware store, a Chanel No. 5 gift set off a boutique shelf, and two bottles of whiskey from underneath Joe's keen eye. These mischiefs were followed by pranks more galling, even malicious. Folks woke to find their cars egged, their gates ajar and dogs loose, their mail scattered across trampled lawns, the flowers beneath their windows hacked off. No coincidence, the petals in Raven's hair. Front Street became Second Street and Second Street, Front Street. Trouble, those strangers, they said.

And then Mr. York broke his ankle falling down the school stairs. Just like that, the Soviet girl went from Red Menace to sorceress, from staging town pranks to jinxing enemy targets, from cracking codes in her attic to brewing potions, the rumors turning downright delicious.

Rumors of the best sort.

The sort Rev. Travers warned against one Sunday in an especially stirring sermon, quoting from no less an authority than Mark Twain—though even that, I came to find out, might've been a rumor.

Taking the pulpit, Rev. Travers had scanned the chapel, searching perhaps for the girl and her uncle, and then settled his gaze on the choir loft. I sat up straighter, my mouth clamped over my bubble-gum braces.

"We begin today with a verse you surely all know well." A hush fell over the sanctuary. "'A lie can travel halfway around the world while the truth is still putting on its shoes.'"

Though it wasn't a verse I'd happened upon yet, it had a nice ring to it, ridin' as it was atop a familiar twang, and I chuckled with the rest of the congregation.

"Of course, we don't need Samuel Clemens to tell us what God told Moses on Mount Sinai"—his tone became grave—"'You shall not bear false witness against your neighbor.' Though we laugh at Mr. Twain, we dare not laugh at God."

With that he beckoned the congregation to turn to James, chapter three. Being that my Bible had somehow wedged itself between the toilet and a six-pack of lilac Zee toilet paper in our backyard shed, I took the occasion of the rustlin' pages to unwrap another piece of gum. As he read the passage, his deep voice a holy rumble, I let myself drift into a fine story about horses and ships and winds.

"'Behold!'" The command jarred me from my torpor, shook the rafters, boomeranged off the walls, below me the congregation roused and beholding. "'How great a forest is set ablaze by a small fire!'"

Up to that point, an uneasy agitation had been creeping over me, so it was a mighty relief to consider he might be talking 'bout arson.

"Brethren, it grieves me to learn that among this flock are those who have been setting forests ablaze." A murmur rippled across the room. "Fires rage in our town, in our church, in our homes. The unkind word, the careless whisper, the harsh rebuke—these are sins enough. What then of gossip? Slander and malice?" The question lingered, echoed. "And rumor?"

But if a rumor were true?

Peering above horn-rimmed glasses, he surveyed the small chapel—the two dozen pews flanked by narrow windows, the elders perched on aisle seats, the choir loft, a simple raised platform—rested his gaze on a yellow-banded straw hat, beneath it the willowy Mrs. Travers. Ben sat slumped to the right of his mother, his head in his hands, his usual Sunday posture. A younger brother squirmed to her left. I imagined a green pallor seeping up the neck of a certain Heather Clark, sitting in a back pew, my vaunted choir seat affordin' me a view akin to the reverend's.

"None can tame the tongue—it is a restless evil. 'With it we bless the Lord and Father, and with it we curse men, who are made in the likeness of God.'" He whisked his Bible aloft, pages fluttering, seemed almost to levitate, as though wind-borne on a gust of revelation. "Seated here today," he continued, his voice wrought in the fires of iron itself, "are those who have kindled fires of gossip, even fueled those already ablaze."

A ray of sunlight fell across the pews, or perhaps an overhead light flickered on.

"'The tongue is a fire, a world of iniquity.'"

I could've sworn he was speaking father to son, Ben slinking even lower in his seat if it were possible. "Life and death—these lie in the power of the tongue."

So it was, our Sunday services, the reverend launching into the direst warnings, pourin' into his sermons a tumble of words so large we all had to hold our breath to make space in the hushed sanctuary. Then to clear the room for more, he'd lapse into down-home talk so simple a toddler could chortle an amen. Though on occasion sweat trickled down his forehead and the veins of his neck swelled fit to burst, he never paraded far from the podium or flailed his arms like some preachers, with hornets down their trousers and tornadoes up their sleeves.

My father said he was the same as the lot of 'em, our Rev. Travers, no more than a slick hawker of religion, a conjurer of conviction and confession, a mesmerizing show-man on the wrong stage, a highfalutin charlatan, and no amount of Mama's chiding or cajolin' could persuade my father otherwise.

But I knew better.

As though I were Nathanael under the fig tree, Rev. Travers exposed my sin one Sunday in a sermon reproach-ing "she of unclean lips." Just the night before, I'd lost my last dollar in a round of Texas Hold'em and, none too pleased, used Joe's salty language right back at him as he pocketed my coins.

The reverend had read my sorry soul. Right then and there I swore to be worthy of my second-soprano post, and next poker game plunked a pack of Bazooka Bubble Gum beside my stacked chips. Soon as my unruly tongue tingled with temptation, I quashed it with a hard chunk of pink flavor. With my mouth full of sugar, there was no room for blasphemy. Rev. Travers had made a difference.

Rumor, of course.

But now I'd seen it for myself. Raven had stood sus-pended above the sea, arms aloft, and vanished. Drowned or doomed, she was gone.

TWO

"SHE STOOD AT the edge, arms straight out like this, and then *poof!*, gone." My arm thwacked Hollis in the chest. We sat on the sea wall, a waist-high stretch of concrete that tracked Front Street, a carpet of sand between us and the water.

"A goose. I know. You told me." Hollis poked a corner of his towel into his ear. "Might have to rename her. Unless, of course, you bother learning her real name."

"You're one to talk 'bout names." I still had one eye on the egret, now bobbing on the buoy. "Whoever heard of a name like Hollis Sweet?"

"Anyone who knows me, that's who." He ducked under the towel, rubbing his sun-bleached hair with fury. His voice became a muffle. "Your name's no Sue, Dick, or Harry."

"My name comes from Genesis. That makes it practically holy. Where's your name come from?"

"Told ya already."

"What, that you were born in Kern County, California, three weeks early and in a ditch?"

"Uh-huh." He pulled on a T-shirt. "In the back of my parents' station wagon. My dad swerved off the road and took out a signpost."

"How come they didn't name you Kern, then?"

"The sign said Hollis." He brightened. "Your preacher might call it a sign from God."

I snorted. "Unless it's a fib."

"Ask my mom." His hair stuck out every which way. "Back then, Hollis was just a Podunk town, nothing but fields and railroad tracks and telephone poles. Now it's got four houses and a bar." A grin broke across his face. "And me, of course. Now, if you'll just hand me my hat there."

I fished a floppy hat from the bucket and slapped it over his soggy curls. "Yeah, well, what about Sweet?"

"S'pose you'll have to ask my dad."

"S'pose I will." But I wasn't thinking 'bout his name anymore. "Mine eyes have seen the glory," I murmured, staring back out to sea. "I reckon a rumor's not a rumor if it's true."

"Reckon not." Hollis followed my gaze. "*If* it's true."

℘

WHAT *WAS* TRUE, I knew, was that when she'd first entered Harford High late winter—the only public high school this side of the highway—our teachers told us to give the newcomer a warm California welcome, though no warm welcome could have thawed her ice-blue eyes. If she had a name, I didn't remember it. No one did, far as I could tell.

Rumor was that she and her uncle had infiltrated America as communist moles from the Soviet Union—why else would they be here? She'd been carted 'cross the Midwest as he took odd jobs, we heard, mostly as a long-haul trucker—what better cover for a spy, gone for weeks on end, no sightings of him, just of her, wandering the cliffs under light of moon. Seemed no one thought to ask about a mother or father.

Rumor was right juicy the first few weeks, then limped along, might've even died out had it not been for a serendipitous sighting one Saturday afternoon at the ramshackle house—a Kalashnikov rifle poking out the attic window. That was all the resuscitating the rumor needed. It was a cold fact now that her uncle was a KGB agent, a communist informant—worse than that, a gunrunner, smuggling revolvers and intel, Raven his stooge, a sort of mute ward tasked with fixin' up false identities, forging passports, plotting the next load site, dismissed at day's end to wander the darkened streets, the moonlit shore, flitting in gossamer scarves and silken skirts, like some nocturnal bird.

I supposed the KGB story did stretch credulity, but rumors are spun from threads of truth. And better fantastical stories for shadowy newcomers than phony bless-your-heart commiserations for a defective brother. Better a raven than an albatross.

Not that I held Raven's nomadic ways against her. I'd been upended myself, carted from the Gulf Coast to the West Coast, only to be cut adrift by an AWOL father, all on account of Dex coming home. Most like, these humiliations fueled the rumors Hollis refused to divulge.

"That's purdy sad," Joe had offered that first poker night, aiming to aggravate me with his phony drawl. Still, it was the only nice thing he ever said to me, but unless pity counts, there wasn't anything *purdy* about it, so maybe it wasn't so nice after all. Dealing me a 2 and a 7, Jake called it a lousy hand, straight unlucky.

And Anna, well, she just started off on some yarn about a stray chicken spooked from its coop by a barnyard cat, darting after t'others, flapping its wings and scootin' in circles. Farmer couldn't settle 'er back in, all pecks and scratches. Took a towel over 'er head to get 'er to see she weren't in danger anymore. Hollis figured it was Anna's way of offerin' comfort, but what comfort there was in a spooked chicken, I didn't know.

Didn't stop Hollis from calling me Scoot on occasion.

The move had been a bust from the get-go, pulling up Houston stakes for San Sebastian mid–eighth grade, just to swap San Sebastian for Harford Beach last summer. It'd been a dreary ninth-grade year, with tenth grade threatening the same. With no say in the matter, I'd found myself a California girl, my old life tucked away, only a slight drawl to betray me 'less I was feelin' spiteful or a certain kind of lonesome—that and my "gothic take on things," according to Hollis. But it was my take on things that made me amusing, he added, which I let pass for a compliment.

Mama was a different story. As my father told it, he'd jimmied Mama out of the Bible Belt, but he couldn't jimmy the Bible Belt out of Mama, and that irritated him plenty, which was fine by me, seein' as he was the reason we were in this mess to begin with. So I didn't begrudge Raven what she couldn't help.

The way I told it to Mama, we might have welcomed her into our midst, though certainly not warmly, had she not been so freakish, staring at us with those brazen eyes, playing deaf or dumb when addressed by teachers, and muttering, always muttering.

She didn't bother coming to school on time, if at all, but when she did, she spooked us good, roaming the halls, wandering in an' out of classrooms, done up in vintage clothes, the kind a thrift shop might carry but hardly ever sell—discarded trunk finds from decades past, musty, garish, worn only for theater perhaps, and always the deepest purples, indigos, and blacks—silky scarves gathered over crocheted shawls, lacy peasant blouses with ruffled sleeves, gauzy skirts layered over mesh stockings tucked into ankle boots, and adornin' her arms, a dozen golden bangles. Her glossy midnight hair fell loose to her waist, sometimes woven with garlands of daisies, violets, or small camellias, white and velvet soft—like she'd only just picked them—sometimes flecked with dried petals strewn like confetti.

"Lord love her. That child got any friends? Think she'll get any valentines?"

"Who'd wanna be seen with a frea—with someone like that?" I'd near knocked over Mama's sun tea. "And we're in ninth grade. No one gives valentines."

"Like what?"

"Like a fortune teller in a travelin' show."

"Now, sugar, that's not kind. From what I hear, that child has no mama or daddy, not even a brother or sister to call her own. Would it hurt you to be a friend? What's that Rev'n Travers always says? Nothing is more unlovely than a person who won't love the unlovely."

"Dad know that?" I said, too quiet for her to catch.

What I didn't tell Mama was that I'd fared no better as a newcomer twice uprooted, Texas about as foreign to my ninth-grade classmates as the Soviet Union. The strangest thing I ever wore was an ugly old pair of cat-eye glasses, right fine for my astigmatism but right woundin' for my vanity, not that I had any. Now, with the broken bridge taped together, I smuggled them on for small-print books, and *that* only till I could unbury my tortoiseshell glasses packed for the second move. But thinking of the U-Haul loaded with our boxes didn't do a lick of good, only made me mad. And thinking 'bout Mama didn't do a lick of good either, 'cause if it had, I'd have been home with Dex instead of baptizing Hollis.

I knew I should be in for it, but that I wouldn't be, because Mama had stopped caring.

₨

My thoughts scattered as Hollis jumped off the wall to corral a small dog. It took a moment to see that the dog limped, a hind leg hovering above the sand.

"Got somethin' in her paw." Hollis had her by the collar, was working a sliver of wire. "Mission accomplished. You're cleared for takeoff." He gave her a pat on the rump, but she pranced behind him, flopping beside us. "Where, oh where does this little dog belong?" Hollis sang, knuckling her head. "Looks like a terrier. S'pose someone will miss her soon enough."

I picked up where I left off. "The way that I see it—"

"With or without your Jane Jetson glasses?"

"Very funny. Ooh-wee, that dog stinks!" I scooted down the wall. "The way I see it, the crimes only started when she came to town. Same with the juju."

"The what?"

And then I told him about that winter morning in our English class, how Mr. York, reading Edgar Allan Poe's "The Raven" aloud, told her for the third time to sit down. He might as well have been speaking Greek, though English probably *was* Greek to her. Her eyes transfixed on him—or on something beyond him, unseen to us mere mortals—she lifted her bangled arms, the bracelets clattering as they slid, and began to spin, slowly at first and then more quickly, a blur of scarves and shawls and tangled hair, and then to sing, a strange, lilting tune, the words a stream of syllables, tumbling without meaning, an incantation. And then with an anguished cry, she fled the room.

Hollis raised an eyebrow. "Everything's bigger in Texas, isn't that what people say?"

"What? Yeah, why?"

"Accounts for your imagination."

"Thought you didn't listen to what people say." That lowered his eyebrow.

Payin' him no more mind, I continued. Two days later while shuffling down the school stairs, Mr. York missed a step and went tail over teakettle, fracturing his ankle.

"And that makes her a witch?"

"She hexed him. Least that's what *they* say. I can't rightly know, but then *you* tell me how she vanished off the pier."

"Didn't see it. And who's *they*?"

"The ones who don't have their head in a bucket. There's more."

"Who'da thought?"

The rest of that week we'd formed tight clusters—*they* did, the kids in our class—whispering among themselves, casting furtive glances her direction, embellishing the incident till no one quite remembered the truth. Had she really chanted a curse? Had she given our teacher the evil eye? Had the hands she'd reached toward him curled into talons? *That* girl, that black magic girl, we—*they*—dubbed "Raven."

"Been brewing potions in the toilet, witch?" they'd jeer. "Gonna hex the principal next?" The girls mocked her, turned their backs. The boys slammed doors on her, shoved her.

"Not me, mind you," I said to Hollis, interrupting myself. "*Them*."

"Wonder where their parents are."

"Parents?" It took a moment to see what he meant, but a towheaded boy near the swings had emptied his dump truck over a little girl's head, 'rousing a wail of fury. "Someone's gonna get what-for."

Sure 'nough, a woman sprang from her beach towel and

pried the kids apart, brushing sand out of the girl's eyes and delivering a swat to the boy's bottom. The smoke from a barbecue wafted from the firepits beyond the swings. Hot dogs, I decided, my stomach growling. Behind us, a motorcycle roared to a stop, exhaust spewin' as the engine revved, went quiet.

"Anyway, as I was saying—what's the matter?"

Hollis had turned out his pockets, upending coins and a hankie. "That figures."

"What?"

"My beef jerky." He groaned. "Gone. Washed away with my sins." The terrier sat up, nose twitching.

"Want a donut? I can hop over to Beach Yum." Though not visible from the sea wall, the donut shop sat between the laundromat and the Fish-n-Ships Diner, the diner easy to spot, thanks to the neon Corona parrot above the door, the blues and yellows a fuzzy sparkle in the sun.

"Sure. Got any money?"

I dug in my wet pocket. "Got a quarter."

"That your poker winnings?" Hollis grinned, fished a five-dollar bill from inside his salt-stained hat. "Your Mama know you've been gambling away your allowance?"

"Haven't neither. Jake always gives back my losings. Anyhow, a girl needs things."

"Like what?"

"Bubble gum."

"And that orange paint all over your mouth?" He swung himself onto the sidewalk. "I'll go. Two donuts coming right up. Old-fashioned for me, brussels-sprout glaze for Scoot."

I made a play for his bucket hat, but he ducked out of reach, laughing as he darted across the street.

The sun warm on my face, I shut my eyes, let myself

drift to the creaking of the swings, the chatter of kids, the crash of sea, then popped 'em open again at the squalling of two seagulls. I tracked the blurry arc of a Frisbee, little boy to dad, bet myself my quarter that a busty girl's bikini halter top would snap. It did, sparking laughter among her friends as she shrieked and slapped at the guy beside her.

"Heads up!"

A hand shot in front of my face, snagging a spinning football before it could knock me silly. Flinching, I squinted toward the voice, shielding my eyes. It was a dangerous voice. Least if the rumors were true.

THREE

"Almost gotcha." He had to be a football player, the way he intercepted the ball, launching it at a couple kids throwing long bombs.

I leaned sideways, the sun ducking behind broad shoulders. "Thanks!"

"Vince to the rescue"—he flashed a smile—"despite my reputation." He slugged his buddy easy in the arm. "Stoppin' trouble, not startin' it. Huh, dude?"

The other guy grunted, face hidden beneath a Dodgers cap.

Vincent Andrews, heartthrob and heartbreaker of Harford Beach—Vintage Heights, to be exact—wore danger like a badge. "Gotta keep a lookout. Easy to find yourself in the line of fire." He looked like a modern James Dean, tight jeans slung with a thick leather belt, faded crew sweatshirt, cigarette between his lips.

"S'pose so." I scratched the terrier, a piece of driftwood in her mouth.

"Does Toto bite?" The voice came rich, like the reverend's but with less twang.

Vince snorted.

"Hey, Ben, how's it going?" I said, seeing only myself in his mirrored shades.

"Makin' it. No kid brother toda—"

"Speaking of going"—I slid off the sea wall—"I gotta git."

"Not so fast." It was a hard truth, but this bad boy had dreamy eyes. "Kid brother? Oh right, you're that new girl from—"

"Texas," Ben finished, smacking Vince on the back. "C'mon, man. Let's get lunch."

Vince shook him off. "Houston, right?" His laugh rolled like his cigarette smoke. "Careful! Gonna catch a horsefly."

My mouth clamped shut.

"Don't worry—I'm not stalking you. Just make it my business to know who's who."

I felt my cheeks flush. "Right nice to make your 'quaintance."

"Ohh, cowgirl's got manners." Dimples lit his chiseled face. "What're you standing for, anyway? Thought we're havin' a little chat." He motioned to the sea wall.

I sat again, glanced at a fidgety Ben.

"Dude, let's go. I'm hungry."

"Thought you came from the South too. Lose your manners in the move?"

Shrugging, Ben tightened the straps of his frayed backpack.

"Speaking of acquaintances"—Vince fixed serious eyes on me—"you might wanna rethink yours." He flicked ash onto the sand. "I've seen you palling around with that commie."

"What?" I choked, same as if I'd swallowed a clump of kelp.

Early mornings, at the first peek of sun, jocks from Harford Beach, Vintage Heights, and even Gulch Run set aside their turf differences to catch the waves, ridin' 'em like pros. On days I could make a quick getaway from the house, I'd watch them from the sea wall or swings, waiting for the local anglers to come strolling by, for Hollis, with his fishing rod over his shoulder and bucket dangling. Vince might have spotted me at my usual hangouts, but never with Raven.

"You seem like a swell kid, so here's another heads-up. Steer clear of her."

"Why?"

"'Cause till she and her comrade uncle showed up, there wasn't any trouble in this town."

"Wouldn't wanna be branded a pinko, would ya?" Ben tussled with the terrier for the driftwood.

"Reckon not." *Whatever that means.*

"Then do yourself a favor and pass on a little message from us." Vince dropped his cigarette butt, grinding it into the sand with his boot heel. "We're on to them—us, the sheriff, the whole town. And cute as you are"—his smile dazzled, showing braces on his bottom teeth—"I'd hate to catch you in the line of fire again."

"Uh . . ." I felt myself bristle and blush, a tangle of fluster.

"She gets it, man. C'mon, I'm starving."

"We'll go when I say," Vince snapped, but laughed as he turned to me. "The Beaver here wants some grub. Could use some beefing up."

Ben clutched his chest. "Ouch, that's col—"

"Don't forget what I said." Vince popped a keychain off his belt loop. "Just wanna keep this town safe."

I nodded.

"See ya 'round, cowgirl."

Twirling the keys, he hopped the wall, nearly colliding with Hollis, who trotted out from between two cars, clutching a white sack. With a startled *whoa!*, Vince straddled his motorcycle, slid his shades down to his nose, and pulled a pair of gloves from his back pocket. Ben settled in behind him, the engine roaring to life. Waving away the cloud of exhaust, Hollis dropped beside me.

"What was that about?"

"Nothing."

"Nothing? Looked like something to me." He dug into the crinkly bag and handed me a coconut-dusted chocolate donut, then tugged a pack of beef jerky from his pocket. "Hey, what happened to the dog?"

We scanned the stretch of golden sand, the beach littered with rotting kelp, striped umbrellas, and picnic baskets. Chubby tots chased the surf, and off-leash dogs bounded after sandpipers, barking in full view of a large sign reading "No dogs allowed past 10 a.m."

"Ha! She must've read the sign."

"Who'da thought?" Hollis laughed.

We quieted for a spell, munchin' on our donuts, the soft waves a foamy ribbon, our legs warm on the sand.

"Didn't know donuts came with baptisms." Hollis licked his fingers. "Guess it makes sense, though, with them both being holy."

I supposed a rebuke was in order, him being newly saved and in need of some sanctifying, but I wasn't thinking of baptisms anymore, or donuts, though I sure liked mine plenty, scraping off the chocolate icing with my teeth. I wasn't even thinking how maybe I'd just fibbed to Hollis. *Them, not me*, I'd said. What I *was* thinking about was whether I'd ever fill out a bikini halter top.

"What did the guys want? And don't say nothing."

"Nothing."

Hollis frowned.

"Okay, something."

"Yeah?"

I puffed out my chest. "I'm turning fifteen next month."

"Uh-huh."

"Do I *look* like I'm turning fifteen?"

He gave my arched body a sideways glance and grinned. "You look like a girl, if that's what you mean."

"Well, that's okay then. I ain't fixin' to be a woman anytime soon."

"Heaven help us on that day."

"What's that supposed to mean?"

"Nothing. You gonna tell me what those guys wanted?"

"They had a message for Raven." I snorted. "Like I'd ever talk to her."

"Thought you weren't mean to her like the others."

I cuffed and uncuffed my pants. "Not exactly. But I'm Florence Nightingale compared to Ben and his buddies."

I proceeded to tell Hollis whole hog the good, the bad, and the ugly. Only not in that order. The bad came first—a near felony. The good came next—penance. Then the ugly— well, that might have included me.

About a month after she arrived at Harford High, some boys—Ronnie, Wayne, and the usual suspects—pelted the new student with a storm of pebbles as she crossed the school parking lot, hollerin' "Go home, commie!" Then from nowhere, Rev. Travers's '53 Ford pickup came barreling, missing her by a whisker as she tumbled into the gutter.

"Your preacher almost ran her over?"

"Hollis Sweet, you know good an' well that Old Clunker's Ben's. Near caused a divorce though."

And how did I know *that*, Hollis asked.

I knew *that* 'cause Rev. Travers had preached a Sunday message on staying united as a family of believers, quoting none other than Abraham Lincoln—or maybe the apostle

Matthew—that "a house divided cannot stand" and mentioning the Old Clunker. At this, the reverend's gaze landed squarely on Mrs. Travers, hands folded on her Bible in the front pew. I near fell out of the choir loft, becoming even more alarmed when he called her a "pickup." But I came to see that the Old Clunker was the pickup truck used for hauling loads.

"Said it was a member of the family." The terrier was back, gnawing on a piece of Hollis's jerky. "Like my father's VW used to be," I added. "But M&M green, not that rusty brown."

The Old Clunker had become a source of discord, the reverend told the congregation, he and the missus quarrelin' over the wisdom of bequeathing the truck to Ben. After much prayer and a little fasting—lunch, I think—the reverend relented. A testing of his faith, he said, and handed the keys over to Ben. For the trouble, he earned himself a pot roast dinner and a house still standing. The Old Clunker became an immediate hit at Harford High, able to lug a dozen surfboards and spew a spectacular plume of exhaust. Anyone could hear that truck buck and cough a mile away, and though it couldn't hold a candle to the spankin' new '71 Camaros all the rage at Vintage High, it held a certain charm. And any wheels were better than nothing.

"*That's* how I know."

Hollis satisfied, I continued.

That some of the guys tried to run down Raven was no rumor, 'cause we saw it with our own eyes from our upstairs classroom. Whether from Ms. Wong's shriek or the Old Clunker's squealing tires, we rushed to the windows in time to catch the shebang mid-show. Two hooded guys had snuck up on Raven and shoved her off the curb. The pickup was churning exhaust and gravel, the bandits were chucking themselves into the truck bed, and Raven lay sprawled on the asphalt. The truck peeled off in a burst of bangs and smoke like it was ready to blow.

Hollis's slate eyes darkened.

"*I* didn't do it. *They* did. And they got what-for, too."

The principal called the sheriff, and the sheriff corralled the boys, but Ben swore up and down he wasn't behind the wheel. Still not a one of 'em would spill the beans, so Sheriff Moretti threatened jailing the whole lot. When Ben finally copped to it, the sheriff called the reverend, and the reverend worked a backdoor deal, said the buck stopped with him, and he'd do better by Ben than even jail could. It was his duty as head of the church family to keep his own house in order.

"Figure that means twice the Bible learnin' along with pullin' up the drawbridge at sunset."

"What dra—"

"I ain't done yet."

Of course the school had to mete out punishment and spared not a boy: a three-day suspension—striking envy in the hearts of all—and hard labor at Raven's house, a once-grand ruin in Gulch Run.

"A month of Saturdays yankin' weeds and haulin' branches. Only that didn't sit too well with her KGB uncle. Aimed a rifle out the attic window."

"Thawt no'un's ever sheen'm," Hollis said through a mouthful of beef.

"Maybe not. But the chain gang sure saw his shotgun." I fished out the last stick. "'Cept Ronnie swore it was the kitchen window."

Word spread like wildfire that he kept a whole arsenal of guns locked up in the lean-to shed, hawked 'em on the black market for a heap of American intel. *Smuggling Soviet guns in and American secrets out,* folks whispered.

"That a fact?"

Reflecting on it later, I could trace the very moment the devil got a foothold in Ben, and it was in church, no less. And by way of his father's orders too, the miscreant hauled up to confess his iniquity before the congregation of Mar Vista Chapel—that of pressing the gas pedal instead of the brake.

Rev. Travers propped him against the podium in a show of contrition, his son's pocked face flushed, hands a fidget of fingers—but whether for what he'd done or for what his father was doing, I couldn't say. The reverend lamented the fact of things but rightly praised his son, an example of fallen yet forgiven man, repentant and thus redeemed. Not stoppin' there, the reverend confessed himself a father negligent, pledged again to set his own house in order, citing Paul's admonishment to Timothy. And he too asked for forgiveness, to which the congregation responded with a chorus of "Lord, have mercy!" and "Hear our prayer!"

Raven rarely came to class after her near death by Old Clunker, and if she did, she didn't stay, wandering in just to wander out again, slinking into corner desks, books unopened, stare vacant. We became used to her erratic ways, kept clear of her, teachers and students alike. If I passed her in the corridors, I'd give her wide berth, near strangled by the thick scent of wildflowers and mothballs. But one morning as I jostled past, she rammed straight into me, my notebook, papers, and pencils flyin', daisies fluttering from her hair.

"For Pete's sake! Watch where you're going."

Her arctic eyes flashed, as clear as the translucent blue beads on Dex's bedrail.

For a moment, I considered that she might be blind and awfully clever to find her way around school and so fool us all. Lickety-split, I wrenched myself away, sure that if I looked too long, I'd see straight into her soul—or worse, that she would see straight into mine. "What is Christian love," Rev. Travers had preached, "if not to love the unlovely?" If ever a time to polish up my soul, it would have been then. But the musty garments, fringed shawls and layered skirts, the rambling words murmured like chants above a cauldron, the unflinching stare of crystal eyes—she was the stuff of sorceress tales.

"I got it, thanks," I'd said, dodging a passel of scurrying legs to snatch my papers. But she squatted with me, reaching for my pencils and murmuring her strange, lilting words, her breath warm on my face—*maynay hemezli leeyuh*, that's how I remembered it to Hollis. A hex, I told him, juju, hoodoo. Just like she'd done to Mr. York.

A strappy platform shoe just missed my fingers as it stamped on my essay about Poe.

"Oh look, it's the choir brat." Heather Clark's voice could unravel a spiderweb. "Finally found a friend, did ya?"

A boy in gray Chucks sauntered up beside her, laugh hollow. Ben, of course. Without Vince to glom on to, he made do with Vince's girlfriend. I traced the platforms to teal knee socks, then to a short plaid skirt, then to a macramé shoulder bag, a bouquet of orange poppies drooping out. A second shorter skirt joined hers.

"Birds of a feather." Trish giggled, twirling her rope necklace like a 1920s flapper.

"You're one to talk, birdbrain!" I snapped, but they were already down the hall, their laughs an echo. Ripping a pencil from Raven's hand, I shoved past her, trying to shake off her cloying scent—cedar and mothballs, dried petals and eucalyptus leaves.

"Did you help pick up her flowers?" Hollis had asked.

"How could I do that? I was trapped and being hexed! Three times she said it, the exact number of a magic spell."

I could hear the chant now: *maynay hemezli leeyuh.*

"You ever consider that she mighta been speaking her native language—saying *sorry* same as you?" Hollis had offered matter-of-factly, not a goose bump on his sunburnt neck. "She's Russian, isn't she?" He paused. "You did say sorry, didn't you?"

"Why would I do that? *She* ran into *me*. Anyway, I know a hex when I hear one."

He chuckled, reeling up an empty line. "Who'da thought? A Bolshevik bewitcher."

I made to grab his hat as he switched out the bait. "Don't you take anything serious?"

"Sure, Scoot. Wanna hear my theory?" He fended me off with an elbow.

"What?"

"Maybe she's just an ordinary girl." He cast his line out to sea. "Like you."

One thing she wasn't, was ordinary. Or like me.

And now she had vanished off the pier.

FOUR

SNATCHING HIS FISHING rod and bucket, Hollis hopped off the sea wall and headed for the pier, the terrier having plunked beside a plump girl lost in a romance novel. Trailing behind, I wished I'd done a better job of saving him. Although he'd been a sport to suffer three dunks, he didn't seem much different for it, no huzzahs or hallelujahs as the burden rolled off his back, though I admit to a dereliction of duty, if through no fault of my own. So far, savin' the heathen lacked the glamour of Sunday morning missionary tales.

The public restroom was 'bout as roomy as a phone booth, dank and buzzing with pesky flies. Yanking off my clammy jeans, I shook out the sand and shimmied them back on. I felt slimier than a clump of algae and hankered to fetch another pair from home, but I had to catch up to Hollis.

Hollis Sweet was my first mission field. I'd spied him one November Sunday as I moseyed 'long the sea wall on my way to Mar Vista Chapel, a 1940s grammar schoolhouse the reverend had converted, being good at that sort of thing. We hadn't been much for church, my father no more interested in inviting God to live with us than Dex. But after he bailed and Mama rented us the shabby bungalow on Front Street—the sea air will invigorate Dex, she'd said—she'd taken up with religion again, a return to her Southern roots. Divine providence, Mama told the reverend, that he too harkened from the South. And maybe it was at that. The way I saw it, Mama needed soul comfort as much as Dex needed sea air.

Mar Vista Chapel had taken us in like the lost lambs we were, assigning Mama to the Sanctuary Beautification Committee and eventually recruitin' me to the chancel choir, jittery as a possum in a trap. But Rev. Travers had worked a miracle in me, stirring up an off-key zeal for the Lord, and that particular Sunday saw me in fine form.

"Do Lord, oh do Lord, oh do remember me, oh Lordy!" my zeal sang as I teetered along the sea wall, Bible perched on my head.

"Don't think he can help it."

A slim but muscular boy stood near the fish cleaning station, rinsing his feet under a low faucet, lanky in cutoffs, aviator sunglasses, and a faded blue canvas hat, his grin impish.

"Thanks!" I returned, realizing too late what he meant. "It's not the voice that counts, it's the veneration."

"Never heard better veneration in my life." He dove for a wayward beach ball, tossing it back to some kids. "Name's Hollis."

"It's Sunday. You oughta be in church, Hollis."

"And you oughta be fishing . . ."

"Eden."

℺

WITH DEX NEWLY residing in our glorified shack, I hadn't had much occasion to consider fishing—or anything 'cept the packing up of one life and unpacking of another. We'd rejiggered the front room to fix a spot for Dex, turned his playpen into a bed—a playbed, we called it—squashed against the back wall, away from the large window framing the sea. A Goodwill couch sagged beneath the scratched pane, the cushions a mottled green paisley. A wicker end table held a lamp and box of cotton wipes, and behind the table stood the Leaning Tower of Pampers. A narrow coat closet stored Dex's paraphernalia—steel leg braces, orthopedic shoes, ankle pads. Mama's rocker sat against a short bookcase.

From the front door, a narrow hallway opened to a tiled kitchen, small as a hen's nest, and to a Tom Thumb bathroom. Between the two, a rickety staircase climbed to two bedrooms, each with corner views of the Pacific. Mama's cot lay buried under boxes, most still packed, remnants of our city life sealed up—my Pollyanna dolls, Mama's cookbooks, my father's backgammon. Mostly that door stayed shut, Mama throwing a sheet on the couch to sleep near Dex, his troubled nights her troubled nights, though she would have said it was no trouble at all.

Beneath my bedroom lay a yard choked with overgrown shrubs, shadowed late afternoons by the Sea Crest Motel. A wooden toolshed abutted a collapsed fence. Though only half-roofed, it held a heap of charm: a creaky workbench below a frosted porthole, rusted tackle hooks on one wall, a sepia map on the other, and a leaky toilet. If the urge hit two folks at the same stroke of midnight, one of them folks—mainly me—would skitter through knee-high cattails and quilled thistles same as if bein' chased by haunts. The weed-snarled yard morphed into a gator-fogged swamp beneath the glow of the motel sign. The crooked shingle on the splintered door—"Welcome to Fishermen's Lodge"—was of little comfort.

Those anguished nights when Dex woke us with blood-curdling screams, tossed and turned and thrashed, our own

Jacob wrestling a mercurial God, his twisted body racked with sobs, when all Mama's lullabies failed to soothe . . . those nights, I would slip from bed with my flashlight and creep out the back door through the moonlit yard, less afraid of the shadows than of the terrors that tormented Dex.

In the cool of Fishermen's Lodge, I'd perch on the creaky toilet seat, knees tucked under my flannel nightgown, and breathe. Sometimes I'd take my leather Bible with me, shine my flashlight onto its whispery pages, and lose myself in miracles—Jesus spitting in the dirt to give sight, walking across a furious sea, waking up a dead girl. Other times I'd pocket my sketchbook and let my charcoal pencil run rampant, conjuring mythical creatures from my father's history books. Always I would wait until the drugs took effect, relaxed my brother's cramping limbs, quieted his sobs, leaving in its wake the curdled breath that washed over our lives.

ⅎ

"WELL?" HOLLIS HAD called. "Church or fishing?"

"You drive a hard bargain." It's what my father would say to me.

Though I hadn't fished yet, I'd watched the anglers many a morning, the weathered men hauling tackle boxes and ice chests, the square-jawed women luggin' buckets. I'd seen the squid baiting and casting, the jigging and reeling, heard the banter and grousing, the cussing after long silences, the shouts at a particularly fine catch.

"Still got my line out." Hollis tugged on a shoe, hopping back as an angler spilled his catch onto the cleaning table.

I nearly succumbed, nearly forfeited my soul for the thrill of a catfish strike. But the Lord never allows us to be tempted more than we are able—I'd read that one night in the Lodge—and the peal of bells from St. Francis, on a hill above Gulch Run, was my way out, reminding me that the only fishing I ought to be doing was fishing for men. But I'd be back for Hollis.

And I had, getting so far as to baptize him, a Roman Catholic, by immersion. Hollis Sweet had no use for church, Catholic or otherwise, and he figured God didn't either. He had it on good authority, he said, that God wouldn't be checking denominations at the pearly gates. That authority was the Good Book itself, not that he'd read it. But he had consulted an exhaustive concordance in the parish library.

"The word 'denomination' is nowhere to be found," he'd announced.

"That's because you looked in the Catholic Bible," I'd countered.

Eventually, I wrested a concession from him, remindin' him that a switch in bait on a slack line is the sign of a seasoned fisher—I'd heard the grumbles of a bad haul plenty of times by then. At the very least, I argued, he ought to consider baptism by immersion, just in case the sprinkling didn't take. And anyway, I needed the practice for my Ecuadorian forays. I'd yet to be baptized myself. Somehow I just didn't feel ready.

Either Hollis feared for the sins that sprinkling missed or he considered a switch in bait a smart tactic. Course, it might have been he didn't want to tangle with the Lord's calling on my life. But no matter the reason, he let me baptize him.

Now, three dunks an' two donuts later, Hollis was helping a couple of the regular anglers load gear into a pickup.

"Say"—I refastened my damp ponytail—"how 'bout a stroll on the pier?" I kicked at a piece of broken glass. "Bet

Jake landed that yellowfin he's been after."

"A stroll?" A raised eyebrow threatened as he tossed the glass into the trash.

"Sure. Why not?"

"Why not? Ten feet down the pier and you're gonna be sick, that's why not."

"Not anymore. I gumptioned myself all the way to the Bait and Tackle Shack yesterday."

"Yeah? 'Bout time you conquered your fear." Hollis looked amused. "And here I thought you were scouting for Raven."

"C'mon. Don'tcha wanna see me make it to the end?"

"Can't. Gotta help my dad." He picked up his bucket. "Doesn't your mom need you soon?"

The answer to that question was always yes, thanks to my AWOL father and gimpy brother, though to be fair, it wasn't my brother's fault. He was what he was, but that didn't mean I had to saddle my life with him. "I got a little time."

"I don't. But I'll see ya later." And without a look back, Hollis headed across Front Street, his gait easy, shoulders sturdy, curls escaping the brim of his cotton hat.

When I walked it alone, the pier made me dizzy, the long stretch of planks crawling and warping as I tried to squint it into focus. If I looked down, I saw churning sea washin' over churning sea, doubling and tripling, and en-visioned my body plummeting to an Alfred Hitchcock death, a silent scream frozen on my lips. If I looked straight ahead, I met a seesaw horizon of endless ocean and my gait became drunken. One false step and I would slip through the gaps—no matter that the gap couldn't fit even a deck of Bicycle cards. If I walked pressed against the railing, white knuckles clamped on for dear life and palms brushed by a hundred splinters, bumping into fishermen and tripping over rods, I saw more water than wood, and with one strong gust of wind, I'd go hurtling over.

Not that I considered myself a coward in most things. Just heights—pier heights and balcony heights and amusement-ride heights—"depth confusion," the optometrist told me, nothing a pair of glasses couldn't fix. Or a steadying hand. It was walking the planks *alone* that got me woozy. I'd never come this far alone before, always stopping at the Bait and Tackle Shack.

I had Hollis to thank for the sick slurping in my stomach.

Fine droplets coated my face as I gripped the railing at the pier end. The sea stretched turquoise into a fog-shrouded horizon, somewhere out there a coastline that meandered east and then south again. To the west, two more piers jutted into the ocean, the nearer one on loan to the San Sebastian university for marine research and closed to locals. Three small coves lay between it and the farthest pier, the last outpost before the coast veered sharply north and vanished.

Hemmed in by the breakwater, an outcropping of jagged rocks and concrete, Alvarado Pier bustled with sailboats and fishing vessels, sea lions sunning on barges and tourists lunching at the Mermaid Café. The lucky springtime visitor might spot gray whales, mothers and calves, migrating north and humpback whales from July to October. Jake had taken me fishing out there once in his *Autumn Rows*, his sister bobbing alongside in *Patches*, a fitting name if ever there was one, what with leaks sproutin' like wildflowers. It had been a one-off, that fishing jaunt, Jake's bones too old and stiff for wedging long spells in a dinghy—and he wasn't about to boot Popeye, the rescue mutt, tail and red-checked bandana flapping in the wind.

Below me, the pier shook with a surge of sea. *Gumption, Eden!* I mouthed, licking salt from my lips. I set one foot onto the lowest rail, eased myself up, and looked down. My stomach lurched, rose to my throat. The pier was nothing but a jumble of beams thick with barnacles, swaying beds of kelp, and tethered ropes, the fall enough to dizzy anyone, most especially a girl without wings. Where in tarnation had Raven gone?

"Goin' for a swim, Scoot?"

I popped up so fast I heard my neck snap.

"Con-tarnit, Hollis! Don't be creepin' up on me like that!" I yanked out my ponytail, hiding my face under a tumble of hair.

"How'd ya make it to the end without falling through?"

"Very funny. Thought you had to help your dad."

"I do. Job got moved to next week. So did you find her?" With the barest hold on the bird-splattered railing, he bent over double and surveyed the tossing sea. "Hmm. Now, isn't that odd?"

"What?" I leaned over, grip tight on the railing. My stomach pitched as I searched the waves, water frothing against the pilings, sure I was about to swoon but determined not to give Hollis the satisfaction.

"Why, that there."

"Where?"

"There, under the pier."

I strained to see what he was seeing, but saw only tangled fishing line, seaweed—I couldn't look anymore, my stomach in full revolt, and sank back.

"What?" I asked weakly.

"All that water."

"Hollis Sweet, you would try the patience of a saint." I fought the urge to snatch his hat and toss it overboard.

"Are you telling me one baptism made you a saint? My, miracles do work fast 'round here." Shoving his hands into his pockets, he did an about-face and whistled his way past a row of tackle boxes.

"Hey, wait for me!"

Heathen though he was, he slowed his pace.

Walking back up the pier was a cinch.

FIVE

TRUDGING DOWN THE beach after Hollis, I let my thoughts stray to Mama, in particular to the penance I'd owe for ditching her. She'd most like be hunched over her nursing books spread 'cross the kitchen counter, scrambling eggs with one hand, turning pages with the other, sighing over a fussy Dex strapped in his high chair, and wearily beseeching the Almighty to redirect her wayward Jonah home.

By the slant of the sun, I figured she had maybe ten minutes before she needed to head to her shift at the clinic, a forty-minute drive south on Highway 1, catty-corner from the county courthouse. While I frittered away the summer, traipsing after Hollis and preparing for the mission field, she was fixin' to step into the workforce—her duty, she said, now that it was just the three of us. *Duty* was about the ugliest four-letter word I'd ever heard, a mess of worry I didn't have time for, and she must have seen it on my face, because she'd looked hard at me and said, "Duty is an act of love, Eden Mae."

Ruing my trials, I veered toward the street with a wave at Hollis, my thoughts drifting back to Raven. In an otherwise ho-hum summer, the strange girl afforded me some mystery, but fact was she taunted me, the very being of her, the way she lived unfettered, roaming free as the bird that folks said she was, doing as she pleased, beholden to no one an' nothing. On days when Dex had soiled his diaper yet again or woken us in the dead of night with howls from the underworld, those days I'd have swapped lives with her. One uncle had to be a heap less trouble than my kin, even if the man was a KGB spy.

Although the mayhem she'd stirred up piqued my curiosity to near distraction—not that I blamed her, tormented like she was, and not that I wasn't grateful for a little distracting—Vince had no call lumping me with her, thinkin' I was a pinko. The only thing pink about me was the tortoise-shell glasses I'd lost.

I heard the putter of my father's VW Bug before I saw it crest the hill. So he'd stayed the night. I hadn't heard him arrive—the creaky front door tattling on our comings and goings. But I should have known. The night had been too still, my sleep too sound. Somehow Dex always knew, calmed into a deep slumber by the father who came, but not for him.

This was the third time in two weeks my father had spent the night. I stamped on a Coke can, crunched it hard into the sand.

If I ran to the end of the sea wall, I could flag my father down, catch him before he headed to the university, the newly hired professor of medieval history. I'd allowed him to sweet-talk me into a donut at Beach Yum a couple times. But now I shrank against the rusted swing set, the cracked seats ridden by a gentle breeze, and waited for the percolating engine to fade, the slow putter up Front Street and then back, once, twice, his last lookout for me. I stomped up the sand-crumbed stairs to the street.

∾

HE HADN'T BEEN right to leave us last August, Mama and me, though I supposed I should be grateful he'd waited — waited until the smoke from my fourteen candles had thinned and vanished, taking with it my birthday wish, waited until the giggles of my slumber party had dwindled into yawns, until the last goodbyes the next day.

A soft rain had dusted the waning tomato vines. I'd hauled Dex's toys from the closet where they'd been stashed since Easter. With each stuffed animal I pulled out, Dex hooted and thumped his chest. Soon hippos and bears flanked him, giraffes and zebras, tigers and Aslan — the stuffed lion Gramma Kay had crocheted for him. After he bored of the wild kingdom, I'd stacked his sponge alphabet blocks for his flailing arms to tumble and popped a record on the turntable, croonin' along. He thumped his chest whenever I stopped. We cut up for a good spell.

I hadn't missed Dex really. Sure, he was my only sibling, and I supposed I was glad for the fact of it, but once Gramma Kay moved into our Houston house on account of her stroke, Mama couldn't tend to them both. It was all right though. Dex had grown into a handful at four, and my father had found us an elm-shaded house near the institution. Mama could still be his mama, feeding an' bathing an' wheeling him about the grounds. "A golden-haired boy with eyes like maple syrup and skin sweet as country milk," she'd wax on, saying nothing particularly poetic about my wooly hair or mud-brown eyes.

Those days, my father taught at the community college, writing his dissertation at night. With Mama tending to Dex and my father tending to book learnin', I didn't see my parents much, except when chores hollered. Mostly I tolerated the school days, counting the hours till the weekends. Saturday mornings meant bicycling from one garage sale to the next with my father, hunting for Topps baseball cards. Sunday mornings meant sleeping in, then working jigsaw puzzles with Gramma Kay. And Sunday evenings I spent with Little Joe Cartwright, watching reruns aplenty, even Mama hooked on *Bonanza*, or maybe on Little Joe, like me.

And then, as though caught in a Texas gully washer, our lives were swept away by the telephone, two jangles in one hour: the first from the hospital, Mama's crestfallen face telling us Gramma Kay had passed, the second from the California State University of San Sebastian, my father's lifted face telling us he'd landed the job.

"Where?" Mama clutched a Kleenex box.

"Small town on the central coast."

"How small?"

"Beaches and rolling hills. No smog." My father reached for her hand. "There's a children's home in Los Angeles."

"Los Angeles?"

"It's close enough. The change will be good for us."

"What, three hundred miles?" She pulled her hand away.

"Two hundred. We'll make it work." He heard me in the doorway, turned. "We'll always be a family. I promise."

That spring, Mama planted tomatoes and cucumbers under a California sun, busied herself outside when my father was inside, busied herself inside when he was outside. Two weekends a month, she'd drive the four hours through congested LA freeways to see Dex, my father grumbling that he'd go when he could, swamped with papers to grade, lectures to write.

As for me, I had a brother on holidays or the odd weekend when Mama brought him home. I didn't know life with him enough to miss him. Sure, I liked his visits, liked making

him laugh, liked his fierce hugs 'round my neck, liked that—
for a weekend anyway—we'd be the Lewis family, together
and complete, a "Dexie day," Mama would say. But I liked
it just as much when he left. He wore me out. He wore all of
us out.

I'd just balanced my birthday tiara on Dex's alligator
seesaw when I heard Mama in the hall, words clipped.

"You promised me, Alex."

"The holidays are hard enough."

"He needs to be home. And not just on Christmas, a
week in the summer."

"He doesn't know the difference."

"You've seen him when we leave, how he cries." Mama
paused. "He's lost weight."

Rain tapped at the windows.

"Give him time to adjust, Elaine. It's barely been six
months."

"You said we'd find options."

"We will."

"When?" She murmured something I lost in Dex's
squeals.

"It's all I can do to keep up with work right now, okay?"

"I'm not taking him back." Her voice caught, steadied.

In the silence, I realized I was holding my breath.

"If he stays"—my father's voice was flint—"I go."

Watching the rain fall in sheets over the yard, I lifted
Dex to the alligator seat, strapped him in, and let the other
end rise empty, my tiara toppling.

That's how Dex came home to stay. Except we didn't
have a home anymore. We pulled the curtains on our shady
ranch house, my father rustling up a condo near the university,
and Mama, Dex, and I pig-piled ourselves into a pokeweed

bungalow to live on sea air and prayers.

Mama, Dex, and I could make a life without him. That's what he said as he balled up his shirts and ties, shovin' 'em into a suitcase, packed up his history textbooks, crammed his lecture notes into his briefcase. Dex coming home meant we had no home. That's what he said as he pounded the For Rent sign into our grass, like he was hammering a nail in a coffin. Did we forget what Dex was? A toddler trapped in a broken ten-year-old's body. *Cytomegalovirus, microcephaly, mental retardation*—one ugly word at a time etched into his medical charts before his first birthday. *Baby boy, Alexander David Lewis II*, the son he'd always wanted, never wanted. Dooming him. Dooming us.

I won't be a prisoner of his needs. That's what he barked as he climbed into his candy-green VW Bug, stuffed with his life.

"And I won't be a prisoner of yours." Mama said it low, real low. But she said it.

"Go ahead, fault me for putting family first."

"But Dex *is* our family," Mama murmured, standing in the fog of exhaust, runnin' her hand through my hair, stroking and stroking till my head hurt. Mama, Dex, and I could make a life without him, he'd said again, rolling up the window. And then he was gone.

And I meant to prove him right, more right than he knew.

ℂ

PASSING A SOUVENIR shop, I caught a murky glimpse of myself in the smudged window, sunburnt and dirt-streaked, a far cry from the slender clerk stocking items on a jewelry rack—starfish earrings, mermaid pendants. Task done, she fetched a stool and stacked beach towels, a floral sundress hugging her tanned frame, an anklet of puka shells above her sandals. She swayed dream-like to a song on the radio, the faint melody drifting through the propped door. The song over, she looked up and tapped her bracelet watch, and the reflection in the window that was me—soaked pants, baggy T-shirt, tousled hair—turned away and headed the last few yards home.

A twig large as the one on the makeshift porch ramp could tumble Dex. Tossing it into the yard, I opened the front door to the smell of sizzlin' bacon and the squall of angry tears. Dex thrashed in his high chair, hair mussed, bib skewed, country-milk face beet red. His glasses dangled from an ear despite the tight band that fastened them, the thick lenses smeared with food. Something greenish, like sea foam, dribbled from his mouth. Glory be, was there never an end to my trials?

"For Pete's sake, Dexie!" Dodging Mama's gaze, I dropped onto a chair. "What's with the hootenanny?" I wiped egg from his cheek, tried to right his glasses, his head jerking every which way. "Ain't no peace in this house," I muttered.

"Where've you been hiding?" Mama stood at the stove, scrambling eggs, her uniform unzipped, voice tense. Somehow, I no longer felt so sure the Lord's work of the morning had been baptizing Hollis Sweet.

"Helpin' at church." *In a manner of speaking.*

She lowered the spatula, gave me a looking over, sighed.

I hitched up my pants, tried to smooth my hair flat. "It was real windy out there."

Long as her eyes didn't fill with tears, I figured I was all right. Since Dex had come home, she didn't know how to get proper mad, just crumpled into a sadness that punched me in the gut.

"Dex's diaper's 'bout as soggy as your pants. Go change 'em both." She drew her words out in the soft drawl of a Louisiana childhood. "Please."

Please? I shirk my duties and she asks me with a please?

"I don't reckon Dad could've spared a precious minute to change a diaper?" The wince on Mama's face made me bite my tongue.

When I returned to the kitchen, warm in a navy pullover and frayed shorts, my frizzy hair bundled into a ponytail, Mama sat hunched at the table, coffee cup in one hand, red pencil in the other, scribbling in her anatomy text. I unbuckled Dex and lifted him to me, his arms squeezing my neck. Even in a soggy diaper, Dex weighed no more than a sack of goose feathers. Thin-boned, doily-delicate, he seemed to float at times, slight as a sunbeam, but in storms he could sink like an anchor, drowning us all. He smelled of fermented baby powder and rotten egg.

"His rash is flarin' up again. Mind your touch."

"Mm-hmm."

"Just a dab of ointment, and pat him dry first. His skin's gotta breathe."

I wrinkled my nose.

"And Eden"—Mama shut her book and rested a tired gaze on me—"don't let him grow roots in his bed. Play with him. He's your brother." Goodness' sake, as if I needed reminding. "Make it a good day. Rosa's due in an hour."

Like he'd know a good day from a rotten day. And what about *my* day? Didn't my day amount to more than changing diapers, mashing peas, and entertaining a stinky, spastic brother? With our TV on the blink, it had fallen to me to keep Dex amused. Sure, he spent a good part of each morning at Hope House, a special-needs school across the highway, and sure, Rosa sat Dex duty several afternoons and after Sunday mass, but like a basket of laundry, he always got dumped on me at the very times I was trying to live my life.

Like now.

Now, I needed to get back to the pier. If she hadn't taken flight—and I supposed it a far-fetched fancy—then I had some investigating to do. This time I'd wear my glasses and take my binoculars. I'd poke 'round the beach, catch her in another act of thievery or plotting more havoc. Anything was better than being stuck here. Hollis would be out helping his dad, the town handyman—plumber, electrician, carpenter, whatever trade a body needed. And I didn't have any other friends to speak of, leavin' 'em behind in San Sebastian. By the time Rosa set me free, it'd be afternoon, and any clues about Raven's fate would be long washed out to sea.

"Confound it anyway," I muttered, dodging Mama's glance and hauling a clamped-on Dex to the bathtub for a hosing.

Rev. Travers had warned us hard 'bout grumbling, so grumble I didn't. Not when Mama told me to work Dex's legs—flex his feet, bend his knees, knead his calves—measure out his seizure syrup, brush his grimy teeth, read him stories, and blow him bubbles, set him on the porch to get some sea air, and, when she arrived, help Rosa without pesterin'. Not when she dashed out the door without so much as a goodbye. Not when Dex lunged for my Dr Pepper, knocking it off the end table and into the Leaning Tower of Pampers. Not even after I'd searched the upstairs closet for a month of Sundays looking for my binoculars.

Only when I nicked my thumb on the razor-thin pages of a dusty ol' book—*Punishment and Torture in Medieval Europe*—did I grumble, except it was more of a holler I tried to squelch with a bloody finger in my mouth.

That's when I laid eyes on the binoculars, fumbling for the box of Band-Aids. Never mind that Dex had been whimpering in his wheelchair downstairs. It gnawed at me some, I guess, but half *my* day hadn't been my day at all. Rosa was the startin' pistol for *my* day. That's when I'd get to the truth of Raven.

SIX

R ᴇᴠ. T ʀᴀᴠᴇʀꜱ ʜᴀᴅ warned me about grumbling that first Sunday Mama had taken Dex to church, before I had been conscripted into the choir. Dex was, she'd said, as much a child of God as the rest of us, created to worship him. I'd uttered not a word but instead had traipsed upstairs to my room, climbed back into bed, and taken ill.

No one knew about Dex back then—no one who mattered anyway. Not Heather Clark with her short skirts, smudged saucer eyes, and copper hair. Not her best friend, Patricia, a shoo-in Skipper doll, same pouty lips, same penciled brows, and sleek sandy hair to her waist. Not chisel-jawed Vince, with his carved muscles and speedster motorcycle. Not the rest of the surfer guys, sun bronzed and oozing swagger. It wasn't that I hankered for their high opinion. Only that I liked staying out of the spotlight, and if Dex was anything, he was a humongous sore thumb.

These were the rich kids, hip and flashy, most from Vintage Heights, a swanky pocket of spacious Spanish-style homes tucked into the eastern hills, overlooking terraced vineyards and apple orchards. Their parents had city jobs— lawyers, doctors, university bigwigs—a few owned seaside inns, and others had inherited their riches, at least according to Hollis. But being rich didn't mean they didn't work hard, he'd added.

"Wouldn't mind working for an inheritance like that," I'd groused. "Some people get all the luck."

Handing me the last pretzel, he'd dumped the bag's crumbs into his mouth and remarked that from what he'd heard, it was a sin to covet, something 'bout an amendment. That didn't sit too well with me, considerin' I was the one churched. If anyone was going to preach, it wasn't going to be him.

Most of the Vintage Heights kids went to Vintage High, a private school up on Ventana del Cielo Drive, with a view that traced the coastline. Those who didn't wore their grievance loud, the boys mouthin' off to teachers and throwing punches in the halls, the girls closing ranks and trading gossip. Heather and Trish glossed over the slight with fuchsia lipstick in February, mauve in March, swapping out lipstick shades as quick as they swapped out crushes. The two high schools—Vintage and Harford—had themselves a rivalry of sorts, mostly settled under Friday night lights, but out on the ocean the only rivalry was between surfboard and thundering crest, a white-knuckle foe that humbled even the cockiest, turning rivals into friends with high fives and an occasional harrowing rescue. But nobody ruled the waves like Vincent Andrews.

There wasn't a girl who didn't swoon over him, except maybe me, the lot of 'em taken in by his devil-may-care swank and rugged good looks. No denyin' the truth of things—the guy was a fox, with his tall, V-cut frame, golden tan, and velvety hair, a sweep of chestnut bangs above sea-green eyes. But I knew a thing or two about foxes, thanks to Rev. Travers, the Lord himself calling out that fox Herod for spoiling the vineyards.

Vince's parents, real estate moguls, had developed most of Vintage Heights, and rumor was their only son would inherit the Andrews Coastal Estates empire, expand their holdings and their name. Whether he felt railroaded or just hadn't taken a cotton to it, the prospect seemed to bore him, if his freewheelin' ways were any indication. A soul in need of saving, I reckoned. It was no secret he was sweet on Heather, and she was just dead gone on him. Why, she'd have sewn his letterman jacket to her skin if she'd found a needle that didn't hurt.

When Vince and Ben weren't surfing, cutting sleek silhouettes on the breaking swells, the two of them could often be seen, or heard, revving Vince's motorcycle, gunning the engine, smoking the tires, and popping wheelies along Front Street. A slick black Suzuki, Hollis informed me, voice hushed same as if he'd caught a twenty-pound halibut off the pier, with red-hot flames blazin' across the tank and leather tassels snapping in the breeze.

Other than smirks at my taped-together glasses and sneers at my sometimes folksy, sometimes sprawled, oftentimes polite manner of talking—addressing adults as *sir* or *ma'am*, remnants of a dimming past—not much attention came my way, and that suited me just fine.

But then Mama had to bring Dex to church.

ᐢᘓ

IT TOOK SOME doing and most of autumn to unhitch Dex from the institution, what with Mama wrangling for physical custody at the courthouse, holding her own against wary medical staff, tackling an ambush of paperwork. Then we'd had to ready our Harford rental for his October arrival, lay a ramp to the porch, rip up the carpet, and tend to any hazards, not that a bird with clipped wings need fear the wind. Dex had a hard time of it those first few weeks, waking to a house he didn't know, to a Mama he hadn't had, smacking his head against the padded rails and howlin', but by December, he'd taken to beach life, or perhaps forgotten institution life, squawking and grinning more than he wailed.

That's when Mama's notion about church set in. Like Mama, I'd wanted Dex with us, even if my father didn't. Maybe I hadn't always, but I did now. *I* knew he was family. Still, I kept to the shadows at school, away from curious glances trying to ferret out my secret. Mama didn't take much to my idea of waiting till Good Friday, an evening service lit only by candles, allowing me to fade into the darkness. Instead, she picked a tropical Sunday morning in March.

So I'd taken deathly ill.

"Eden?" Her powdery scent wafted up the stairs. "You ready?"

I burrowed lower under my blanket. "Is Rosa here already?"

"Rosa isn't coming today. You know that."

Dex squealed at Rosa's name, nothin' but a coincidence, but irksome. I felt my fever spike.

"Is Dex coming?"

"You know good an' well he is."

I forced a dreadful cough. "Might be catchin' a touch of something."

"We don't wanna be draggin' in late."

Blankets muffled my ears.

"Eden . . . come on now, sugar."

I wasn't fooled for a second. She figured to catch flies with honey, that's what. While occasion might call for sweetening, it was always *sugar*, never *darlin'*. *Darlin'* was a name reserved for Dex.

"Don't you want to see your friends? Caroline Clark's daughter, Heather—"

"Heather?" I bolted upright. "That snob? She's so stuck up, she'd drown in a rainstorm!"

"Eden Mae! That's no way to talk. Where's your Christian charity?" So much for honey. "I don't have the patience for this. It's been a trying morning."

Trying wasn't the half of it, Dex making a mess in his diaper the minute I wrestled it onto him, slapping the applesauce from his spoon, the gooey mush flying into my hair, banging his head against the high chair, grunting and snatching his tongue. *Uhng uhng uhng!* And then laughing like a loon.

So what? Every morning was rough. And every afternoon and every evening. And every single day and every single night of the rest of our lives. Why the urgent need for celestial light and hymns *now*? Dex wouldn't even know he was in church, let alone how to worship. And what kind of creator would make him, anyhow?

"Now, Eden."

I cracked open my door, ready to plead a case of the vapors, the collywobbles, sudden apoplexy, anything. At the bottom of the stairs, Mama clipped on a pearl earring and tucked her Bible under her arm. Dex sat beside her in his wheelchair, strangely calm, his downy blond curls combed back neatly, his slack, shrunken body smart in a crisp plaid shirt and knit vest, beige trousers cuffed above heavy black shoes. He looked at me through crooked glasses, his maple eyes enormous, a silly grin spreading across his face of its own accord. There wasn't a single thing he could *will*, all of it just happening to him, pretty near same as me.

"Don't forget your tithe, sugar."

I must have gone pale.

"Just one dollar—ten percent of your allowance." Mama gave a tired smile. "We're barely gettin' by on your dad's salary. But soon as I'm done with school and bringin' home a real paycheck, I'll tuck in a little extra."

Making ten bucks stretch over thirty days was a feat beyond my best hand. What with Max Factor's hottest new lipstick and my weekly prescription of Bazooka, I had no choice but to ante up my collection plate money at Cappy's.

The trek downstairs felt like braving a wind tunnel, the fifty cents dumped in my patent purse like parting with diamonds.

Mama straightened the bow on my ponytail as I locked the front door.

I followed half a block behind them all the way to church.

Ascending to the pulpit, the reverend swept dark eyes across the chapel, across a somber and mostly gray-haired flock, across Mama seated at the aisle next to a dapper Dex, the reverend's gaze lingering a spell on the child in the wheelchair, and then across the ripple of restless boys and tittering girls. He'd pondered each of his stumbling sheep with furrowed brow and tight lips and then had settled on the last pew, where I slumped alone, no kin to anyone there, fixin' his gaze on me and reading my failings like a collection plate tally that had come up short.

"Do you feel burdened, dear family? Beleaguered by trial, besieged by tribulation?" If not for his three-piece suit and polished black shoes, he might have been the family doctor come to call, his voice gentle, probing for what ailed our souls.

Yes, sir! Only it was my body wantin' saving, for at that very moment, a dreaded *bzzz* signaled I was indeed under siege, by a sand wasp no less—harmless if left alone, Hollis later informed me. But even as I slapped my rolled-up bulletin at it, I knew my troubles went far deeper.

"Do you, like Job, cry out in bitterness and despair against the weight of your misfortune? Or do you, like Paul, find strength in adversity, giving thanks and trusting in God's providence?"

Only thing I had in common with Paul was a thorn in the flesh, two if the wasp got me. That and lousy vision.

"To grumble—even in the depths of adversity, the dark valley of despair—is to question Almighty God, a God who loves us and wills for us only good, who restores our soul and leads us in paths of righteousness."

I slid lower in the creaky pew, dodging the wasp and the prick of my conscience, and set my ruminations on Mama, her head tilted toward the reverend, hair tied into a silk scarf, one arm resting on Dex's wheelchair. Mama never grumbled, not even when Dex wailed fit to wake the dead, keeping us from a wink of sleep, for nights on end some weeks. There she'd sit in the shadowed front room, or on a porch step, rocking him by moonlight, from her lips the sweet incantations of hymns and Scripture. Mama's exhausted calm at daybreak, without even a harsh word to me for givin' Dex the stink eye, seemed awful unnatural. I reckoned she was 'bout as unnatural as Paul.

I swatted at the wasp again.

"Consider the Israelites."

I was happy to oblige, my own soul a murky and dismal place.

"God performed mighty miracles for the people of Israel. He raised up Moses to lead them from Egypt to the Promised Land. He parted the Red Sea with Pharaoh's armies close behind."

A baby whimpered; several people coughed. A deacon shifted in his seat near the choir loft. In the hush, I squinted at the corner window, the bottom sash open, allowing a soft breeze—and, sure as shootin', the wasp. Beyond the dirt parking lot, a lazy ocean curled against the shore. Above the rippled murmur, I heard Dex squawk and saw Mama lean into the aisle, hankie in her hand, most like wiping drool from his chin.

"He guided them through the desert with a pillar of cloud by day, a pillar of fire by night. He rained down manna, bread from heaven, for sustenance."

Now I chafed right along with the Israelites, vexed at the trials of a wilderness no fault of their own. At least I'd been spared the prying eyes of the starched flock, having trailed a good twenty paces behind Mama as she'd entered her usual front pew, Dex burbling and bouncing in his wheel-chair, every scrubbed neck craned their way. Ditching Mama for the back pew, I'd found myself behind the Barbie brigade, girls cast in California cool, dolled up in Hollywood dreams, older by a year, hankerin' to be noticed as much as I wasn't, with all the ease and chatter of a once-upon-a-time, of a Texas no longer mine.

My seat afforded me a close-up view of Heather's purple tie-dye shirt, macramé hoop earrings, and polished-penny hair, coiled like cotton candy. Trish wore her dark-blond hair down, probably slept all night in curlers to get the cascading bouffant wilting in front of me. With each breath, I inhaled their citrus hairspray till I became fair intoxicated. But at least they couldn't see my burning shame.

"Gimme your wrist," Heather whispered loudly, digging in her leather clutch, Julie elbowing her with a *shh!*

Trish stuck her arm out obediently as Heather held a

glass vial to it, spritzed, then doused her own wrist. A wave of floral perfume mingled with the hairspray.

Heather never paid Rev. Travers any mind that I could tell—and Trish wasn't about to cross a street that Heather hadn't crossed first. Done with their toiletries, they took to doodlin' on the church bulletin, their pencils busy on a photo of "Ms. Henrietta Pringle, Missionary of the Month," their giggles hushed. When they lifted their bent heads, Ms. Henrietta Pringle sported muttonchop sideburns and a mustache.

The wasp alighted on a beaded handbag, then crawled down the clasp, where I lost it as Heather filed her nails, turquoise powder dusting the seat cushion. Only Heather could wear her hair in a flaming plume a foot high and not look stupid. *No less impressive than the pillar of fire that led the Israelites through the wilderness,* I mused. I had to lean a bit to the right, past the Shekinah glory, to see Rev. Travers.

"Yet the Israelites grew impatient, weary, disgruntled—took to bellyachin', we'd say in the South—lifted their voices against Moses, declared captivity in Egypt better than death in the desert."

I watched the wasp float near Ronnie, take stock of his rumpled shirt collar, his layered shag, then flit away. I was no better than an Israelite. Swapping my bulletin for a hymnal, I comforted myself with the lyrics of "Blessed Assurance."

"So he gave them up to their unbelief, gave them up to the wilderness. How he grieved for his people, stiff necked, wayward—yet loved. How he grieves for us."

A hearty "Preach!" erupted from the center pew—the retired Pentecostal pastor, most like—sending Mr. Brewster, our postman, springin' out of his seat, with Mrs. Brewster snatching him back before he was fully uncoiled.

"Likewise, God may be leading you through a desert.

You may be tempted to doubt, to fear, to grumble. You may long for hope."

I needed a little hope right then, for the wasp now rested on my sleeve, its wings silent. Lord a'mighty, I was a goner.

"My beloved family, let us with Paul 'rejoice in our sufferings, knowing that suffering produces endurance, and endurance produces character, and character produces hope, and hope does not disappoint us.'"

I let out my breath as the wasp resumed its erratic flight, circling above Heather's updo. Trish unwrapped a piece of saltwater taffy and popped it into her mouth.

"God leads us through the desert, not to abandon us, but to deliver us to the Promised Land."

The reverend's voice, which had swelled to an impassioned crescendo, plunged like a meteor, leaving a cratered hush in its wake. "A promised land not of milk and honey but of love, joy, and peace—the fruit of the Spirit."

"Fruit?" Heather hissed, leaning into Trish and pointing toward the front pews. "Looks like *she's* been blessed with a vegetable."

In a serendipity of grace, the wasp nestled into Heather's flouncy plume.

Whack!

The shriek that met my heroism brought the congregation to a sudden gasp—and the wasp to a sudden death.

That's how I found myself drafted into the choir, robed in amethyst satin and zeal for the Lord, my rehabilitation complete. As Mama often said, God sure does work in mysterious ways.

SEVEN

I TOLD HOLLIS afterward that Divine Providence had landed the wasp on her pouf, my quick wits converting the hymnal into an instrument of deliverance and my valor sparing Heather a vicious assault. Though he'd raised an eyebrow above his aviators, he allowed me my story. I suppose my explanation to the church elders might have raised a few eyebrows as well, what with Heather flailing in the pew, caterwaulin' that she'd been attacked, but the elders asked for none, instead swiftly escorting me into Rev. Travers's office to await rebuke.

As for Mama, she'd wheeled Dex home ahead of me, waiting at the front door only to sigh, "Oh Eden Mae, I'm just so sorry."

Sorry? For what? Sorry that she'd insisted on taking Dex to church? Sorry she couldn't trust me not to make a spectacle of myself? Or the kind of sorry she'd stammered into the choking exhaust of my father's VW last summer as he'd pulled away from our San Sebastian house, her kitten heels sinking into the damp lawn, her hand stroking my hair? The memory seared, welled in my eyes.

The sermon must have skidded to a stop, the benediction to a rushed amen, for in a blink an' a breath, the reverend walked into his office, leaving the door open. In the narrow corridor, two elders stationed themselves like the cherubim at the Garden of Eden, 'cept not to keep folks out but to keep me in, scowls as good as flaming swords.

Rev. Travers made a beeline for the window and opened the Venetian blinds. "And you are?"

"Eden, sir. Eden Lewis."

Sunlight washed the dark room. "Let there be light!" Tugging off one shoe and then the other, he shrank by two inches and then some. "New brogues. Haven't broken them in quite yet." He set the wing-tipped shoes beneath the window and sighed heavily. "As for you . . ."

I took a sudden interest in my scuffed Mary Janes.

"Do your shoes pinch too?"

"What?"

But he'd slipped a notecard from his pocket. "'Ruckus in pew 11. Popsicle violins.'" His brow furrowed. "Ah! 'Possible violence.'" He gave me a severe look. "Have you anything to say?"

"No, sir."

"No? 'Be ready always to give an answer to every man that asketh you a reason.'"

"Yes, sir." But it was too late to plead ignorance of either Scripture or my crime. He'd settled into his chair and was holding the murder weapon.

"Time was of the essence, sir."

His horn-rimmed glasses now on his nose, he opened the hymnal. "A bug, smashed between hymns 62 and 63."

"A wasp, sir."

"And these?" He extracted a few strands of red hair.

That was a bonus. "Heather's hair was a casualty of war, sir." It's what Hollis had said when I'd asked about a hook-shaped cut on his hand.

His glare gave way to a warm laugh. "All's fair in love and war, is that it?"

I didn't know anything about love when it came to Heather, but I did my best to look stricken, lowering my eyes to contemplate the tragedy of scuffed Mary Janes.

"Now, now, it's not so bad as that." He turned a framed photo toward me. "Last summer at the bluffs—the missus, Joshua, Benjamin." Elephant seals sprawled on the sand behind the windswept family. "But then you must know Ben from school. He's in eleventh grade. What are you? Tenth grade?"

"Ninth grade, sir."

"Ah, a young'un. Ben's birthday's next week—seventeen years old."

Same age as Hollis, though Hollis seemed a good deal older than Ben. Taught at home with his siblings, he'd graduated at sixteen to learn carpentry with his dad. Real life, he'd said, not book learning, though he didn't disparage scholars none, saying it took both kinds to make the world go 'round. Still, he said, nothing like duty to make a man grow up quick. And he wouldn't have it any other way.

"Time waits for no man." The reverend spoke to the photo now, brows furrowed again. As he studied it, I ventured my own studyin'.

Above the sanctuary pews, Rev. Travers loomed, swelled, fair leapt over the pulpit and into our laps. But here in his office—a plain, bare room hemmed in by solemn bookcases, Rev. Travers shriveled into a pitted prune, swallowed by a behemoth of a desk, a word I'd come across in Job. Not a hair on his head whispered out of place, and not a thing in his study, either, 'cept on the desk itself, that is. Books, loose papers, pens and pencils lay helter-skelter, one thick book smack-dab in the center—*Matthew Henry's Commentary*, far as I could make out. A striped tie dangled off the corner of the desk, held fast by a dented tin of Kiwi shoe polish.

Up close like this, I could see waxy dew beaded into the creases of his forehead, catch a whiff of his cologne—cedar, cinnamon, and pepper—even count the gray flecks clinging to his jacket collar. His hair, slicked into glossy black ripples, looked near unnatural, like he might've touched it up with the shoe polish on his desk. Even his voice, so mighty and spellbinding above the congregation, had gone soft now, settled low, easy as dust.

He stared long at the photo, like he hadn't laid eyes on his family in a year, though they always sat just 'bout chained to the front pew, Josh and Ben shackled either side of the missus. I reckoned brothers never did outgrow the itch to sock each other.

"Where were you born, child?" He gave the picture frame a swipe with his sleeve, leaned forward, and folded his hands, nearly knocking over a bottle of Old Spice.

"Sir?" I wondered if there was a right answer. Funny how when *he* called me "child," I felt a nice kind of drowsy, but when Joe called me "child," I wanted to kick him in the shins.

"Elaine Lewis—your mother—she's from Louisiana, isn't she?"

"Shreveport."

"Ah, Shreveport. That explains the music in her voice . . . and yours. Were you born there?"

"No, sir." As soon as I said it, I knew the right answer would've been *yes*, and under most circumstances I'd have stretched the truth, seeing my neck was in a noose. But there was a holy presence in Rev. Travers's office that terrified the lies out of me. "I was born in Houston Methodist Hospital. Lived there till last year. In Houston, I mean. Course, I spent most summers in Shreveport visitin' my grandparents. Then

Gramma Kay came to live with us."

"How about that? I had a Gramma Kay too!" Just like that, his stern brow went lax and he began to sing, low and easy. "We're a walkin' case of the blues, oh what're we gonna do-ooh? Gramma said to kneel and pray, joy is just a step away. Goin' back to Houston." He let slip a small chuckle. "Dean Martin, pastor style. You know it?"

"Sure I do." And I hated it. Whenever it came on the radio, my father would belt out the chorus, swapping *Houston* for *Frisco*.

Rev. Travers fished a peppermint out of the collection plate and tossed it 'cross the desk. "Go on. It'll clear your head." He unwrapped one for himself.

Spitting my bubble gum into the crinkly wrapper, I popped the peppermint into my mouth. "Thank you, sir."

"We've got somesink in common, child." The reverend's cheek bulged.

"We do?"

"Okra—fried, pickled, grilled. Isn't a way that I don't like it. And I wager it sets you to droolin' too."

Mercy's sake, the reverend was a betting man. But now I *knew* the right answer. "Fine eatin', that. Mama makes a mean gumbo, but I like pecan-fried okra best. And sweet potato pie."

"Now you're talkin', child. I'm a Tennessee boy myself." I near expected a burst of peacock feathers from his backside. "Know what that means, don't you? Means we understand each other." Picking up the shoe polish, he set it to rolling from one side of the desk to the other, pushing paper clips and pencils aside, the tie slipping clean off to the floor.

It was a puzzler how three states between us made for understanding, or maybe it was the okra, but one minute I was low as a snake's belly, and the next I was sittin' pretty.

"And what that means"—he rolled the tin back to his other hand—"is that you'll be joining the choir."

I nearly choked on my peppermint.

"We're alike, you and me." His slight twang unfurled, softening just like Mama's. "It's not easy uprootin' and startin' over. My boys, well . . . it's not easy." He dabbed a hankie to his forehead. "You have a heart God can use."

And so I found myself sentenced to the choir, though the reverend might've considered whether I had a voice God could use—"that child couldn't carry a tune in a washtub," Gramma Kay used to chuckle. Whether I should be right ashamed of my punishment or happy as a pig in mud, I couldn't decide. That is, until one Sunday in the church restroom.

Heather's whine had cut through the flush of a toilet, declaring to someone in the next stall that *she* ought to have been asked to join the choir, not that redneck twerp. "Too late now. I wouldn't join that riffraff choir for a million bucks."

I'd just wiped my mouth clean of my Courageous Coral lipstick, no trace left for Mama to spot, leastways from a distance.

"Oh look, it's the riffraff herself." Heather banged her way out of the stall, one hand holding a small mirror, the other applying eyeliner. "Don't think I'm gonna let it go, twerp."

A second toilet flushed, and Trish emerged, toilet paper trailing from the chunky heel of her shoe.

"You talking to me?" I donned a wide-eyed stare in the sink mirror.

"C'mon, Heather." Trish stuck a lollipop in her mouth. "She'tha norbody."

"Actually, I'm a second soprano." Before Heather's envy could work itself into a sputter, I sashayed past them out the door. "And wouldn'tcha know—I've got a solo next week."

I figured a fib told in the ladies' room didn't count the same as a fib told in a church pew.

Mama never again mentioned that day, nor did she ever again bring Dex to Sunday service. She seemed content enough to sing him Southern hymns in the porch shadows of a warm summer evening, her melodies carried on a harmony of ocean waves.

And though I had no more close encounters with Rev. Travers, I considered him a giant of a man. No more encounters—that is, until the shooting on the beach.

EIGHT

DULY WARNED 'BOUT the fate of the Israelites, grumble I didn't. Not when I dragged out toy after toy for Dex, not when his squeals darkened into squalls, not even when hunger pangs sent me foraging to quiet our bellies, the coconut-sprinkled donut of the morning a sweet memory. To Mama's cold fried chicken, I added canned peaches, Dex in hog heaven, each tickin' minute on the wall clock drawing me closer to my stakeout of the pier.

Leaving a mountain of dirty dishes in the sink and a pile of crumbs beneath the broom, I waited for Rosa on the front porch, sitting astride the handrail, filing my nails into the almonds Heather always showed off, 'cept mine looked more like armadillo claws.

Dex sat slumped in the cobwebbed shadows of a gnarled bottlebrush tree, large eyes tracking a hummingbird. I'd scrubbed his face with the dish rag, raked my fingers through his sticky tangles, and wrested his floppy feet into Mickey Mouse socks, feet that'd never walk, at least of their own accord. Now and then, I'd peer through my binoculars, sharpening the busy shoreline, the wading children, the sailboats bobbing beyond the buoys.

My 'dillo nails beyond savin', I sat on the porch step and cracked open a dusty book I'd unearthed from the upstairs boxes. The title read *Philosophical Perspectives of Medieval History*.

"Little Piggy's Trip to Market," I announced to Dex, wiping my smudged glasses with my sleeve. That Mama let my father dump his spare books in her bedroom—stacked in boxes on her unused cot, no less—irked me, but I aimed to make good use of 'em.

Course Dex didn't know the difference, wouldn't have known Humpty Dumpty from President Nixon if the giant egg had somersaulted into his lap and said *howdy-do*. Leastways, that's what we all figured. Not that it mattered. I read for me, took a kind of comfort in the frayed covers and dog-eared pages, liked puzzling out the margin scrawls in my father's handwriting, red check marks, parallel lines, the smattering of *e.g.*, *i.e.*, *cf.*, asterisks, and exclamation points. Seemed like he talked to his books more than to us, seein' how they'd whisk him behind closed doors evenings and weekends.

Clearing my throat, I read to Dex like it was gospel, tripping over five-syllable words, skidding across tight rhythms, lurching through meaning, and feeling smarter by the paragraph.

"'Appearing in the seventh century'"—I rolled out my storybook voice—"'the bestiary, or "book of beasts," captured public imagination, weaving descriptions of animals with allegorical lessons.'" I eyed a bumblebee buzzing 'round the scarlet bristles overhead, picking back up once it darted off.

"'Written primarily in Latin, the bestiary taught religious truth through animal lore, often using lavish and fantastical illustrations for the illiterate.' That's you, Dex."

He whimpered, eyes glazed behind his slipping glasses, mouth slack, breath ragged in bursts of sour air.

"Deaf, dumb, and pretty near blind." I sighed. Not even lavish and fantastical illustrations would mean anything to him. "'The caladrius, for example, is a snow-white bird that foretells whether a sick person will live or die.' Not to be mistaken for a goose, Dexie." I studied his shadowed face, his lips parted in half-sleep, drool puddlin' at the corners, and sighed again.

"'If a man is to die, the bird turns its face away from him, but if he is to live, the bird looks into his face and breathes the sickness into itself.' Glory be!"

Dex stirred.

"'Then flying toward the sun, the caladrius releases the disease to be incinerated and flung to the four winds.'"

With no illustration, I tried to imagine the caladrius, but got distracted instead by a mottled seagull landing on the sea wall, more scamp than saint. I squinted at a note scribbled in the margin: *Aviarium* or *Book of Birds* c. 1132–1152, illustrated in *The Aberdeen Bestiary*, England. That's what I'd do then—go plunderin' my father's boxes again.

"'The caladrius represents Christ, who is pure white without a trace of black, "who did no sin, neither was guile found in his mouth."' Well, I'll be tar-nated. It really is the gospel!"

In the distance, the bells of St. Francis clanged once.

"Upsy-daisy, Dexie Day!" Balancing *Philosophical Perspectives* on the porch rail, my glasses on top, I righted Dex and wiped his chin. "It's one o'clock, and ya know what that means, don'tcha? That means she'll be coming 'round the corner!"

He broke into a wide grin, rocked side to side.

"That's no way to play patty-cake." As I slapped his hands together, he chortled and threw himself on me, arms slapping at my neck. I let him clamp on, his breath warm and stale. I could afford to be kind. Relief was on its way.

Peeling Dex off, I uncapped a bottle of bubbles and blew fat, shimmery spheres, sweeping the wand into a torrent of silvery orbs, laughing with him as the bubbles floated beyond reach.

When we'd tuckered ourselves out and Rosa still hadn't come, I allowed myself the first grumble of the day. "Where *are* you, Rosa slowsa Mendoza?"

Dex had sunk back into his stupor, silky lashes drooped over glazed eyes, left cheek squashed against a bony shoulder. The sun reached through the shrubs and into his corner of the porch, throwing soft rays across the rise and fall of his chest. It wasn't like him to sleep so easy during the day, or even at night, for that matter. Truth was, his sleep seemed an ever-elusive yearning—more ours than his.

With a snoozin' Dex safe in his wheelchair, I saw my chance. Wouldn't take but three minutes to slip around the corner and scout the hill for Rosa, who often parked behind the fire station. Slinging my binoculars 'round my neck, I catapulted down the stairs. If she caught me deserting my post, it'd be my earthly end, her tongue thwacking me like a stick upside a piñata.

℘

ROSA LIVED ON the north side of the ravine—a ravine carved by Diablo Creek, a graceful meander most days but a right viper when the heavens let loose—though I had never been to her house, never been to the north side at all. "Gulch Run," we called the smattering of houses that made up the shantytown beneath the Solana hills. Rosa didn't much like me callin' it a shantytown, boasting it had near two hundred folks, hardworking men tending the orchards and vineyards or mining the quarry on the other side of the ridge, harder-working women keeping the men sober and their young'uns fed. And besides, had I ever heard of a shantytown having a post office? No matter that it was a one-window operation at a two-pump gas station.

When I'd asked Hollis about Gulch Run, he'd told me the town lay 'cross the highway, a couple miles down a potholed country road dotted with shacks, rusted cars, scrub oaks, and the occasional wayward cow. You'd spot the bell tower of St. Francis first, the sun-flecked church perched on a grassy knoll. Below that would be a snatch of streets and rundown stores, the ravine winding to the west. Best way to get there, he'd said, was on the heels of autumn, with a few hours to spare, and by way of a footpath through the sprawling ranches and apple orchards, totin' a picnic basket stuffed with sandwiches and then restuffed with plump Fujis and Winesaps.

But if you were driving, you'd take the second turn off the highway, just past the gas station. You'd follow the road a spell till it narrowed and caught up to a gravel lane that veered south, a shortcut that hauled you over a wooden bridge straddling the ravine and then crested two hills before spilling you into the pint-sized town. Except the bridge wasn't there anymore.

"Flood washed it out." Hollis had sounded wistful. "Most people stick to the paved road now. It gets you there too, and a whole lot quicker, but it's not near as fun."

"Quicker? Then how's a washed-out bridge a shortcut? That's as bananas as a post office at a gas station."

"It's just a mail drop. And plowing through the creek, that's a hoot, long as the water's not too swift."

Rosa had picked up where Hollis had left off, but giving directions in reverse, coming toward Harford Beach. Now, a decade after the floods, she'd told me, most of the Gulch Run dwellers just walked the half mile from the ravine along the footpath, vying with cars for the smidgen of road to the highway. But every now and then a jeep or truck would brave the washout an' splatter its way across in a swirl of sludge and smoke. *"Idiotas!"*

The ravine snaked lazily through weeds, eucalyptus trees, and poison oak, slithered past the crackerbox houses toward the sea, such a slow, meandering sort of ravine, that no one was prepared for the storms that winter of '61—frog strangler, we called 'em down South. Certainly not Rosa, Antonio, their nine children, eight chickens, and two dogs. They, along with other bunkered families, watched from tin shelters as howling winds buffeted the coast and relentless rains stirred the ravine into a raging leviathan, spewing charcoal froth into the ocean, uprooting trees, and plunging shacks beneath its current. That January the creek became a river demonic, worthy of its name, Diablo. God's mercy that not a house was lost, though the mud stayed ankle-deep through two summers. Now, though, the ravine was sawin' logs, Diablo Creek no more than a sluggish broth.

Raven lived there, somewhere, out on Ravine Road. That was no secret. With men needed to harvest grapes and blast limestone, a town of sorts had sprung up along the gulch, the outskirts settled by a steady trickle of down-and-out migrants. But rumor erected, whisper by spine-tinglin' whisper, a mansion of gothic proportions, a maze of twisted passages, dark rooms, and endless doors, with an attic sinister as a witch's cauldron.

Hollis wrote it off as bunk, said the largest house there belonged to the Honorable Mac MacDougall, the local drunk and self-appointed mayor of Gulch Run. Now in exquisite shambles, the once stately home had been built by Mayor Mac's grandfather, a landowner who planted his fortune vine by vine just to produce a grandson who drank it away bottle by bottle. Even then, the house held no more than seven rooms if you counted the sunroom out back. Mayor Mac and his pap lived there still.

"Why would anybody wanna live in Gulch Run?" I asked Hollis once. "In tin-can houses, trash dump on one side, smelly ol' creek on the other."

"It's not so bad." Hollis threaded a squid tentacle on a hook. "It's got character. And," he added with a grin, "a post office."

And it was home to Rosa, her husband, and their nine children, two occupyin' the house in a Catholic state of grace—never having reached their first birthdays—hiding lizards under the bedspread and twirling the curtains on the dog days of summer, she insisted.

"Their tooths, I put under pillow same as all childs. Always the peso from *el Ratón de los Dientes*. If he win at the craps."

"What tooths?"

"The tooths from *bebés*."

"But spirits have no teeth."

"Then what I find when I sweeping, heh?"

Señor Mendoza worked the orchards in season and played Cayote off season, a back-alley dice game, Antonio a better gambler than husband. Two stray cats in a barnyard, all claws and hisses, Rosa told me. And then to the din had come the cries of *cariños*—*uno, dos, tres*—all in crescendos so quick she had no time for tears. This she told me that first week she came to watch Dex.

"How'd you have so many kids with all that scratching and spitting?"

"Eh? You think if fighting, you no can loving? Sometimes loving better."

Mama hired Rosa a month after our move to Harford Beach. With my father MIA, tackling Dex early mornings was like ropin' cattle, rushed and messy, Mama racing to the clinic, uniform half-zipped, hair mussed, taking the snaky hillside roads too fast. Until Rosa arrived an hour later, I wrangled Dex on my own, dashing to school in mismatched shoes, hair rattier than Mama's.

"Dexie couldn't ask for a better big sister," Mama had soothed that first morning. "Rosa's here for the both of you, sugar. And mindin' Dex when I'm on call or in class ain't so bad, is it? Just a couple afternoons a week." Tacking a list of emergency numbers on the fridge, she'd reminded me that the LUV ladies would pop by at a moment's notice—more like *without* notice, but fine by me.

If I grumbled, only I knew about it. On Rosa's afternoons, I felt like Christian in *The Pilgrim's Progress*, dropping to my knees at the cross, burden rolling off my back.

"I thought he carried a burden of sin."

I could always count on Hollis. "A burden is a burden. Anyway, as the Good Book says, don't judge another till you've walked a mile in their moccasins."

All I got in return was a raised eyebrow.

Mama hiring Rosa—a Christmas gift from the Good Lord himself—meant fewer dreaded hours cooped up in our drab rental, fetching flung toys, wrestling off and wrangling on diapers, keeping an ear out for the sounds of fretful sleep. Had I doubted the power of prayer before, I never would again, leastways not until the next calamity came beggin' for a miracle.

Mama had introduced Dex to Rosa by means of a Saturday afternoon stroll, wheeling him down the porch ramp to a fit of squeals and paying no mind to my protestations of homework. Dragging a good ways behind Rosa, I hid beneath a ten-gallon sun hat, brim tugged low. Mama pushed Dex along the sea wall, rattling off a list of dos and don'ts, pausing now and then to straighten his glasses. Rosa, smelling faintly of cilantro and onions, kept up a steady stream of *sís*. I let my steps lag. When we were out and about, Dex was Mama's business, not mine.

As we neared the swings, catcalls greeted two bikini-clad girls scampering across the sand. Surfers swarmed the sidewalk, leaned against a beat-up Chevy van, stacked glossy surfboards, their wetsuits peeled to their hips beneath the balmy January sun. Slugging each other, they cut up over somethin' and passed a paper bag between swigs. Somebody fiddled with a radio knob, landing on a blast of bluesy piano and thumping bass. Though I couldn't make out their chatter, every so often I caught a *bitchin'* or a *far out*.

Mama kept right on by 'em, weaving Dex to one side when they wouldn't budge. Rosa had to lean in to catch Mama's instructions. Yanking my brim down farther, I slowed my pace, paused, gave the sea wall a lazy kick, twiddled with my shoe. I didn't fall back in with Mama till she'd crossed the street to double back along the storefronts, ducking between cars but casting a quick glance over my shoulder to make sure nobody'd clocked me.

Even with my vision, I recognized Vince—deep tan, all muscle, louder than the rest, a cigarette hanging from his lips. The others were just a smear of faces, likely rich kids from Vintage Heights. Even Anna, who allowed folks their ways, noted their smug privilege with a curt "Idle hands are the devil's workshop." And it was no secret how Joe saw 'em, always blowing into his liquor store for beer they weren't old enough to buy. "Punks. Spoiled and bored and courtin' trouble," he'd say. "I'd take one GI for ten of 'em." Fact was that if the Vietnam War dragged on, they'd be GIs, like it or not.

Then I saw her, a flutter atop the sea wall beyond them, all indigo scarves and sheeny skirts, a shifting blur, ebony hair pinned with flowers—Edgar Allan Poe's raven among the bleached blondes strutting in Coppertone and crocheted bikinis. Like a loosed spirit Raven was, roaming free, unfettered. Not even the school principal could settle her into a classroom for long. She was a lot like Hollis that way, ruled by nothin' but her own whims.

Now she faced the sea, shoulders squared, head high, hands shielding her eyes. I half figured she might take flight. Instead, as if she'd felt my gaze, she turned and scanned the sidewalk. I hurried to join Mama across the street.

"Won't be but a minute." Mama had parked Dex in front of Beach Yum. "They've still got a day-old dozen. You can take one to your friend over yonder."

Before I could kick up a fuss, Mama had ducked through the beaded curtain into the bakery.

"Con-demmit!"

"*Tu madre,*" Rosa huffed, brushing against me, "*es una buena mujer.*" Callused fingers wrapped around mine—the one an' only time we might've been friends—her stout frame blocking all way of escape. "She good mama."

What I wouldn't have given for a bad mama at that moment.

"Here you go, sugar." Mama was back in a jiffy, handing me a white bag. "Run that on over to your friend now."

Run I did, across the street, past the Chevy van, my hat pulled so low over my face I could barely see—just asphalt, sidewalk, the sea wall, Raven's ankle boots, the donut bag, more sidewalk, aspha—

"Hey!" I felt my hat sail off my head.

"Whoops, did I blow your cover, Natasha Fatale?" Heather sneered, tossing my hat into the van. From the back seat came a shriek, Trish bobbling my hat like a hot potato, then throwing it onto the pavement with a loud *ew!* Her giggle sounded like nails on a chalkboard.

Oh, for the gumption to let 'em have what-for, but any comeback would've just added fuel to the fire, the surfers laughing, all eyes on me. Snatching my hat, I pulled it low and didn't come out from under it for a week.

Over donuts and sweet tea that afternoon, Mama laid claim to Rosa as the family we so badly needed, leaving me to show her the ropes—wasted breath, of course. The sooner Rosa learned Dex's routine, the sooner I could hightail it out of the house. If my eagerness to help surprised Mama, she didn't let on as I launched into my own list of dos and don'ts, a zeal that knew no bounds till it collided with Rosa's ire.

"*Ay caramba!* What tell you me? I can change diaper," she said as I showed her how to calm a cranky Dex, "can feed *bebé*, can walk *bebé*," as I showed her how to buckle his clunky shoes, strap on his braces, lock his knee joints. "You think I no care for *bebés*? I *madre* to *nueve chamacos*! *Nueve!* *Uno, dos, tres*, uf! *Nueve!*"

"He's not a baby." I fetched his glasses from under the couch and snugged them on his flingin' head. "He's got special needs. If he throws off his glasses, you must say *No!* and put them back on."

"Heh! What tell you me?" She caught his fist just as he was yanking them off again. "This child same all other childs. Who mama here? You or me?"

I didn't bother to remind her that he had a mama and she was at work.

"You," I said glumly.

And that's how Rosa became my deliverance and my doom.

After her brisk walk from Gulch Run along the ravine path, down the dusty roads, across the highway—or from the parking lot by the fire station, if Antonio drove—and up the seven steps to our porch, Rosa would stop at the front door and look skyward. "*Santísima Virgen María, Madre de Dios y Madre nuestra*, all the good I done Lupé, Eloisa, Beto, Carmen, Javier, María, and Guillermo, and never I forget my Evangelina and Eduardo, same I do *mi tesoro*, Alejandro Dex." Pursing her lips, she'd add, "And this Eedee Mae, ay!" She'd mutter this prayer with a frantic sign of the cross, her heavy bosom heaving with the burden of her piety. Rosa Mendoza was the devout Roman Catholic that Hollis was not.

And Rosa, who was never late, was more than an hour late today. Condemnation.

NINE

"Ow!" My binoculars trained on a dirt-streaked pickup across from the fire station, I'd collided with my deliverance herself, Rosa charging down the hill holding a large grocery bag.

"*Santo cielo!*" she cried, green apples tumbling.

The pickup honked, made a U-turn. Antonio waved out the window.

"Excusa me, *señori*—oh, is you." Rosa's eyes narrowed as she stooped to gather the apples. "What happen? Why you not to Alejandro?"

"Why you so late?" I scrambled after an apple rollin' down the gutter.

"*Mucha* trouble, *malvada. Bendita la Virgencita!*" She bathed my face with the stink of garlic as we dropped the apples back into the torn bag. "What wrong with Alejandro? *Vamos!*"

"Nothing is wrong with Ale—Dex. He's fine, asleep on the por—what trouble?"

Pushing past me, she fished two apples out from under a car, a trail of Spanish in her wake, her walk so brisk I had to jog to keep up with her.

"The holy church, de-sacreded! And now bruised apples, who will eat?"

"I will. I love bruised apples." I took a bite of one to prove it. "Whaddya mean de-sacreded? Wait, you mean *desecrated*?"

Rosa's delay took a back seat to this new turn of events.

"How? Who?" Raven had returned front and center.

"How I know who?" Rosa chugged steps ahead of me, huffing as she neared our house. "Bad person, that who."

"What did they do?" I tore after another rogue apple.

"Grafti! Grafti on the church. *Sacrílegas. Terrible* words, I no say. *Qué mal!*" She looked to heaven and made the sign of the cross. "*Y la hermosa angel*, the window, *quebrada*! Ay!"

"Grafti? What's grafti? *Graffiti*? On the Catholic church?" It had to be. No beautiful angels graced the plain windows of Mar Vista Chapel.

"*Sí, la iglesia de San Francisco*," she informed the gutter, her skirt hiked up to reveal folds of legs stuffed into knee-highs. "*Las ventanas de cristal de colores, destrozadas!* Is a seen, *pecado*, a seen to de-sacred a church. *El padre*, he pray, he pray for the seener and he wash the seen. All morning, he wash, I wash, *rojo* like the blood. *Horrible* the words, *horrible* the pictures. I wash. I clean. I late!"

A motorcycle engine drowned out Rosa's next words, and I glanced up to see Vince buck through the stop sign, leather jacket unbuttoned, cigarette between his lips, and behind him, Ben, wavy hair brushing his collar, cowlick defiant. They'd taken to cruisin' Front Street near a dozen times a day now that school had let out, blipping the throttle at the intersections, rattling windows with every downshift, then burning rubber from the stop signs. And, as if the rumble and whine didn't draw enough stares, they'd spruced up those flashy flames licking the gas tank.

Above the purr of the bike, I heard a wolf whistle.

"Now there's a sight to give a guy sore eyes!" Vince's laugh rang out, unmistakable. "And right next to our cowgirl cutie too."

Ben leaned sideways to catch a glimpse of Vince's latest target, but turned away quickly as they roared past.

Vincent Andrews sure thinks he's all that. I frowned, for a moment distracted from Rosa's news and feeling my cheeks burn. If he'd been a playing card, he'd be a wild one—an ace or a deuce, no one knowing which way he'd land. I couldn't puzzle him out any more than I could puzzle out Rosa's scrambled English. Had to admit it, though, if not for him, I'd be grinnin' all gums like ol' Seadog Smitty. Still, I didn't blame Joe for looking askance at the James Dean wannabe, hotshot gonna-be senior, a rebel without a cause—least till the commies drifted in.

We had that in common anyway, Joe and I. The rough edges that snagged many a heart rubbed me like sandpaper, despite the silver spoon in his mouth. I wagered a thing happened to a guy when he turned eighteen, put a chip on his shoulder, made him dare the world to a fool-crazy dustup before it—and the war—swallowed him whole. Leastways, that was Hollis's guess 'bout what chased his cousin off to Canada, "mighta dodged the draft, but can't outrun duty." Or maybe it was just a taste for trouble before he'd be saddled with a suit, tie, and his daddy's shoes, giddy-upped into runnin' the family business.

I felt a kind of pity for Rev. Travers, seeing firsthand the truth of Paul's warning to the Corinthians that bad company corrupts good character, though who was corrupting whom caused no little discord during choir practice, pitting the alto against the tenor. The tenor prevailed on account of his deeper voice, reciting the old saying that the preacher's kid raises more hell than the devil's own. Then again, I'd sat through enough sermons to know that where there's a problem, there's a parable. It was no secret that the reverend intended Ben to attend seminary—better than a pigsty, I reckoned, for bringin' the prodigal home. If I'd been in Ben's shoes, a PK on display, I might not much care for the noose of religion either, but fact was I had enough trouble in my own shoes. And the way I saw it, a thing became a noose only when it was forced on you, the way Dex had been forced on me. Religion on Mama was a halo.

Another motorcycle vroomed past, a flash of metal and bare skin, Ronnie at the handlebars, a girl pressing into him, all curves and lashing blond hair, the faint scent of suntan oil in the fumes. The two bikes rumbled side by side now, their own parade down Front Street. Watching them, I felt a kind of pity for myself too, the sour grapes kind, though I'd learned to content myself with Hollis, poker, and religion.

"What'd you say?" I caught up to Rosa. "Pictures of what? Blood?"

"*Rojo* like the blood, *hoz y el martillo*. What you call—hammer?"

"Hammer? They broke the window with a hammer?"

Rosa's tone stopped me cold. "*Qué mal*, Eedee Mae!" Barreling up the porch steps, she saw what I couldn't. "*Vergüenza*, Eedee Mae! *Inaceptable!* Alejandro, ay, ay! He go for you! See you did!"

From the third step, I peered past Rosa. Dex, fast asleep in his wheelchair not two minutes before, now flopped in a heap of limbs and sobs on the porch, his legs crumpled beneath him.

"What kinda seester, you? You no buckle him? *Qué mal!*" Rosa dropped the grocery bag, apples scattering again, scooped his twisted body to her bosom, and plopped herself down on the porch with a grunt. "What you say, *mi tesoro*, heh?" She wiped his face with her thumb. "What you say to Rosa?"

Whenever he cried or wailed or bleated his *uhngung gung uhgn*, she'd take his hands in hers, tilt her head, and ask him, "What you say?"

"He doesn't say anything!" I'd finally blurted one day. "He just makes noises. They don't mean anything."

"Uf! You not listening him," she answered. "You listen, you hear what he say."

What he say, if anything, only God knew. Certainly not Rosa. I gathered the scattered apples to her coos and his cries and piled them into an empty flowerpot. Rosa watched my every move as she rocked Dex, his sobs replaced by hiccups.

"Down the stairs he maybe fall. *Vergüenza.* Why you no strap?"

I shrugged and squinted at a sidewalk crack.

"How many times I tell you?"

"*Qué mal!* I didn't mean to. I just forgot."

"*Poca memoria*, eh? What say mama when I tell her you forget?"

"My mama?" I looked as stricken as I knew how.

"Heh!" Rosa seemed satisfied. "No, I say *nada* to mama, no worry mama. But you ask God forgive you. This your *hermano.* How you leave him no strap?"

"I'm a wicked girl, that's how." I could feel something harden and sour inside, and the last of my saintly virtue at Hollis's baptism tumbled from my heart, same as Rosa's *manzanas verdes.* "You've never liked me anyhow. Always I make you mad." I sounded like her, my words mixed up just like my thoughts.

"Like you? *Niña tonta!* I no paid to like you. I paid to care Alejandro. You, I for to pray. Where you go?"

"Where I go?" Rosa had a way of making me feel like I was five. "Reckon I'll go drown myself in the sea."

"Mmm," she said, not looking up.

But an idea was takin' shape even as I spoke. "I'll tell you where I go. I'm going to church. Gonna confess my wicked ways." That got me a look. "And *then* I'll go drown myself in the sea."

"*Muchacha traviesa!*"

As I stomped off toward the fire station, I could hear Rosa snorting and fussing by turns, irritable *Eedee Mae*s followed by tender *Alejandro*s. She couldn't know it wasn't my church I was fixin' to visit, but Hollis's church, *her* church, St. Francis Roman Catholic Church, the scene of the crime, and that confessing was the last thing on my mind. I wanted to poke around the church a bit, see the *grafti* myself, or whatever traces were left, the blood on the walls, the shattered window. The pier would have to wait.

And then, if I still had time, I'd scout out Raven's house, see the gabled ruin of my imaginings in all its grand glory. Ravine Road couldn't be too far beyond St. Francis, surely an easy switchback or two toward the gulch. I'd lay bets there were nefarious goings-on to uncover. *Like a new crop of weeds taking over the backyard?* It was just like Hollis to put an oar in uninvited where there was a chuckle to be gotten. I had a ready answer: *For me to know and you to find out.* Couldn't sort the truth of the rumors till I braved the trek. What was to say I wouldn't find something that would tie Raven to the spate of crimes? Or prove her uncle a KGB spy, even the head of a smuggling ring? I might even catch a glimpse of Raven herself, pacing the attic, long as her uncle wasn't aimin' a rifle out a window, same as Ben said. The thought sent chills down my neck. Wouldn't that be a hoot to tell Hollis?

If *muchacha traviesa* was what Rosa thought of me, then I had nothing to lose.

My time was my own now, and I intended to be beholden to no one, same as Raven, same as Hollis, to be free, loosed from the shackles of my life.

TEN

BY THE TIME I reached the ravine, a low bank of fog had crept over the shore, venturing no farther than the sea wall at last glance—a glance accompanied by a vexed *con-tarnit!* when I realized I'd gone off without my binoculars—but chilling the breeze that followed me toward St. Francis. I'd simmered down some, my pace slow and a little uncertain, no less bitter but less interested in immediate drownings.

Only one vehicle passed me, a pickup stacked with surfboards, chugging the opposite direction along the shoulder, from the vineyards into town most like, kickin' up such a tornado of dirt that my eyes teared up. Not until the clattering contraption had barreled by with staccato honks and a shout from an open window did I realize it was no ranch rig but the Old Clunker herself. I swung 'round too late to see who'd shouted, inhaling exhaust and dust, but couldn't dodge the hurled words. *Commie lover!* That's what she'd jeered, red hair whipping as she leaned across the driver, someone else to her right. I hadn't seen who was driving, but I'd know Heather anywhere.

Quitting the potholed road for a footpath, I cut through a thicket of oaks, the steeple of St. Francis 'bout swallowed by their branches, walking myself bang into headstones, mossy slabs chiseled in eroded, near unreadable script. The graveyard dozed in shadows, no hint of breeze, dank and musty, tinged with the decay of bones and buried memories. A shiver shook my spine. Not that I fancied spirits running amuck in my house, but Rosa's way of keeping alive the dead, her twins whisking about her rooms, makin' mischief of one kind or another, seemed less fearsome than trying to hush restless bodies in moldering coffins. None too eager to creep 'long the ashen markers, I clung to the outskirts. I had no intention of stirring up ghosts.

A dozen more paces and I'd entered the shadow of St. Francis itself, the bell tower soaring above me, the adobe walls a yellowed ivory, the wooden beams cracked and splintered, the old church like a sea-battered sailor, worn by decades of ocean winds and harsh California sun. Smack middle of a patch of lawn sat the fountain of Rosa's laments, water frisking into two basins, bursts of flowers like a skirt at its base—the yellow and purple pansies taking me back to weekends kneeling in the garden with Mama, she patting the dirt around the new shoots, me despairing of ever telling one flower from another.

"In every pansy is a butterfly." She'd traced gentle fingers against the buds. "You'll see."

And I did, the deep purple wings unfolding into yellow petals beneath May skies.

"Won't ever forget a pansy now," she'd said.

But seeing them here beneath the fountain, I almost wanted to.

Quiet as a church mouse—fittin', given the circumstances—I looped the fountain. If there'd been any graffiti on the mottled stone, it wasn't there now, not at first look-over anyhow. Past the fountain, wide steps led to two arched doors flanked by Bible stories narrated in stained glass. I gave it a hard squint, could just make out a shattered angel. If not for the sawtooth pane and glistening shards, I might've fallen into an oil painting, what with the tidy rows of flowers, the splashing fountain, the sun-dappled steeple.

Who'd have thought that a church this side of the ravine, and a Roman Catholic one at that, could be so quaint, even holy, and, except for the busted window, so peaceful? *Yep, who'da thought?* I could hear Hollis gently mock. Our seaside church, or rather our rejiggered schoolhouse, with its A-frame and plain windows, had neither fountain nor garden, only a stout turret, room enough for one dull bell, and a dirt parking lot. The beauty of Mar Vista Chapel, I reckoned, lay in the fiery truth of Rev. Travers's sermons.

Picking my way through the flowers, I crouched beside the fountain. "*Rojo* like blood," Rosa had said. But though I scoured it, the fountain gleamed—no trace of graffiti, no blood-scrawled profanities, nothing. "I clean. I scrub." *And, Rosa, you done washed away all the tellings.*

Plenty aggravated, I dug in my pocket for my last piece of gum, the crinkle of the wrapper loud as rattlin' bones. No sounds filled the air 'cept for the slap of water flowing into the basins. No birds called, no leaves rustled, no bells clanged. Seemed the ugly vandalism of the morning had stunned the venerable church silent.

One wooden door stood ajar, inviting me to come on in. Most like, the priest—what did Rosa say his name was?— would be kneeling at the altar, calling down righteous judgment on the vandals. The holy man would be easy to spot, stooped from the weight of mankind's sins, grizzly white beard sweeping the floor, sandaled feet shuffling in an ancient gait. All the priests I'd ever seen were older than the moon, leastways the ones illustrated in my father's medieval history books, or maybe those were magicians, but I supposed they all amounted to the same thing.

Squeezing through, I shed sunlight for a sanctuary muted in dusk. It took a moment for my eyes to adjust, but when they did, I had to pinch myself.

I'd clean done a time travel, stepped into another century. The church glowed, filtered light falling from the vaulted ceiling onto a tile floor. The rows of stained-glass windows blurred and shifted like a kaleidoscope. Statues lurked in various corners, though it took some mighty squintin' to be sure they weren't real folks—saints in supplication and sorrowful women, though come to think of it, they might be one and the same.

Front and center stood the altar and above it slumped a wooden figure on a cross. It 'bout stopped my heart to see Jesus draped in red tapestry and sunbeams. And Hollis hadn't breathed a word about it, the fantastical doings of St. Francis, saying only, "Aw, it's just a church. Nothing so grand as the great outdoors." Maybe not, but grand enough for a reverential whisper.

"Lordy."

"Yes. He does show up now and then."

I nearly swallowed my gum. A man sat facing the back wall, legs splayed from a low stool, boot tips pointed up. A bucket sloshed beside him as he dunked his arm into it. He didn't bother to turn, just wiped the wall, then his brow, the sponge dripping water onto his jeans.

"The Lord is always welcome here, and so are you." He leaned back and surveyed his work. "Even if you are the vandal."

"Me?"

"Maybe. Returning to the scene of the crime."

A door creaked open, and a shriveled woman ducked behind the altar, duster in hand.

"I'm not the vandal. But I know who is—maybe. I wanna tell the priest."

"The thing about a maybe"—he dropped the sponge into the bucket—"is that it's just as good as a maybe not." He rose, grunting, and reached for a Stetson perched on a statue of Mary—least she seemed blue enough to be Mary, though the cowboy hat perked her up considerably. Creasing the crown, he made to put it on, then thought better of it.

"So what can I do for you? I'm Father Miguel."

With his red-plaid shirt, faded Wranglers, and silver belt buckle, he could have passed for a ranch hand—and one not much older than Hollis, by the looks of his tufted face. But the stiff white collar told a different story, one I wasn't sure I was buying.

"I thought priests had to be old."

He grinned. "We get old real fast. All those sins on our shoulders."

I'd been right about something anyway. "I thought you were a ranch hand. Sir."

"I thought you were the vandal." He had as easy a way as did Hollis. "Of course, if you *are* the vandal, I'll hear your confession."

"Lord a'migh—no, thanks." I had trouble enough 'fessing up to Mama. Wasn't about to confess to a ranch hand.

"Ask, and the Lord will forgive."

"That's what the reverend says. Only I haven't got any wrongs needin' forgiving." Now that I knew he wasn't any ol' ranch hand, I polished up my tone. "If I did, I'd take it up with God direct-like." At his amused look, I added, "I'm not Roman Catholic. Sir."

"First Protestant saint, I see." He chuckled. "Well, we'll let that ecclesiastical muddle slide for now. I still don't know everyone in the parish. Got assigned here last month. Interesting place, this Gulch Run."

"Yes, sir." I could think of a heap of other ways to describe it, but minding my p's and q's required silence on the topic. "Can't say I'd know, sir. I live in Harford Beach."

"What's with the *sir* now? I liked being a ranch hand better."

"Yes, si—"

"So you came all this way to tell me who *maybe*"—he stepped aside—"did this?"

Water stains darkened the wall, leaving trails that began far above my reach, even on tiptoe, the red scrawls washed into pinkish whispers—unfamiliar letters paired with symbols. But there were English letters too, forming words I could just make out, and above them, barely visible, a semicircle, like a crescent moon.

"Death to U," I read, squinting my fiercest. "What does that mean?"

"That a soul is in need of prayer."

Seemed a priest walked in those cowboy boots after all.

"Is it blood?"

Crash!

I jumped, and we both turned to see the old woman snatch a toppled candlestand off the floor, kiss it, and set it back on the altar.

"Blood? No, nothing so sinister. Just red spray paint."

I cocked my head, wishing I were taller. "What does the moon mean? And why does it have a capital *T* over it?" Then it came to me. "No, not a moon—a bow an' arrow! No, wait." I remembered Rosa describing it, asking for the English word. "A hammer. But what's a hammer and a bow supposed to mean?"

Father Miguel slid a finger across the mark. "A sickle."

Hollis would tell me later that anyone could spray paint anything and that a hammer and sickle might be the symbol of communism, but that didn't mean Raven or her uncle had done it any more than did the scrawled "Death to USA." But we both knew that was just plain bunk. Who else would hate America—and the Americans who'd sniffed them out?

We did *not* both know, Hollis countered, telling me not to put words in his mouth. By my reasoning, I argued, it had to be her uncle, seein' as how high on the wall the symbol was, 'less she really *did* turn into a raven, an idea Hollis allowed might have merit had any black birds been spotted hauling spray paint outta town. And, he added, don't even start on Rosa's declarations of blood.

"A sickle? Good Lord!" I couldn't hold back, not even in front of a priest. I'd seen what I'd seen, and no amount of a doubting Hollis was going to change that.

"Best not to read too much into it." He stretched, rolled his shoulders, arched his back. "The Good Lord alone knows the heart." Picking up a dustpan, he headed to the shattered window, greeting the cleaning woman in Spanish as she hobbled past.

"How'd they break the window?"

"Lug wrench, maybe. Or a baseball bat." He heaved open the doors, letting in a cool breeze. "So you're not a vandal come to confess and you're not a Roman Catholic. Who are you then?"

"Eden."

"Like the garden?"

"Not very original, but Mama insisted."

"I'd say that's about as original as it gets. Does your mama have a name?"

"Elaine."

"Hmm . . ." He poked a broom under a pew, frowning at the tinkle of glass. "Don't think I know any Elaines. She have a last name?"

"Lewis."

"Elaine Lewis?" He leaned on his broom. "Sounds familiar. Ah, I know. Rosa—she works for your mother, doesn't she? Takes care of your brother?"

"No, I do."

He gave me a sideways look.

"I mean, sometimes. When I'm not in school." What business was it of his, my family?

"Rosa's a kind woman." He dumped the shards in the wastebasket. "I'll have to thank her for sending you to help me."

Before I could object, Father Miguel had retrieved his bucket, fished his sponge from the murky water, and steered me outside, ducking inside briefly to rassle Mary for his hat. "You tackle the steps. I'll finish sweeping here. Watch out for glass."

I might as well have been the vandal come to pay penance for all the elbow greasin' I had to do. For the next half hour, I scrubbed the stone steps, and not even for graffiti, just for the usual dirt and grime. "And cigarette butts, bleh," I grumbled, scraping the mucky ends into the bucket. "A priest who wears a Stetson and smokes!"

We worked quietly, only the scritch-scratch of the broom and the splash of water shaking up the hush, the breeze cooler, the sun a coin sinking beyond Gulch Run. I let myself imagine a crazed Raven pacing her gabled attic, skirts swishing, scarves fluttering, itchin' for moonlight to set her free, imagined her morphing as the first beams spilled across the floor, skirts and scarves warping into glossy feathers, bangled arms fanning into nightmarish wings, imagined her flinging open the cobwebbed window to soar into a charcoal sky, to wreak mischief on a sleeping town, blood dripping from her talons. A Bolshevik bewitcher, same as Hollis had said.

The quiet grew even quieter, the shadows longer, my imaginings more chilling, until the shrill clang of the steeple bells fair made me jump out of my skin. Then it hit me—I was alone. I listened for a moment but heard only my own breathing. I hadn't heard Father Miguel leave, though 'less a haunt roamed St. Francis, the cowboy priest had to be ringing the bells.

Trying to shake off the jitters I'd pothered myself into, I wrung out my sponge, set it next to the bucket, and skittered down the path, coming to a sudden halt at the road, my skin in prickles.

Someone was watching.

I whirled around, lassoed by an unearthly gaze. The church stood silent, the steps stark but for a smatter of leaves. I squinted across the church grounds, the flowerbeds, the fountain, the path to the hillside graveyard, stopping short of the tombstones, having no hankerin' to behold ghostly shapes, and instead scanned the trees along the road.

No one. Not even a rustle.

But I wasn't alone. Whether it was my own shriek that catapulted me or the cries of a dozen crows erupting from a nearby grove, I couldn't say. But with a profane holler for divine intervention, I lit down the road in finer form than I knew I had, runnin' as though ghostly shapes *were* upon me, certain that the eyes I felt belonged to Raven and hearing, over the screeching birds, the ring of shrill laughter.

ELEVEN

We slept a restless night, Dex's moans not like his usual cries, instead groans that burst into occasional sobs, sounds that merged with the bland voice of Mr. York reciting into my restless sleep, *darkness there and nothing more*. Peculiar. I hadn't tried to memorize the poem. *Wondering, fearing, doubting*—still the words came with each tortured moan—*dreaming dreams no mortal ever dared to dream before*. I lay upstairs, hot despite the ocean chill seepin' through the open window, *all my soul within me burning*, and tried to imagine what dreams tormented Dex. *'Tis the wind and nothing more!*

But it was no dream that finally rousted me from bed and through the back forty to the Lodge, my head pounding, my stomach in wobbles. He moaned, I reckoned, from his tumble on the porch, red and purple bruises stamped 'cross his paper-thin skin, a casualty of my rush to steal the afternoon for myself. I was a sorry excuse for a sister. Even if he didn't or couldn't know it, I did. My conscience pricked, kept me from sleep, the lone comfort being I had a conscience at all.

Inside the Lodge, I sat on the toilet lid, Jane Jetsons pinching my nose, flashlight balanced on the water tank. A spider hovered in its beam, dead still—or maybe just dead—but not taking any chances, I swung my legs to the side and propped my sketchbook on my knees. Dex's cries were no more than a night wind through the cattails.

I drew no better than I sang, but these pages mattered only to me. For weeks, come late night, it was my sketchbook I reached for, not my Bible, carrying it to the Lodge like a dog with a bone, worrying its pages with scribbles. I liked the scrape of pencil, the shaping of form and dimension, the emerging.

Ever since Raven arrived, seemed I mostly drew eyes—children's eyes, classmates' eyes, dragons' eyes, even fish eyes one Saturday at the pier, bored with my slack fishing line. But not 'cause I wanted to. Just that whenever I tried to add a nose, lips, cheekbones, the outline of a face, the unruly sketch would give way to disjointed scrawls, the scribbles of a five-year-old. No amount of wrestling or wishing summoned anythin' but eyes—almond, sunken, squinty, wide, the lashes silky, sometimes stiff, the pupils eager, sometimes empty, the eyebrows arched, sometimes furrowed. But never an entire face. Dex's moonlit eyes, Mama's weary eyes, even my father's hard eyes—all stared at me as I flipped through the pages for a blank space. Finding one, I drew.

Had I bothered to look up, I might've seen a glimmer of moon wreathed in wisps of fog, the blinking trail of a far-off plane, the flutter of moths 'round the motel balcony lights—the usual nightscape. But I was fixed on the strange lines unfolding beneath my charcoal pencil.

Three curved marks down, one shorter mark to the side. Rounded points on the ends, sharp talons in dark stabs. A raven's claw, like the illustration beneath Edgar Allan Poe's poem, the one Mr. York was reading aloud when Raven rose to cast her spell.

I swept the line upward to form the leg, shifted to curved

strokes—the soft underside of the bird's body—layered a flurry of feathers, smeared the charcoal with my fingers, worked full tilt, fierce-like, dabbing short marks to flesh out the breast. I erased, tried again, erased again. I blended more. But no matter what I did, the raven refused to appear. Sliding my pencil back 'cross the belly, I drew tail feathers, arced 'em into a cresting wave, hopin' the momentum would spit forth the back, the neck, head, and beak. Instead, from the sweeping curves and smudged feathers stared an eye. An eye brushed with velvet lashes, deep with shadowed swirls, bold, searing, and locked on me. An eye with the claw of a raven dripping from it.

I studied the haunting eye my pencil had drawn, considered the rage and sorrow, Dex's forlorn cries louder, more urgent. Mama would be exhausted, rocking Dex all night and then rising for her shift at the clinic. I'd need to pass on my morning fishing with Hollis again, stay home and tend to Dex while Mama readied for work. And what hope of a return to Gulch Run with such a burden of chores? That thought made my pencil scar the white paper with jagged lines, the bars of a prison with an eye peerin' through—an eye that was no longer Raven's, but mine.

I'd go anyhow. If I left at first light, maybe I could sneak back without Mama any the wiser. I'd stick to the backroads, skirt St. Francis, track Diablo Creek through the ravine, and cut 'cross the shantytown to Raven's house. Without hard facts, Hollis would chalk my suspicions up to rumor and Southern imagination, with reason to mock me but pity to keep himself in check, neither of which I wanted. I needed to return, needed to prove the truth of what I already knew.

The balcony lights of the Sea Crest Motel dimmed, went black. From the cold seat of the toilet, I heard the quiet roll in, the lap of ocean waves mixin' with the steady sobs of Dex. I closed my sketchbook, feeling bone tired. Tomorrow I'd find out the truth.

<h1 style="text-align:center">TWELVE</h1>

Tomorrow came with a blast of late-morning sunshine across my pillow and the heavy grind of the Thursday garbage truck. I jolted upright. Condemnation. Mama hadn't woken me. Neither had Dex's usual yammers and squawks. Mighty peculiar, that. Chokin' down a particularly fine swear I'd heard Jake mutter over a mucked poker hand, I yanked on my jeans, still coated in sand from Hollis's baptism, and sprinted down the stairs. Dex sat wedged between the couch and the bookcase, a pajama sleeve snagged on his wheelchair spoke, whooping as the garbage truck revved its engine extra loud for him, the driver waving at the boy in the picture window.

"Lord a'mighty, can even smell it from here! Or is that you?" Unbuckling Dex, I swung him to my hip. A glance at the kitchen clock told me Mama had just left.

Propped against a box of yesterday's Beach Yum donuts was a notecard in Mama's steady hand. *Gave Dex codeine at 3,* the note said, a dose fit to topple a mad elephant, I knew, Mama resorting to it only when she'd been utterly trampled. *Didn't want to wake you. Please see to Dex.* See to Dex? How could I *not* see to Dex? *You will need to*—and the list seemed endless—*change his diaper, put on his T-shirt and khakis, give him his calcium, scramble him eggs, wash the dishes, exercise his legs, and play with him until Rosa arrives.* Oh, and *Please remember to oil the hinges on the front door.* Mama had told me at least three times to oil them, yet still she said "please." *Thanks, Eden,* the note ended. *You're our angel.*

I frowned at that last bit, seeing what my father saw, even as I felt my anger surge toward him, that Mama's wishful thinking didn't make it so, but yes, I would and I did. And when I was done, I did even more. I spritzed and patted down his hair, cinched my Astros cap on his mussed curls—one my father and I had bought for a quarter at a garage sale—strapped his legs into his braces and sturdy shoes, and shared two donuts with him before settin' him in his wheelchair. The only thing I didn't do was oil the door hinges.

"Can't stop living just 'cause we overslept, y'know," I said, nearly forgetting to buckle the chest harness. He grinned and hooted, flapping his arms 'round my neck while I adjusted his glasses, his sour-curd breath washing over me. "Gulch Run will just have to wait, Dexie," I said, trying not to inhale the stink. "Meanwhile, might as well make the most of being stuck together."

By way of reply, he burbled a string of *uhngs,* agreeing with me, Rosa would have said, but I knew they meant nothing.

Although plenty irked that I'd slept through my recon of Raven's house, with hours to kill before I could roam free, I also felt rested, resurrected in soul and body and altogether dandy. No need to take it out on Dex. But no need to stay cooped up in the house all morning either. It'd call for some disguising, but long as I stayed low under my sun hat and kept to the pier, I should be safe.

"We're gonna have us a fine day," I sang, grabbing my hat, a pair of dark sunglasses, and a baggy jacket I zipped to my chin. "See the pier?" I pointed out the window. "That's where we're headed. It's a bridge to the edge of the world. You ever walk on water, Dexie Day? It's not so bad if you don't look down."

He threw himself back against the chair, gurgling and laughing, and slapped at his Astros cap, his elbow barely missing my sunglasses.

"What you say, heh?" I copped my best Spanish accent. "You like the *océano*? The sparkles? Sissy likes 'em too. But they aren't real, Dexie. Touch 'em and *poof!* they vanish. *Sí,* it's true. The beautiful things, we can't always hold. Where do they go, *mi tesoro*?"

I was dropping pearls more to myself than to Dex, but he squealed and babbled.

"And the sea will sing to you, same as Mama."

If dappled sunrays and cadent hymns could calm him, then I reckoned a thousand dancing suns and the steady roar of swells might work a similar magic. Then, while Dex snoozed, I'd give Hollis the what's what, report the hard-to-scrub facts of St. Francis, ask him to scout out the Soviet den with me. Might even poke around the end of the pier, solve the mystery of Raven's flight.

"And y'know what else, Dexie Day? You're gonna meet Hollis."

Though long past the best fishing hours, I wagered Hollis would be pulling in a final haul or helping the other anglers with theirs. Sure, Hollis knew about Dex, had most like caught a glimpse of him on evening walks, though I hadn't mentioned the fact of my brother exactly, and he'd never asked. Somehow I didn't mind so much if Hollis knew. Hollis Sweet had been born sworn to secrecy. Even getting him to tell me the tides took twenty minutes of plying—high tide for surfperch and white croaker, low tide for halibut. He said it was to teach me how to read the moon myself, but it was no use. Why bother learning what came second nature to him? And whenever I'd hazard a guess, he'd tell me I was a day late and a dollar short.

Now seemed as good a time as any to properly introduce Dex. Anyhow, I needed to see how Hollis's salvation was progressin'. He was under orders to memorize the Lord's Prayer. To hear him tell it, he talked to God regular, but the only prayer he knew, he'd gotten from *The Old Farmers' Almanac*, reciting proudly one morning the lone part he remembered:

> *God grant me a little more time*
> *To pick up my rod and cast my line.*
> *When I am feeble, old, and gray*
> *Please don't take my rod away.*

"Lord a'mighty, Hollis Sweet! That's no prayer," I'd said. "That's a sacrilege."

"Then how come it's titled 'A Fisherman's Prayer'?"

"There isn't a single holy thing in it."

"Might be in the part I can't remember," he offered, breaking into a whistle.

For a moonshine certain, I wasn't the only one needing some learnin'. I resolved to redeem the morning best I could, given his failings and my trials.

"Hey!" I hollered as I pushed Dex down the pier, the wheels swerving with my vigorous wave. The few lingering fishermen barely blinked, true to form. When you'd lived years enough fishing a roiling sea, sweltering under a blazing sun, years enough to harden your face into leather, casting out and reeling in countless lines until your bones dried brittle and your hair faded white, years enough to boast and drink and brawl and spill seafarin' tales that'd singe the coarsest beard, not much turned your gaze. That's what I figured anyhow.

"Hey yourself," Hollis returned, his shout snatched by a gust. He'd set up camp midway at his usual bench, two fishing rods braced against the railing. Fixing my sights on the Bait and Tackle Shack to quell my stomach, I steered the wheelchair in fits and starts across the planks.

"Holy smokes, not like that!" Nearly tripping over his tackle box, Hollis covered the distance between us in a few long strides and grabbed the wheelchair.

"This here's Dex," I said, relieved to let Hollis take over.

"How do you do?" He tipped the rim of his bucket hat. "That's some rough riding. Whatcha say we ditch the throne?" Dropping into a squat, Hollis unbuckled the tight straps and scooped Dex into his arms. "Why, you wouldn't snap my lightest test!" Hollis turned wide eyes to me. "I've got bait weighs more than him."

"He's 'bout seventy pounds wet. But you don't have to carry him. He can walk."

"Well then, let's see your stuff, matey."

As Hollis lowered Dex's legs, I took hold from behind, slipping my arms around his gaunt chest, steadying him as his weight shifted to his braces. Careful not to look between the planks, I let go his hands and backed away. "C'mon, Dexie. Walk to Sissy."

"Uhngung gung!" Grinning ear to ear, Dex lunged forward, his wayward steps startling a pigeon from the railing to the lamppost. Hollis at his elbow, he slapped one shoe after the other, feet twisted inward, body rocking on his toes, somehow not pitching over, his arms in erratic thrusts and swoops. Dex's walk was the mechanical lurch of Frankenstein's monster. A toddler bouncing in his stroller quieted and pointed, his mother crouching to wave his hand with hers. An elderly couple slowed to give a thumbs-up. An angler nodded.

"Attaboy, Dexie. Come to Sissy."

Near bowlin' me over, Dex shrieked with glee.

"What you say, heh?" I teased, turning him toward Hollis. "See that silly hat? Get it for Sissy!"

For a good five minutes, we cheered him on, clapping when he fell into us, launching him back and forth until his legs began to wobble, his squeals to peter out.

Before Dex could collapse into wails, Hollis swept him into his arms as easily as if he'd been a rag doll and, whistling a catchy tune, carried him down the pier to his fishing post. A snatch of wind near took Dex's baseball cap, but Hollis snatched faster, plunking it down on his own head, over his own hat. The wheelchair rattled as I pushed it behind them, making sure to set my feet squarely on each plank, between the gaps a surging ocean I tried not to see.

"Here"—Hollis slid his ice chest aside with a foot—"how 'bout a front row seat?" He set Dex gently into his wheelchair, fastened the harness, and snugged the Astros cap on Dex's head. Then from his tackle box, he plucked a crumpled red flag, pressing it to Dex's palm and folding the small fingers over the pole. "This here is a windsock. Tells me which way the wind is blowing." He knotted a piece of twine 'round Dex's fist. "Your job, matey, is to hold on tight."

Dex took no notice, his fist pumping with a mind of its own, but when the windsock caught the breeze and ballooned open, he threw back his head and hooted, his baseball cap tumbling to the ground, his arms thrashing, and if not for the straps restraining his shrunken body, he might have taken flight.

Threading bits of anchovy onto his two hooks, Hollis cast the lines away from the railing and settled himself on the bench. I followed suit, bumping against him to avoid a fresh bird splatter. As he handed me the smaller rod, he seemed to see me for the first time. I could feel his quizzical eyes sizing me up—my baggy sweater, my dark sunglasses, my enormous movie-star hat.

"That's quite a getup. Hiding from the paparazzi?" If anyone could tuck a chuckle inside a comment, it was Hollis.

"Did you hear about St. Francis?"

"I did." He fixed on something in the distance.

"Well, I *saw* it."

He continued to stare.

"Well? Aren't you gonna say anything?"

"Sure. There's a pod of dolphins near the Pirate Caves. Just saw one breach."

I searched the sea. "All I see are whitecaps."

"Gotta look harder."

I looked harder, but whether the water churned from breaching dolphins or breaking waves, I couldn't say. "Sure. I see somethin', I guess. Don'tcha wanna know what *I* saw?"

"Figured you'd tell me."

"Well, maybe I won't."

"Okay." He pulled a stick of beef jerky from his pocket, chewed it slowly.

What Hollis lacked in curiosity he made up for in patience.

"Fine," I blurted, unable to stand the silence any longer. "I'll tell you."

Hollis let me talk, his stare never wavering from the distant dolphins, but asked no question and offered no comment, either because his mouth was too full of jerky or because he had no mind to encourage my imaginations—that is, till I called it flat out, sayin' trashing America had Raven and her uncle written all over it, even Father Miguel almost said so, or maybe just her uncle or maybe just Raven, but at any rate, the only two communists 'round these parts.

"How do you know they're communists?" he finally said, swallowing his last bite.

"They're from Russia, aren't they?"

"You from Texas?"

"Yeah. So?"

"That make you a longhorn cow?" Grinning, he stepped to the railing, tugged on his fishing line, sat back down.

"All right, smarty-pants, then who do you think did it?"

"Can't say."

I waited a moment, hoping he'd say with a little time. Beside us, Dex's arms had dropped into his lap. He gazed at the waves, mesmerized.

"But who do you *think* did it?"

"I don't think anything."

"You have to think *something*."

"Don't either." His fishing line shuddered, jerked. Rising, he reeled it in, checked the bait, then cast it farther out. Clouds gathered on the horizon.

"You know the talk as well as I do—KGB spies, Kremlin stooges. Even the sheriff says so. No trouble till they came to town."

"Talk doesn't mean anything."

"Then howdya explain the hammer an' sickle?"

"I don't." He nodded to Anna as she lumbered toward the street, a frayed satchel and fishing rod slung over her stooped shoulder, rolled-up cuffs scraping the planks.

"What's that supposed to mean?"

"It means we don't know."

"*I* know," I said. "And I'm gonna prove it too."

"Yeah? How so?"

"I'm going back to Gulch Run."

Dex sighed, his eyes now closed, his breathing slow, the windsock still flappin' in his hand.

"And do what? Break into her house?"

"Maybe."

"Last I heard, trespassing's a crime." The easy cheer of Hollis's voice fell away.

"Got a better plan?"

"Plan for what? Bailing you out of jail?" His jaw tensed.

Anything I might have wanted to say stayed shut inside.

Even sitting next to me on the bench, he was a full head and shoulders taller, licks of gold-tinged hair coiling against his T-shirt collar. He shifted his gaze from the horizon to the cliffs that hid the Pirate Caves. As the sun disappeared behind a cloud, the ocean darkened into a deep plum. Though he knew I studied him, he didn't blink.

"Wanna come with me?"

"No thanks."

"You don't wanna catch the vandal?"

"Don't wanna waste my time chasing rumors."

THIRTEEN

We sat in silence awhile and then some, Hollis reelin' in three croakers, my line snagging a hunk of kelp. I figured now wasn't the best time to demand a recitation of the Lord's Prayer, so I busied myself shooing away pigeons, pointing out bobbing sea lions, swatting flies off Dex, drowsy in the warm sun, and scouring the pier for Raven. Anglers sauntered past, took their posts against the railing, cast their lines. A few sat on overturned buckets, jolted awake by an occasional jerk on slack lines followed by a fast reel up an' over. I manned the rods while Hollis cleaned his croakers, until a lunge and strike spurred me to my feet, now my turn to hoist up an' over the tiered slats, and this time an honest-to-goodness fish.

"Heya, Anna!" Hollis called. "Going back for more?"

Anna, returning from the cleaning station, rod still slung over her shoulder, trundled toward us. She peered into Hollis's ice chest with a snort of approval, and then bending over Dex asleep in his wheelchair, considered him a long moment.

"Meet Dex," Hollis said. "He's my weatherman."

Anna's next snort softened, and she touched Dex's cheek with a gnarled finger. "Ain't he a fine one." She could've been talking about a fish. "Brother?" Her smile revealed one gold tooth and several missing ones.

I grunted. "Caught me a big ol' perch. Say, where's Jake today?"

Jake was her older brother, my poker mentor and nemesis, a downright scoundrel and a perfect gentleman, showing me how to win but never letting me. They almost always fished together, Anna and Jake, among the oldest of the Harford anglers, waiting for the running tides and then casting lines two hours before or after high tide.

"It ain't being a scoundrel to play poker better than you, Swee'Pea," Jake had told me, sliding my coins into his lumpy fishing bag. "Though I haven't learned you half-bad."

"When you gonna learn me the half-good part?" I'd countered, fixin' to fold again and staving off the urge to swear with another chunk of Bazooka.

He came by his fish the same way, I soon discovered, fishing better than the lot of us but tossing most of his catch in Anna's bucket and his gear in her satchel, his own duck-cotton duffel occupied by rolled-up newspapers, a bologna sandwich, and a tin flask. When I asked him about the "medicinal tincture," uncapping the flask one foggy morning for a sniff, he snatched it back, recapped it, and informed me the elixir was Gramps's secret recipe and secret meant secret. But if I was going to insist, which I was, it was a medley of glycerin, lemon, and honey, with a "splash" for good measure. Made the heart sing, he said, to which Anna, baiting her line, had snorted. He told me not to get any ideas, and had I ever seen him drunk? What *thut* had to do with anything only piqued my suspicions.

"His legs still hurting?" Hollis continued, scooting over on the bench.

"All of 'im's hurting." Anna flumped beside us with a grunt. "Ain't nothin' doing for it." A spot of rouge on each cheek and a bandana 'round her hair were her only nod to the feminine graces, and though I didn't say it, seemed she and Popeye shared a wardrobe. "Nothin' 'cept drink."

"Yeah." Hollis handed Anna a stick of beef jerky. "Suppose it's his one comfort."

"One misery chasin' down another. Damn mule." Anna could swear just as sweet as Jake. "But I allow it."

"That's a trial," I offered, ruing the burden of brothers. "Ain't for the faint of heart."

"Heart's fine. In his bones." She gnawed at the jerky, muttered under her breath, the words lost in the roar of waves. "Fool notion, them sea walks. Swears by 'em, though. Says they quiets the tremors."

"S'pose it gives him some peace," I tried again.

"Don't give me no peace. Every day, far as the buoy. High tide, low tide."

"Yeah." Hollis could make one word say so much—that he knew, that he hated that he knew, that time stole what it gifted, that a man's way ought to be respected.

"Pa tried lickin' him once. 'Nother fool notion, that." She took a toothpick from her overalls pocket and chewed it. "Only made Pa cry."

"Yeah."

A couple more minutes dragged by. A seagull squawked above us, skimmed the water, circled back to the railing.

"We keeps an eye on 'im, me an' the hound."

"Sure you do."

"Could walk 'imself straight into a riptide."

"Or a shark," I volunteered.

"Nah," Hollis said before she could snort. "Jake's too smart for that."

"Pish! He's all fool."

A gust covered us in ocean spray, pelted us with the scents of kelp, gutted fish, and cigarette smoke. I closed my eyes and let myself drift.

ॐ

Long before the rumors began, I knew Jake ailed, but not because he looked pale and gaunt. He didn't. Fact was, he could have been kin to an ox, broad chested and just as hairy, with biceps that bulged beneath his faded denim shirts and quads thick as pier pilings—unruly as one too, payin' no mind to anyone 'cept Anna. Proud of those muscles, he was, for what they could do, hauling abalone traps in his younger years and a skittish lump of dog across the pier in his older ones.

It took some cajoling, but give him a pretty-please smile, a run of winning poker hands, and a swig of Gramps's elixir, and Jake would roll up his sleeve to lay bare a hula girl inked over a faded scar, grinning as she shimmied 'cross his twitching arm, grass skirt swaying and sultry eye winking. Anna would scowl and tsk, but one time I saw her trace crooked fingers along the scar.

"Gruff if needed," Hollis conceded, "but a regular gent."

What with his chuckles through cigarette smoke at my bad poker face and his raspy laugh at my losses, I saw more gruff than gent, irking me plenty. "Better luck next time, Swee'Pea," he'd say, without a shred of sincerity. But I couldn't stay irked long. Even though he stole me clean every Friday night at Cappy's, he always ponied up my losings the next week, covering for Joe, who never did. I never made money, but I never lost it either. Far as I could see, my sins tallied up the same after gamblin' as before.

If not for Jake, I'd have never seen the inside of Cappy's storeroom, much less dealt cards at the card table. Joe would've made sure of that. Cappy owned the cheapest—and best—eats in town, offering crispy fish-and-chips, hearty clam chowder, and Pedro's Mexican "surprise of the day," even to Pedro. Tourists knew the corner diner as Fish-n-Ships. Locals knew it as Cap's Diner. To me, it was just Cappy's. Every Friday after shooing out the last dawdlers, Joe would flip the door sign to "closed" and turn the lock. We'd file past the kitchen into the storeroom for the debauchery that was penny-ante poker. I supposed it might've been the ruin of me if my trainwreck family hadn't already been.

It began innocent enough that first Friday of Christmas break, Jake's scruffy mutt dragging me into the diner close on Jake's heels seconds before a scowling Joe slammed the door. Sidling past a tsking Anna, who rummaged through the produce boxes, I'd hunkered cross-legged on the dusty floor, offering a knee to Popeye's snout. Hidden by shadows and cigarette smoke, I'd breathed soft as a ghost so as not to draw Joe's ire, wallowed in the stench of beer and sweat, waited out the stretches of silence broken by insults, studied the crinkled brows of the men fingering black chips, and puzzled at profanities bandied like terms of endearment. Shelves filled with bulk goods lined the walls, alternated with sketches of fishing vessels.

The briny aroma of Anna's clam chowder mingled with Ernesto's cigar, a chowder more onion than clam, if sniffing were any clue. Shuffling in from the kitchen, Anna announced she was headed to Mayor Mac's with his weekend grub. When Joe jumped up to grab her coat, she scooched a creaky chair to the table and motioned me up from the floor. If I'd had any buttons on my sweatshirt, they would've busted, and that's before I got dealt my very own hand of cards. Of course, that set Joe off like a fire alarm, a near riot ensuing.

"Ain't playing with no kid!" He had thrown down his

cards, his glare ordering the others to do the same on pain of death.

It took Jake pounding the table and calling a vote to silence the men's bickering. He gave a stirring speech first though, saying I was a stray just like Popeye—

"Ha!" Joe had blurted. "Mangy, both of 'em!"

—and needed taking in. And anyway I'd be permitted only on Fridays—that was low-stakes poker night. The other days would be off-limits, which was fine by me, seeing as I had homework most nights and Dex always. The way Mama heard it, "Poor old Anna, sweatin' over Cappy's stove, stirrin' and fryin' for those two sickly gents up yonder Gulch Run. Sure would like to lighten her load." Mama had little choice but to remark on my charitable initiative—the duration of which got me only as far as the chopped onions, Jake proffering me his hankie and a seat next to him. Never could figure how Mama didn't catch on.

Anna counted the raised hands: five *ayes*, zero *nos*, and one abstention, that being Joe, who clamped both hands around a bottle, the left keeping the right from hurling it, I reckoned. I thought the appeal to democracy mighty Christian of Jake, though I doubt he'd have presumed himself worthy.

That he was sick, real sick, hit me like a bolt one particularly rousing poker night, Jake standing so suddenly that his chair toppled and then stumbling to the bathroom, where even the slammed door couldn't muffle the retches. As if on cue, the gripes and curses grew louder 'round the table, beer bottles got banged down, chairs got scraped against the floor, cards got slapped face up, the din enough to give Jake his privacy, but through the ruckus I heard Joe tell Cappy to put Jake's tab on him, he was taking him home.

Joe owned Lucky Liquors & Sundries, a market of sorts

on Second Street, catty-corner from the diner, and supplied Cappy's with beer, the only alcoholic drink on the menu. Joe's surly ways met their match in Cappy, not that Cappy was surlier, unless he had to be, but that he was a legend, a real sea captain, with a bum arm he got aboard a Navy destroyer when a torpedo struck the hull, shrapnel lodging in his shoulder—that was the rumor, anyway, and he didn't deny it.

Cappy fried up the best fish-and-chips on the coast, beer-battered and drenched in Tabasco sauce, a one-armed culinary whiz. Jake ordered it every Thursday, Friday, and Saturday night. By Sunday, he rued, his stomach was a burning hellhole. He had no choice but to quell it with Gramps's elixir—at least until the next Thursday. Gramps and Cappy were keeping him alive by turns.

℘

"OF COURSE YOU'RE worried about him," Hollis said softly, startling me from my musings.

"That old mule? Pish!" Anna tugged a whisker on her chin.

"Good catch today?" I tried to peek in her bucket.

"Yup, strange enough."

"Why's that?"

"Sea's foamin' charcoal. Fish sense a storm an' ain't biting."

It was a marvel how Anna, Jake, and the other anglers, even Hollis, could read the sea and know which fish they'd hook—or not hook.

"Lucky t' catch two." Anna tilted her bucket toward us. "But they's big 'uns. Takin' 'em over to Cappy's. He'll cook 'em up tasty, just the way Jake likes."

"But nowhere near as tasty as yours."

Anna smiled at Hollis, her faded eyes 'bout disappearing into the folds of her leathery skin. "Hush now. Can't go lettin' Cappy get wind of it." She hauled herself up from the bench, scanned the darkening sky, the slate sea. "Storm's headed in. No fishing t'morrow." Then she looked at Dex, his head resting on his chest, saliva dribbling down his chin. "You take care, li'l bub," she said, though to Dex or to Hollis, I didn't know.

"You take care, yourself." Hollis gave her a wave as she started up the pier, a heavy sway of an old woman, taking one slow plank at a time.

"Well then," I ventured after a few moments, an angry wind ripping through my knit pullover. "Guess I'm going to Gulch Run alone."

Hollis nodded toward the horizon. "Guess you're not going at all. Storm'll be here in twenty minutes."

Ten minutes later, the rolling thunderheads opened in gray sheets on the far sea. But Hollis hadn't waited. We'd piled our gear into the wheelchair and dashed up the pier toward the street, Hollis cradling Dex, his feet pelting the ground in long, steady strides, hollerin' at Mayor Mac, perched on the sea wall in his usual stupor, to take cover. I fell back, the wheelchair swerving side to side as I pushed it up the sidewalk, past the souvenir shops, and into my front yard.

From the safety of my porch, we watched the rain gather speed across the tossing waves, hasten toward shore, pour in torrents over the town. Dex whimpered, rocked his head. I knew those whimpers. They were the prelude to an all-out squall of his own. I hadn't remembered to pack his crackers and juice. And no doubt his diaper needed changing. Rosa would be here soon, giving me what-for. There'd be no Gulch Run today.

"Con-demmit!"

Hollis side-eyed me as he set Dex in his wheelchair. "Something you wanna say?"

"No. I mean, thanks. For gettin' me an' Dex home." Sometimes I didn't have a lick of manners, that's what Mama said.

"Sure." He pulled up his collar. "I'm going back for Mac. I'll see you later."

"But it's raining."

Slinging his fishing rods over his shoulder, he grabbed his bucket. "You don't say." He patted Dex on the little fist still clutching the windsock and ran down the porch steps.

"Don't get wet!" I called after him.

"Wouldn't dream of it!"

I watched Hollis scurry 'cross the street toward the pier, lashed by rain. Soon as this confounded hurricane stopped, I'd head to Gulch Run, with or without him.

FOURTEEN

For two days, fierce winds battered Harford Beach, remnants of a distant tropical storm, roilin' the ocean into a witch's cauldron, howling—Mama said—like a death rattle, the rain in slanted torrents against our faces pressed to the windows, Mama's face worn, raked with the worry of slick roads to the clinic, Dex's fraught, ashen, mine a glower in the streaked pane. The stately palm trees along Front Street swayed and lurched, the fronds bucking and occasionally snapping. Screaming gales snatched shingles from roofs, ripped apart shop awnings, hurled massive waves onto the pier, shearing off the railing near the end, the shredded boards tumbling into the frenzied sea. From upstairs we watched construction workers don yellow slickers and galoshes to tackle the pounding surf. Working by flashlight into the night—pulsing fireflies encased in jars of rain—they secured dangling planks, cordoning off the breach with vinyl caution tape and orange cones. News reports cited concerns for weakened pilings.

With daybreak on Saturday, the last clouds dissipated, wisps of cotton under a jaunty sun, the washed skies a brilliant blue. Not foolish enough to brave the tempest for our Friday poker match, Anna had called the game off, and I'd headed to bed early, sleeping a dead man's sleep, undisturbed by dreams or by Dex.

Still in my nightgown, I puttered 'round the kitchen, stirring up a mess of oatmeal and humming hymn 43, heaping on butter, brown sugar, and chocolate chips. Dex fancied the sweet lumps same as me, gurgling and dribbling oats down his chin. Mama, reading the weekly *Harford Herald*, coffee cup to her lips, raised no complaint, reminding me to add banana—for some nourishment, I guess—and wash my dishes.

"Eden Mae, must you use every pot, pan, and spoon for a simple bowl of oatmeal?" There was no edge to her voice, only a purr and a drawl, her words a stretching cat. Reaching across the table, she wiped Dex's chin, her bathrobe slipping from her shoulder. On those rare days when she had neither clinic nor classes, she reverted to an earlier mama, the mama I'd had before Dex came home to stay, before my father left. With long sips from her coffee, she remarked now and then about some story in the *Los Angeles Times*, passing her bowl to me for another ladle of oatmeal.

I was helping myself to a third serving when the grinding rumble of a Volkswagen engine twisted my stomach. I dumped my bowl back into the pot. "What's he doing here? Y'all goin' somewhere?"

That'd be just my luck, stuck home babysitting. Finally, a day without rain, without choir rehearsal or chores, without Dex duty. I hankered to cut out soon as I could, swing by the pier to badger Hollis a bit, maybe prevail on his defective sense of reason, and then hoof it to Gulch Run. Busting into Raven's house no longer needed doin'. I'd had a think about that, about what Hollis had said, and recalled that scuttlebutt placed the smuggled guns in the lean-to shed. Gratifying as a snoop might've been, that revelation came as a mighty relief. Couldn't hardly be a crime to check a shed, 'specially one chock-full of contraband. My parents weren't going to saddle me with Dex this time.

But Mama was already in the hall and opening the front door. I could hear my father's pleasure at the aroma of coffee, my mother's offer to make him a cup, could hear their voices grow louder through the hallway, could feel my hands clench.

"Good morning, Eden." My father strolled into the kitchen like he owned the place.

"Is it?" I muttered.

Dex broke into lunatic grinning and threw himself forward. Dumb brother. Seein' my father always sent him giddy.

"Hey, hey, Dex. How you doing, buddy?"

I hated my father calling him buddy. He wasn't his buddy. He wasn't even his son. He was something to be locked away in an institution for useless kids. To Professor Alexander Lewis anyway.

"Sure a lot of commotion at the beach." My father peered into my pot of oatmeal. "Mmm, scrumptiferous! Got enough for me?"

"What commotion?" I hoisted myself above the sink, hoping for a view from the window.

"Looks like something washed up during the storm."

"How 'bout I check it out and let you know?" I offered, scoring a two-for-one ticket out of there.

"Eden Mae, don't you step outside this house till you've washed these dishes."

"Course, Mama. Wouldn't think of it!" But I did think of it, making a to-do of clattering pots in the sink to await water, soap, and someone else's hands.

Before Mama could pour my father's coffee, I skedaddled

upstairs, yanked on my cutoffs, threw my bedspread over my dirty clothes, and jammed my feet into my cheap Rexall thongs by the front door, leaving it ajar. No squeaky hinge was 'bout to waylay me.

"Con-demmit!" I sputtered, dodging cars and hopping the sea wall. If I'd been on my game, I'd have been first on the beach, ahead of the knot of people now gathered between the firepits and bluff. A cold gust pierced my shirt, the storm's last hurrah, as I raced down the shore. Though I'd grabbed my jacket, I couldn't be bothered to unwrap it from my waist as I approached the clustered bystanders, several of them restraining dogs. A barefoot figure in a bucket hat stood slightly apart from them, arms crossed, muscles tensing beneath short sleeves.

"Hey!" I skirted mounds of kelp, putrid relics from the storm, and came up panting beside Hollis. "What's goin' on?"

"Dead seal."

"Is that all?" *Shoulda gone to Gulch Run.* "Sure seems a big fuss. I mean, it's awful sad, but—what?"

Hollis, taller than most, could see over the crowd, and whatever he was seeing paled his face. I pushed past him.

"Call harbor patrol!" someone shouted.

"We did," someone else replied.

"What's takin' 'em so long?"

"Senseless!"

Edging through the crowd, I recognized a few surfers—Vince, face grim, Ronnie, Wayne—their wetsuits rolled to their waists, surfboards propped beside them. Teen girls huddled nearby, whispering, gazes lowered. Squeezing forward, I gazed down too.

Amid the fly-ridden kelp lay the mottled gray seal, its small body motionless, waves slapping its hind flippers. I might've taken it for a barnacle-crusted rock. A woman knelt at its side.

"What happened?" I asked as she rose.

"Pup's been shot."

"Shot? Who'd do a thing like that?"

"A sicko, that's who."

"Move aside, folks. Coming through." A yellow-vested ranger brushed past me, behind him two more men in harbor patrol garb, one with a walkie-talkie to his mouth. On the street, a large van cut its ignition beside the sea wall. I could just make out the words SHP MARINE UNIT splayed across it.

As the first ranger waved us back, the two others knelt beside the seal. Wriggling their fingers into tight gloves, they felt along the body, brushing sand off the flippers, and then probed the small head, from the twin nostrils flanked by stiff whiskers to the glazed obsidian eyes, embedded like flat stones, to the bullet hole like a third eye between them, matted with blood.

"Found the casing," a ranger said. "Headstamp's got a star."

Dropping their voices, the trio took a heavy-duty bag from the approaching van driver.

Not keen on seeing what was next, I fixed my gaze on the breaking surf. Foamy water rushed the shore to form eddies around the kelp, slid back into the ocean. Somewhere out there was the seal's mother. *Left her pup to forage for food,* someone had said. Had she returned? Did she know? Was she watching from the swells even now as the rangers slipped her pup into the body bag, lifted him gently, carried him to the street? The thought too sorrowful to ponder, I tried instead to figure whether the tide was rollin' in or out.

West of the pier, the coast lazed another half mile, the sand littered with cigarette butts, bottle caps, bits of driftwood. At the farthest point, where sand collided into cliffs, the surf dovetailed with the sea wall, swallowing the last sliver of beach. Just before the pier, a lanky form trudged with familiar strides to the swings.

"Hollis! Wait up!" Though he slowed his steps, I had to jog to keep up. "Why would anyone shoot a seal?"

"You tell me." He nodded toward the street. "That your priest?"

On the sidewalk above the firepits, Rev. Travers watched the rangers lower the bagged seal into the van, same as us, same as the crowd. Seemed his wardrobe hadn't a pair of casual pants in it, dressed like he was in black trousers, button-down shirt, and tie, his suit jacket dangling over his shoulder. He even wore his brogues. Or maybe he was just always on call.

"S'pose he's prayin' against the principalities. And he's a reverend."

Hollis shrugged but said nothing, only strode more quickly toward the stairs, kicking up sand as he went.

"Bet she did it. Same as she vandalized the church."

"Huh?"

"Raven."

"That's a leap." He reached for his Chucks, tucked inside his bucket. "Why would she do that?"

"Why wouldn't she?"

"This isn't like the other stuff."

"Maybe not, but I'd wager it's the same hateful person who wrote 'Death to US—'"

"There's lots of hateful people. They don't go around shooting animals."

"Then how do you figure it?"

"Listen, Eden, just because you want something to be so doesn't make it so." He yanked on his shoes, leaving the laces untied. "I'll talk to you later, okay? Gotta fix a fence with my dad."

It wasn't okay, but I had to hand it to him. No one could shut a person down more polite than Hollis. Fine, innocent until proven guilty. All the more reason to prove it.

I watched him hop the sea wall, cross the street, and break into a lazy run past Cap's Diner, take the corner at Lucky Liquors, lope across the pay-to-park lot, and disappear somewhere in the maze of residential streets at the far edge of town.

Hollis—who came and went as he pleased, who shifted shapes like a cumulus cloud on a blustery day, unfettered and wise as the moon for all his almost eighteen years—had parents, a fact that dumbfounded me every time I remembered it. A mom and dad and a slew of sisters, some grown, maybe two or three at home, though seemed to me they were most of 'em married and with a posse of children astride their hips.

Hollis, who always turned to wave, didn't.

I eyed a sunning lizard—nope, just a stalk of kelp—and considered that I ought to get on home too. I'd promised to report back, jaw 'bout nothing with my father, stack an' whack block towers with Dex. I considered for all of ten seconds before my good sense kicked in. It wasn't just the prospect of misery that kept me from heading home—I stamped hard on the kelp pods, but they were too fresh to pop, soft and squelchy—it was that I had some serious thinking to do.

Tramping to the swings, I wriggled onto a cracked seat, the rubber warm, kicked off my thongs, and buried my toes in the sand, pushing off and swaying gently at first, then pumping higher. The beach swarmed with sunbathers and sand sculptors, the havoc of the storm quickly forgotten but for piles of deadwood and debris. Pigeons and sandpipers pecked among the litter. Children romped past, grabbed empty swings, soared for a while, jumped off. A dog lunged for a Frisbee. From the street, a radio blared Stevie Wonder. Must be gettin' on half past nine, I calculated, glaring at a freckle-faced boy who'd wandered up with a wistful look. I pumped harder.

"That's a leap," Hollis had said, but my gut said otherwise. Before the Russian girl and her gun-totin' uncle darkened Gulch Run, nothing more disagreeable than oil slicks drifting in from sea and hardening into tar had disturbed the town, nothing more dangerous than an occasional sailboat stranded on the far reef, the sailors towed to safety by harbor patrol. I supposed the leap might have been from the sacrilegious to the sadistic, vandalism of a church one thing, the shooting of a seal another. But serial killers often started out persecuting cats, didn't they? And they always started out being bullied. Raven had certainly been that, shunned at school, taunted and tormented.

The way I figured it, she and her uncle harbored a whole heap of grievances, though whether the one or the both, I couldn't rightly say. What seemed a leap was thinkin' anyone else had such a hefty score to settle. Soon as I could, I'd return to Gulch Run, find Raven's house, see what I could see, maybe sniff out a trail of blood or, at the very least, a stash of red spray paint, lay to rest the rumors by proving them true. I'd bet my last dime the shed held secrets.

Next to me a shirtless boy took his own flying leap from his swing, tumbled onto the sand, and scampered off. The empty swing continued on alone, slowed, then hitched. I whiffed the woody scent before I saw her, the fragrant petals scattered in her hair, the sprigs of dainty camellias, the silk scarves and layered skirts, the musk of clothes packed too long in mothballs. I felt her eyes bore into me as she halted the ebbing swing. For a heart-thumping moment, I considered hopping off my swing and hotfootin' it home, certain she had read my suspicions and was about to cast a ghastly spell on me. But she closed in, blocking my path, and I had to drag my feet to keep from hitting her.

Without so much as a flinch, she unclenched her cupped hand. In her palm lay a gold chain.

I shook my head. "No, not mine. Thanks though."

Taking it by the ends, she draped it across her neck. It looked vaguely familiar, like a necklace Gramma Kay often let me wear, her vanity table cluttered with costume jewelry, but Gramma's gleamed more rust than gold, time gnawing off the plating. Now it lay buried in a moving box somewhere, a last gift to me. Was that it? Was Raven gifting me a necklace? Whatever for? Did she think tossing her a donut months ago meant we were friends?

"Uh, thanks, but you keep it." I walked my swing backward and perched on the rubber edge. Raven would have to move or be hit.

But she remained fixed, even as I swung at her, and again I skidded to a stop. We stood so close that I could trace the weave of flowers in her hair, the twining of green stems with daisies and lavender. Her pale eyes were the translucent blue of Dex's beads.

"See!" She thrust the chain at me with one hand, with the other pointed toward the rocky cliff that hemmed in our stretch of beach, forming a small inlet. Near the washed-up kelp, a few stragglers wandered into the surf.

I nudged her hand away, the chain spilling to the sand.

"I told you"—a motorcycle idled behind us, forcing me to raise my voice—"it's not mine. I don't want it."

But she'd already spun away. Her sable skirts fluttering against her ankle boots, she strode toward the pier.

Thrusting my swing at the freckled boy who had circled back, I dug out the half-buried chain and brushed off the sand. Chunky links, a broken clasp. Not a gift then. Most like, she'd figured it was mine, lost when I'd jostled my way to the baby seal.

Kree-ar! A seagull landed at my feet, squawked again. Fearin' a gull grab, I pocketed the gritty chain—rebuking any curses Raven might've put on it—and scoured the pier.

By the time I spotted her, she'd already reached the midway point. I had no time to lose. Within a minute, I too was on the pier, swerving between folks enjoying a Saturday stroll, so fixed on keeping her in my sights that I forgot to dread the gaps, slowing only a smidge at the caution tape and cones but taking a sharp breath at the gouged rails, the hole wide enough to swallow a car.

And then she was gone.

I pulled up short, just yards from the pier end, searched right and left. I'd lost her, distracted by the gaping death drop. With nowhere to go, I doubled back, scanning the pier more slowly. Ahead, noisy kids crowded the Bait and Tackle Shack, jockeying for a closer look at the fishing rods and swappin' quarters for licorice sticks. Beyond it, cables dangled from towering winches. A fisherman dozed on an ice chest, his fishing rod lodged between the planks. Pigeons squabbled and perched on the splattered railing. But no Raven.

Vanished. Again.

"Con-*dem*-nation!"

The fisherman popped open an eye, peered at me, settled into snores.

I might as well have been a cow stuck in a mud pit, flummoxed as all get-out.

"Basil!"

I turned to see a toddler in baggy swim trunks making a beeline for the winches, his mother sprinting after him. She reached him just as he tripped on a snarled net, his screams piercing the air.

And then I saw it.

A glint of metal.

Squinting, I walked toward the shine. I'd never paid mind to the winches, cables, and ropes cluttering the other side of the Bait and Tackle Shack, never noticed the hatch-grip handle jutting from the pier floor just inches away.

A trapdoor. But to where? Only restless sea lay beneath the pier.

It took two hands and a grunt, but I wrested the hatch open, wincing at the frigid spray of waves. A ladder led to a narrow dock, two dinghies bobbing between the pilings, one straining against its tether, the other capsized. Some of the anglers owned dinghies, I knew, Jake an' Anna both, but I'd always figured 'em to be docked at the Alvarado Pier, along with the sailboats and skiffs, protected from Pacific swells by the breakwater.

"Lord a'mighty!"

Raven, her skirts gathered into her bangled arms, was scrambling into the upright dinghy. Unlashing the rope tether from the dock, she flung it into the boat and yanked the starter cord.

Bang! The hatch slipped from my grip. Jumping back, I raced to the opposite railing and leaned over as far as I dared, chancin' I'd plummet headfirst. But I couldn't lose her!

She'd cleared the pier and was scudding toward open sea, her shawls snapping like schooner sails. I watched the dinghy pick up speed, watched it veer eastward and hug the coastline, watched it thread through low fog near the Pirate Caves, watched it until I lost her, at last, in the mist.

FIFTEEN

WIND WHIPPING THROUGH my thin shirt, I dashed to the street, my head a jumble, zigzagged back to the swings to retrieve my jacket, sidestepping beach towels and sand-castles, vaulted over the sea wall, skidded across the street, and fairly fell through the glass door of Lucky Liquors, knocking over the Budweiser sandwich board.

"Dammit! Now look what ya done." Joe stood atop a stepladder in aisle 2, a case of beer balanced on his shoulder, a pen jutting from his teeth, across his unshaven face a scowl fit to kill.

"Sorry. Didn't mean to." I propped up the sign and, tucking my wayward hair into my ponytail, tried to compose myself without becoming the lady Jake said I wasn't.

"That's not the way it was." His glare could wither a fork.

"Lordy, Joe! I said I was sorry." I adjusted the lopsided sign and gave the glossy model a pat. "There, how's that?"

"You here to buy something?"

"Might be." Digging in my pocket, I pulled out a piece of gum loosed from its wax paper and flecked with lint. The chain felt grainy against my fingers. "Want some?" Before he could snap back an' wither me further, I popped it into my mouth. "Say, where's Jake?"

"What's it to you?"

"Just wondered." I picked up a magazine and tried to

look interested in the cover girl, her pouting lips strangely like Trish's.

"You buying that?"

"Uh, no."

"Wrinkle it and ya are."

I replaced it carefully on the stand. "So you haven't seen Jake today?"

"Dunno." Joe stepped up a rung.

"You dunno if you've seen him?"

"Maybe I didn't see him. Maybe I heard him."

"Huh?"

"Maybe he yelled 'hello' to me." Joe didn't bother to look at me, likely reckoning I'd been sufficiently withered. "And maybe he didn't."

"You mean after his ocean walk?"

"Couldn't say." He stopped on the next rung, nudged a teetering six-pack farther onto the shelf with his elbow.

I might as well have been talking to a fire hydrant. "Didn't he get his morning paper and smoke a pack on the bench, like always? You woulda seen him. Or leastways seen Popeye."

The case of beer on Joe's shoulder tipped forward, steadied.

"Dunno." Joe could make even his voice glower. "And supposin' he did? I don't see what business that is of yours, missy. He's got enough troubles without you pestering him."

"And *I* don't see what business it is of *yours* whether it's my business." Joe didn't like me much, so I didn't like him much either, all my Texan manners evaporating in the heat of my temper—or his. "Do you know where he is, or don't you?"

"Don't."

"When are you gonna know?"

"Tonight. Got a rained-out poker game to make up."

That news I was mighty glad to hear, having forgotten 'bout it in the calamity of the morning. "Guess someone was planning on telling me?"

"Your invite is for Fridays. This here is Saturday." Joe unloaded the crate from his shoulder to the top shelf. "We done here?"

"Aw, c'mon. I just wanna know where Jake is."

Joe landed on the floor with a thud and planted himself in front of me, so close that I took a step back, nearly toppling the Budweiser sign again.

"You gonna buy some liquor?"

"No."

"You gonna buy some cigarettes?"

"No."

"Then you've got no business in this store. This store's for gents and drunks, missy."

"Maybe I'm gonna buy some sundries."

"Then you're outta luck, because I ain't selling any."

"How can a store called 'Lucky Liquors and Sundries' have no luck and no sundries? Gonna have to rename it plain 'Liquors.'"

Seemed there was still withering to be had.

"Okay, Joe, you win. See, Jake's dinghy's been stolen. I gotta tell him."

"Whaddya mean 'stolen'?"

"Same as your whiskey was." I pointed at a bottle labeled *Jose Cuervo*.

Joe's naturally cross face grew two shades crosser. "You saying you stole my tequila?"

"Mercy's sake, she stole that too? And now she's made off with Jake's dinghy."

"She who? And how come you're so sure it was Jake's?"

"I'd know that old dinghy anywhere. It don't say *Autumn Rows* for nothin'."

"You ever thought maybe you should mind your own business?"

"Fine. I'll find Jake myself, tell him he's been robbed and you don't give a hoot."

Truth was, if Jake wasn't at Lucky's, I had no clue where he'd be. Not a morning went by that he didn't emerge from the sea at sunrise, bathed in foam and fog, to lumber up to Lucky's, plunking on the wooden bench out front, shootin' the breeze as Joe unlocked the store, Popeye snuffling under Jake's feet. I supposed Jake lived on the outskirts of Harford Beach, but he could have lived in Gulch Run or Vintage Heights for all I knew, though I'd have laid my bet against Vintage Heights. 'Bout a decade past, brother and sister had come back to the old homestead, "as good for the one as t'other," Anna had said.

"Jake don't need no trouble from you. You git on outta here and don't come back." He folded the stepladder behind the counter and opened the cash register, pausing to count the bills. "A liquor store ain't no place for a kid, or haven't ya heard? How old are you, anyway? Eleven?"

Joe sure could vex me, but I wasn't about to let him gloat over the fact. "Well, we got that in common. Math ain't my best subject either."

"Thought I told you to git."

"I'm gittin'," I muttered, adding under my breath, "soon as I'm good an' ready."

And I wasn't ready yet. If Jake was going to make himself scarce, then he'd just have to wait. No telling if I could chase him down before noon. Anyhow, he'd know soon enough. It was Raven needed chasing. When better to see where she'd gone? But how? Hollis had an old rowboat up at his house, but his little sisters let go the paddles to a watery grave. Not worth a bucket of warm spit that, 'specially being that his mom had planted flowers in it. Besides, Hollis was clear on the other side of town, repairing a fence. Then I remembered Mariner's Cove Boat Rentals.

"Say, Joe, do you sell cards?"

If the only thing between me and Raven's secrets was a dinghy, and the only thing between me and a dinghy was money, well, it was a longshot, but if I played my cards right—meaning, asked Jake real sweet-like to cut me some slack—a couple winning rounds of poker should do it. I was pretty near certain I could rent a dinghy for four bucks at the Alvarado Pier.

"Cards? What kinda cards? Christmas cards?" He chuckled.

I glared at him. "Playing cards."

With a snort, he started punching numbers on the cash register. "Listen here, missy, even if I had any, I wouldn't sell 'em to you."

"Why not?"

"'Cause I ain't even open yet. You see this sign, the one you *didn't* knock down? It says 'Store Hours: 10 a.m. to 10 p.m.' And you see that clock?" He pointed to the wall. "It don't say ten. Or can't you read?"

"If I had a deck, I could practice five-card stud, maybe win me a pot tonight."

Joe shook his head. "What's your angle anyway? First you're all in a dither to save Jake's dinghy from pirates, and now you're scheming to cheat him at cards."

"Who said anything 'bout cheating? I'm gonna practice up, that's all."

Just then the door opened, and Cleo, a tenth-grade classmate with the most bloomin' afro I'd ever beheld, poked his head in.

"We ain't open yet!" Joe snapped. "Give her fifteen minutes, will ya?"

The door swung shut.

"Kids!" he groused, looking at me like he'd just now seen me. "You still here?"

"How come you don't like me, Joe?" *Same as Rosa*, I thought.

"You're a kid. And you ask too many questions." He foraged behind the counter. "Here. Take your cards. That'll be two bucks."

I held the red-and-white Bicycle pack to my nose. "Says right here fifty cents."

"It's two bucks when the store's not open."

"Well, I ain't got two bucks." I tugged my pockets inside out. "See?"

My lipstick, a wadded napkin, and the gold chain fell onto the floor, the lipstick rolling between two metal kegs. As I dove for it, Joe scooped up the chain. "Where'd you get this?"

"Well, I guess that's my business." I grabbed at it, but he dangled it above my reach. "C'mon, Joe. That's mine."

"Ain't neither." He peered hard at it. "Real gold. You steal this too? You kids are all the same. Barging in here, wasting my time, fishing around for money you ain't got." He dropped the chain on the counter like it was a rattlesnake. Snatching it, I shoved it back into my pocket.

"How 'bout I write an IOU for fifty cents?" I smiled sweetly.

"See this here?" He tore off a box flap and began scrawling huge letters across it. "Says 'KIDS STAY OUT.' That means you." Ripping a wedge of masking tape, he slapped his makeshift sign across the pearly teeth of the Budweiser girl. "That means those punks waltzing in here thinking I'm gonna sell 'em beer. Hooligans. The whole lot of 'em. Surfer kids, preacher kids, fat-cat kids, good-for-nothing kids. Thieving kids like you. Thinking I'm not gonna ID 'em. Thinking they can pull a fast one on Joe."

It was quite a speech for Joe. A terrible pang shot through me, a stab right in the center of my heart. Here I was, aiming to be a missionary to the Aucas, devoting my every moment—well, on Sundays anyway—to the learning of Scripture and bettering of my soul, yet when opportunity presented itself to reach the lost, what was I doing? Standing in a liquor store, wrangling for playing cards, and talkin' a streak of mean to a near heathen in need of saving.

"You oughta try church, Joe. It's awful nice."

He stared at me like he didn't know whether to laugh, snort, or spit.

"And they don't have to know about the poker."

He decided to snort.

"Here's your damn cards." He tossed the pack across the counter. "You'd better hope you win tonight, 'cause you owe me. Now scram. And give that chain back to whoever you stole it off. No-good thieving kids."

Or whoever Raven stole it off, you mean. Someone was missing it, that was for sure, but I'd figure out who in short order. Fact was, I had another bee in my bonnet, as Gramma Kay would say, and it was buzzin' something fierce. Unless she aimed to abscond for good, Raven would have to return in Jake's dinghy soon enough, but now—with Raven seabound and no way to follow her yet—an old gabled mansion waited across the ravine, the rooms laden with secrets and likely

Joe's whiskey bottles. Temptation beyond what I could bear sent me hightailing it out of Lucky's and into Gulch Run. And, if rumor were true, toward a whole arsenal of smuggled guns locked up in the shed.

SIXTEEN

S UNLIGHT FILTERED THROUGH the trees as I tracked the ravine into Gulch Run, the gully awake with the quiet rush of stormwater. Above, birds chirped, flitted from branch to branch. The narrow road, rutted with potholes and littered with glass and gravel, stretched into a blur. I quickened my pace. Though she'd steered the dinghy toward the Pirate Caves, there was no telling how long Raven would be gone—or even if the caves had been her destination. She could return within an hour or within four hours. She seemed to be everywhere at once anyway, always leaving her mark but never gettin' caught.

A garbage truck rumbled past, filling my nose with dirt and exhaust. In the distance, the whistle of a train blared, and I pictured Jake clumping down the steps of a passenger car into a leap of paws and tongue and tail.

80

T HAT WAS THE story, at any rate. A brindle hound of patch-work pedigree, Popeye had been dumped near the railroad tracks, booted by a traveling circus, the pup unable to clear the flaming hoops unsinged on account of his bum eye. He didn't budge for a week.

"Just sat there, growin' roots, patient as the day is long."

"Took a liking to you?" I'd asked Jake, calling a bet.

"Nope. Couldn't get within ten yards without him baring those fangs."

I pried Popeye's jaws open and raised the call. "He doesn't have fangs."

"Did then." Jake turned up his cards. A full house.

I had two pair. Baring my own fangs, I shoved my chips across the table.

Popeye, with his limp ear and squinty eye, rode herd on the lot of us those Friday nights, thunking a paw on the table to signal a bluff. Leastways that's what Cappy claimed, smacking the paw with his schooner's cap and calling him a fink. Popeye didn't mind none, just put the other paw up at a safer distance.

"So whadja do?" I pushed my ante into the pot.

Jake leaned back, examined his cards, exhaled a ribbon of smoke.

"Waited for him to quit waitin' on them that wasn't coming back. Nothin' but skin and bones, but he wouldn't so much scoot to—"

"Watch it." Cappy cut the deck with his good arm. "There's a lady present."

"*Dama*," Pedro chimed. Pedro had been washing dishes at Cap's Diner before Cappy was born, least so he said. When Cappy bought the place—a rockabilly hangout for greasers shut down after a kitchen fire smoked out a mischief of charred rats—Pedro had announced, "I no leave." And no leave he had.

"A girl," I corrected.

"*Mija*." Pedro tugged his goatee and grinned.

I gave him a thumbs-up. "You took Popeye food though, didn't ya?"

"Bacon an' eggs. Gulped it right down." Anna nodded.

"You gonna deal me a card or what, missy?" Joe slapped his cards on the table.

I slid him two.

"That bag of bones, he wasn't thinking too clear." Jake discarded three cards, picked up three more. "Knew I'd have to outsmart him."

Joe grunted.

"That's what happens when yer heart is broke, Swee'Pea." Jake took another drag on his cigarette, his cough a harsh rattle.

"How'd you outsmart him?" I frowned at the deuce under my palm.

"Caught the afternoon train and hopped off at the lone oak."

"What lone oak?"

"The one he were sittin' under."

"Thought he got chucked at the way station."

"Ain't the first dog to like that tree." Jake guzzled from his flask, but his cough had the best of him now, and he hacked and spit and swore a torrent. Anna thrust a glass of water at him, which Ernesto knocked over as he pounded him on the back. Jake snatched up his cards in the nick of time, but the glass shattered on the floor.

"Blast it! How many of me glasses yeh gonna break? Last week 'twas that fink of a dog."

"Whadda you care?" Joe popped open a beer can. "Anna's the one always cleans it up."

At that very moment, she shuffled from the closet, armed with a broom and dustpan.

"Popeye's not a fink, are ya, boy?" I kissed his snout.

"You clowns wanna be evicted?" Whether Cappy was talking to me or Joe, I didn't know. Cappy was always threatening to evict someone or other, Pedro and Popeye most often.

"I no speaka de English," Pedro would reply, stacking and unstacking his chips, while Popeye's paw thunked.

"Señor Cappy," Pedro now said, "I no break the glasses. I take them home. *Mi reina,* she like them." He shrugged as Jake winked, Ernesto patting them both on the back.

"Ooh la la!" Joe batted his eyelashes.

"By thunder, how's a man s'posed to run an honest business with all you crooks? I'm gonna evict the whole lotta yeh."

"You mean to tell me that Popeye"—I retied the mutt's gingham bandana—"just up and followed you home? I thought he wasn't budgin' for nothing, that he was waiting for someone."

"Right you are. He was waiting fer me."

"You windbags done strolling memory lane yet?" Joe snarled.

I had three deuces and two sixes. I raised.

"Saw me climb down that train, and a load of hurt toppled off them scrawny shoulders. Huh, boy?" He met Popeye's woof with a knuckle rub under the chin. "He knew I'd come fer him."

"What bunk." I rolled my eyes.

"Bunk or not, you shoulda folded at that deuce, Swee'-Pea," Jake said with a laugh, turning up a straight flush.

Popeye might not have taken an instant liking to Jake, but he had a right soft spot for me, licking me back to life after a dead faint upon first acquaintance.

It'd been a month of fitful sleep in our fusty new bungalow. I'd woken to an autumn sky still dark, feeling mad, all mixed up inside, haunted by an elusive dream, and staggered to the beach, thinkin' to toss some pebbles into the water or maybe wander to the swings, though the shore lay shrouded in chilly gloom. I'd slung a jacket over my nightgown and soon yanked up the hood, flicking off my thongs and letting the wet sand squish between my toes. I could hear the lap of water, a seagull's cry, the low chatter of fishermen, but dense fog bleared sight, not much different from the fog of my sleep.

And then it appeared, rising from the mist like a mythical creature straight out of *The Aberdeen Bestiary*, bounding full speed toward me.

"Good Lord, it's the hound of the Baskervilles," I gasped, keeling over with a thud. Next thing I knew, the phantom dog was licking my face, slobbering on my nightgown, and nosing in my jacket pocket. Before I could fully resurrect, he dashed to the water's edge, beef jerky between his teeth, and plunked himself on his haunches, his gaze trained out to sea.

"Whatcha lookin' at, boy?" I crouched beside him and squinted into the haze.

Didn't take but two minutes before I had my answer. Barkin' to wake the dead, the fiery fiend leapt up and charged at a figure breaking through the swells, the man striding to shore like a Greek god, wild beard and burly frame, tattoos sprawled across his chest. Tail wagging, Popeye romped in zigzags 'cross Jake's path, pouncing on us both, a regular twister loosed from Tornado Alley.

"How come his left eye's all squinched?" I'd asked Jake through a mouthful of donut one morning, the three of us sitting on the bench outside Lucky's.

"Came that way."

"You gonna have it checked?"

"What fer?"

"He might be blind." I waved my hand in front of Popeye's face. He tried to lick it.

"He's got one good eye, don't he? And a fair smart nose. Sniffs out them bluffs."

ℰↃ

I COULD'VE USED Popeye's nose right 'bout now to sniff out Raven's house. I'd decided to circle the shantytown, hike the back way to remain unseen. But somehow I'd gotten turned around. The dusty stretch seemed too familiar—an overgrown lane that snaked below St. Francis, a trail that led through an oak forest, a descent into underbrush, shoulder-high ferns hugged by poison oak, the leaves tinged red—*leaves of three, let it be*, Hollis cautioned—the split into two dappled paths. I didn't need Hollis to tell me I'd taken the wrong one—or to warn me I was treading through tick territory, not to mention rattler.

By now I should have stumbled upon the ruins of the once-grand estate, now a Soviet den, but the only stumbling I did landed me a skinned knee and scraped elbow. The sun climbed with me, melting the shadows, the uphill slog spitting me onto a ridge fit for a postcard: a sweep of hills sprigged with vineyards, a plunge to a coastal curl, the squat belfry of Mar Vista Chapel, the shimmer of ocean. My stomach fixin' to pitch a fit, I staggered on, paying no heed to the dangers most like prowling the shadows, from rattler territory into the range of mountain lions.

After a spell, the trails blurred together, spangled by the same trees, the same prickly shrubs, the same black-berry bushes. Had Hollis been alongside, as he ought, he'd have said something 'bout seeing this bent oak double now, sent me tromping toward that tall pine, took me 'round the eucalyptus grove. He'd have picked me a less tart black-berry, saying to my puckered face, "The sweet ones grow in the sun."

Breaking through a thicket onto a gravel road, I took

stock of things, wiping the sweat from my brow. The sun hung like a hot skillet in a cloudless sky. High noon, I reckoned, lamentin' my lousy sense of direction.

For half a moment, I felt an overwhelming urge to flop down into the dirt and have myself a proper bawl, and then, as though I'd conjured a genie and made a wish, I saw it, tucked behind a tangle of dense trees, a house so small and plain that had I sneezed, I'd have missed it—a rutted drive, a weed-choked yard, a collapsed porch, and one sorry gable, the double windows spalled and cobwebbed, coated in grime. That, leastways, was real as rumor—and the telltale sign I'd hit on KGB headquarters. But not a lick of likeness otherwise to the sinister manor confected by delicious lore. The house sat mute and lonesome as the crumbled tombstones at St. Francis, and sure 'nough, leaning against it and shrouded by gnarled trees, the fabled shed.

I stole toward the house on tiptoe, wincing at the gravel crunching under my shoes, my own breaths the chug of a Texas dust storm. Though mighty relieved I didn't have to brave the house, I'd have to front it. The shed stood on the far side. I paused, ear to the wind, alert for any sign of life, human or haunt. Nothing but the distant wail of a train.

"Gumption, Eden, gumption," I whispered with the echoes. "Ain't nothin' to get so riled up ov—"

A streak of fur shot from under the porch like its tail was on fire, a scrawny thing, its yowls near sendin' me into a swoon. Whether chased by some basement dread or unleashed to wreak hoodoo, I'd no time to consider, striking my best Bruce Lee. The cat went stiff and backed away, hissing at my karate chop. As it slunk across the road, my heart pounding, I knew two truths for a moonshine certain: Of course Raven would have a black cat. And if anybody'd been home, they'd have ushered me to the pearly gates by now.

My breath ragged, I snuck past the porch—mud-brown paint peeling off the front door, screen askew—made it all of three steps, when the shrill ring of a telephone blew my gumption to smithereens. Now a demon cat myself, I bolted to a back window and dropped like a sack of sugar.

Five, six, nine rings. Nothing. I peeked through a dirt-streaked windowpane. Staring back at me was a dead spider and my own scared face.

But I was almost to the shed. The backyard showed a mess of shrubs and bristly weeds and—*well, ain't that a sight.* In a far corner, yellow stalks rustled low, with a scatter of violets and daisies nearby and, over yonder, a bush dusted with blooms. "Can always tell a camellia by its petticoats," Mama'd said one Texas spring day, handing me a spade. "The belle of a Southern garden."

A sweet fragrance drifted 'cross the yard, strong and creamy, not a bit like Mama's camellias. I glanced at the house, tried to picture Raven slippin' out at dawn, water jug in hand, saw her crouch to pat fresh soil, pull stubborn weeds, and pluck blossoms for her hair. It came easier to imagine her hacking flowers from beneath unsuspecting windows.

But it was something, this, her bit of wild earth.

With the cat eyeing me from the road, I crept 'cross the yard to the shed. The rotted door hung askew, jammed into the dirt, just open enough for me to squeeze through. Shapes formed as I blinked into the darkness—a toppled wheelbarrow, a ladder, empty crates, a workbench. Cobwebs threaded the rafters like lace.

No buckets of blood. No baseball bat or spray paint. No guns. A bust.

A whole lotta nothin', I'd have to admit to Hollis, swatting at a mosquito. Time to fold my cards and clear out, I reckoned, except—

I peered into the shadows, emboldened by a fresh piece of bubble gum. The workbench could use a look, anyhow. I inched farther into the shed, sidestepping a canister draped with a dirty rag and catching a whiff of gasoline.

Sunlight splintered through a grimy window, spilling across a table heaped with odds and ends: a garden spade, a pair of work gloves, loose nails, a half-case of Smirnoff vodka, crumpled newspaper, a box of macarons, a toothed iron ba— wait, what? I'd never seen a cookie box stamped with an encircled star and labeled—I squinted, a bubble popping onto my lips—*380 Ammo 9mm Makarov*.

Not macarons. Ammunition.

As I reached for the box, my elbow knocked somethin' clean off the workbench, sending it crashing to the floor. I froze, ears perked like Popeye's one, eyes fixed on a rolling can, the crimson cap spinning to a stop.

Glory be! She *was* the vandal!

In a flash, my vexation somersaulted into triumph, my busted day into a scooped pot. Lordy, what would Hollis say now? What cou—

Crunch.

A thousand spiders scuttled up my neck.

Crunch.

It was getting louder, closer, twigs snapping, then footsteps, then—

SKRITCH!

—talons on glass!

Had an Egyptian plague been loosed on me, I couldn't have lit out faster, flying from the shed like a bat out of hell, tearing 'cross the dirt drive, into the street, and down the hill, running pell-mell toward the ravine, yowlin' right along with the cat.

Only when I plowed into the shantytown itself did I breathe easy. I'd had the road to myself 'cept for a motorcycle swooping past in a cloud of dust. No one had followed me, I'd made sure of that, so I eased my pace, clacking a stick along a chain-link fence.

I found myself on the town's main street, most like only street, unpaved and edged by run-down houses and cluttered yards, the rare flower patch, a tire swing on a leafless tree, barking dogs. Somewhere a door slammed. A woman hollered. Two boys on bicycles skidded to a halt near a mailbox, jumped off, and skulked into the house. Though I walked in the sun, my skin prickled at the strange doings of the shantytown.

She'd been there—at the shed—same as she'd been at St. Francis. Never mind that I'd last seen her miles out to sea, bouncing across whitecaps. *A sorceress has her ways.* I'd felt the sear of those cool eyes as I stood in the cobwebbed shadows. Was she fixin' to return the murder weapon, stash it with the spray paint and ammunition? Or had she stowed the gun in Jake's dinghy to hide in her lair, another treasure buried at the Pirate Caves?

Sure wished I had Hollis to kick my musings around with, but all I was kicking was broken glass as the road wound 'long the mucky creek to the highway. I could hear him now—and truth was, it went down pretty much the way I'd imagined.

"Lots of people have spray paint and ammo."

"Red spray paint? And ammo with a star?"

"Bet my dad's got both in the garage."

"I'm just connecting the dots."

"Sounds more like you're playing Go Fish. How'd she get back to Gulch Run so fast? And so what if she did? Last time I checked,

a body has a right to be at their own house."

Such a long speech would eat up his quota of words for the day, *that* I knew, so though he wasn't much likely to say it, I'd lay odds he'd think it.

"And I don't see how you poking around is a help to anyone. Unless you're planning to go to the sheriff?"

"Can't do that yet."

"Why not? You're so certain."

"I am certain. But I don't have enough evidence."

"Then what do you have?"

Rumors. That's what I had. So far I hadn't breathed a word of my suspicions to anyone but Hollis, mindful of Rev. Travers's exhortation by way of the apostle James: *How great a forest is set ablaze by a small fire!* In that, at least, I felt righteous.

Before I knew it, I'd wandered onto a trail shaded by eucalyptus trees, my feet slipping on loose dirt an' leaves, the paved road snaking above me. My stomach was a wobble of hunger and worry.

Maybe Hollis was right. What evidence did I have? The faded scrawl of a hammer and sickle, the carcass of a shot baby seal, a can of spray paint, and a box of ammunition. *Adding two and two and getting five.* Then to his voice came another: *Ay! Why you no tell shareef? Qué mal, Edee Mae!* These voices I expected, their rebuke familiar. It was the next voice that caught me up short.

Like a rogue wave, it washed over Rosa's words, soft and teasing, faint at first, then louder, erupting into giggles, and then another voice, a sweet-talkin' one. I squinted through the trees into the ravine. Stormwater flowed down the embankment, spilled into Diablo Creek. Spanning the swollen current was a footbridge. And on the footbridge, enfolded in someone's arms, stood a copper-haired girl, her cheek pressed against his letterman jacket. The trees hid his face, but there was no mistaking *her*.

Romance. That was something I had no time for, 'less you counted my crush on Little Joe Cartwright, though I'd given the notion a good mull one afternoon, courtesy of a twitterpated couple sprawled near my beach swing. A dog lay beside them, ears flicking sand fleas, contented same as me. But *he* must've said something *she* didn't like, 'cause quicker than a hiccup, she was shoving him off, slapping herself free of his tangle of arms and scrambling to her feet. She tore across the beach and into the waves, the dog on her heels. One minute, all was right with the world, the next, sand was flyin' and the dog had picked sides. Seemed an unnecessary complication to my already complicated life.

"But she has the gun!" The words quavered above the soft rush of the creek. "She's gonna bury you."

"She won't get the chance."

I crouched, straining to hear.

"What if you're too late? Or Ben does something stupid again?"

Through the leaves, I saw him tilt her chin up, sweep aside her falling hair. His voice came low, calm, butter on a biscuit. "We've got this, babe. Don't worry."

Her reply lost itself in the whistle of the rumbling train now hugging the hillside, but I'd heard enough. They were on to Raven too.

Wait till Hollis gets wind of this, I gloated.

Ch-ch-ch-ch-ch!

The sound came from a thick shoelace in the grass, a moving shoelace, a slithering-over-my-foot shoelace. Choking back a scream, I hopped madly, sending a half dozen pebbles bouncing down the embankment. For a horrified second, I went stiff as a fence post, just long enough to see the love-birds look up sharply, Heather locking wide eyes onto mine. I didn't wait for Vince, breaking into a sprint back to the road, back to the highway, running as though pursued by a howl-ing horde of Gulch Run hobgoblins. I had only myself to blame for stirrin' 'em up. Again.

SEVENTEEN

"**W**HERE HAVE YOU been?" My father stood on the porch, arms crossed, filling the doorway with his question.

What with the dead seal, stolen dinghy, and Gulch Run hobgoblins, I'd forgotten. Plain and simple. Or maybe I'd never remembered. Condemnation. "Awful bad business at the beach. Seal got shot."

"And it took you all day to find out?" His eyes were the same maple as Dex's but brewed a storm. "Your mother's at work, Rosa doesn't come for another hour, and you're God-knows-where. I have a faculty dinner to prepare for tonight. Care to explain?"

"Sorry," I mumbled, studying a crack in the bottom step. No use tryin' to talk my way out of this one.

"Left Dex to fend for himself, is that it? Look at me, Eden."

I glanced halfway up, at his fingers drumming on the doorjamb, at the gold band he still wore, clenched my own hands.

"I asked you—"

I could feel him take stock of my mud-caked tennis shoes, my skinned knee, the streaked dirt on my shorts.

"Are you going to tell me where you've been?"

"Around."

"Around?"

I knew I was skating on thin ice, but I didn't care.

"Not around here, that's for sure." When I volunteered nothing more, he shrugged. "All right, you win." He waved me into the house. "You can keep your where-to-bouts to yourself. Go clean up." My father, the university professor, made up words on the fly, silly, stupid words, words that used to make me laugh. "But hurry it up. We need to talk."

Great. And there was no "we" about it. *He* had a mind to talk, not me. I wanted to wish him away, hole up in my room, and not come out for a month of Sundays. He was the same shiny bubble breaking from the wand, teasing, swirling, drifting out of reach, gone. Just to reappear again. A bubble I wanted to pop.

"Uhng!" Dex flailed at the marbles on his playbed, brayed his nonsense chorus, gurgled and guffawed. Dex, the source of every prob—

I sighed. Fact was, if I were to quit my lyin' ways, I'd have to admit that I was a worse source of my problems. But still I paid him no notice, even when he caught sight of me and let loose a mighty shriek, his arms reaching for me. My entire afternoon would be spent wrangling him, and I didn't see that I should start now.

"Eden."

I headed up the stairs.

"Eden!"

I paused, gripped the banister.

"Eat anything besides oatmeal today?" I willed my stomach to stop rumbling. "How 'bout second breakfast, Pippin?" He sure could sound like a dad. "I'll whip up a batch of stacktacular pancakes. It'll have to be quick, but I've got a little time for my girl."

To my horror, my eyes brimmed with tears. "I'm not

hungry," I snapped, taking the stairs two at a time.

Back downstairs, I lugged Dex from the playbed, still grunting his stupid *uhngs*, fished his fingers out of his mouth, where they yanked his tongue, and straddled him across my hip. I'd washed the grime of Gulch Run off my face and pulled on a sweater and jeans, though I reckoned it was my insides needed cleanin' most. I'd made sure to transfer my loot from my shorts to my jeans pockets—my lipstick, the gold chain, the pack of gum, and my two-dollar deck of cards. Soon as Rosa came and I'd waved my father off, I aimed to play myself a few hands of poker.

The thin strains of a penny whistle caught my ear, pulling me to the window. A man in coveralls straddled the sea wall, beside him a pigtailed girl skipping rope. I squinted at the blues melding on the horizon and tried not to hate how stuck I felt.

"Coming?" my father called from the kitchen. He'd emptied half our cabinets onto the counter and was pouring batter on the griddle.

Strapping Dex into his high chair, I held a lidded cup to his squealing mouth. "What you say, heh?"

"Ah, whipped cream!" My father's head emerged from the fridge. "Want some?"

I didn't want whipped cream, and I didn't want pancakes. And I definitely didn't want time with my father.

"No thanks," I said, as he eyed me.

"Can't say where you've been today, but my money's on swamp fishing. Works up a fierce-alicious appetite, I hear." He shook the can of Reddi-wip and popped off the cap, near the same shade of red as the spray paint cap. "What do you say?"

"All right," I relented, hoping that if he fed me, he'd

leave. I didn't think I could stand another mangled word or another rankling comment.

Though I'd determined not to be hungry, I inhaled a stack of three pancakes, tearin' off soggy bits to pop into Dex's mouth.

"Likes his whipped cream, doesn't he? Chip off the old block." My father squirted a tower of white foam onto Dex's tray, laughed as Dex slapped at it. "That's my boy."

"Your boy?" I stopped chewing.

He set down his fork. "You ever going to stop being mad at me, Eden?"

I figured he didn't really want an answer.

"This wasn't my choice, you know."

The lump of pancake caught in my throat.

"Here." My father pushed my glass toward me.

I pushed it back.

"Okay, fine. We'll discuss it later." His jaw tensed. "I get it."

It's not okay, and you don't get it, I wanted to scream. *And it was your choice!* Why was he even here? This was *our* house, Mama's and Dex's and mine, on *our* beach, not his. I scraped back my chair and dug in my pocket.

"May I be excused, please?" Sometimes I hated my Texan manners.

"What's that? Baseball cards?"

The words jolted me into shared memories, Dad and me huntin' through board games at Saturday garage sales, riffling through discarded junk, trading high fives at the occasional dog-eared Topps baseball card to add to our collection— Hank Aaron, Mickey Mantle, Roger Maris, Willie Mays. Never could find a Reggie Jackson card. I shoved the deck back into my pocket.

"Bicycle cards." I dumped the rest of my pancake in the trash and wiped Dex's chin with a dirty napkin. "Thought I could learn solitaire."

"Solitaire? How 'bout a game for two?"

Was there no getting rid of him?

"No thanks."

"Hearts? Crazy eights? Gin rummy?" He flicked the *Harford Herald* at a fly, missing. "Of course, there's nothing like a fanta-stake, excell-ante round of poker."

Oh Lordy, he knew. Now I'd get busted for this evil too.

"Poker? But, uh, don't you have to bet?"

"Yep. We can use pennies."

"You'll have to teach me." I couldn't believe my fibbin' tongue. Didn't matter though. The whole day had been a gamble. "Mama wouldn't like me playing poker."

"Or me. We'll have to hide the evidence."

"Uh-h—"

"Haven't played since, oh, I guess my college days. Wasn't half-bad." He grinned. "Don't look so surprised. Contrary to popular teenage belief, parents are people too. And they were young once." Gray hairs flecked his furrowed brows. "Sometimes they even remember what that was like."

How parents could turn chitchat into lectures made my head spin. Just as I was chewin' on whether another thirty minutes of my father was worth a few poker tips, cilantro-laced air gusted into the kitchen, the front door slamming.

"Ay, *perdón!*" Rosa must have been a tornado in another life, the way she always blew in on a blast of broken English and bad timing. "Señor Lewis! *Hola, hola!*" She bustled toward the sink, crowding us like a latecomer in a church pew, and thunked a paper bag sprouting lettuce leaves on the counter. "I late? Ay, ay! You waiting long? *Lo siento*, I sorry!"

"You're not late, Rosa. Right on time, in fact." My father patted the chair I'd just vacated. "Here, catch your breath."

But Rosa marched straight to Dex, who was squawking and banging his spoon, and kissed his bobbing head. "Look I bring you, *mi tesoro*! Green apples you like *mucho*! See, they no bruise. They *perfectas*, same you."

I had never hated green apples so much.

"Rosa—" my father began.

"You go, okay, Señor Lewis? I here." And then as though seeing me for the first time, she flung out her arms. "You. You!"

Lordy, now what?

"Eedee Mae!" She fairly sang my name. "*Buena muchacha!*"

"Me?"

"*Sí, sí!* I make you tamales." Diving headfirst into her bag, she surfaced with a bundle of corn husks wrapped in twine. "You good, good girl."

This was shocking news, and not just to me. I saw my father's eyebrows arch.

"*Sí*, Eedee Mae. Father Miguel, he say what you do. You clean church. You wash. You sweep. No more the grafti." Although my head did not receive a kiss, Rosa did squeeze my cheeks. And she had made me tamales.

"So that's where you were. Why didn't you tell me?"

I shrugged, grateful to let the details slide. What matter *which* day? Anyway, I *had* been in Gulch Run all morning. It was practically the same thing.

Rosa tugged an apron over her floral dress, tied it beneath her ample bust. "No worry, Señor Lewis. I care for *chamacos*." Dishes clattered into the sink. "You go. Eat tamales." She shooed my father with a soapy wave.

"Actually, Rosa"—he nudged her from the sink, coaxing

the sponge away—"how would you like the night off?"

"What?" she and I said together.

"Sure, why not? No reason to stay now."

"But what about your faculty dinner?" I stammered.

"*Ay caramba!* I make you miss dinner? Uf!"

"No, you made me a better dinner. We'll heat up these tamales. You just get on home to your husband."

I saw my night at Cappy's swept right off the table.

"My husband? My Antonio? Heh!" She gazed at the ceiling and pressed her palms together in prayer. "*Padre, dame paciencia!*" she beseeched the light fixture. "My Antonio, he shoot the craps, drink the mezcal. He no be glad I come home. I come home, he go outside to chickens." She made such a racket clearin' the table that I had to strain to hear her. "He like sleep with chickens more he like sleep with me."

"You have eight—"

"Nine," I interrupted.

"You have nine children, Rosa. I think he likes you more than the chickens."

Rosa considered a moment. "*Sí,* okay. Sometimes my Antonio, he like be with me. Sometimes he no drink. *Una, dos, tres* weeks." Her face softened at the memory, or perhaps wish, and then hardened just as quickly. "But he drink tonight, I throw him to chickens!" That fate decided, Rosa wrapped her apron around my father and grabbed her shawl from the chair.

"You be good boy, Alejandro." She kissed Dex on the head again. "*Tu padre es un buen hombre.*"

After the front door banged behind her, my father rolled up his sleeves and sudsed the mixing bowl, while I mopped Dex's face. The sun scattered angled rays across the tile floor, and I knew the ol' geezers would soon be cutting the deck and calling bets. My chance of shaking my father was about as likely as a pig flyin'. I'd have to wait a whole week to rake in the poker pot—and rent a dinghy.

"What time does your mom usually get home?" My father tossed me a dish towel.

"Ten thirty. Maybe eleven."

A few long minutes ticked by, no talking, just him washing the dishes and me drying them. Dex cooed and grunted by turns in his playbed, the plink of marbles mingling with his barnyard noises. A sour stench drifted into the kitchen.

"Ohh, that's a beaut!" My father stepped into the hallway. "Does he just lie in bed all day?"

"Not when Rosa's here. She doesn't give him the chance."

He chuckled. "What about when she's not? What do you do with him?"

Do with him? Didn't he know the answer from Dex's holiday visits? Or had he been too busy fussing over his students to notice us?

"We stack blocks with him, sing silly songs, read stories. Mama an' I take him for walks. He likes reaching for the streetlights, the moon. Even the stars."

"Can't mean anything to him."

"Does it have to?" I muttered, adding more loudly, "We do what we've always done."

My father cocked his head at me, my slumped shoulders, my sullen face. I thought maybe he'd order me to stop slouching, to look sharp, the way he used to. Instead he swung his briefcase onto the table.

"Tell you what. I need to make a few calls and prep for next week's faculty meeting—which I *won't* be missing. Dex can nap, and you—"

"I can do homework." I remembered too late that it was summer. "Or read."

"Sure." He looked hard at me. "What happened to your glasses?"

"Only need 'em when I read."

"Huh. That's good." He didn't seem convinced. "And then how 'bout we get some sea air. Maybe take Dex to the pier. Does he like the pier?"

"I guess."

"Well, since you're guessing, what do you guess we'll do afterward?"

"Play cards?"

"Bambingo!"

EIGHTEEN

WHY THE SUDDEN interest in Dex? I fumed, climbing the stairs. Wasn't it enough that my father had to hang around our house all day? Tried to play dad with me? Now he had to play dad with Dex too?

My bedroom door banging shut with more oomph than I meant, I shoved a pile of clothes from my bed to the floor, fished my sketchbook out from under the covers, and drew the usual sweeping contours that refused to be anythin' but another eye. I sketched for a while in the dimness of my room but must have nodded off, my father's voice startling me.

"Ready, Eden?" He rapped on my door.

"Sure," I mumbled, dragging myself off the bed and trying to remember what in tarnation I was supposed to be ready for.

"Well, let's go then."

"Oh, right, okay." All I wanted to do was sink back into my warm stupor—that is, if I couldn't make it to Cappy's for our poker game. Without bothering to look in the mirror, I yanked my ponytail free, refastened it, knotted my jacket 'round my waist, started down the hallway, remembered my sketchbook, doubled back to shove it under the covers, and trundled down the stairs.

My father glanced at Dex gurgling in his playbed, tickled his toes. "Ready?"

"Sure, in like an hour, after I change Dex's diaper, put on his pajamas, strap on his br—"

"Eden!" he snapped, as though fixin' to scold, then paused. "I'll help with your brother."

My brother, but not your son.

I dragged Dex's braces out from under the couch, same place I always jammed 'em, too lazy or too hurried to bother with the closet and not figuring the point anyway, not since I got stuck playing guardian angel.

That's how Mama painted it, in celestial hues and hushed Southern awe, not just another worrisome chore, but an ordained blessing. "Gracious, sugar, you sure do have a way with our Dex," she'd say. It was true, I reckoned. Mama and Rosa could strap his braces and attach his shoe stirrups well enough in the calm, but when a thunderstorm struck, lashed across his features, unloaded torrents of tears—sometimes sudden as summer squalls, other times a fury of twisters— Dex wouldn't let a prayer near him, what with his thrashing and screaming, his creamy skin blotched red, his huge sobbing gasps. Even Mama couldn't soothe him still. But soon as I'd croon, "Say, Dexie, how 'bout a walk with Sissy?" he'd go limp, all coos and smiles, letting me clamp the metal braces on his legs without so much as a whimper.

Once off the porch ramp, he'd romp like a colt loosed from a barn, pitching pigeon-toed and wobbly, crippled legs stiff in heavy shoes, paying no mind to coaxes or shouts, needin' chasing and steering, his fingers yanking his tongue as he squealed.

Course I'd never suggest a walk if I could help it. Bad as it was putting up with his screeching inside, it beat risking a sighting outside—a carload of guys staring, a crowd of girls snickering—the encounter humiliating enough, but the gossip and torment to follow? Lordy, there'd be no livin' it down.

When I did walk him—best done on moonless nights or foggy dawns—I'd grip his hand, keep him close and my ten-gallon sun hat closer. Oh, I supposed the stray fisherman or ranger saw me from time to time, and one dusk I'd spotted Raven twirling in the surf, feathered skirts bunched in glittering arms, and ducked beneath my brim. But along with my Jane Jetsons, Dex was my secret. If Mama noticed my aversion to daytime walks, she didn't say.

"'For he shall give his angels charge over thee, to keep thee in all thy ways,'" she'd utter by way of send-off, leaning over the porch rail to watch us circle the streetlight. "You're Dexie-Darlin's angel, Eden Mae, a gift from the Lord."

No other praise could've made me more miserable. Maybe I didn't want to be a gift from the Lord. Maybe the Lord should've consulted me, though at the time I wasn't on speaking terms with him, same as my father, not until Mar Vista did a mighty work in me. And I was fixin' to take that mighty work to the tundra of Ecuador, though come to think of it, I could've started closer to home, 'cept now my father and I weren't much on speaking terms. He'd had little use for God, being weaned on California hedonism, but assured Mama he'd give the Almighty a chance. Then Dex was born.

On the rare occasion when I struck a truce with God, and that seemed less and less lately, Mama's words filled my heart with pride—and not a little consternation that, according to the Good Book, the proud of heart will not go unpunished. Mostly though, I grumbled at the weight of my halo and wondered at the fairness of God, how it was that he made *me* a gift but Dex a burden.

I yanked a Pampers from the Leaning Tower, setting off an avalanche.

"I got this, Eden."

"You sure?" I couldn't remember my father ever touching—much less *changing*—Dex's diaper, not even on holiday visits.

"I'm sure." He pinned a squirming Dex to the carpet with one hand and shucked the dirty diaper with the other, his fingers clumsy, the fresh diaper twisted. "Clean tooty booty—check. Dry pants—check. Now for the braces."

It took some doing, but together we wrestled Dex still enough to strap his thin legs into the metal contraptions, buckle his shoes, and zip his jacket.

"Lookin' good, champ," my father said, carrying Dex to the porch.

I tugged my hat over my eyes.

"Doubt you'll need that. Sun's almost down."

I shrugged.

"Can you even see?"

"Perfectly." If he gave me a side-eye, I didn't see it.

"How long can he walk?"

"Twenty minutes most. Should be in bed by seven thirty. Mama comes at nine."

"Soon as he's tucked in, it's showtime. Just gotta make sure the old gal doesn't catch us." Winking, he set Dex on his feet under the streetlight, steadying him between us.

My father was as good as his word too, the two of us guiding a lurching Dex to the quiet pier, not saying much, anything we might have said lost in the whoops and hoots of a boy set free, plunging forward, rigid legs faster than his body could keep up with, "grinnin' like a possum," Gramma Kay used to tease. We took a breather on a splintered bench, keeping tight grips on Dex as he tried to lunge for a seagull, watched surfers amble from the waves flashing "hang loose" signs, families pack up their blankets, the sun sink into the distant sea. How long we sat there, I didn't know, but I was glad for the silence, on it the whisper of a poem.

On the morrow, he will leave me, as my Hopes have flown before.

The moon was a rising marble by the time we climbed the porch steps. My father had to carry Dex the last stretch up our block, the braces that had given his legs wings now chains of iron. The front door squeaked open.

"Wore him out, didn't we?" My father intercepted the braces before I could shove them under the couch, stacking them in the hall closet.

His Big Bird pajamas buttoned and teeth brushed, Dex babbled as I laid him on his mattress, purrs and snorts mostly, wouldn't let go my finger.

"Guess that's done then." My father peeled off his desert boots and headed to the kitchen.

"He sleeps with Aslan." I unearthed the crocheted lion from under the blankets. "And he needs his night music." At the click of the tape deck, the rich baritone voice of George Beverly Shea filled the house. "The Golden records are for daytime."

"Can't say I've ever played poker to gospel," my father called, scraping back a chair. "At least your mother can't object to that."

I knelt by Dex's playbed, my finger still in his grip, and ran my hand 'long the glassy beads lining the rails, watching them spin. It didn't sit right with me, my father being here, in our home, at our table, shuffling my cards. It was one thing to crash a Saturday breakfast, but another to settle in like he owned the place. He'd outstayed his welcome, and the house felt too small for the four of us.

That was just it. There wasn't a four of us. My father

had made sure of that. But here he was, like a tick on a dog. And here I was not minding, as long as I got some poker practice out of it.

"I'm a Benedict Arnold," I informed Dex, his glazed eyes fastened on the slowing beads. And all 'cause I itched to beat Jake, pocket some cash. But I needed a dinghy. And neither Hollis nor Joe had seen fit to help me.

"O, the wonder of it all!" George sang from the tape deck.

Plodding to the kitchen, I glanced out the front window at the soft creep of fog. There was still a chance I could make it to Cappy's, catch the last few rounds, spring a trick or two on Jake, courtesy of my father. Wouldn't that be a hoot. Even as I was takin' a shine to the idea, I was onto myself. Sometimes the only way to endure a bad situation is to count your chickens before they hatch.

NINETEEN

MAMA CAME HOME just as I called my father's bluff, trumping his hand with my royal flush and scoopin' up the pot, mostly pennies, but a smart glint of silver too. In the hullabaloo of my win, his loss, we didn't notice the telltale hinges, Mama padding down the hallway so softly that her surprise at seeing my father still at the kitchen table was met with our own. In one fell swoop, I whisked the cards beneath a napkin, the coins already a bulge in my pockets.

"Hey, Mama." I scratched my elbow ferociously, irked at a new mosquito bite.

"Alex?" She stood in her stocking feet, an armload of books clutched tight, canvas bag slipping from her shoulder. Her face was a pucker of worry, as rumpled as her uniform.

"Whoa, let me take those." My father rose, but she leaned away, gripped her books more tightly.

"Why are you here? Is something wrong?" Her eyes darted to me. "Where's Rosa?"

I paused mid-scratch, hoping my father had forgotten he was only here 'cause I hadn't been, too busy sniffing 'round Gulch Run to spare a thought for Mama or Dex.

"I gave her the night off."

"Why? Is it Dex?" Mama was already in the living room, dumping her books on the couch. I trailed behind her, stashing the cards in a potted plant, my father patting soil over them. Dex lay tangled in his blankets, wheezing breaths like a teakettle and clutching Aslan's mane.

"Nothing's wrong, Elaine. We went for a walk, put Dex down, and played some po—"

I shot my father a look.

"—gospel music. Didn't need Rosa, so I sent her home."

Where the easy banter of the morning had gone, I didn't know, though I supposed Mama no more fancied my father settin' up camp for the day than I did.

"Did you give him his erythromycin?" Mama took the syrup bottle from the bookcase, her bag falling to the floor, her words clipped. Mascara smeared a cheek.

"Yes'm. He's fine. We don't need Rosa when I'm here."

My shoulders sagged under his strained tone, sad and angry all at once. Or maybe it was me who was sad and angry.

Stop slouching, his glance ordered me.

"But you're *not* here, Alex. That's why I hired Rosa."

A squall was coming, and I wanted no part of it.

"Rosa brought us tamales, Mama. Would you like one?"

"Tamales?" She stared at me as though I'd spoken Waorani, the tongue of the Aucas.

"Count me in," my father called, reaching the kitchen before us and pouring himself the white wine Mama used for seafood gumbo. "You mind?"

"Actually I do. I mind you parking in my driveway. I mind you sending Rosa home. I mind—"

"Y'know what? Keep your wine." My father dumped his glass back into the narrow neck, sloshing Chablis onto the counter. "Doesn't go with tamales anyway." He attempted a laugh.

"Would you please—"

"Don't suppose there's beer in here?" Before Mama could

answer, his head was inside the fridge. "Aha! My Corona! Forgot I put them there. Let me guess—you mind that too."

Their voices locked in a wrestle of low words, I backed into the hall toward the front door.

"You set one foot outside that door, Eden Mae—" Mama lassoed me with a tone reserved for my father. "Go straight up to your room and take those smelly sheets off your bed." Her voice softened. "Probably where you got that bite."

Just hearing the word made my elbow itch. Two minutes in her shed an' Raven had zapped me. "Yes, Mama."

But she'd shifted her scold to my father, the edge back in her voice. It might cost me a month of chores and a share of my salvation, but I had places to be—and places not to.

Commanding the door hinges not to squeak, I eased on my tennies and tiptoed outside. By my reckoning, Cappy would be fryin' up a second batch of fish fillets, Jake would be nursing an Olympia, and Joe would be counting both his chips and his lucky stars—*finally, a poker night without any no-good thieving kid.*

ℰ℩

A THICK HAZE blanketed the poker room, a weave of Cappy's pipe, Jake's cigarettes, Ernesto's cigar, and a small grease fire that Pedro was dousing with baking soda and a torrent of Spanish curses. Joe had taken his sweet time unlocking the front door, first heading off Jake, who struggled to rise from his chair, and then moseying through the diner toward me, pausing to straighten the menus on the counter, move the trash can, fiddle with the blinds. I must have stood shivering in the fog and rapping on the window a full five minutes.

"You want something?" he said when he finally cracked open the door.

"Nice to see you too, Joe."

Squeezing past him, I threaded between tables to the storeroom, stacked with bottled sodas and bins of potatoes, and squatted beside Popeye, lapping water from a salad bowl. The old dog pelted me with wet kisses, then perched on his hind legs, a white paw poised on the table, his tail thumping.

"Heya, Popeye. You winning?" I stroked his scruffy head, untwisted his bandana. "Hey, Jake."

"Where ya been, Swee'Pea?" Jake eyed the steaming platter making its way from the kitchen on Ernesto's shoulder, the tray teetering as he nicked a basket heaped with fish strips.

"Noodlin' catfish in the creek," I quipped, awed by Jake's ritual of double-dunking his fish strips into a bowl of Tabasco. His appetite was back, an observation that cheered me mightily. Maybe those morning sea walks were patching him up after all, worth the threat of riptides and sharks. Though I was itching to report what I'd witnessed—Raven's brazen thievery of the *Autumn Rows*—a glare from Joe told me now was not the time.

As Cappy nudged a chair toward me, the kitchen door swung wide, and in lumbered Anna, a heavy pot hitched to one hip, a bag of rolls to the other. Joe, gentleman that he was to everyone but me, hustled to her aid, setting the pot on a diner table and holding up her coat.

"Off to Mac's," she announced, as though we didn't already know.

Once or twice a week, Anna carted whatever fixin's she could scrounge up to Mayor Mac and his pap, holed up east of Diablo Creek. Ma had given up the ghost sixteen years before at the age of eighty-two—"just a spring chicken, she was"—and ever since, Pap had lain prostrate with a grief so severe he couldn't hardly remember his own son's name. It had fallen to his nameless son to care for him, which His Honor managed fairly well when he wasn't drunk and even better when he was. Between the Mar Vista Ladies United Visitation Ministry—known simply as LUV—and Anna, father and son were properly fussed over, though to hear her say it, she didn't feel a lick sorry for 'em, milking sympathy nigh on two decades, and wasn't aimin' to convert the ol' codgers. She just fed 'em. Like the Gospel story, no matter how scant the loaves and fishes after a busy week at Cappy's, Anna never failed to multiply the scraps, rustling up a pot of hearty stew or clam chowder fit to last for days.

"How come you bother with a no-good drunk and his crazy pap?" I'd asked her once.

"I'd bother with you if ya needed botherin'."

I couldn't argue with that—and knew better than to try. Anyway, they paid her in gossip, which she served up hot to the rest of us.

Anna drove a wood-paneled station wagon, dented and rusted through, usually returning from Gulch Run within the hour—unless she had to track down His Honor, camped under a bridge or cradled in a gutter. Once back at Cappy's, she'd settle herself on a corner barstool, high enough to keep a sharp eye out for poker cheats and near enough to monitor Jake's sips of Gramps's elixir. Then to the clink of chips, she'd settle into ruminating aloud for our benefit, tidbits doled out like the Milk-Bones she tossed Popeye. Last week she'd been grim.

"Mac gots the gout in 'is big toe. Bad flare-up this mornin'."

From the collective murmur at this revelation came a gruff voice. "Schmuck needs to lay off the booze. Me too."

Jake uncapped his flask. "Course, keeps me alive."

"*Cómo?* Who this Schmuck?"

Anna kept right on. "Made me take off 'is sock an' examine it."

"Pretty."

"Gout the size of a pea. I seen worse. But I ain't smelled worse. Foot stunk t' high heaven."

"I'm tryin' to enjoy me soup, if yeh don't mind."

"Figured I could take care o' both at once, the stink and the gout."

"What'd ya do? Chop off his foot?"

A spate of chuckles met Joe's question.

"Sure did. But stucks it in a bowl of ice first. He didn't feel nothin'."

Jake hooted. "Mac likes you coddlin' him. Taken a fancy to you, he has." He blew a cigarette ring at her.

"Pish!"

Mac and his pap's doings duly reported, she'd set about sweeping and scouring like she owned the joint, spraying surfaces with a vengeful mix of white vinegar, bleach, and formaldehyde—least that's what Joe said—provoking curses and cries of suffocation. The diner spick-and-span, she'd resume her seat and scold our cheating ways, but we all knew what lay behind her gossip and gripes, could see it in the dim gray eyes that followed Jake.

A blast of cold air told us Joe had opened the door for Anna, the chowder sloshing as she shuffled outside. He straddled the threshold, allowing himself a rare laugh and shutting the door only after the chug of her station wagon had died out. On his return he switched off the lights but one, the ceiling lamp casting a dusty halo above us.

Cramped on rickety chairs around the square table, the

men stacked their chips to the pop of beer cans, lunker burps punctuatin' poker calls, but not a soul drunk or even tipsy. They could drink a sailor dry, what with all the practice they got, and anyway the only rule Cappy enforced was to play sober. I never did think to ask when sober wasn't sober anymore, but it was a hard-and-fast rule, one I had no trouble keeping, downing a Dr Pepper most nights. Gambling and swearing burdened my soul enough, or on second thought, perhaps not enough. No need to add drinking. And though I never touched a drop of the nasty stuff, tonight I needed something stronger than soda.

"Coffee?" Cappy knit his bristly eyebrows together. "Yeh sure? Been sittin' in the pot since morning. More like battery acid now."

"I can handle it." I poured myself a cup and sidled back between Jake and Ernesto.

Ernesto was Pedro's brother. At least Pedro claimed him as a brother, though I couldn't figure it. Ernesto was darker than a Van Gogh night and just as silent, but Pedro swore on his mother's grave that they were blood brothers—never mind that his mother was alive and well in Tijuana. Ernesto didn't claim to be Pedro's brother, nor did he dispute it. In fact, he never said a word, merely twisting the ends of his handlebar mustache. The only thing to come out of Ernesto's mouth was the stink of a fat cigar and the sweetest tunes ever to swell from a harmonica. While I wouldn't bet my bottom dollar on it, seein' I needed it to rent a dinghy, I'd a hunch Ernesto had taken a liking to me as much as Joe had taken a hating. He smiled at me now, his harmonica wedged between yellow teeth.

"Five-card stud. You in?" Joe barked.

"I'm in." I fished three quarters and five nickels from my pocket.

Cappy slid a stack of red and black chips across the table.

"Gonna last more than one round tonight?" Jake coughed between cigarette puffs.

"Not only that, I'm gonna clean you out."

He grinned, leaned into Popeye, paw ready on the table. "Hear that, boy? Them's fightin' words."

"You'll see. I got wised up."

"Ya don't say. Catch that, Popeye?" He lifted the dog's limp ear to make sure.

"Yep. Get ready to fold."

"You two gonna yak all night or ante up?" Joe glared at me. "What's all over your mouth?"

I puckered my lips and sat up taller, pushing out what chest I had and giving my ponytail a pert swish. "Max Factor UltraLucent Whipped Creme Lipstick." I felt myself blush. "Proud Pink Frost. Wanna borrow it?"

I didn't dignify Joe's snort with so much as a glance.

A flushed Pedro scraped up a barstool and perched above the rest of us, mopping his brow with a dishrag. His goatee glistened with oil.

"Git down off of there," Cappy growled, flapping his bum arm. "How yeh gonna play sittin' on a totem pole?"

"Is no place for me." Pedro tossed a five-dollar bill at Jake.

"Move that girl," Joe said. "She ain't got no business here."

"I'll say who has business here." Jake hauled Popeye onto his lap, the hula girl shimmying under his sleeve.

I scooted over.

"Plenty room for yer skinny butt. *Ándale!*"

Joe smirked. "You gonna play poker with a gorilla on your lap?"

"Unless you want him?"

Joe made like he was 'bout to spit, threw the deck of

cards on the table instead, and swore unmentionables. Leveling a mournful one-eyed gaze at Joe, Popeye scrambled off Jake's lap and tucked himself in a corner. Pedro dragged over a footstool, sat down, and propped his chin on the table.

This time Joe spat. "I ain't playing with no midget."

"This table, it's for four chairs." Pedro tugged at his goatee. "This game, it's for six peoples and one dog. You wanna *me* sit on your lap?"

"Deal the cards." Cappy emerged from the kitchen with a glare. "If you dimwits don't drop the Three Stooges act, I'll fire the lot o' yeh. And quitcher damn swearin'."

"Why? Ain't no ladies here." Jake winked at me.

"We don't work for you," Joe muttered.

"And you ain't about to, neither. Not a full deck between yeh."

"*Oye*—where's my chips?" Pedro reached for a stack of black chips but accepted the soggy french fry Jake offered instead.

"This ain't poker. This is a doggone sewing circle." Joe swore again. "I ain't playing with a bunch of grannies."

"Cut the blasted deck!"

In this way, Cappy and Joe bossed us through a night of five-card stud, seven-card stud, and Texas Hold'em.

I was mulling over my three jacks and four junk cards when a gust of cold air cleared the smoke above our table and Anna shambled in with news that silenced us all.

"Take a load off." Cappy waved his bum arm at the barstool. "I'll raise an' draw two," he added, swiping the cards Pedro slid him.

Jake eyed his sister through a smoke ring. "What took so long?"

Anna hoisted herself onto the stool with the aid of Joe, sitting as high as Pedro sat low. "Mayor Mac had some talkin' t' do."

Popeye uncurled himself and ambled to Jake.

"Yeah? What kind of talking?"

"He actually had something worth listening to?" Joe raised the bet.

"Saw who killed that seal." The dim lamp swayed with the gust that had followed her in, threw shadows across her wrinkled face.

Cappy grunted, sorted his cards. "Malarkey. That lush couldn't see straight if a ruler hit 'im between the eyes."

"Musta been a yardstick. Sleepin' on the stairs down by the sea wall, trussed up in that ratty bedroll. Gunshot waked 'im. Swore on 'is honor."

"Bah! He could swear on his grandmother's grave—wouldn't make it true."

"She dead, his grandmother?" Pedro made the sign of the cross. "*Qué triste.*"

Ernesto patted his shoulder.

"Said a girl was standin' over it." Anna set her jaw. "Holdin' a gun."

Joe cussed, though whether at our interrupted game or at the revelation, I didn't know. Afraid I might cuss too, I took a hefty gulp of coffee.

"What girl?" Jake asked.

"Gypsy lass holed up in that rundown shack past Gulch Run."

The coffee spluttered out my nose.

"Trouble started after they moved in, her and her uncle."

"Don't mean much, Joe." Jake tossed a red chip into the pot.

"Means fifty bucks for cam locks. Where's her folks, anyway?"

"Can't say." Anna shook her head. "Uncle's gone weeks on end. Child roams like a lost thing. Ain't right."

"Now don't go getting soft on commies." Joe called a bet.

Cappy raised. "If it's Mayor Mac, it's the liquor talkin'."

"Sheriff Moretti don't think so."

"Whaddya mean?"

"He were there, at Mac's. Said others seen it too. Got statements."

"Who?" Jake licked Tabasco off his knuckle. "No one's out that early 'ccpt me and Popeye—and a few surfer kids on dawn patrol."

"Yep, them. The one with the Harley. And those beach bunnies."

"Well, I didn't see nothin'."

"Pish! Were t'other side of the pier. Near the inlet."

"Harley? You mean that punk Vince? If that's a Harley, I'm Ernesto." Joe spat his toothpick onto the floor.

Ernesto beamed.

"Vince, that's the name. Couple other surfers too."

"His stooge? The preacher's kid?" Joe's eyes narrowed. "They're Tweedledum and Tweedledumber."

"Can't say." Anna took a glass of water from Cappy. "Boys told Moretti they heard the shot from the waves. Rushed ashore an' tried t' catch her. Girls swore it too."

"No foolin'."

No condemned foolin'! I'd known it. And I knew where she'd pilfered the gun too. My chair creaked under my fidgets, me and myself debating which I was rarin' to do more—tell Jake about his dinghy or tell Hollis about Raven's guilt. Guess Hollis wouldn't be so high and mighty now.

"Why in the blazes would she shoot a seal?" Cappy returned to the table, beer bottle in hand.

Revenge! I had to take another gulp of coffee to keep from blurting the truth.

"Don't make sense," Jake said. "Maybe the odd mischief here or there. But killing a pup?"

"Kids these days."

"Nah, pranks is one thing. But takin' a life, that's evil. Can't figure the girl fer it." Jake seemed to debate with his flask, lifting it to his lips, setting it down, finally letting Anna coax it from him.

"Ain't no whys to evil sometimes," she said.

Hell-bent on revenge, I wanted to say. *That's why. Hates the lot of us, hates this town, hates America. Plain as the nose on your face.*

"She's *loco* in the *coco*, that's why." Pedro gave Ernesto a knowing look. "*El que es perico, donde quiera es verde.*"

It was Pedro's default answer to life's inscrutables, according to Cappy, one I heard often.

Ernesto smiled tooth to crooked tooth, as though he'd just been complimented.

"We gonna play or wh—"

"Let her talk." Jake held up a callused hand. "Those beach bun—girls. What'd they see?"

"Told Moretti they saw 'er standing over somethin'—kelp or driftwood, till they got close—and then the surfers running from the water, shouting."

"And His Honor? He saw the actual shooting?"

"Snorin' off a bender on the stairs. Said a holy ruckus waked 'im, then *bang!* He knew it was her, hoverin' over the seal. Said he'd know those black skirts and wild eyes anywheres."

"Even dead drunk? Even in the fog?"

"Just sayin' what I heard."

"What ruckus? Thought the gunshot woke him."

Anna shrugged. "Can't say Mac didn't change 'is story."

Considering the lengths folks had to go to rouse His Honor after a bender, that he woke up at all was remarkable.

"Aw, he's a fool drunk." Jake wiped fish crumbs from his beard.

"Ain't sayin' otherwise. But he's an honest drunk."

"Did they find the gun?" I asked, awash in a storm of questions but able to spit out only one.

"Not yet. Waitin' on a warrant t' search her house. Uncle's been took in for questioning."

"Yeh know if they arrested the girl?"

Anna rose from the stool, grunting as she arched her back. "Gots to find 'er first. Poor thing."

Poor thing! How could Anna not see the facts staring her in the face?

"Can't arrest someone on a might." Jake retied Popeye's bandana. "Need evidence."

"And quick-like." Anna exchanged glances with Jake. "Seems folks made up their minds a'ready."

"That's a helluva tale, but you done yet? Game ain't gonna play itself."

"Brush up yer solitaire."

"Might win, Joe." Anna could hold her own. "That ain't the worst of it."

Joe fell silent, cut the deck for Pedro.

"Mac saw the girl point the gun at Vince, heard her say he's next. Kid's real shook up."

The room couldn't have gone more dead had it been full of stiffs.

"Bah! He 'eard that?" Cappy flung his bum arm into Pedro's chest. "Bubble-wrapped on the stairs like 'e was?"

"Can't say. We wasn't there."

"You gonna deal me a card this year?" Joe groused. "Like playing in a funeral parlor. Who wants a beer?" Without waiting for an answer, he slid a bottle at Jake. "Now deal, dammit."

Whether the doings of the gritty coffee, Anna's particulars, or my father's poker tips, I surged with a vim and vigor that saw me sweep the next three rounds, biding my time, sizing up the odds, keeping a sharp eye, making bold calls, and scoring a grand chunk of change. That last hand was all my father—and Popeye's paw.

Jake's grin showed a broken front tooth. "Mighty nice, Lady Luck."

"Why, Jake"—I puckered my Pink Frost lips into a movie-star pout—"you just called me a lady."

He blew a smoke ring my direction, to which I stuck out my tongue.

"Aw, cut the mush. More like the brat cheated."

"I don't cheat." The very thought chagrined me. "I've been baptized."

"Not sure it took."

I paid Joe—and my fib—no mind, scraping the pile of chips toward me and stacking them. I'd have some confessin' to do before bed.

"Might as well keep the pot on the table, missy. You're gonna lose it next round anyway."

"Ain't neither. I'm out."

"Whaddya mean, you're out?" Joe snatched Ernesto's cigar from beneath his mustache and dunked it in Jake's Tabasco. "Damn stinkin' cigars."

Ernesto replaced it with his harmonica and blew a hearty blast.

"Damn stinkin' harmonica." As Joe made to grab it, Cappy slapped him with his hat, but like a bull seein' red, Joe turned on Pedro. "I ain't telling you again, sizzle boy. Deal the cards."

"I'm out, Cappy." Now with the funds to rent a dinghy, I'd sense enough not to push my luck—and some serious thinking to do. I'd a hunch where Raven had fled to—and where she'd stashed the murder weapon—so now it was a matter of tracking her down. Anyway, a heavy dread had settled in my stomach. Mama would be waiting for me, sighing and rocking Dex, beseeching the Almighty to bring home her—and his—wayward child. Guess Ben and I weren't all that different. Plus, I had to pee somethin' fierce.

"Cashing in yer chips?"

"Yes sirree, Jake. Four bucks fifty." I made sure Joe took notice.

"Good riddance," he huffed. "Finally a man's game. And

it's two bucks fifty. You owe me for the cards."

Confound it. I'd forgotten. How was I supposed to rent a dinghy now?

Joe nabbed two bills from Jake, waved them in my face, and then stowed them in his wallet. "Thanks, missy."

I shoved a dollar bill and six quarters into my pocket, the coins clinking against the gold chain.

Ernesto stood as though to speak—a first if he had—took a deep breath, pressed his harmonica to his lips, and launched into "La Cucaracha."

"Cut that racket! Gonna smash *you* like a cockroach."

Ernesto grinned at Joe and bowed to the rest of us. Slipping his harmonica into his apron, he produced another cigar, slick as a pickpocket.

"Night, Anna. Thanks for the game, Cappy."

Rousing herself from a light doze, Anna patted my hand. "Mind yourself, li'l lass."

Cappy blew me a kiss with his good arm.

"Don't get yourself mugged going home." And just in case I thought he might care, Joe added, "At least not till you're out of earshot."

But Jake called a seventh-inning stretch, steadying himself against the table as he rose, Popeye at his heels, and walked—more like hobbled—me outside.

Rushed by chilly sea air, we stood beneath the neon Corona sign, the parrot perched on flickering yellow letters and flanked by a palm tree. It took the quiet of night to hear the low, steady hum of the electric colors. Cap's Diner didn't sell Corona, but Pedro insisted on hanging the sign, replying to Cappy's "Bah!" with his go-to Mexican proverb: *El que es perico, donde quiera es verde.* It translated, Pedro told me, to "The parrot, he is green for always," even though the Corona parrot was mostly purple. What that had to do with beer—or any-thing else—no one knew. He'd lugged the sign onto the bus from Tijuana, that and pruning shears, figuring that if he couldn't find work cutting chili peppers, he could cut hedges.

Jake puffed on his cigarette, setting off a torrent of coughs.

"Aw, Jake. Smoking's gonna kill you."

"Sure might. If I live long enough." But he didn't lift it back to his lips, instead flicking the ash onto the ground and staring out to sea.

As much as I itched to report what I'd seen from the pier, I considered Jake's ailing heart and tried to mind my words. "I'm not wantin' to stir you up—bring on palpitations and such—but your dinghy, your *Autumn Rows* . . . Raven stole it."

Jake just stared at the waves like he hadn't heard a word, the fog a slow creep of white over midnight blue. His ciga-rette smoldered between his fingers.

"Aren't you gonna say somethin'?"

"Sure." The cigarette was back in his mouth. "My heart's just fine. The aching's in my bones."

I frowned. "Wish it weren't anywhere." *And wish I had Hollis's words or Mama's comforts.* But I just had me. "That all you gonna say?"

"Okay, Swee'Pea, I'll say something else. My dinghy is just where I left it, docked at the pier."

"But I saw her take it!"

"Guess she brought it back then."

The door opened, and Joe stuck out his head. "Finish your Cracker Jacks yet?"

"Take a leak, bub. Make it a long one."

Joe slammed the door.

"He don't like me much."

"Joe don't like anyone much." Jake brushed ashes from his flannel shirt.

"Even gripes at Popeye." I gave the sniffing hound a noogie. "He's plenty nice to Anna, I s'pose."

"That he is. Ain't no reason not to be."

"Ain't no reason not to believe her either. Raven shot the seal, and now she's on the run. They're commies, Raven and her uncle, and you know it."

"Yer wrong there. I don't know it. And it's not Anna I'm doubtin'."

He could be infuriatingly like Hollis, going tight-lipped on a dime. Maybe all those lone hours over a fishing line rusted a fisherman's tongue.

"But you *do* know they're trouble. She made off with your dinghy!"

"Who says I didn't let her?"

"You *what?*" I should have figured Jake for the softy he was. Of course he'd do some fool thing to aid a stranger come to town. Hadn't he taken in a dog too dumb to leave the train station? Hadn't he called a democratic vote to give me a spot at the poker table? "Why'd ya do that? She's wanted by the sheriff!"

He dropped his cigarette butt onto the sidewalk and ground it with his toe. "I don't see what business that is of yers, Swee'Pea."

"Mayor Mac saw her. Anna said so."

"Mayor Mac said he saw a girl near the seal. He said he saw a whole bunch of girls near the seal. Why, His Honor seems to have seen a regular Girl Scout meeting take place near the seal. But I don't recall anything 'bout him seein' the shooting."

"Well, he heard it. Said a gunshot woke him, right after the ruckus did."

"So which is it?" Jake leaned against the diner, wheezed.

We watched a sedan make a U-turn at the end of the street, roll past. I stroked Popeye's head, tried not to fault myself for fretting Jake. "Either way, he saw Raven point the gun at Vince and heard her say 'you're next.' That's what he told the sheriff."

"You ever known Mayor Mac to talk sober? To see sober?" He rasped the words. "You ever known Mayor Mac to *hear* sober?"

I hadn't known Mayor Mac at all, truth be told, just seen him around, usually flopped on a bench, grinning when he wasn't snoring. But I knew what folks said, that he'd been a fine honorary mayor, wranglin' some hard men and doing right by Gulch Run, deserving of whatever pleasures were left to old folks, a souse but a charmer, giving the town character and endless occasion for charity. And who could blame him, anyway, with a pap that didn't remember his own son's name.

"It isn't just Mac. The surfers and those girls saw her too."

"That's the story." Jake lit another cigarette.

"Whaddya mean, the story? You think they lied?"

"Couldn't say. But there were mighty thick fog." A cough rattled Jake's chest again. "You never lied?"

'Cept for the flask poking from his pocket, Jake could have doubled for Rev. Travers right then, reading the truth of my fibbin' ways on a street corner, smoke in eddies above his head, stripping my soul bare. Just like the reverend said, my sins were finding me out.

"Well, if I did, I didn't aim to."

Popeye raised his head, gave me a once-over, his squinched eye wide.

Wasn't a lick fair, shifting the conversation from Raven

to me, and though I supposed I'd confabulated here and there, I was in no mood to be contrite about it now.

The diner door opened again to show Joe wreathed in scowls, then slammed shut.

"Sure played a mean hand today. Gonna put yer winnings in the offering plate tomorrow?"

He had me with that. "Naw. It'd be a sacrilege."

He snorted. "So's swearing. And spreadin' rumors."

That they were, but Bazooka had done wonders for my mouth, and a rumor wasn't a rumor if it was true.

"So's smoking. You're gonna kill yourself."

"Don't have to. Already dyin'." A coughing spate choked his words. "Go on, boy," he wheezed as Popeye sniffed at a trash can. "Get Swee'Pea on home."

Popeye plodded beside me along the darkened storefronts, lifted a leg at a fire hydrant, nosed a candy wrapper, and then parked himself at the cross street. With a parting pat on his head, I strolled the last block alone, past the souvenir shop and motel. Reaching my yard, I stopped to look back. Jake cut a dark figure beneath the soft shimmer of the Corona sign, a smear of moonlit fog and shadow. He might've been anyone, even a stranger in town, but for the large dog beside him and the glowing ember between his teeth.

TWENTY-ONE

S LEEP CAME IN fits and starts, my sheets twisting 'round my legs as I kicked them down just to yank them back up, sweaty and chilled by turns. Twice I stumbled downstairs to pee, too tired for a midnight trek through the cattails but too awake to drift peacefully off, a riptide of chaotic images and thoughts sucking me from rest.

Mama hadn't waited up for me after all, the porch quiet and empty, the house dark. Her Nightwatch Blue Corvair still hugged the curb, but only a trashcan claimed the driveway, and even Dex slept easy, nestled against a pyramid of stuffed animals, the room bathed in a gentle spill of street light. Before heading to bed, I had mumbled a prayer into my toothbrush, first thanking the Good Lord for my winnings and then repentin' of them, ill-gotten as they were, but mighty glad for 'em anyhow. Next, I'd rued my many failures—and occasional fibs—in particular, that I was a lousy sister to Dex and a sorrow to Mama, but stopped short of confessing them as sins, since under the circumstances, they couldn't be helped. Finally, I begged tolerance for the irreverence of my prayer, offered through a mouthful of toothpaste instead of properly, on my knees by my bed, hands folded.

"For the spirit is willing, but the flesh is weak," I'd reminded God, trudging the stairs to my room. Plumb worn out, I'd burrowed beneath my blankets without bothering to pull off my jeans or sweater and beckoned sleep to come.

But what came instead were jumbled bits of the day, the week, snatches of conversation, scents—seaweed and dried flowers and cigars—a swirl of faces and muted voices. And into the shifting kaleidoscope entered the thrumming of wings, the swoop of a bird, a dazzle of white, a swan perhaps, drawing into itself the colliding hues, the sounds, calling the commotion into calm, swelling, sinking with the heaviness, falling, until with a surge, breaking the plummet and wheeling into an upward soar, and as I dreamed, the ice wings spread, their span as far as the east from the west, the bird climbing on feathered strokes, on currents of blue, soft rustlings of incandescence in motion, snow into sun, not melting, only reaching. Then, in a tumble, the sky collapsed, inverted, became sea, a tossing foam of grays and greens, and the feathers dripped with deep indigos, rippled into scarves and shawls, the swan's neck ebbing, alchemizing into a shimmering dance of black plumage, into flows of billowing hair, and the soaring caladrius was now a plunging raven, hurling itself toward an angry sea, a crazed girl on the edge of a pier, falling in slow motion. As a silent cry bubbled in my throat, the raven-girl turned cobalt eyes on me, her gaze holding and slipping, like fingers on a ledge, and then down she crashed into the waves, shattered, and in the suspended moment of dreams, splintered into crystal galaxies across the sea.

I woke in a sweat, the house so still that I could hear the far lap of surf. The fluorescent Sea Crest Motel sign—minus the flickering *M*—cast an eerie beam onto my floor and across my alarm clock. A quarter to three. Con-tarnit! I had church in the morning! With the rained-out poker night of Friday made up on Saturday, tomorrow had become Sunday—and tomorrow was already today. The storm had thrown me off, scrambled the days. And we were rollin' out a hymn I'd yet to learn. Now I was wide awake and rankled plenty.

Groping the floor for my choir folder, I swung my blanket over my shoulders, sending my glasses flying and me fumbling to perch 'em on my nose. A frumpy superhero flickered in my mirror as I tiptoed downstairs. The Lodge seemed as good a place as any to practice singing, but as I waded into the weeds, a thousand stars rushed at me, diamonds flung across a velvet sky, swept clean of the earlier thick fog. Whether it was the pulsing stars or the slapping waves, something drew me to the front of the house, and I settled myself on a porch step.

The salty breeze clearing my head, I angled hymn 22 toward the streetlight and hummed a few bars, then croaked the words softly so as not to wake Mama.

I was sinking deep in sin, far from the peaceful shore,
Very deeply stained within, sinking to rise no more,
But the Master of the sea heard my despairing cry,
From the waters lifted me, now safe am I.

In the distance, a buoy clanged — an E-sharp, I decided, adjusting my pitch. I sang the verse again before launching into the chorus.

Love lifted me,
Love lifted me!
When nothing else could help,
Love lifted me.

The blunt rap of shoes halted me mid-note.
"Hello?" A man stepped from the shadows. "Eden?"

He wore a thin corduroy coat over his suit.

"Reverend Travers?"

"Bit late for choir practice, isn't it?"

A musky scent mingled with the smell of decaying kelp.

"I couldn't sleep." I tried to rise, got tangled in my blanket, and stuck out my hand instead. "Hello, sir."

"No need to get up." He leaned against the porch rail and patted my hand. "Okra and sleepless nights, another thing we have in common."

"S'pose so."

"It's a magnificent night to be awake." He tipped back his head and gestured to the sky. 'The heavens are telling the glory of God.' A psalm of David."

"Reckon he couldn't sleep either."

The reverend laughed, his eyes tired but warm without his glasses. "David's woes kept him up at night. And those sleepless nights gave us the psalms."

"Goliath will do that to you," I offered, right pleased with my biblical literacy.

"One of his easier battles." He knotted his brows. "You haven't seen Ben wander by, have you?"

"No, sir. Not many wander by this late." A taxi crawled past. "Maybe he's with Vince."

"You know Vince?"

"He saved my teeth from a football."

Rev. Travers chuckled. "Quite the hero."

"S'pose. But trouble, accordin' to Joe."

"Joe?"

"He owns Lucky Liquors."

"Got a thirst, do you?"

"Lordy no. Lucky Liquors *and Sundries*. Anyhow, Joe doesn't like me much. Thinks I'm trouble too."

"Two hoodlums in a pod, huh?" Though he said it with a smile, worry laced his voice.

"Leastways, if Ben's with Vince, he ain't lost," I added, by way of cheering.

"Isn't he?" He folded his handkerchief into a neat square. "But you, what woes are keeping you up?"

That I couldn't answer without letting on about Raven—*rumors and hunches*, he'd likely say, maybe quote a verse or two—or without confessing my gambling ways. No, I wasn't about to open Pandora's box, but he spared me spinnin' a yarn.

"Ah, I know. Forgot to learn tomorrow's hymns."

It wasn't the whole truth, but truth enough. "Just polishing 'em up, sir."

"Sounded pretty good from the street."

What distance could do to improve a situation.

"If only all woes were so light." He frowned. "Terrible, what happened to the seal pup yesterday."

"A right tragedy, sir."

"That woe weighs heavy on Ben's heart. Wishes he'd been there to prevent it."

I couldn't help but envy that Ben was spared the grisly sight, unlike me and Hollis.

We stayed quiet a moment, him slumping against the rail, me pondering the woes that kept us up at night, the both of us watching the night sky as though it were alive. The stars seemed to fall toward me, to hurtle and then catch, their steady twinkles like the lights of a celestial city, the vast spread of collapsing heavens making me dizzy.

Beyond Front Street, the slate sea was a shimmer of silver. I hugged my knees, warm in my sweater and jeans, grateful I'd stumbled into bed without putting on my nightgown.

Sometimes a fool thing can work to your advantage. It should've struck me more peculiar than it did, the crossing of our woes in the wee hours—no sleep for Southern folk bein' the eleventh plague of Egypt—but the night loomed too majestic to feel anything but small and strangely alike, just two people beckoned awake.

"He counts the stars and calls them by name. A name for each star. Isn't that a wonder?" Rev. Travers spoke softly, without the force volleyed from the pulpit but just as hypnotic. "Seem close enough to pluck, don't they?"

"A star in my pocket"—I rubbed the crick in my neck—"now that'd be a wonder." I reached into my jeans and up-ended two packs of gum, my lipstick, the gold chain, and my poker winnings, sending several quarters clinking down the steps.

"That's quite a haul."

Good Lord, I've been caught red-handed. "For the collection plate, sir," I mumbled, snatching at my coins. But he was fixed on the hodgepodge.

"Looks like you already have a bit of shine in your pocket."

"This?" Relief flooded over me. "It's just a broken chain. Not even mine." I pried the chain from the heap, still coated in sand, and handed it over, quickly stowing my dirty money.

He dangled it at eye level. "No cross?"

"No, sir, and no locket either."

"I see. Where did you say you got it?"

"I didn't. Raven gave it to me after sh—after the shooting. Dunno why."

"Who?"

"Raven. The Soviet girl."

He tilted his head.

"The commie from Gulch Run. Reckon she swiped it off someone in the crowd."

"Mind if I take it?" Not waiting for a reply, he tucked it inside his vest pocket. "The owner will be missing it."

So he meant to find Raven, wrangle out a confession! He'd shepherd her into returning the chain, show her the error of her ways, be the missionary I wasn't. The poor man would be workin' double time once he discovered the depths of her depravity.

"Her name is Raven?"

"Yes, sir. I mean, no, sir, not her real name anyway."

"'A good name is more desirable than great riches, than silver or gold.'"

How anyone, even a pastor as fine as Rev. Travers, could quote the Bible on a dime was a marvel. Was any occasion known to man without cause for a holy word from Scripture?

We lapsed into silence again, listening to the ebb an' flow of the ocean. From the wilderness behind my house chirped a chorus of crickets. The minutes stretched on, distant and endless like the canvas of stars above us, so many minutes that I felt my eyelids droop.

"The wrong things mattered." Shadows reached across the reverend's face.

"Sir?"

"Moses warned them." He seemed to be arguing with the bottlebrush tree. "The father's sins visited upon the son."

A strong wind had picked up, chilly gusts that made me glad for my blanket.

"My father left us." My voice shuddered. "For no reason. And now we're stuck with his sin."

"Yes, I heard." Easing himself onto the bottom step, he patted my hand again. "I'm sorry, child."

Tears sprang to my eyes.

"There are many ways we leave each other." He sighed. "And many reasons. Some good, some not, all breaking our hearts." As if comfort lay in the constellations, we both surveyed the glittery sky. "You know those stars God calls by name?"

I nodded, wiping my face with my blanket.

"Sirius, Polaris, Alpha Centauri," he recited, his voice rich and tender, same as Mama singing her lullabies. "Vega, Altair, Antares, Rigel, Capella, Arc . . . oh dear, I've forgotten that one."

I laughed.

"You, Eden Lewis, are more precious to him than even these. Fearfully and wonderfully made. Fearfully and wonderfully *loved*. You. Your mother. Your father. Your brother. Down to the least of us."

Rev. Travers maybe, with his eloquent homilies and zeal for the Lord, and Mama certainly, cradling in her riven heart the darlin' boy my father had discarded. But Dex, wonderfully made? And me, wonderfully loved? Then why did my father leave us?

"We have that in common too, child—the need to forgive."

The way I saw it, forgiving needed asking, and asking needed admitting you'd done wrong. Being as how that was an impossibility for my father, like the sun rising in the west, I figured it didn't cost me none to agree with the reverend. "Might forgive him—least consider it—if he'd own up to bailin'. Do it even quicker if he moved us home to Texas."

"With God, all things are possible. Even forgiveness."

That was fanciful thinking if I'd ever heard it. With or without God, it would never be possible to rewind time, go back to the family we were, before 2122 Grand Avenue, California, back to our house in Texas, Dad waking me to biscuits and gravy and thunderstorms, Gramma Kay braiding my hair before school, Mama looking in on Dex at the residential home next door, family being the way family was meant to be. What bunk.

"I don't mean forgiving *them*—Ben, your father—though of course we must. I meant us."

Well, that didn't make a lick of sense. What did I need forgiving for? "He promised we'd always be a family."

Rev. Travers rose, brushed a leaf off his coat, and studied me. "It's a hard lesson, Eden. We mustn't let the wrong things matter." It was what he'd said to the bottlebrush. "Where there are promises, they will fail. Where there are dreams, they will die. But love never fails."

He had lapsed into the pastor of Mar Vista Chapel, and I was his lone congregant, 'cept instead of sitting on a velvet-cushioned pew in my Sunday best, I was tangled in a blanket on a cold cement step, and instead of towering from the pulpit, he was leaning on my porch rail. It was, I realized, a sermon just for me.

"You've read Paul's chapter on love, haven't you? First Corinthians 13? If you speak in the tongues of angels, but do not have love, you are only a clanging cymbal. If you have a faith that moves the sea—"

"Isn't it a mountain, sir?"

"Ah, so you have read it. Here in Harford Beach, we can move seas." A smile crossed his weary face. "If you have a faith that moves the sea, but do not have love, you are nothing. And if you bear up under promises broken, but do not have love, what have you gained? 'For now we see through a glass, darkly; but then face to face.'"

"That's a fact," I said, rubbin' my smudged glasses with my sleeve.

"Love, that is what matters."

"Yes, sir," I said dutifully. But I knew better. Not even love could make us the family we used to be.

"Gracious!" He squinted at his watch. "Time to get some shut-eye. Can't be late to my own sermon." He flipped up his coat collar against the wind, smiled at me. "We'll wait for them, Eden. Just as God waits for us." A hint of cologne spiced the air.

I watched him walk into the beam of the streetlight, don the clinging glow for a moment, and then shed it for darkness, his wing tips a fading *clack, clack* up the sidewalk. A minute later, a car drove slowly past, down the hill, and into the night.

TWENTY-TWO

IF MAR VISTA'S choir sounded less like a cat fight that morning, it might have been because a certain second soprano lay fast asleep tangled in sheets woven from cotton and musical notations, a misfortune not entirely of my doin'. After seeing the reverend's car off, I'd traipsed back to bed just to be jolted awake by the blare of the Harford fire engine roaring from the station.

Mama and I had learned to weather the nocturnal sirens—not the sirens themselves, but the terror they riled up in Dex. Springing from the couch, Mama would douse his howling sobs in living water—that being Bible verses and hymns—while upstairs I'd mash my pillow over my head, prayin' she wouldn't call for backup.

The Harford Beach Fire Station sat opposite the Sea Crest Motel, mostly out of sight and mind, but on a rugged coastline, a calamity or two was bound to happen—a shipwrecked fishing trawler, a drunken row at the firepits. Gulch Run and Vintage Heights had their share of mishaps as well, dutifully reported in the *Harford Herald*, but most times nothing more alarming than a cow on the train tracks or a rockslide across a hiking trail.

During the day, the sirens didn't seem to wail much, or if they did, they got lost in the din of traffic. But come night, the sirens set Dex into conniptions like to wake the dead, his shrieks a piercing reminder of what he didn't understand and what we couldn't soothe.

℀

"WHAT THE—FOR God's sake!" my father had bellowed not a month ago, a siren blasting us awake and flooding the house with pulsing red light. He'd crashed on the couch, tired an' worn thin from waiting for Mama, a pink birthday card and ribboned box sandwiched between medicine bottles on the bookcase. Before he could call upon God again, Dex let loose a scream that rattled the windows. Shaking off the rubble of an exploded dream, I stumbled downstairs, nearly colliding with my father as he snatched his jacket and barged out the front door.

"Well, looky that, Dexie, you scared Dad off. Shh, shh. Nothin' to get worked up over."

I swung Dex from his playbed just as Mama rushed in, brushing past my father's tantrum and into my brother's. Hauling the cartoon-clad tempest from my hip, she flumped into the rocker.

"Hush, little baby, don't you cry. Mama's gonna sing you a lullaby," she crooned, kissing his tear-soaked cheeks. The wails of the fire engine had faded, with them the putter of my father's VW Bug.

The kitchen light too harsh to brave, I fumbled in the dark for the kettle and cranked the burner all the way up, frettin' the water to bubble double-quick. Mama's smile had been weak but grateful.

Setting her teacup on the bookcase to cool, I knelt beside the rocker and caught Dex's fist, his palm hot and moist as I uncurled his fingers. "Hey, Dexie Day, such a ruckus!"

He yanked his hand back, smacking himself, and howled even louder.

"Glory be, Dex!"

"Go to bed, Eden. He'll be okay."

Nothing sounded better than bed, but Mama's duty needed easing. Switching bait, I dropped my voice to a whisper. "What you say to a star walk, Dexie?"

He shuddered and hiccupped.

"That's better. Ain't at all neighborly to be kickin' up such a fuss. Let's go have some fun, you an' me."

Mama stood beneath the streetlight watching as I led Dex along the deserted shops, the street silent but for his labored breaths, the swash of waves. Making a U-turn at the corner, I steered him past our yard, toward the scrubby hillside to the dead end, and then in another U-turn home.

The birthday card and ribboned box sat on the bookcase for a week.

Mama let me sleep in the next day, sending me to school with a note: *Please excuse Eden Mae. She is late on my account. Sincerely, Mrs. Lewis.* I shoved the note across the office counter and glowered as it fluttered to the floor. Her name was Elaine.

ℇ

ONLY A MONTH ago. And now, again, the sirens had wailed, wrenching me from the grip of a bad dream. I'd listened to Dex's howls from under my pillow, coming up for air after they finally petered out. But I couldn't sleep.

Shuffling downstairs, I found the front door ajar and Mama on a porch step, cradling Dex and singing.

Oh, happy day (Oh, happy day)
He taught me how (He taught me how)
To watch and pray (To watch and pray)
And live rejoicing every day (Oh, happy day)
Oh, happy day (Oh, happy day)

A blue dawn rose over a sea of fog. Mama heard the hinges, took in my tousled appearance.

"Go on, sugar. We're doin' just fine. Get some sleep."

A high sun woke me a final time, sent me shambling to the kitchen, where I poked my toast and pushed away my orange juice. Mama sat across from me, dolloped honey into her tea.

"I missed church," I announced, though this was news to no one.

"We all did." She let the spoon clatter to the table and rubbed her temples. A sorrowful pang pricked me, same as if I'd swallowed a wasp. Just 'cause I'd sunk back into sleep didn't mean she had. Fact was, she'd probably rocked Dex through daybreak, praying over his tortured body, not to mention my wayward soul.

Dex sat cattywampus in his high chair, eyes glazed, Mama nudging his mouth open for another bite of Rice Chex. All that raisin' Cain left us worn to the bone. I huffed a sigh at him, but he only babbled and pulled his tongue, saliva trickling from his mouth.

"We were gonna sing a new hymn." I didn't know why I was so out of sorts. Sleeping in should've soothed my woes. My mind drifted to Rev. Travers combing the dark streets, searching for Ben. I supposed he'd gotten 'bout as much sleep as Mama. Preaching after a night of woes had to be a woe itself.

"You'll get to sing it again." Mama's was a tender sigh. "Missing church pains me too."

What pained me wasn't missing church, though the reverend's sermons did keep me on the straight and narrow, leastways for a spell. What pained me was missing an occasion to look down upon the congregation from the choir loft—most specially Heather Clark. 'Cept, on further consideration, something had changed between us yesterday in Gulch Run, and I wasn't too keen on discovering what.

Mama's tea finished, she clipped the stems of dandelions picked from among the cattails, *weeds*, according to my father, who had dumped the yellow flowers from a vase one afternoon.

"Weeds are only those things we don't want," she'd replied, rooting for them in the trash.

Prettying up our rental mattered, Mama said, though it'd take more than wildflowers to pretty up the mess of diapers, dirty dishes, and unpacked boxes. Seemed an ugly truth stayed ugly no matter how gussied up it was. But I reckoned, like the reverend had said, she had her reasons.

"Who needs sirens when you've got Dex," I grumbled.

"I know, Eden. A trying night." The weeds looked almost respectable as she arranged them in a frosted bottle and placed them on the windowsill. "Not nearly so trying as for that family in Gulch Run, though. Heard they almost lost their house to the fire."

I wasn't much listening, rassling a spoon from Dex's fist before he launched it, my sleeve coated in soggy cereal. "Fire? What fire?"

"Strange, the goings-on in this town," she continued, more to herself than to me. "They do say trouble comes in threes. Hope this is the last of it." Dex's grunts had grown steadily louder, more insistent. Mama took a dishrag to his face. "Would you like Sissy to play alligator with you?"

But I'd seen the writing on the wall and was already bustin' tail, jamming my feet into muddy shoes.

"Eden Mae, you're not to—"

Slamming the front door, I vaulted down the porch steps.

TWENTY-THREE

THREES. WHAT HAD Mama meant by *threes*? The town had suffered a spate of petty crimes for months, pranks and five-finger discounts mostly, but then had come the slurs and smashed window at St. Francis, the shooting of the baby seal, and now a house-guttin' fire. But fires happened, didn't need sinister reasons. Likely some hippie dozed off puffing demon weed, a vice I was proud not to have. It was Gulch Run, after all, repository of every kind of riffraff. Seemed smokin' and drinkin' and carousin' were next-door neighbors to poverty, supplying the Honorable Mac MacDougall with mayoral duties aplenty. Or maybe it was poverty caused the vices, allowing a body momentary escape.

Come to think of it, we'd been forced to live lean since my father walked out, what with his place, our place, Dex's school, and Rosa stretchin' his paycheck an' then some. And I'd been forced to take up gambling to lift myself out of poverty, that and to allow God his due. Well, to afford a dinghy anyway—still a buck fifty short. I reckoned it wasn't very charitable of me, harumphing 'bout the heathen like I did. Though unlikely I'd ever be worthy of my amethyst choir robe, I'd start by not reading more into a fire than was there.

Shoving my hands into my pockets to check my loot—minus the gold chain—I made for the pier, skirting the colorful spread of beach towels and dodging a beach ball. Hollis greeted me through a mouthful of sandwich—peanut butter and banana. I wrinkled my nose. Three small fish wriggled inside his bait bucket, sloshing water.

"Pish!" I said in true Anna form. "You call that a catch?"

"Aren't you s'posed to be in church?"

"Not if I don't wanna be."

I glanced at the square belfry of Mar Vista Chapel peeking above the rooftops, imagined the congregation filing out, shaking Rev. Travers's hand, remarking on his eloquent sermon, hollerin' after their young'uns.

"To what do I owe the pleasure of your snit today?" A grin slipped into his question, chafing me all the more.

"I'm in no snit. And even if I were, I wouldn't tell you." I resisted the urge to stick out my tongue.

"If you say so." With a mock tip of his hat, he hooked a fish on his line.

"Fact is," I began some moments later, "I'm particularly fine."

"Oh?"

"I won the pot last night." I jingled my pocket.

"Nice. No small feat with those card sharks."

"It ain't a sin if it's for a good cause."

"Didn't say it was."

"Some might say so."

"They might."

"Don'tcha wanna know what cause?"

Hollis raised an eyebrow. "Probably not."

"I'm gonna rent a dinghy."

He cast his freshly baited line over the rail.

"Gonna take it to the Pirate Caves."

The hard part done, I caught him up on yesterday's

doings, doling out the details slow to hold his ear—my trek to Gulch Run that *happened* to deposit me at Raven's house, the unlatched shed door *inviting* a peek, the *accidental* un-earthing of spray paint and ammunition, the twigs snapping underfoot and talons scraping the window, *not* that I was *inside* the shed, then down to the ravine, the pleas of Heather and assurances of Vince, their voices so loud I couldn't *help* but overhear.

"Course if I had a boat," I said, real casual, "I could get to the bottom of it all."

It went down pretty much how I'd figured on my way back from Gulch Run, mulling things over to the crunch of broken glass. Only Hollis didn't say I was playing Go Fish or that I should invest in an abacus to work my sums. He didn't say anything at all, not even to give me what-for about med-dling. Fact was, he stayed quiet as a church mouse for a good long spell. By and by, I lost track of the time and the number of empty lines he reeled in. Might have dozed off once or twice. Even nibbled my way through a pack of Fig Newtons stowed in my jacket pocket. It wasn't till he hauled in a whoppin' bug-eyed red fish—a rockfish, he informed me—that he spoke.

"Did you hear about the fire last night?"

"Me an' the dead. The blessing of bunkin' across from the fire station." Now that he was feeling chatty, I came back around to the issue of finances. "Guess I'll have to rent me that dinghy—'less you got connections."

"Nope."

"Could I borrow your dad's? Just for a couple hours?"

"She's in the shop. Engine's on the fritz."

"Then how 'bout loaning me some money? Costs four bucks a day, long as it's not on the weekend." I recalled the sign outside Mariner's Cove Boat Rentals. "That leaves me one dollar and fifty cents short."

"Three dollars and fifty cents. Summer price is six bucks." Nothing about Hollis's tone suggested he'd loan me the difference.

"Six bucks? How am I gonna get that?" I kicked at a loose nail.

"You could get a job. I hear they're hiring barnacle scrapers for the buoys." He dodged my swipe, chuckling.

"Don't you take anything serious?"

"I'd say a fire's pretty serious. Looks like it mighta started in the shed." He squinted out to sea, tugged his hat lower over his eyes. "Then jumped to the house."

"Shed? What shed?"

"Some teens partying in the ravine saw smoke, booked it to the house. They dragged a man from the flames just in time."

"What man? You mean . . . you mean *her* shed?" I gaped like a hooked catfish. "Her *uncle*?"

Hollis nodded. "Sheriff's saying it's likely arson."

"Why would someone wanna burn down the house?"

Even as I asked the question, I already knew the answer. *She'd* done it. She'd discovered they were on to her—Sheriff Moretti, Mayor Mac, Vince and Heather—so she'd set the shed ablaze. Probably hoped it *would* catch that rattletrap house on fire, a real slick ruse to shift suspicion off her and her uncle. Or maybe she'd gone madder than a hatter, decided to break ranks with her uncle, possessed with a vengeance that saw no loyalties.

"Well, I'll be tar-nated! She burned down her own house."

"Why would she do that?" He seemed to have his own ideas. "Endanger her own uncle?"

"If you'd pull your head out of your bait bucket, you'd know why. She's lost the plot!"

Hollis's eyebrow outdid itself. "To think I called you ordinary."

Another thought struck me. "She wasn't there when it happened, was she? They would've had to drag her out too."

"So?"

"Don'tcha see? That proves it."

"No, I don't see." Hollis peered at me over his aviators. "Just 'cause she wasn't in the house means she set the fire?"

"You have a better explanation?"

"Sure. She mighta flown out the attic window."

I met his snicker with an eye roll. "Got any other suspects?"

"Weren't you at the shed yesterday?"

"Me?" I gawked at him. "You telling me, Hollis Sweet, that *I*—" But I was seized with the realization that I *had* been at the shed and that someone, someone with razor blades for nails, had seen me. "What kinda hogwash is that?"

"No different from yours." Hollis shrugged and collected his gear, slingin' his fishing rod over his shoulder. "Anyway, you asked."

As he sauntered toward the beach, I tried to gather my wits about me, think through my next steps.

"Wait!" Catching him at the far bench, I grubbed up two pieces of bubble gum from my pocket.

He stopped whistling long enough to pop one into his mouth. "Thanks."

"Betcha five bucks," I said, the words garbled around my gum.

"On what?"

"That Raven set the fire and then lit outta Dodge in Jake's dinghy. Bet she's lying low at the Pirate Caves."

"You don't have five bucks."

"Well, I'm gonna scout it out anyway. You comin' with me or not?"

"Not." He rubbed his forehead. "I'm getting lunch. Must be after three."

"You had lunch."

"I need another one. Fishing does that to a man." His grin faded. "Don't go looking for trouble, Scoot."

His gait easy as he crossed the street, I dithered over whether to badger him for more particulars, which somehow he always had, or to try my luck at scoring a dinghy. Before I could settle on a course, I heard the rustle of skirts, inhaled the must of dried flowers, and Raven brushed past me, swift, sudden, like a spirit just loosed from a body, darting toward the far end of the pier.

I sprinted across the street, nearly dropping Hollis to the ground as I collided with him.

"She's headed to the caves, Hollis! Now's our chance!"

"Holy smokes, Eden!" His bucket swung wildly. "Chance for what?"

"You know very well what. To see where she goes!"

"Why don't you just ask her?" He snatched his hat off the pavement.

"You comin', or am I goin' alone?"

"How do you plan to do that?"

"Gonna take a dinghy."

Hollis furrowed his brows but kept walking. "What dinghy?"

"Any dinghy. Whatever dinghy is at the dock. Maybe Anna's."

Only thing was, *Patches* had sprung another leak a couple weeks back and awaited fixin' at the Alvarado Pier. Still, a small leak might take well to a triple wad of chewed gum.

"Anna give you permission?"

"She will." I dogged him down the sidewalk.

"You know how to handle a dinghy?"

"Can't be that hard."

"You'll drown yourself."

"I surely will. That's why you've got to come with me."

"Might drown you myself." He nodded at two fisher-men lounging outside Beach Yum Donuts. "Hey, Smitty, how ya doin'?"

"I'm going with or without you, Hollis Sweet."

Hollis stopped in front of Lucky Liquors and looked me square in the face. He wasn't the only one. Joe glared at us from behind a pyramid of beer cans in the display window. "And then what?"

He had me there.

"Ever consider going to the sheriff with what you know, let him figure things out?"

That was just it. I didn't *know*. Not unless you count rumors and sightings and hunches the same as knowing a thing. If I hadn't been scared off the shed—if I hadn't been trespass-ing—I could be forkin' the evidence over to Sheriff Moretti right now. But even though Raven had beaten me to it, torched the whole lot, she hadn't beaten *me*. I'd find the gun. Vince and Heather knew she had it, and I knew—well, had a pretty good idea anyhow—where it was.

"I aim to, soon as I'm certain. Don't you wanna know where she goes? What she does?"

"Nope."

"Aren't you a mite bit curious? A baby seal got mur-dered, for Pete's sake!"

"Nope. Got my own business to mind."

"Well, I've got business too, *town* business—why, it's a downright civic duty."

"Will miracles never cease. A duty you wanna do?"

"It's not funny, Hollis! C'mon, we're gonna lose her." I tugged his shirt, sloshing the fish in his bucket.

"I'm not stealing a dinghy."

"It's not stealing if we just borrow it." *Unless*, I realized after the fact, *you're Raven.*

"Either way, not taking something that's not mine. That'd make me a thief. And I've been baptized, or maybe you don't remember?"

He could be maddening, and at the worst times too. "I'll drown. You said it yourself. Would you rather be a thief or a murderer?"

But he'd gone deaf as a post, and with a two-finger salute to Joe, busy planting an American flag atop the Olympia pyramid, he trudged off, bait bucket slapping his legs.

She might have had three minutes on me, but if I girded up my loins—a fine phrase I'd heard in church—I'd surely catch her. Returning Joe's scowl, I dashed back to the pier, jostling several anglers as I skirted the orange cones, my stomach somersaulting with each glimpse of waves between the planks. It came to me as I pell-melled down the pier that it was Elijah who'd girded up his loins—or was it Elisha?— and that there was wisdom in heeding Scripture. Clutching the end rail, the damp wood splattered with bird droppings, I scanned the rocky coast.

Nothing. I was too late, and Hollis was to blame.

Unless she'd doubled back to shore while I was wranglin' with Hollis, she'd likely be tracing the same voyage toward the Pirate Caves. I'd just take my chances on drowning and do the same.

I spotted the hatch quick enough, thanks to a board propping it open, but lugging it up took all my strength and an imprecation or two. My feet groping for the ladder rungs, I resolved not to mind the abrupt eclipse of sun, the groan of kelp-twined pilings, the cold prickle of mist, but mind I did, my stomach rising to my throat.

Gumption, Eden, gumption, I mouthed, my grip fierce as I searched the battered dock, the jouncing dinghies, the shadowed—

There it was, still tethered but straining at its rope, Jake's dinghy, across the hull the faded red words *Autumn Rows,* and in it—the wind whippin' her skirts and cascading hair—stood Raven, her hand outstretched.

TWENTY-FOUR

We stood there, under the pier, the sea spitting froth against the barnacle-crusted beams, Raven caped in wind and spray, and I tangled in second thoughts and a slew of *condemnations*, our eyes locked, hers cool and hard, mine wide with mounting terror. Before I could figure what had me most spooked—the girl, the sea, or my stupidity—I felt myself climb into the dinghy, grasping her hand to avert a near tumble.

Tossing the mooring rope into the dinghy, Raven straddled the bench across from me, bunching her skirts to her knees. One, two, three times she yanked the starter cord, the motor sputtering as the air filled with the sharp smell of gasoline. For a moment, I thought I heard my name shouted, thought I saw a coltish form running along the pier, but the motor roared to life, waves thrashed the *Autumn Rows*, and it was all I could do not to be sick.

Lurching, we cleared the tethered dinghies, the dock dwindling as we hurtled east, bouncing across whitecaps, hugging the shore. No longer tucked beneath the pier, I shivered, water stingin' my face like swarming bees. Raven thrust a life jacket at me.

"Take."

More English—I knew it! All part of her commie ruse.

"Take!" she said again.

Snapping the last buckle in place, my fingers stiff and

disobedient, I set my sights to the north, tracking the coast-line, a shore that crept upward like a waking dinosaur, to shift from flat sandy beaches to stone ridges to towering cliffs, hidden within them coves like crescent moons. Behind us the pier shrank rapidly, lookin' every bit like a pokey centipede, beside it sailboats that might've been pinched from Dex's bathtub. Harford Beach stretched golden, streets crisscrossed, shops and houses terraced atop each other, the drowsy town hemmed in by barren hills, and Mar Vista Chapel giving me what-for from the fuzzy belfry. Good heavens, if only I'd gone to church—and stayed there.

I dared not glance at Raven for fear she would read my suspicions and heave me overboard, tried instead to fix the blurry landscape in my memory, but I could smell the attic musk of her clothes, the earthy sweetness of her petaled hair, and even her babblings, snatched by the wind, carried a scent like winter rain, the rain of Edgar Allan Poe's raven.

I betook myself to linking
Fancy unto fancy, thinking what this ominous bird of yore—

Condemnation! It was *her* stare spooking me at the church, *her* laugh ringing from the woods, *her* nails clawing the shed window. The broken chain was no token of friend-ship, no lost heirloom to return—it had been ripped from someone else's neck and dangled like a hangman's noose to threaten mine. And now here I was, at her mercy.

"Land's sake, child! Don't you know that curiosity killed the cat?" Gramma Kay had grunted, working my six-year-old head free from between the bars of the iron gate marked "Zoo Employees Only."

"But I saw a kangaroo!" I'd exclaimed once she'd pried

me loose. "Sadisbaction brought me back!"

"No such doin', honey. Your Gramma Kay did."

But adrift on the Pacific, my fool head caught between steely gusts and fantastical imaginings, there was no Gramma Kay, and betting on satisfaction suddenly seemed a dangerous play.

They'd been trouble from the second they set foot in Harford Beach, Raven and her uncle, like rattlers in the weeds, lurking behind every petty crime, every spiteful act, from the injury of Mr. York to the torching of the shed. No doubt gettin' mowed down in the school parking lot had spiraled the spectral misfit into madness, her classroom hocus-pocus escalating to slaughter on the beach. *Ain't no whys to evil sometimes.* Anna's voice echoed in my head. And now Sheriff Moretti, Rev. Travers, the whole town were bird-dogging this conjuror of evil.

But I'd found her first.

With a hard slap against the waves, Raven veered abruptly north and bore full throttle toward a wall of rock, cutting the motor within inches of ramming it. She paid my yelp no mind, instead steering the dinghy inside a narrow cove, beneath the cliffs a row of arches—so these were the Pirate Caves! Jumping into the shallows, she hauled the dinghy ashore, first pulling and then pushing it onto the sand, the water tugging at her skirts. At some point I had stumbled out too and was pushing beside her.

Before I could catch my breath, Raven had darted across the beach, disappearing into a cave. I followed but held up at the dark entrance, blinking. I could just make her out in the shadows, clambering over a heap of rocks and up a boulder, her hands groping the ledges, her feet testing sunken ridges.

It's now or never. I tried to swallow my fear along with the gum stuck to the roof of my mouth, near chokin' on both. Wasn't this what I'd aimed for from the start, to trail Raven to her hideout, sniff out her secret stash, prove the rumors true? With a last uneasy glance at the dinghy, I plunged inside the cave.

Day turned to dusk as I crept deeper, the cave cool and dank. I pictured the shore retreating, framed in scalloped rock, but I knew how Lot's wife ended up and wasn't fixin' to turn any more petrified than I already was. Sunlight snuck through the sandstone roof, cast a spotlight on Raven as she shifted her weight. Straining on tiptoe, she eased a bundle from a jagged shelf, heavy by the way it unsteadied her, then lowered it into my outstretched hands before dropping lightly beside me.

Well, I'll be, the cave whispered back as a knotted scarf fell away under her fingers, revealing a glossy, hand-painted keepsake box. Like something straight out of an Arabian folk tale, a story shimmered across the lid in a whirl of colors. Turbaned peasants crowded a golden street, waved palm branches, as a procession of elegant courtiers marched toward a turreted palace, on their shoulders a velvet mat, and on the mat a princess with flowing black hair.

"*La Bayadère.*"

I started. "What?"

As she pried the lid open, a shiver skittered down my spine. What I expected to see, I couldn't rightly say. A Chanel No. 5 gift set, a hammer and rope, Joe's whiskey? Or something more menacing, the likes of hoodoo dolls, amulets, or potions? The scents of leather and candle mingled as she dug through odds an' ends: a satin ribbon, tarnished coins, a bouquet of withered flowers, a ballet slipper, a book—*I knew it! A grimoire like* The Key of Solomon . . . *or a Soviet ledger full of spy codes!*—the maroon cover mottled, faded. Gripping it, she ran from the cave.

Good Lord, she was stranding me, leavin' me to languish with the dead pirates, only my sun-bleached skeleton left for Hollis to mourn. With not a moment to spare before the cave came crashing down on me, I tore after her, shielding my eyes against the bright sun till I spotted her, a vague silhouette perched on a boulder by the water. I dashed toward her, slowed, stopped. She was reaching for my hand.

"Uh . . . no heights."

Whatever English she might've known failed her—and me—as she seized my wrist and yanked me up the rock and then down beside her.

A leap to solid ground wouldn't have broken my neck, maybe twisted my ankle or skinned my shin, but she'd opened the book, the frayed cover on my knee. Pasted in neat rows were yellowed newspaper clippings, the ink faded, the photographs gray. Even with my nose to the paper, I couldn't make heads nor tails of the squarish alphabet—Russian, I reckoned— but the photos I could read, curtained stages with costumed dancers, men poised in tights, women buoyant in tutus.

But a single ballerina graced every page, her poses captured mid-motion. One photo caught her in flight across a snowy stage. In another she melted into a man's embrace. In others she arched like a rainbow, held aloft by clustered dancers, her lithe body adorned with sheer ribbons, sequined blouses, netted skirts. Raven's murmurings rose and fell as she turned the pages.

"Who is she?" I didn't know why I whispered.

I hadn't paid much mind to her murmurs, but at my question she looked up, spoke slower, her words crisp, clipped, like she was stirrin' up some kind of spell. *Dzyatur kosschum horayografya*—leastways, that was the best I could figure.

You ever consider that she mighta been speaking her native language—saying "sorry" same as you? Hollis had asked when I fretted 'bout her hexing me with her mumbo jumbo. Truth was, I couldn't be sure she *wasn't* hexing me even now, but I'd allow Hollis his say.

"*Dzyatur kosschum horayografya*," she repeated, lingering on the last page, on the last photo, a photo she touched. Her finger, light as my charcoal pencil on shadows, traced the woman's upturned face, the shoulders draped in scarves, the dark hair crowned with flowers. And though the ink bled, I could almost see in the ballerina's eyes the same translucent blues of Raven's.

Clasping the scrapbook to her chest, her own petal-strewn hair cascading over it, Raven rocked, same as how Mama rocked Dex. It didn't seem right to watch, so I gazed out to sea. The tide had ebbed, leaving shells and clumps of kelp. *Sugar,* I heard Mama counter, *that child has no mama or daddy, not even a brother or sister to call her own. Would it hurt you to be a friend? What's that Rev'n Travers always says? Nothing is more unlovely than a person who won't love the unlovely.*

And then Raven was scrambling down the boulder, the scrapbook now in my lap. She unlaced her boots, peeled off her shawl and hip sash, shed her outer skirt. Clad only in a white chemise, she became a waif, smaller, lighter, no longer a raven. Pressing a finger to her lips, though I hadn't said a word, she tilted her head, and as if hearin' a voice from the cloud above Mount Tabor, she broke into a smile so radiant I'd have swallowed an entire pack of Bazooka.

"Wh—"

But she'd spun and scampered toward the surf, gauzy white scarves trailing. Sweeping her bangled arms to the sky, she rose on her tiptoes, and there, on the packed sand, among the scattered seaweed, she began to dance.

"*Bourrée*," she called, flitting from one end of the small beach to the other, ankles crossing, fingers brushing the clouds. Lifting her chin, she let her arms sink, dipped them in a slow float, raised them again, dropped them, her scarves billowing, like making snow angels in the air.

"*Port de bras en avant.*" She bent forward from the waist, swooped into a low dive, coasted backward with tiny, swift steps. Arching up again, she leaned over an outstretched arm, her gaze intent on something in the distance, but all I could see was sky and sun and endless sea.

As though no longer bound by gravity, she drifted forward, her feet in rapid flutters, her skirt rippling. She was a caged bird loosed, soaring, her bare arms spread like wings, her feet leaving the sand in flight. I strained to hear the music she danced to, for a moment fancyin' I did, in the roaring swells of sea, the lap of waves against the *Autumn Rows*, the moan of the marine breeze.

Confound it, Eden Mae! I nearly shouted. *How will you make sense of this to Hollis?*

Her dance was a snake charmer's flute, and I the cobra, too hypnotized to strike. She was no more innocent for the theatrics, still a girl gone mad. I tried to shake the spell of her pungi, the plea of her innocence, recalled the rumors of a witch girl spreading raven wings and hurtling from her attic, screeching omens by dead of night, saw again the hammer and sickle, the shattered stained-glass angel, the small, still body of the baby seal, bullet hole between unblinking eyes, heard again the screams of the fire engine racing toward a shed ablaze, the screams of a man dragged from a flaming house—remembered, but only dimly, faintly, the memories dissolving like wisps of summer fog. I forgot even the panic that had almost suffocated me as she'd steered the dinghy across open sea, as Harford Beach faded and the Pirate Caves emerged.

Whether Tempter sent, or whether tempest tossed thee here ashore . . .

Raven bowed out of the dainty steps and surged into grander prancing ones. *"Pas marché sur la pointe."* Her body glided, a swan on a pond, arms wafting to her side, arching back up, three, four, five times, scarves like feathers 'cross her arms, rising, falling, rising.

"Arabesque." Balancing tall on one leg, she swept the other behind her, her right arm reaching toward the horizon, the left in line with her raised leg, her face tilted upward.

Desolate yet all undaunted, on this desert land enchanted—

"Glissade, saut de chat!" she sang, sailing in light skips across the sand, leaping into a split, toes pointed, her circled arms framing her face. Landing softly, she sank into a deep curtsey, her head bent low, her tangled hair grazing washed-up kelp, the petals fluttering loose.

Tell me truly, I implore.

She dances, but she packs a pistol. She scrawls slurs on a church, but she lingers over old photographs. She sets a house ablaze, but she frolics to phantom music. She pitches and shrieks over rooftops, but she floats and sings across wet sand. She stirs up red mischief and mayhem, but she renders into art the sacred, a transfigurin', as though she'd beheld the glory of the Son.

I couldn't figure it. No dots connected. *Last I heard, there were no dots in Go Fish,* Hollis would say, *had* said in his way. There was no denying it. I'd taken leave of my senses, been charmed by the pungi, bewitched. It was a once-and-gone magic, out here at the Pirate Caves, that's all. *Bewitched?*

Hollis chuckled in my head, an eyebrow raised. *With your gothic take on things, that'd be a waste of a good spell.* Well, if I *had* taken leave of my senses, they'd creep back tomorrow like the tide, now ebbing into a darkening sea.

"*Divertissements!*" As she called out, it hit me too late I should've clapped, but now she burst into a sequence of skips and twirls, the sun sloping, the air chilly, and just as my skin started to prickle and my stomach to growl, she halted, looking at me like she was seeing me for the first time, and came runnin' back, threw on her bolero and skirt and sash, layered her scarves and shawls, yanked on her boots. Grasping the hand she offered, I dropped beside her.

The scrapbook cradled against her chest, she sprinted to the cave, now a dimly lit dungeon, stopping so abruptly I near plowed into her. She tucked the scrapbook into the keepsake box and knotted the lid closed, the shiny Arabian folk tale dulled by long shadows. Again she scaled the boulder, felt for the hidden shelf. Finding it, she nudged the box inside. It snagged, teetered. She pushed harder, jostling it over the ridged lip, but as she did, something dislodged, tumbled out, glinting and clanging, landed at my feet. Before I could jump or holler, before the echo had decayed, she'd vaulted to the ground, sheathing it quickly with her skirt, and scrabbled back up the boulder.

But not quickly enough.

In the dying light, I saw it, the black barrel, the russet grip, the stamp at its base—an encircled star.

I came to my senses.

TWENTY-FIVE

THE RETURN TRIP chilled me despite the shawl Raven draped over my shoulders, the waves a merciless pummel against the dinghy, the wind savage, and by the time we reached the pier, my fingers were near frostbitten. Steering through the pilings, she tethered the boat and hauled me onto the dock, brushing my fumbling hands aside to unbuckle my life jacket. As she tossed it into the *Autumn Rows*, I noticed a skiff bobbing beside Jake's dingy, water sloshing a good three inches inside—*Patches*, Anna's boat. I wouldn't have gotten far had I taken it, but for half a heartbeat I sure wished I'd had the chance.

Had a swamp gator been after me, I couldn't have bolted the dock any faster, letting Raven's shawl fall to the planks. As I rushed past her, Raven grabbed hold of my sleeve, but I yanked my arm free. All the way back from the Pirate Caves, I'd avoided her gaze, had instead faced the shifting shoreline—the rock-hewn cliffs, the peekaboo coves, the golden bluffs, now a rich chestnut in the tuckered sun. Even as I'd squinted at the coast, another landscape took shape, one inside me, one of my own doing, leavin' me all kinds of mixed up, mad, and troubled. I'd found what I'd set out to find: the flight of Raven, the whereabouts of the gun— the truth within the rumors. But I'd stumbled upon another secret too, one that whispered from the pages of a scrapbook, in the barefoot steps of a ballet, one I hadn't wanted to know, one that pulled at me like an undertow.

And goodness' sake, what would I tell Hollis? That I'd nearly fallen under her spell, nearly let her draw me in, nearly bought the myth of her dance, the story of a girl draped in sunlight and memory, a raven reborn as a swan? That even though the trance had been broken, I still almost believed her innocence? No. No one needed to know 'bout my cockamamy notions.

Hollis. I was in no mood to talk to him. And I was in no mood to meet Raven's eyes.

She grabbed at me again, this time latching on to my arm. Before I could wrench free, she whisked a white camellia from her hair and slipped it into my jacket pocket.

"I don't want it!" I shouted, scrambling up the ladder.

If the pier by dawn stained me seaweed green, the pier by dusk blanched me clamshell white. What light there was smeared and scattered, revealing to my warped eyes a fleet of ghosts riding the seething waves, planks that bucked like a dragon's tail, a mirage town on a far desert. As I pelted toward the street, my foot hit a safety cone, and I tripped, the caution tape a snare of tangles dragging me to my knees. *An accident waitin' to happen*, Mama would've said.

The fog reached the sea wall before I did, crested and slunk into town, swaddling the streetlights and muting their glow. Cheery jukebox tunes floated through Cappy's propped door, the Corona parrot a dull pastel in the thick cotton. Children straggled behind parents. A dog barked.

Raven hadn't followed me, hadn't even left the dock that I could see, most like stricken with the horror of thinking me a friend. If she had her wits about her, she'd be back in Jake's dinghy, hightailin' it to the Pirate Caves, hell-bent on pitching the gun, sinking it a hundred fathoms deep. By the time I cleared the pier, my head pounded fit to split. I leaned against the streetlight and closed my eyes.

"You okay?" Hollis's voice emerged from the fog before he did, his brows furrowed.

I closed my eyes again, grateful for the breeze washing over my face.

"Carnival's coming to town this week." His voice seemed to rise from a well.

Though a stretch of minutes since we'd docked, I could still feel the buffeting of waves against the dinghy, still felt unsteady, qualmish. I opened my eyes, fixed on something miles away, tried to carve shapes from the blur. "She thought she could play me."

"What do you mean?"

There was no other way to make sense of it. She'd wanted me to follow her, had all but knocked into me, spurred me into a pursuit down the pier, had even propped the hatch open for me.

"I need to tell the sheriff."

"What did you find?"

"The illusion is true, the old hag an' the girl."

"What?"

"In the sketch. They're both there." My tongue felt thick, my skin flushed and clammy. "She did it . . . but she couldn't have." *This must be how Mayor Mac feels when the tremors set in.* Even my legs ached. I sank onto the sea wall.

"Okay." Hollis eased beside me, took off his creased hat, ran his fingers through his mashed curls. "Wanna tell me more? Did she have the gun?"

"Maybe." *Maybe?* Good Lord, what was wrong with me? Why couldn't I tell Hollis what I'd seen? "She had a scrapbook."

"A scrapbook." It wasn't a question, just an echo.

A VW Bus stacked with surfboards rolled past, its sliding door splashed with a peace sign and psychedelic flowers. Across the street, shop owners locked up for the night.

"It's all right, Scoot. You don't need to tell me."

If I hadn't been so dog-tired, I would have thanked him.

We sat without words for a long moment, the rise and fall of the sea in cadence with our breaths. A pigeon pecked at a scatter of sunflower seeds, no hint of iridescence in its gray feathers.

"She wanted me to see."

"See what?"

For now we see through a glass, darkly; but then face to face.

"She wanted to show me. Why?" I knew I was being impossible, that it wasn't right, asking Hollis what he couldn't know.

"Maybe . . . maybe she figured it was the only way you'd stop."

"Stop what?"

His gaze tracked a red convertible as it growled past. "Nothing. Just thinkin' out loud."

It wasn't like Hollis to think out loud. Seemed whatever he said, he first sifted through a gold miner's pan. Whenever a question met with silence, I reckoned he'd mined all the gold, talked himself done.

"What's that supposed to mean, the only way I'd stop? Stop *what*?"

"Chasing her. Pestering her." His voice softened. "Like a blue jay."

"I'm not chasing *her*!" The furnace burning in my head exploded into rage. "I'm chasing the truth!"

"Sure you're not running from it?"

It was all I could do not to shove him off the wall. Who asked for his two cents anyway? I wished to high heaven I had let it be, just shut my trap and kept Raven to myself. A wave of nausea threatened, but I gulped hard and breathed deeply, let the creeping fog cocoon me.

A rusty pickup rattled past, shuddered to a stop down the street, the Old Clunker herself, radio thumping. I shut my eyes. A hint of smoke wafted toward us.

"I'm tired." *Bone-weary*, I thought, too worn for another word.

"Yeah." Hollis punched his hat, slapped it back on.

"You got curls like Little Joe." I blinked back a surge of tears.

"Yeah?"

"Yeah."

We sat beneath the streetlight, saying nothing. Any other time I'd have hounded Hollis for answers, demanded a response, harangued and badgered him, his silence intolerable, would've talked a blue streak till his good humor frayed thin, till out of sheer annoyance he finally said what I wanted to hear, satisfying me at least for the moment and then doffing his bucket hat in defeat and runnin' a hand through his tousled hair. But tonight I was grateful for his silent ways. Tonight my eyes stung, my thoughts caromed.

This I sat engaged in guessing, but no syllable expressing—

"Oh, hello." Hollis rose, offered a smile. "I'm Hollis."

But Raven planted herself squarely in front of me, smelling of sea and revenge. Though I stood too, I had no smile.

And then, as if the fog had swallowed the town and left only us, no Hollis beside me, no couples ambling by, no cars cruising the street, just me and *the fowl whose fiery eyes now burned into my bosom's core*, she clutched my wrists, her nails digging into my skin, and spat three words.

"Liliya. My name." Flinging my wrists free, she turned heel and was gone.

"Well, she—" Hollis caught sight of something on the sidewalk. "What's that?"

At my feet lay the crumpled camellia.

Picking the flower up, he studied it, then studied me. "You don't look so good, Eden."

I didn't feel so good either, drenched in sweat despite the chill, my knees 'bout to buckle.

Is it so hard to love the unlovely?

Hollis nudged my elbow. "C'mon. I'll walk you home."

We'd passed the laundromat when the Old Clunker sputtered to life, jolted forward, and spewing exhaust, peeled away from the curb. As Hollis would point out later, oftentimes when we don't see a thing, it's 'cause we poked out our own eye.

TWENTY-SIX

I woke the next day with a fever. Canceling her morning shift, Mama ordered me to bed, taking up post beside me in snatches while Dex napped, her silver-flecked head bent over *Pharmacology for Nursing,* urging sips of honey tea and nibbles of dry toast, and heading downstairs only to rinse the washcloth she held to my forehead and open the door for Rosa.

My fever raged, and I kicked off my sheet just for Mama to re-tuck it beneath my chin. If I opened my eyes, the room swayed, the walls closing in on me, warping in waves, framing Mama's face as it wavered above me. If I closed my eyes, the murky curtains behind my lids rippled and folded, became ocean currents breaking against my temples, slapping the dinghy, whisking me back across the Pacific, lurching me toward the cliffs, into restless sleep, and we were at the cave, on the shore, only it was Dex with me, not Raven, and he was in motion, whirling, caught up in her ballet—*bourrée, arabesque, saut de chat*—his legs no longer crippled, but sturdy, supple, lifting him in flight over the swash of sea, his outstretched arms strong as he soared, and I longed to join him, to dance in the joy of a boy perfected, to hear his secret music, but I sat on my rock and watched because I knew I never could, the moment his and his alone. The sun beat down on me, hotter and hotter, scorching the sand, and then came the breeze, the wind off the sea, and a sleep so sweet.

By late afternoon I felt well enough to curl on the couch with my pillow, Rosa now able to keep an eye on both her wards, freein' up Mama for a run to the grocery store.

"And the pharmacy, if you don't mind, Rosa."

Rosa not only didn't mind but fairly pushed her out the door, barking in broken English that she could manage for an hour or for a month, *it make no difference* to her. After all, she'd raised *siete niños*, hadn't she? And did they wait their turn to have *the feber or runny the nose, heh?* And the chicken pox! *Ay, ay!* All seven at once!

"Eden," Mama called from the hallway, "feelin' up to a visit from Dad?"

"What for?"

"For about ten minutes." She poked her head around the corner. "I could ask him to come over tonight. Y'all can play cards."

Con-demmit, so he'd told her about our poker game. Wasn't anything private in this stupid family that wasn't even a family? I buried my face in the cushions. *If I can't see them, they can't see me.* Wasn't that how it worked, those childish games we had no hope of winning? Even so, I heard bits of their backroom chat, Mama's sigh, Rosa's consolation, their murmured conspiracy at the front door, something about chicken soup and ginger ale. I hated ginger ale.

From my nest of blankets, I heard Rosa knocking about in the coat closet, Dex's braces clanging, then emerge to restack the scattered foam blocks, chattering in Spanish.

"He doesn't understand." I opened one vexed eye. Dex straddled her hip, pulling his tongue.

"Ah, the feber better, heh, Eedee Mae? No more sick?" Her palm, coarse against my forehead, felt cool, even soothing. Dex dribbled on my arm.

"I no better." The edge in my voice lingered.

"Aha! Then no *necesitas* leesin."

"How can I not listen? And why do you even talk to him? He doesn't know English. He doesn't know Spanish. He doesn't know anything."

"He know. He know *mucho*. He know the heart." She thumped her chest with her fist. "*Verdad, mi tesoro?*" She switched on the table lamp despite the streaming sunlight. Through the tilted blinds, I saw beachgoers stowing umbrellas in their cars, brushing sand off their legs.

"So late! What time is it, Rosa?"

"Snack time." She planted a kiss on Dex's head as she grunted after a wayward sock.

"Confound it! I've lost a whole day." I hoped Hollis had kept a lookout for Raven. But then why would he? I'd told him nothing about the caves—nothing that made sense, any-way. I wondered if he had missed me at the pier. Fishin' by his lonesome probably made for a right quiet time.

"You find it *mañana*."

"Find what?"

"The day." Rosa disappeared into the kitchen, then re-appeared with a box of graham crackers. "You want?" she asked, the rocker creaking as she flumped into it.

I shook my head.

Breaking apart a cracker, she lassoed a bouncing Dex, now in his playbed, and pried a piece past his fingers and tongue. She munched her own cracker.

"He isn't supposed to eat in his bed."

"*Ahí viene el avioncito . . . brrrrr!*" She zoomed another piece into his mouth.

"Rosa?" I threw off the blankets to see her better. "You ever heard of somebody changin' shape?"

"*Cambiar de forma?*" She wiped Dex's drool with her sleeve. "You see shape my stomach? *Bebé uno, dos, tres*—uf!"

"Not like that. I mean into a rat or bird or whatever."

She huffed and stopped rocking, her chin bunching into two. "*La Lechuza.*" Touching her forehead, her breast, and then her left and right shoulders, she uttered a fervent *amén* and fed Dex more cracker.

"What's that?"

"*La cruz.*"

"Not that. The *Lech*-thing?"

"*La Lechuza.* The *abuela* my Antonio, she change. She *bruja*, witch."

"She is?"

"No *is.*" Rosa had finished her cracker and was now eating the rest of Dex's. "She dead."

"How did you know?"

"She no breathe."

"I mean, how did you know she changed shape? What shape?"

"Ahh. She change in the night. Day, *abuela.* Night, *búho*—huu huu!" She flapped her arms, then pointed toward the evening sky. "I see her *en la palma.*"

"An owl? In a palm tree?" That her husband's grandmother turned into an owl—and at *night*—near proved that Raven could turn into a raven.

"*Sí.* She sit. She watch."

"What did she watch?"

"All what happens in *hacienda.* She *búho.*"

"Did she cast spells? Or brew potions?" I made a stirring motion with my arm, nearly knocking over the lamp.

"*Pociones?* Heh! She no need *pociones.* See everything,

know everything. My Antonio's *madre y padre*, they can no secrets." She peered down her wrinkled blouse after a fallen cracker crumb.

"But did she hex anyone?"

"No, no. Only *Lechuza* do—what you call? Spellings?"

"Spells. What spells?"

"Take soul of *bebés*."

Batting his marbles, Dex launched into a barnyard of sounds, from whinnies to clucks to oinks. Rosa pinched both cheeks and patted his head.

"What babies?"

"How I know what *bebés*? The *bebés* who no souls."

"How can a baby have no soul?"

"No *bautizado*, no soul." Rosa sprinkled Aslan with invisible water.

"Mercy!" That shined a right new light on infant baptism. Even if sprinkling was no ticket to paradise, infant baptism had kept Hollis out of the clutches of *La Lechuza*.

Before I could call Rosa's theology into question, the front door let out a squeak, a dismal reminder of my dereliction.

"Hey there, sugar." Mama glanced at me from the hallway, arms loaded with grocery bags. "How's my girl?"

"*Mucho* better, *sí*?" Rosa unwedged herself from the rocker to place a sticky hand on my forehead. "She *no tiene más feber*." Satisfied I wasn't bound for glory just yet, she sighed a *gracias a Dios* and scurried into the kitchen.

Rosa was nothin' if not full of surprises.

The rustle of paper bags and murmur of voices must've eased me back to sleep, because only a minute later Mama was waking me to a house thick with the smell of simmering onions, bay leaves, and rosemary.

"How 'bout a little soup?" she urged.

"Sure." Too groggy to disagree, I dragged myself upright.

"Stay put, sugar. I'll bring it to you."

Mama settled beside me on the couch while I ate—a hearty chicken soup with rice and bits of okra, a vegetable my father couldn't stand—her sweet tea and a surgical text perched on the end table. Antonio had fetched Rosa, she told me, with a loud honk that Rosa met with a smack upside the head. Dex slept in his playbed, his mouth parted in wheezy breaths, his cheek smashing Aslan.

"Glad you feel like eating." Mama wore a soft smile. "You've been scarce 'round here. Probably wore yourself out."

I made a show of slurping my soup.

She squeezed my toe. "Care to tell me where you were yesterday?"

Yesterday. Was it just yesterday? Yesterday seemed a year ago. Oh, the agony of not knowing the goings-on of the town while I languished on death's door. "Sorry you had to miss work today, Mama."

"Joyce—Ms. Keller swapped shifts with me." She handed me a napkin. "And I needed to swing by Rexall anyhow. Now we're stocked up for another gully washer."

"Uh-huh." Was I that sick?

"Guess who I ran into at the deli—Rev'n Travers! Said hospital visits make him hungry."

"Hospital?" I dropped my spoon, seized by a vision of Mr. York, tail over teakettle. "Did something happen to him?" Went in for a confession, came out with a concussion, most like.

"Goodness, no. He and a couple LUV ladies checked in on the man pulled from the fire. Poor dear's got to stay a few more days, but looks like he's on the mend."

"Oh. Well, that's a fine thing."

"Know what the reverend told me? It was his son who saved the man! Imagine that!"

"What?" Hollis had mentioned teens in the ravine, but— "You mean Ben?"

"Well, one of the boys. He and his friends were out searchin' for a lost dog when they smelled smoke."

"Lost dog? That's hardly—" I bit my tongue.

"Hardly what?"

Hardly the truth, leastways the *whole* truth. They'd been partying. That's what Hollis had said. Drinking an' carousing an' most like smoking pot, causing no end of grief for the reverend, up all night roaming the deserted streets for his wayward son. I guessed sometimes it paid to be in the wrong place at the right time. Ben had become a ticker-tape hero. Rev. Travers would be mighty pressed hauling him before the flock this go-round, despite Ben's trespasses—which, come to think of it, included a yarn 'bout a lost dog.

"Who'da thought?" I said, in true Hollis form. "If that wasn't a stroke of luck."

"Providence, not luck. See how good our God is, hearin' our prayers?"

I glanced at Dex, still curled in sleep. "Sure, real good," I muttered, my head throbbing.

"Oh, and your beau stopped by earlier. He wanted to know if you were all right." She swirled her glass, the ice cubes clinking. "Seems you had a fishing date this morning."

I nearly choked on a celery chunk. Hollis Sweet, my *beau*? Good Lord. He was my mission field! And anyway, I could still see ninth grade in the rearview mirror, with trepidation enough fitting into sophomore shoes, let alone dancing shoes. Beaus were for, well, for Heather and Trish. Pretty girls with pretty pouts. They certainly weren't for anyone as unladylike as I had folks believing. I supposed when I was sixteen like them, I might reconsider—both beaus and Hollis. Till then, I had Little Joe.

"That's just Hollis, Mama." I felt a tingle creep up my face and blew pretend steam from my spoon. "He's friends with the whole town. Anyhow, he's Roman Catholic. But I've been showin' him the error of his ways."

Mama swallowed this information like she did my father's Corn Flakes casserole, picking up her glass, gazing into it as if reading tea leaves, then putting it back down. Whether she was mortified I was fraternizing with a Roman Catholic or pleased I'd introduced him to Rev. Travers's truth, I couldn't be sure.

"And how's he takin' to it?" she finally said.

"Oh, he's swell about it. He isn't much for church, but he sees the sense of religion. Leastways he let me baptize him."

She gave me a look so peculiar I figured I'd finally done something right. I allowed myself a moment of righteous pride, careful not to sin in doing so, though it was a blurry line. Mama had to see that what I lacked in holiness, I made up for in zeal. I resolved to remain humble while she praised me.

"Well, he sounds like a fine friend, this Hollis."

And that was all. She reached for her textbook and, balancing it on the armrest, took her red pencil to the margins. I reckoned her mind was too crammed with femurs and tibias to bother much with praise.

"'Dem bones, dem bones, dem dry bones, O hear the word of the Lord,'" I croaked, peering over her shoulder and sneezing violently.

"Not on your sleeve!" Mama handed me a tissue, and I sank back against the cushions.

Parting the blind slats, I squinted at a street cloaked in the usual fog eddies, a night descending. "An entire day shot." I punched my pillow. "So much mighta happened!"

No sooner had I said the words, *heard* myself say them, felt the hot ire on my tongue—untamable evil that it was, full of deadly poison—than I wished I'd kept my mouth shut. Hadn't Mama lost a day too, my fever the reason she'd skipped her shift at the clinic, even missed her evening class? Sure, she could've left me with Rosa—or worse, my father—but she didn't, instead making me tea and toast, stirring up chicken soup. A sadness caught in my sore throat, a sadness that I always had to be me, that I couldn't somehow be better than me, like Mama was, ever so much better than herself.

Eden Mae, I wanted her to say, *do you ever stop your wallowin' long enough to consider the trials of anyone else?*

Because I deserved that. But she wouldn't say it any more than she'd say to my father that our busted-up family was his doing, or to God that the feeble, hurtin' boy now whimpering and moaning was *his* doing. Mama was as perfect as Dex was imperfect—but even perfect people wearied, and Mama, nestled in the couch corner with her head bent over her textbook, had one more trial than even I did, and that was me, so it seemed the least I could do was forgive her the lack of enthusiasm over my evangelistic efforts.

"I'm sorry." She patted my foot. "Each day has its own troubles, Eden. It's how we bear them." She meant well, leaning into Scripture for comfort, but I would've appreciated a how-to manual.

As if on cue, Dex woke with a wail that worked my last nerve, and Mama, without so much as a sigh, lifted him gently from his playbed and brought him to me.

"Just for a minute while I fetch his medicine."

I held him on my lap, his shrieks angry, his honey-flecked eyes pouring tears. I could calm him, I knew, hush his sobs, his unknowable fears. I could sing "Old MacDonald," make all kinds of critter noises. I could bounce him on my knee, promise him a moonlit walk with Sissy. I could flick off the lamp, raise the blinds, and let the hazy glow of the street-light mesmerize him. But I didn't. I let him holler and waited for Mama to come back, clampin' him till the pink goop dribbled down his chin. Before she could cap the syrup bottle, I thrust Dex at her and slid off the couch.

"Night, Mama."

"Need anything? A glass of water?" Shifting Dex to her hip, she brushed the curls from his blotchy face, nestled her mascara-smudged cheek against his slobbery one, against his tears and snot. Dex hiccupped, burrowed into her. "There's aspirin on the counter. And lozenges."

"I'm fine." Another sneeze erupted. "Just a bunk day, that's all."

When I glanced back from the stairs, the room had gone dark except for the sparkle of black sea beyond the picture window. Only the slow creak of the rocker told me anyone was there.

TWENTY-SEVEN

MAKING A GETAWAY the next morning didn't come easy, what with Mama fussing over me, peering down my throat, taking my temperature, heaping more eggs on my plate, and taking my temperature again. By the time I wrangled free to find Hollis, crews had emptied most of the carnival trucks, put chain-link fences 'round the public parking lot—a patch of mostly nothin' till the summer tourists descended—and begun setting up rides, game booths, and food stands.

I circled Harford Beach twice looking for him, trudged the shore inlet to cliff, a volleyball clipping my shoulder, a sneaker wave soaking my shoes. I swept the pier with my binoculars, none too eager to brave the woozy trek in my infirm condition. I scoured the streets, corner to corner, even traipsed past Hollis's shingled house, glimpsing his aproned mother pinning shirts to a clothesline. I'd met her once briefly, when she'd come scouting the beach for Hollis.

Before I knew what possessed me, I hollered a howdy and helped myself to one of the white pickets, leaning on it ever so casual. "Fine day to be hanging clothes, Mrs. Sweet. I mean, if you have to hang clothes." I worked a bit of Southern charm into my voice. "Maybe you remember me? Hollis's friend from Texas? Been huntin' high and low for him. Don't suppose he's home?"

"No, dear. Haven't seen Hollis yet today. Edith, isn't it?"

"Eden. Eden Mae."

"Oh yes, such a lovely name."

"Thank you, ma'am. Why, that reminds me, I've been wondering 'bout—that is, Hollis says you named him after a town in Kern County."

She flashed a Hollis grin, amused and sweet and maddening all at once, and pinned up a pair of jeans. "Now there's an idea—Buttonwillow Sweet." Her laugh tinkled like wind chimes. "No, he's named after his great-grandfather Hollis, father's side." She yanked a towel from the laundry basket. "Hollis Percival Lavinia Sweet of Kent—he's lucky we stopped at Percival."

"Then he wasn't born in the back of a station wagon?"

"He most certainly was, three weeks early and a stone's throw from the Highway 46 watering hole. Didn't mind the herd of Angus looking on, but the stink!"

"Musta been a right misery, giving birth in a ditch—and under a toppled signpost too."

"Dear, it was unfortunate enough without embellishment." She paused to study me. "I remember now—you and Hollis were teaching that scruffy mutt to dive for fish."

"But *he's* the one—oh, never mind." Hollis had whatfor coming, that was for sure. "Stink, you say?"

"Nothing like the fresh scent of manure. Didn't think the poor baby would take a second breath."

"Mighty fittin'," I said, keeping to myself just what exactly was fitting, and it *wasn't* being named after his great-grandfather. "It's good to have the facts, Mrs. Sweet, though I reckon Hollis might need some remindin'."

But she was wrestling a tangle of sheets onto the clothesline and had been swallowed whole.

"And we won't be naming any son of ours Percival," I finished.

Aside from that serendipity, I'd wasted two hours of my morning ferreting for Hollis. Not only hadn't I seen a lick of him, I hadn't seen Raven either. That, at least, would have made the search worth my soggy shoes.

"Hey, Scoot!" A chipper voice shouted me back from a third sweep as I stomped past Lucky's, flushed and sweaty.

Hollis waved at me from the tailgate of a cargo truck, where he sat between two other orange-vested men, all three chowing down sandwiches, hard hats clamped to their heads. As I moseyed closer, I made out the festive lettering on the side panel—*Midway Marvels*. Hopping off, Hollis gave the men a nod, grabbed his sack lunch, and steered me toward a stone wall, where he resumed his sittin' and his sandwich.

"For Pete's sake, Hollis. Where have you been?" It took me two jumps to hoist myself beside him.

"I'm working the carnival. Do it every summer." He slurped a loose strip of ham from his sandwich. "Pays good money."

"Coulda told me."

"Just did. Wanna pickle?" He clawed off his hard hat, his mussed curls in a fringe 'round ruddy cheeks, set it next to my binoculars.

"No thanks. Seen Raven?"

"Your loss. And might be one in that tree." With a chuckle I didn't share, he added, "How you feeling today?"

"Good enough to head back to the caves." I plunked his hard hat over my ponytail. "When will you be done?"

He rooted around in the sack. "Pretty soon. All I got left is a banana, two bags of potato chips, three peanut butter cookies, a Slim Jim, another pickle, and a carton of orange juice. Unless I swing by Lucky's for an Eskimo Pie." Grinning, he patted his flat belly. "Then I gotta get back to work."

"That's not what I meant. Lord a'mighty, you sure eat a lot."

"Gotta fuel these muscles."

I rolled my eyes at his flexed bicep but figured if I let him chew in peace, he'd finish quicker. A loud squawking drew my gaze to an oak tree, where a small gray bird swooped from the branches after a big ol' red-tailed bird. Both birds soared and dipped, the little one darting right an' left, pecking at the red-tailed bird, and the red-tailed bird dodging it and trying to break away.

"Such a bully." I squinted after them. "Pesterin' that eagle."

"Hawk." Hollis pinched open his juice carton. "Small one's a mockingbird. Must have a nest in that tree. Only blue jays pester without reason."

I stiffened, something hovering on the edge of my memory. "So how 'bout a straight answer? When will you be done?"

"Late. Lotta booths to set up, rides to test." He burped politely, but I could still smell pickle and orange juice. "Carnival starts tomorrow night. Wanna go?"

"Sure. Well, maybe. I wanna go to the caves."

"Ya don't say." He pulled out a bag of chips. "Doesn't mean we can't go to the carnival."

"I have to watch Dex. Aren't you takin' your sisters?"

"Course I am. All day Saturday." He licked salt off his fingers. "What about Thursday night? Got Dex duty then?"

"Dunno. Ain't no rhyme nor reason to my Dex duty."

"Well, if you're free, we're on. There's a roller coaster, a super scrambler, and bumper cars for ground squirrels like you." He let me take the biggest chip from the bag. "There'll be fireworks near the pier too, three barges shootin' 'em at once. Gonna be groovy, man." He winked.

It occurred to me that he wasn't much different from Popeye when the excitement set in, his slate-blue eyes bright, his head cocked.

"Yeah, okay." Didn't seem right to refuse such eagerness. And I supposed the carnival could be fun. "You don't got anything to tell me, do ya?" *Like maybe the sheriff's already locked Raven up or a posse's run the commies outta town?*

"Nope."

"Would you tell me if you did?"

"Yeah, absolutely. I'd tell you if I had something I wasn't gonna tell you." He laughed.

"Hmph. Well, I got stuff to tell *you*—to show you. At the caves."

That landed a glance, but he only balled up his paper bag and, tossing it, watched it sail in a smooth arc toward the trash can. "Swish!" He dusted off his hands, faced me. "Okay, I'm listening. But ten minutes tops—then I'm back on the clock."

And I didn't waste a one, spillin' the whole story, from Raven waiting for me on the dock to me shucking her double-quick soon as we got back, throwing in every little detail— some of 'em twice—done talked myself out, if that were possible. Every little detail, that is, except Raven's dance, maybe because it didn't seem to matter or maybe because it didn't seem worth remembering. Point being, we needed to fetch the evidence. That was all that mattered. Get the gun, the keepsake box—anything that would help the sheriff.

"Think you could find the cave?"

"Might take some doing." I'd already considered the slim chance of *that*.

"Same 'doing' it took to find her house? Should I pack a sleeping bag?"

"Well, ain't you a hoot 'n' a holler?" I drawled, sticking out my tongue. "S'pose we'll have to follow her."

Hollis gave my ponytail a tug and, returning his hard hat to his head, greeted three crewmen striding out of Lucky's, unwrapping Fudgsicles.

"I don't know, Eden," he finally said. "It still doesn't make sense. Why would she burn down her own house, try to kill her own uncle? And I don't really like the idea of chasing her. How 'bout we let Sheriff Moretti handle this?"

"Like he'd believe me—you don't even believe me. Just my gothic imagination, right? How 'bout *you* help *me* get the gun?"

"Tell ya what. If I can scare up a dinghy, we'll follow her tomorrow. But only to see where she goes, okay?"

It wasn't okay, but it was something. And chances were he'd change his mind by the time we got there, see the stakes for what they were. I'd take these cards and play 'em like aces. Poker had taught me that—and how to keep a game face.

"Oka—"

But Hollis had hopped off the wall and was bounding across the street. As I slid to my feet, my sigh gave way to a smile. On my binoculars lay a pack of peanut butter cookies.

With nothing left to do but wait for tomorrow, I drifted toward the unfurling fairground and watched the crews ready the midway. We'd missed it last summer, Mama and I doing our own readying in the bungalow, lugging boxes up the porch steps to carousel melodies. The traveling carnival was back by popular demand, so Hollis said. It was a noisy affair, the gravel lot teeming with workers putting together a fairground, erecting tents and booths, hollerin', and roping off sections. We'd likely see a run of tourists, triple the usual number, leastways for the first couple days. Tolerable, I'd give it that, maybe even welcome—I liked a carnival as much as the next person, providing my feet stayed on the ground. Welcome, that is, long as we had our town to ourselves the rest of the year. *Our town.* Peculiar that I would say *our.* My life had been in the city, at 2122 Grand Avenue, San Sebastian, in the dappled house shaded by sycamores. That's where it should have stayed. Better yet, in Texas.

Leaning against the chain-link fence, I counted the trucks as they rolled 'cross the gravel, the ground shaking. Men unloaded heavy equipment, set about raising a carousel, seemed to holler it into existence. They spread a canopy of bright colors over the beams, anchored the canvas to the middle pole. Beyond the carousel, a crane hoisted steel rods up to the sky-high frame of some death-defying ride. Another crew pieced together a kiddie coaster, unloaded bumper cars, tied a rope of rainbow flags to a game booth.

Right in the thick of the bustling lot, a dozen men scrambled beneath the Ferris wheel tower, steered tractors and forklifts across metal plates, shouted orders to one another. They guided the last gondola into place as the crane operator lifted it, snapping and bolting it to the outermost ring. Even from the sidewalk, I could hear the hum of a motor breathing life into the massive structure. My stomach somersaulted.

Why in tarnation did the carnival have to come today? The sooner we raided the cave, the better. Odds were, we were already too late. Raven had most like stashed her loot elsewhere—or worse, destroyed it, pitched the gun into the ocean and swept the cave clean. And what an exasperation *that* would be, a downright disaster, nothin' doing for it 'cept call in deep-sea divers or a Navy submarine. It was far-fetched hooey, of course, imagining a submarine, but Mama's way out of a calamity was to find the comical—or so she used to say, before calamity landed her a knockout blow. Condemnation! Another lost day.

Each day might have its own troubles—couldn't argue with Mama or the Good Book—but I aimed to give tomorrow a run for its money. The way I worked it, Hollis and I would stake out the pier, station ourselves at our usual bench, fishing rods over the railing, keep a lookout—the rush of ruffled skirts, the waft of woodland blooms—shadow her to the dock, allow her a head start, and then trail her, stayin' out of sight. Once she veered into the cove, we'd cut the motor, drift on open sea and wait, far enough not to be pegged but close enough to—*glory be, I mustn't forget my binoculars.* Or maybe we'd take cover under a bluff till she set out for Harford Beach.

Whose dinghy didn't much concern me—that was a detail for Hollis—so long as we were back by six sharp. Mama wouldn't have but an hour after her shift to shoo Rosa home, dump some Hamburger Helper and last night's carrots in a pot, and load herself and her textbooks into her Corvair. Once she left, I'd be stuck with Dex.

But another hitch needed smoothing. With the carnival in full swing, drawing revelers and hell-raisers like fish to a hook, the sheriff and his deputies would be runnin' themselves ragged, breaking up more than one drunken brawl. We'd have to hide the gun until the dust settled.

What we'd do if the gun *wasn't* at the caves was another of Hollis's details.

In the grinding and rattling of machinery, I didn't hear my father's VW till he'd pulled up to the curb, the idling engine 'bout as welcome as a hornet's nest.

TWENTY-EIGHT

MY FATHER ROLLED down the passenger window. "Eden!"

I moseyed along the fence, the construction racket making for a fine excuse not to hear a thing.

"Eden!" He laid on the horn, jarring me to a stop. "Shouldn't you be home?"

My answer was to resume my walk, his VW Bug puttering beside me.

"Your mom told me you were pretty sick."

She also tell you about payin' me a get-well visit?

"I'm fine." My ponytail gave a pert swish.

"Glad to hear it."

Glad enough to drive off now your conscience is clear?

"Feel up to some clam chowder at Fish-n-Ships Diner?" He grinned. "A souperrific bread bowl?"

"It's Cappy's. And no thanks." I kicked the fence, suddenly riveted by a crewman chasing a flyaway red-striped awning.

"Coke?"

"No."

"Milkshake? I could go for one."

"No thanks."

"Are you going to say no to everything I ask you?"

"I'm not hungry."

When there was no follow-up question, I stole a look at

him. He was staring over the steering wheel, straight ahead, his lips tight. The hair along his temples shimmered with a new gray.

"Thought maybe some of that glacial ice thawed when we spent the day together, played poker."

So I'm the glacier and you're Mr. Sunshine? One evening of your best behavior and now life is hunky-dory, huh? The ol' Band-Aid fix while the family bleeds out.

"Well?"

"Think I'll watch the construction for a while."

"How 'bout a movie instead? *Chitty Chitty Bang Bang*'s playing at the drive-in."

"Yeah, no. I'm not six." The fence rattled under my kick. Fact was, six or sixty, I'd watch a documentary on lawn-mowers at the Moonrise Drive-In if it was showin', the giant screen looming big as Texas and the popcorn buttery as Mama's cornbread. Sometimes my own notions hit me like a boomerang.

"You drive a hard bargain. See you at dinner then."

Confound it. If he was going to live with us, he needed to *live* with us. I had an address for just the place: 2122 Grand Avenue, San Sebastian.

He stuck his head back out the window. "Hey, almost forgot. Grandpa and Madge are driving down to Palm Springs next week. They'll want to see you."

"Well, bless 'em. They wanna see Dex too?" That kind of gumption could get me grounded, but my father just shook his head and put the Bug in gear.

I didn't bother waving as he drove off. And I didn't let Rev. Travers's voice barge into my head either. But I no longer cared to watch the crews set up, roaming willy-nilly instead—three turns 'round Harford Beach, from the carnival grounds to the overpass where the highway crossed the cliffs, down to Front Street, lollygagging at the swings for a cookie break, then tracking the sea wall to the inlet before doubling back past my house—the candy-green VW snug against the curb—up the weedy hill to the edge of town, and then along tucked streets. Though I kept a coon-dog lookout, I caught neither hide nor hair of Raven. Most like she was conjuring up more mischief at the Pirate Caves or lurking around Gulch Run, burying her guilt in the ravine, maybe poking around the scorched ruins of the shed, sleuthing for anything that might give her away. One thing was for sure—she was duckin' the sheriff's keen eye. That was something I'd bet my last dollar on.

Before I lost myself between reverie and rage again—and between the highway and the golf course—I cut my loop short and veered back toward the carnival. With any luck, I'd catch Hollis packing up for the day, run tomorrow's plans by him, fix a time for our morning rendezvous, and get down to brass tacks. I jogged across an intersection clogged with cars leaving the beach, the peak tanning hours fading with the sun, and turned onto a cross street.

"Hey, boy. You here alone?"

Popeye lay flopped outside Lucky's, snout on his white paws. He stretched as I scratched behind his ears, snuffling my cheek with his wet nose.

"Ooh-wee, you stink!"

He smelled near as rank as Ernesto's cigars, like a canine gumbo of tobacco, seaweed, and dirty water. The glass door swung open, and out came a woman crowned in pink sponge curlers, toddler in tow. The little girl bent to pat Popeye's head, blowin' kisses as she trailed after her mother.

"Ever the charmer, huh, Popeye?"

The smattering of folks who rose with the sun—anglers,

surfers, delivery truck drivers, shop owners, Hollis and me, excepting when Dex threw a monkey wrench into the works—had gotten used to Popeye claiming the wooden bench till Jake shooed him off. On the cusp of sunrise, the large mutt could be spotted on the seashore—or tripped over in the fog—waiting for Jake to emerge from the sea. Then man and dog would trudge the waking beach to Lucky's, settle themselves onto the bench, and ease into the day, Popeye with a hearty strip of bacon, Jake with a smoke and the *Los Angeles Times*, then coffee and a cinnamon roll, which he polished off with a bologna sandwich.

Hollis and I tagged along on occasion, Jake grousing at first but tolerating us on condition we keep our own company and not his, which we took to mean as long as we didn't badger him like Anna did, what with her frets about his ocean walks, sharks cuttin' their teeth on him or riptides sweepin' him off to China. He was at his gruffest best.

But Popeye at Lucky's in the early evening and without Jake, now that was peculiar.

"Don'tcha fret. He always comes back."

Like Jake, Popeye wasn't much for talking, instead circling once and then folding himself under the bench, bandana sideways.

Had Jake been in the store, Popeye would have been too. Joe allowed no tommyrot, but he allowed Popeye. Squashing my face against the store window anyway, I peered directly into the brazen baby blues of the Budweiser girl, behind her a mess of blur. No Jake to be seen. I helped myself to the bench, the wood warm on my back, a fuzzy snout on my foot.

"Pish! Look atcha!" Anna trundled out of the store. "Throwin' me over for a beauty, eh?" Popeye's tail thumped as she rubbed his belly.

I grinned. "Ain't no beauty for that mangy beast but you, Anna. 'Cept maybe Jake."

Cuffing my knee, she near cratered the bench as she sat, just a mite less husky than her brother. An amber bottle poked from her paper bag.

"You ain't seen nothin'." She tipped the bag to reveal something red. "An apple a day, doc says. That's all ya seen." She leaned into me, her breath like moldy cheese.

"Sure."

"Course, between you an' me, Gramps's elixir, that's the stuff."

"Does it help?" I scootched sideways.

She swelled into the space I'd vacated, her wrinkled lips sprouting whiskers. "Keeps the dreads away." She righted herself. "Swaps 'em, anyway, one dread for t'other."

"Like choosing between bad and worse, I reckon."

"Gots t' play the hand y'got." Anna swallowed hard.

"Or bluff the one you don't." By way of cheering, I added, "Bet he's a swell brother."

"Pish! He's an old mule." A blast of Roquefort sent me backward. "But kin gots to take t'other the way they is." She stuffed the paper bag into her satchel, the whiskey bottle jutting out again. "It ain't the dying saps a body. It's the living."

"He's not dying yet, is he?" Popeye had moseyed out from beneath the bench and now rested his chin in my lap. I twiddled his floppy ear.

"Nah. Plasterin' the kitchen with fish guts last I seen."

"He says he's gonna teach me how to whittle an arrow."

"Ha!" Though she spat the word, a smile touched her lips, softened her crinkly eyes. "Only ever done that once before."

"Done what?"

"Taught a girl t' whittle an arrow. Then he married 'er."

"Jake? *Married?*" Hardly seemed possible. Come to think of it, I hadn't put much thought into folks' lives before I happened along.

"Ain't cared for another since."

"But he . . . how come . . ."

"Ain't my story to tell." A shadow flickered across her face. "Just kids then, but you never forget."

That Jake had a wife once—"Is she the hula girl on his arm?"

With a loud snort, Anna patted my knee again. "S'pose you'll just have t' ask the old mule yourself."

Rooting through her satchel, she dug out something that looked like bait—squid or maybe anchovy—catapulting Popeye out from under the bench. As he gobbled it down, two teens, laughing and trading jabs, kicked open the liquor store door. The slighter one had a face full of pimples.

"Hey, bud." Ben squatted to give Popeye a knuckle rub. Though not as dark as his father's, Ben's shaggy hair boasted the same thick waves.

Behind him, Vince studied Anna before turning sea-green eyes and boyish dimples on me. "Well, howdy." Slinging his letterman jacket over his shoulder, he chuckled. "From commies to grannies. We need to find you some friends."

"Got plenty," I said, *and if you mean Heather, no thanks.* "This is Anna."

"Hello." Ben stood, hiking his beat-up backpack into place. "Nice dog y'got here. Sorta the mascot of Harford Beach. Don't know his name though."

"Popeye." Anna blew fiercely into a hankie pulled from her sleeve.

"Does he like spinach?" Vince smirked, let Popeye sniff his fingers.

"Likes anythin' gots anchovy in it."

"He's a better man than I am." Vince made such a ridiculous face that I laughed despite myself. "Better man than you too, huh, cowgirl?"

"By like a mile." I frowned as I thought of my father's go-to at Little Caesars. "Always pick 'em off pizza."

"Can't say it don't make 'im thirsty," Anna added.

"I bet. Dude!" Staggering, Ben righted his backpack as Vince yanked a canteen free.

"What, don't wanna share your holy water?" Popeye lapped from Vince's cupped hand in a gusto of slurps. "Way to go, champ."

Anna squinted hard at Vince. "You them boys run into the burning house?"

"Yeah—us and a couple others." Straightening, Vince punched Ben. "Ben here's the real hero. Saw the fire first."

"Smelled it."

Anna grunted and lumbered to her feet. "Best get on."

"Us too." Ben tugged his Dodgers cap from his back pocket.

"Your moms waitin' dinner on ya?"

Glory be, my father would be settling himself at our kitchen table right about now—'less I'd frostbitten him into leaving early. I could only hope.

"Nah," Ben answered as Vince broke off a weathered piece of wall, muttering. "Gonna meet up with Sheriff Moretti."

"Moretti?"

"Says we can help him close the net." Vince ground the brittle flakes between his fingers. "We've got a duty to our town."

"Yeah." Ben slapped on his cap. "Everything hit the fan when *they* showed up."

"Ain't wrong, that." Shifting the heavy satchel to her hip, Anna nudged Popeye with her boot.

I squatted for a furry hug, near suffocated by a stench like wet socks.

"You best get on too, lass."

"Give Jake a holler from me!" I called as she trudged across the street, Popeye ambling behind.

"She's all right, your granny." Vince dug a pack of cigarettes out of his jacket pocket. "Bet she'd want you to turn over the gun."

"What?" My breath caught.

"We saw her give it to you, that bird girl." He stuck a cigarette between his lips, clicked his lighter, once, twice,

"Yeah, the pier isn't the best place for fraternizing with the enemy," Ben added.

"She didn't give me any gun—and can't rightly say she's an enemy."

"You admit it then?" Vince took a drag from his cigarette, flicked the ashes. "That you're friends? I go out of my way to warn you that she's dangerous, and you blow me off. Ouch."

"So much for 'United we stand,'" Ben chimed.

"You've got it all wrong."

"Do we?" Vince thumped Ben's shoulder. "Gee, Ben, musta been another cowgirl we saw struttin' outta Gulch Run."

"Naww, this town ain't big enough for two cowgirls."

"Or two commies."

"Yeah, okay, I was there, but I was just—"

"Aiding and abetting? Look, I don't know what BS story your pal spun you, but plenty of us saw her kill the seal pup in cold blood. Holy"—Vince swore a word Mama would've doused with bleach—"she threatened to shoot *me*! Don't you give a damn?"

"Sure I do."

"Then why are you helping her hide the gun?"

"I'm n—she doesn't even speak English!"

"You don't have to defend yourself, Eden." Ben spoke gently. "Just give us the gun. It's evidence."

Vince nodded. "Hey, we get it. New kid on the block, kinda weir—different."

"Weird?"

"Like unique, y'know?" Ben offered.

"Exactly. It's easy to fall in with the wrong crowd, especially when things are rough at home. But now's your chance to do the right thing."

"I'm not weird!" I tossed my shoulders back. "Things are fine at home. And I don't know anything 'bout a gun."

Vince shrugged. "Suit yourself. Just hope the Russki doesn't put her next bullet through you."

I flinched. *And why not?* She'd trusted me with her secret, and I'd turned on her. "Why would she do that if we're friends?"

"Commies don't have friends. They have useful fools. And from where I'm standing, you're no longer useful."

"Come on, work with us." Ben inched closer. He had his mirrored sunglasses on now. "This doesn't have to get ugly."

"What's that supposed to mean?" The girl starin' back from his shades looked cool as Mama's sweet tea, not a thing like me.

"It's real simple, cowgirl." Vince blew a lasso-shaped smoke ring. "Either you help us put that freak away, or we tell the sheriff you're her accomplice."

"Hardly." But wasn't I? I hadn't meant to be, but somehow I found myself harboring her secret.

"Okay." Vince's smile didn't reach his eyes. "Gonna ask you one more time nicely. Where's the gun?"

Ben shifted uneasily from side to side.

Shrugging, I tried to push past Vince, but he stamped a harness boot onto the bench, hemming me in.

"Let me by." I winced at the stench of wool and sweat.

"We're not finished."

Almost in tandem, Ben flanked Vince, both guys so close I could count the pimples on Ben's nose, smell the tobacco stink of Vince's breath.

"You know, sweet thing" — Vince twirled a chunk of my hair 'round his finger — "you're not blond enough to play so dumb."

"Leave me alone!"

"Afraid I can't do that." He sighed, still twirling my hair. "We don't stand for commies, see? Until those two Russki moles started stirring things up, nobody had problems with nobody. Just a mind-your-own-damn-business American town, a little on the dull side" — he laughed — "nothing more criminal than rolling joints."

"Then *she* shoots a seal." Ben cracked his knuckles. "The Bolshie is armed and dangerous."

I swatted at the smoke in my face. "*You* ran her down in the school parking lot."

"The hell I—"

"That?" Vince grinned. "Ben got a tad too fired up, patriot that he is. Just a warning not to mess with our town. Right, Ben?"

"Yeah." Ben eyed the store. "C'mon, dude. Gonna miss Moretti."

"Moretti can wait. We got business here." He ground his cigarette butt into the wall, inches from my shoulder.

"Last chance. Give us the gun, and no one has to know you were in on it."

"In on *what*?" Even as I said it, I knew they were right. I *was* in on it.

Joe's face appeared at the window.

"Told you the blond thing isn't gonna work." Vince yanked my coiled hair, caught the wrist I lobbed at him, gripped hard.

"Ow! Let g—"

"Cool it, Vince." Ben jerked his head toward the window, but Joe's face had disappeared. I'd never been so sorry not to see him.

"You haven't got anything on me!" I spat. "You're just playin' Go Fish."

Vince laughed but let go my wrist. "Hear that, Ben? She thinks we're playing games." His eyes narrowed. "No one's playing games but you. That said, between two KGB spies, one pinko cowgirl, and your charity boyfriend, looks like I've got myself a full set."

"You're gonna scalp me!"

Though he released my hair, his leg still fenced me against the wall. "Guess you'd rather join your bird friend in a cage than protect your fellow Americans." He leaned within an inch of my face, his nicotine breath gagging me. "Or maybe we'll shake the gun out of that retard brother of your—*gah!*"

I jammed my elbow into Vince's ribs, doubling him over and shovin' my way free, only to collide with Ben, my thumb catching and twisting on a chain spilling from his crewneck.

"That's *it!*" Armed with a push broom and a death glare, Joe charged at us, the door flinging with such force it lodged open. "Git! The lot of you! You no-good, thievin' punks. I ever see you around here again, you'll be wishing your moms hadn't born you!"

Raising his hands in mock surrender, Vince swaggered backward, then lit across the street, Ben close behind. Though I hardly needed rescuing, I was mighty glad to have it anyway.

"You too." Joe wheeled toward me. "*Git!*"

By the time I climbed my porch steps, I was breathing easier, but my chest still thudded like a runaway mule. *In on it . . . her accomplice.* They'd watched us from the Old Clunker, saw us link up beneath the lamppost—Raven, me, and Hollis—took our bickering for conspiring. Fact was, they were right. Keeping her secret meant I *was* an accomplice, guilty as sin for stayin' quiet. Hollis and I had to beat 'em to the sheriff. Hollis—Lordy! The last thing he wanted, getting mixed up in it, but the very thing I needed. He'd have to help me now. Tomorrow couldn't come quick enough.

Lying in bed hours later, the motel sign flickering shadows 'cross my walls, I rubbed my thumb, sore where the cross had caught it, turnin' things over and over, wondering how chasing the truth had tangled me in a lie. The answer floated beyond reach as sleep pulled me under, the evening blurring like my vision. Only scents lingered, the odor of mangy dog, of cigarettes, the sickly mix of sweat and leather, and ever so faintly, the sharp, sweet fragrance of flowers.

Then, methought, the air grew denser, perfumed from an unseen censer—

My eyes flew open.

She'd been there—Raven! Before I could latch on to where or why, my breaths slowed, my eyelids drooped, and sleep overcame me.

TWENTY-NINE

By the time Hollis unhitched himself from carnival duties the next day, the sun had crested, and I was near beyond redemption, vexed and agitated.

I'd woken to a twilight moon, a crescent over the breakwater, and made my getaway through the back door, noting with relief that my father's car was nowhere in sight. Flumping onto Jake's towel, I'd eyed the bologna sandwich peeking from his canvas bag, my stomach rumbling.

"Say, Jake—"

"Back soon, Swee'Pea." He buckled his duffel. I supposed it was his flask wantin' protecting.

Nestled against a warm Popeye, I gnawed my lip as Jake waded into the surf, as he let the ocean take him, the waves slapping his ankles, swirling 'round his knees, swallowing his shoulders, washing the ache from his bones, fainter and farther into fog and foam. Scanning the horizon, a warp of pinks threaded between blues, I kept a lookout for sharks or spectral girls and commanded Popeye do the same. But I spotted only the bobbing smudges that were buoys, their bells clanging. A pelican flopped down near the surf, waddled on webbed feet, its head tufted yellow, its beak holding . . . what? I grumbled the fact of faulty eyes. Though the sun wasn't much more than a yawn, I fretted aloud that Jake was takin' too long, that Hollis was runnin' behind. A scruffy paw on my sore thumb hushed me, and I twirled Popeye's ear.

We saw him surface at long last, bit by bit—beard silvered with salt, brawny shoulders dappled with foam, thick legs a slog through the swells, the old fisherman rising from the sea, restored.

"How can you stand it, Jake? Ain'tcha frozen?" I passed him the towel Popeye and I had been sitting on.

"Head to toe and then some." He panted above me, his heaving chest covered with coarse gray hair. "Nothin' like being numb to make ya feel alive."

"Doesn't seem any point to aches and pains," I mused, "'cept to knock you to your knees. Least that's what the reverend says. Course, if that's where the Good Lord wants us, what'd he give us feet for?"

Though Jake snorted, he set furrowed eyes on me. "What's got you so gl-glum?"

"Nothin'."

"Gotta work on yer poker face, Swee'Pea." He could barely finish the words, his breath labored, his gruff voice thin.

"Nothin' a donut won't fix anyway." It wasn't right to burden him with my woes, seeing as how he was in a fight with his own body. "'Just a spoonful of sugar' an' all."

We sat a spell on the sand, watched the waves break, the dawn sky splinter gold, waited till Jake's breaths came regular again, till Popeye nudged him up and to the street. I tagged behind them to Lucky's, Jake dropping heavy onto the bench, sucking in sharp. He didn't let on, but I knew he wasn't near as numb as he was playing. Popeye felt it too, laying a paw, then another, then his whole head on Jake's lap.

"Callin' my bluff, eh, boy?"

Catching the quarter Jake tossed me, I scurried to the

newspaper stand by the laundromat and then to Beach Yum Donuts, buying a Boston cream donut and a cup of coffee—both paid for out of my poker winnings now that rustlin' up a dinghy was Hollis's detail.

Jake snuffed out a cigarette as he took the paper and coffee, and minding his orders to "keep my own company and not his," I busied myself with sucking the cream out of my donut, sharing my last bite with a panhandling Popeye.

We lazed on the sun-warmed bench a good half hour, Jake smoking his pack while reading the paper, Popeye flopped beneath us, me blowing pink bubbles, then peeling splats off my nose, worryin' the minutes like Rosa worried her rosary beads. As the morning wore on with no sight of Hollis, I wheeled from concern to annoyance to downright vexation. In the distance, the carnival stirred awake—crews hollering, machines whirring, a traffic controller blowing a whistle. From inside Lucky's came the clatter of window blinds snapping up, the slam of a cash register drawer. Joe poked out his head, dealt a grunt to Jake, a scowl to me, flipped the "closed" sign to "open."

Another quarter hour and Hollis's fate had taken a dire turn, his goose not just cooked but burnt. Jake had drifted into an uneasy sleep, head sagged forward, snores rattling his chest. Nothin' doing for the either of 'em, I paced the sidewalk, from Second Street to Front Street, down Front Street to the corner Rexall, and back again.

"Whoa—hello." A ranch hand steadied me. "Forget to turn on your blinker?" From his Stetson hat to his leather boots, clerical collar to belt buckle, bolo tie to blue jeans—and for a little extra shine, a wide grin and easy stride—the cowboy priest was a marvel of ministry.

"Sorry, sir. Wasn't payin' attention."

"Now, was that so hard?"

"What?"

"Confessing to a priest." Father Miguel laughed, his gaze falling on Jake. "Hmm, wait here. Just gonna duck inside." Tipping his hat, he turned into Lucky's.

"Well, I'll be tar-nated!" I plopped down next to Jake, who twitched and rumbled, a one-man band of wheezes and snurgles. *Will wonders never cease?* I wagered Father Miguel was fixin' to accessorize his priestly getup with a six-pack of Budweiser. But when he walked out, he carried only a flat paper bag.

"Fine cattle dog, this one." He scratched Popeye behind the ears.

"Naw, just an old circus dog."

"Now, maybe. But there was a time." He lifted the mutt's eyelid. "Looks like a bull got him."

"Ya don't say! A cowboy dog." I had a whole new respect for both dog and priest.

"Yessir, we all have a past. And sometimes it's brutal."

Jake burbled and popped open an eye.

"How are you, my friend?" Father Miguel rested a hand on Jake's shoulder. "Feeling all right?"

Jake's one eye blinked. "Feeling? Overrated. Not worth the having."

"I can think of better places than a bench to catch some z's."

Jake tried to rise but slumped back down. "Waitin' fer Anna. Ain't she come yet?"

"Not that I've seen." Though he spoke gently, Father Miguel's voice held worry. "You sure she's coming?"

"Can't remember." He tugged at his beard, his thick brows furrowed. "Aw, heck. S'posed to meet her at Smitty's."

"That's only 'bout three blocks from here," I said, having spotted Seadog Smitty hosin' down his fishing gear just the day before, right along with the neighbor's windows.

"That's an easy walk if you're up to it, Jake," Father Miguel coaxed. "Let's get you home."

At the word *home*, Popeye woofed and wriggled out from beneath the bench, plowing into my legs.

"C'mon, pardner. Heave-ho." Taking Jake by the elbows, we eased him to his feet.

Jake fussed some but let us steer him toward the edge of town. We didn't talk much—counted the trucks clattering away from the carnival, groused 'bout the skunk stink in the air, nudged Jake's wobbles with a repeated "attaboy."

We'd managed several blocks when Anna chugged by in her Woody, the station wagon pitching and clanking.

"Gots caught up at Mac's," she said as we bundled Jake inside, Popeye bounding into the cluttered back seat.

Shutting the passenger door, Father Miguel stuck his head through the open window and mumbled somethin'—a Hail Mary most like, which, thanks to Pedro, I'd learned was a rosary prayer for good luck. Roman Catholic though it was, the fact of it gave me comfort. Lord knew my prayers over Jake had more to do with winning the poker hand than winning his soul. I resolved then and there to pray for Jake's troubles before tendin' to my own.

"Hold up, Anna," Jake blurted, fumbling in his duffel bag.

"Pish!" Anna snorted, waving a bicycle around her car. "Got us a traffic jam."

"Here y'go." Jake stuck his arm out the window. "Go on—take it."

"But Jake—"

He slapped his bologna sandwich into my hand.

"Do somethin' about that belly racket, would ya? Anna's gonna force-feed me her fish-and-chips anyway—habanero hellfire."

"Ain't no better dread, you old mule." With another *pish!*, Anna peeled away from the curb.

As we watched them drive off, Father Miguel pulled the paper bag from his back pocket. "Postcards."

"What?"

"Postcards." He tipped the bag toward me. "My fridge is already stocked with beer." His grin flashed teeth too white for a smoker—or a drinker.

"You sure you're a priest, sir?"

"You sure you're not the vandal?" He laughed, then grew somber. "Good of you to care for Jake like you do."

Good I wasn't, leastways by Auca missionary standards, and come to think of it, if anyone was good to anyone, it was Jake to me.

"He's an old mule," I said. "And he don't mind I'm a young one."

Father Miguel laughed. "Sounds like a friendship made in heaven."

We parted ways at the next corner, Father Miguel swiveling to wave as I headed into town, his boots a tinny *clack, clack* along the pavement.

By noon and with no sign of Hollis despite having cased the town twice, I'd lathered myself into a panic, my ears on high alert for police sirens, my stomach a slurp of undigested bologna, and then a glimpse into Beach Yum Donuts had me turn heel and duck into the laundromat. Sitting at the counter, chattin' with the bakery girl, was Sheriff Moretti.

Con-demmit! My heart thumped hard against my ribs, though what I was so worked up about, I didn't know. Reckoned it was my guilt tumbling like the clothes in the washing machines, wanting yet not wanting to confess to the sheriff. For all my morning frets, I hadn't spotted Raven—or Vince and Ben, for that matter. What could I tell Sheriff Moretti? That I'd seen the gun? *You sure you saw a gun? With your screwy eyesight? In the moonlight of a cave? A star with a circle? Lucky to see that through a magnifying glass.*

I had nothing.

"Lordy, it's like Hurricane Beulah done set up camp here," I muttered to the dryers, a row of rattling cyclopes, the sweltering steam and thick fumes of Tide chasing me outside. Raking my hair over my face, I scurried down to the beach.

I'd bored of the swings and was dragging a stick through the sand, lookin' for an unbroken shell, when Hollis vaulted over the sea wall and near on top of me, his lunch sack spilling from his back pocket.

"Hey, Scoot!"

A bottle cap at my feet riveted me, so much so that it rendered me deaf.

"Sorry about this morning," Hollis said, giving it another go. "Guess you're sore at me."

Before I'd decided whether to notice him, he scooped up the cap and flipped it like a quarter. "Heads!" he called, catching it on the back of his hand.

That got him a glower.

"Had to work the carnival." He lobbed the cap into a trash can and plopped onto a swing. "Crews needed an extra hand. But"—he winked—"I got us some comp tickets."

"Us?"

"Sure. For the rides tomorrow night."

Though plenty nice of him, he wasn't getting off so easy.

"I'm not riding anything that leaves the ground."

"What fun is that? I was thinking we'd hit the Ferris wheel first." He grinned and then grew sober. "So have you seen her?"

I was fixin' to lay into him when the foolishness of doing so gave me pause. The fact was that Hollis hadn't a lick of reason to help me track Raven, as far as *he* knew anyhow, or to rustle up a dinghy. A further fact was that she hadn't showed anyway. And the final, most persuasive fact was that, obliging as he was, he might prefer an afternoon of fishing to my badgering, never mind that mine was a righteous wrath. Reelin' Hollis in meant casting slow and steady.

"Not yet." I unwrapped a wad of bubble gum and squinted at the comic. "I'm Bazooka Joe. You're Jane. 'Knock, knock.'"

"Who's there?"

"'Opportunity.'"

"Opportunity?"

"'Don't be silly, Jane. Opportunity only knocks once.' Well, would ya look at that. Confirmation in a comic strip."

Hollis groaned. "You still wanna follow her?"

"Lordy, Hollis. We have to!" Though a touch of ire seemed justified, I checked my tone. "I don't have a choice now. They think I'm in on it." *And you too*, I didn't add.

"Guess you better tell me then."

So I did, recounting my run-in with Vince and Ben, leaving nothing out about me and everything about Hollis.

He listened without a word as we strolled the pier, his slate eyes distant, his jaw like stone. I spilled the details pell-mell, muddling up the order a bit, interrupting myself with afterthoughts, changing details I couldn't rightly recall, dodging the ones that implicated him, a haphazard tellin' with almost no room to breathe. But Hollis asked no questions. Not until we were seated on a couple ice chests midway down did he say anything, and only then after staring out to sea for a good long while.

"They bother you again, you let me know."

"Joe had my back."

"I mean it."

"Okay, fine—er, thanks."

He stopped wringing his hat and punched it back into shape. Calluses padded his fingers, most like from tying knots and baiting hooks, or maybe from swinging his dad's hammer and sawing wood, the back of his hand sporting reddish scrapes and a flaky scab. I waited till he cinched his hat back over his windblown locks.

"That all you've got to say?"

A paunchy fisherman snored on a bench beside us, his rods propped high against the railing.

"Could be a bluff." Hollis studied a bag of pickle spears rummaged from his crumpled lunch sack.

"How do you figure?" I knew enough to know that until you called it, you didn't know a bluff for a bluff. It was a hunch till then.

"Doesn't add up. And Vince is bad news." He sounded just like Joe.

"Only if you're on the wrong side of 'im."

"And you're not?"

"You know I'm not. I'm no pinko."

"It's not what you are or aren't. It's what he thinks you are."

"Then he's the dumb blond." I felt my cheeks flush, my skin bristle. "Why would they wanna bluff anyway? They're patriots."

"Yeah? It's a fine line between patriot and vigilante." He swallowed the last of his pickles. "Snooping after Raven, that's one thing. But keep away from Vince."

If I'd been ready with a snappy retort, his face would have shut me right up. As it was, I opted for spitting my gum over the railing and unwrapping a fresh piece.

From our ice-chest seats, we commanded a wide sweep of the horizon, east toward hidden inlets and caves, south 'cross a shimmer of sea, and west to the rocky breakwater. We watched a small truck jounce to the Bait and Tackle Shack, the driver hopping out to unload fishing gear. Just beyond the shop, cables dangled from winches, below them the hatch to the dock.

"What do you mean, vigilantes?" I pressed.

"Saving Raven's uncle from burning to death mighta made them heroes, but they still view the guy as a threat." His tone was somber. "Bet they'll stop at nothing now. Dead set on protecting the town from the Red Scare, a.k.a. him and Raven—and now you."

I couldn't figure how partying in the ravine made anyone a hero. If they'd reached the house five minutes later, Raven's uncle would've died. Reckoned running through flames to save a life gave a body the right to feel like hot stuff. I smirked. And now I supposed Vince had moved on from James Dean and fancied himself Clint Eastwood, takin' matters into his own hands. He'd lasso Raven before she could shoot again—that's what he'd promised Heather. Playing bounty hunter was all fine and dandy long as my neck stayed clear of the rope.

"Any which way, I gotta get that gun to the sheriff, and quick-like. Otherwise, it'll look like I *am* an accomplice."

"Are you?"

My gum lodged in my throat. "Wh-*what?*"

"Think about it, Eden. Where were you when the seal was shot?"

"In bed."

"Anyone see you?"

"Who sees you when you're in bed?"

"Maybe you wandered down to the beach early that morning. Same as you do when you meet up with Jake and Popeye."

"Wouldn't they have seen me? Or Mayor Mac?"

"Maybe."

"Whose side are you on anyway?"

"Where were you when the shed caught fire?"

"She didn't give me the gun."

"*I* know the truth. But you got too close. You were at the church after it got tagged. At the beach after the seal was shot. At her shed. In the cave with her. Who's to say you're not covering for her?"

"Why would I do that?"

"Why was she waiting for you at the dock?"

His question pulled me up short. Why *was* she waiting for me at the dock?

"What are you saying? That she's tryin' to frame me?"

He removed his hat, punched it twice, tugged it back over his matted curls. "Dunno. I'm just not sure you're reading the cards right."

"Then help me get the gun. You said you'd handle the dinghy. By gum, I'll *stea*—borrow one if I have to!"

"Don't you ever listen? Told you I'm not going ashore."

"If we're gonna help Sheriff Moretti"—*and me*—"we have to follow her. At least to see where she goes."

"Holy smokes, Eden. You ever consider that's exactly

what the guys want, for you to lead them to her? She's too slippery for them—but you, you're like bait on a hook. They'll catch you both red-handed."

That was a wild card I never saw coming—maybe 'cause there aren't any in Texas Hold'em. Or Go Fish. Alligator jaws gripped my chest. "Got any better ideas?"

"Yeah. Leave it alone."

"Leave it alone? You promised to help me."

"Helping you looks different today than it did yesterday."

There was nothin' more to say, that was plain as day. Hollis had reneged on his offer to take me to the caves. Whatever I had to do, I had to do alone.

THIRTY

HOLLIS COULD SIT only so long on the metal chest, his legs bunched up and restless, before he up an' left me, ambling over to lean beside a fisherman baiting a line, most like wishing he had his rod. With a whistle at a young boy's catch, he helped wrangle the thrashing fish loose with a pair of pliers, then loped down the pier to untangle a busty girl's line from a kelp bed. I'd never fill out a halter bikini top.

With no Hollis to pester and no Raven to trail, I paced the planks, crossing them with care. But avoiding the gaps meant looking down, and looking down meant seeing the frenzied sea. Feeling queasy, I flopped back onto the ice chest, soon to spring up again and start all over. Like a coon dog waitin' on a hunt, Mama would've said. I paced, sat, paced, caught bits of small talk, braced against the occasional gust of salty wind. The odor of fish guts and seaweed only made me feel more sick.

"Reeled in four black perch this morning." At first glance, the voice seemed to come from a jellyfish, the man's white hair hanging from a sock cap in stringy patches. "Six yesterday." His words creaked and wobbled, and I figured him to be as old as the barnacled pier pilings.

"Yeah?" someone else said.

"Been a good week for 'em."

"Where they biting?"

"Second pier. See those crossbeams? Just up from 'em. Shallow end."

"Don't know nothin' 'bout that pier, but me and Hank seen a school of rockfish here last night," a woman's voice cut in. "Got a dozen strikes right off. Took in eight, 'bout yea big."

The afternoon stretched on like that, lazy as a yawn, unruffled by my pacing, and still no sign of Raven.

"Condemnation," I muttered, watching the sun scatter itself across whitecaps as it arced toward the farthest pier. Plopping on a bench, the wood bird-splattered and flaking, I helped myself to Smitty's buckets, flippin' 'em over and resting a foot on each, not a bit the lady. My insides felt sour as one of Hollis's pickles and shook up, like the baking soda volcanos we made in grammar school. That got me to thinking about Hope House, wondering if the staff made baking soda volcanos for the kids. Wouldn't that be a hoot for Dex!

I reckoned he'd be there 'bout now, in the jungle-themed classroom, slapping at Magic Bubbles—"a tracking exercise for hand-eye coordination"—or bouncing across therapy mats. Even as I pictured him at play, I sighed, seeing the lie of it in the dipping sun. Fact was, he'd be home now, school long over, Rosa changing a last dirty diaper, Antonio's horn blastin' a Spanish curse, Mama scraping clumps of macaroni and cheese off the walls, scribbling red notes in her textbooks, and me—me, way out yonder and then some, shirking my duties, just a possum playin' dead.

Still, every kid should get to watch a volcano erupt, retarded or not.

A yelped *Got 'im!* jarred me out of myself, but only for a moment, and then I was back to ruminating. Why hadn't she come? Or had she? Slipped out at the crack of dawn, steered unseen to the hidden coves, stripped the cave of every trace of her crimes. I kicked at a pigeon grubbing for bait scraps, flinching as it flapped up an' over me. Didn't matter which way I read the cards, seemed like they were stacked against me.

The fishermen started to pack up their gear, stowing lures and sinkers in tackle boxes, gathering buckets filled with the day's catch. Still, I waited.

By the time Hollis made his way back, the emerald sea had deepened into twilight blue.

"Smitty's heading out. Needs his buckets." He rapped my knee.

I let my legs drop, but not without a huff. "I'm not leaving."

"Didn't say you had to."

"Maybe she's waitin' for it to get dark."

I might've been the groan of a rusty fish hoist, the way Hollis paid no mind, sauntering to the faucet to rinse tackle, throwing fish guts over the railing. I'd hoped he'd argue with me, see that I couldn't be persuaded, relent his stubborn ways, and sit with me till sunset if need be. Or even better, rustle us up a dinghy. But the only arguing he did was with a feisty jacksmelt determined to hurtle out of the ice chest.

"Think I'll sit a spell longer."

"Suit yourself." Hollis handed the nested buckets to a shriveled stump of a man who snorted and wheezed as he plunked them inside four others.

"Got meself loaded down." Smitty grinned widely, revealing a stretch of toothless gums, and dug in his coverall pockets. Out came a ball of twine, two knives, rusty pliers, one rubber glove, several orange bobbers, a pair of broken sunglasses, and a small radio. He set the jumble inside the top bucket.

Hollis chuckled. "Those are some deep pockets. What happened to your tackle box?"

"Oh yeah, lots! Fish were bitin' all right." Smitty gave a thumbs-up.

"Tackle box, Smitty, tackle box! What happened to it?"

"Eh? Oh. Hinge broke off."

"Better get yourself a new one."

"Sure did. Caught me a real big 'un." Beaming, Smitty hobbled off, the bucket tower near toppling him. When Hollis joined him, plucking the topmost buckets to dangle beside his own, I realized I no longer wanted to suit myself.

"Why didn't she come today?" I said, catching up to them. "Where is she?"

"Maybe the hospital?" At my blank look, Hollis added, "With her uncle."

"You mean the one she tried to murder?"

He arched a salt-flecked brow. "Last I heard, he was recovering at Laguna Vista."

I'd been tossing around the possibilities, but that was as far-fetched as a hog flyin'. Raven visiting her uncle? He was a Soviet spy, a KGB operative, a gun smuggler, hard-drinking, hard-swearing, working her to the bone, more comrade than family—

Hollis seemed to read my thoughts. "You ever met him?"

"No."

"You ever seen him?"

"No. But he aimed a gun at Ben. A Kalinkadink."

His other brow spiked. "Sure that's a gun?"

"All the guys saw it, pointing straight at 'em from an upstairs window."

"You see it too?"

"No. But I saw the ammo in the shed."

Hollis slowed, fixed on something past the yellow caution tape.

"What?"

"That pigeon."

I squinted, trying to see what he was seeing.

"It's missing a leg."

"Huh. Wonder what happened."

"Maybe tangled itself in some fishing line. Or could be it was born that way."

"Well, I sure wouldn't be hoppin' on one leg near the railing."

"You would if you had wings." As he spoke, the pigeon flicked its feathers, a shimmer of greens and purples, spread its wings, and flapped off. "See? Makes no difference in flight." Hollis lit into a whistle, soft and airy.

We'd just caught up to Smitty when a harbor patrol truck rolled slowly past us, the driver waving folks aside, and stopped three-quarters down the pier. After shouting a few stragglers clear, two men began unloading barricades beside the safety cones, placing them end to end, a row of striped wooden sawhorses.

"'Bout time," I said. "It's a wonder no one's fallen overboard."

"Probably prepping for the fireworks. At least they're letting people on." Hollis held up a hand. "Listen. It's started."

From beyond the crisscrossed slope of streets, above the rooftops of souvenir shops and greasy spoons, came the tinny tunes of carnival music.

"Think I'll head over," he continued, plunking Smitty's buckets back on the tower and patting the old codger goodbye. "I'm under orders to win stuffed animals for my sisters."

"Wish I could come." I allowed my voice a note of self-pity. "Gotta watch Dex tonight."

"We'll go tomorrow. That is, if I don't spend all my money tonight." He jingled a handful of coins in his pocket. "Might have some left for you—unless I need caramel corn."

I gave him a flat tire, laughing as he splashed me with fish water from his bucket.

"Don't forget to watch the fireworks!" he called, hopping away while tugging his shoe back on. "They'll be shootin' 'em from the barges at nine thirty. And no fog tonight!"

I watched him jog across the street, wave at Joe standing outside Lucky's, then melt into a gathering crowd.

What a bust today had been, and now tonight too, stuck at home with Dex, waiting for the hammer to fall. Takin' my sweet time while it was still mine, I tromped to the swings, but they were swarming with Brownies. The little girls sat two on a seat, their yellow scarves fluttering like butterfly wings against their brown dresses. Drawn by the charred tang of an outdoor grill, I neared the firepits, where a posse of teens roasted hot dogs, their surfboards propped against the sea wall. Beyond them, other teens, sun-bleached an' coated in sand, bumped volleyballs over the sagging nets, called shots, their faces too blurry to make out. A sour whiff of booze halted me, steered me toward the surf, but not before I caught sight of the Old Clunker, parked by the sea wall. A few spaces over, Vince's tricked-out motorcycle rested on its kickstand.

Slogging through the sudsy foam, I tramped under the pier, then hauled myself up the stairs to Front Street, meandering in the general direction of my house. The carnival sounds grew dim but still bewitched me—the jangled swells of music, the rumble and groan of rides, the bellow of hawkers and buyers. I found myself again envying Hollis's carefree ways, his answering to no one and nothing, 'cept maybe the tides and his mom's summons for chores, his dad's for repair jobs, and consoled myself that at least he'd made room in his unfettered days for me.

What I didn't envy was his breezy lack of curiosity—and math skills. *Doesn't add up*, pish! I'd worked the sums just fine, excepting I'd somehow gotten added in the final tally, but I was fixin' to subtract myself real soon.

Con-tarnit! Where *had* Raven gone off to? It'd take more imagination than I could muster to see her comforting her uncle in the hospital. Now *that* didn't add up.

"Hey, watch it!" Two girls flounced from a boutique, forcing me to swerve into the street.

"Sorry," I mumbled, but the girls moved with me, blocking my path.

Ugh. As if running into Vince and Ben outside Lucky's hadn't been unlucky enough, now Heather and Trish faced me, hoggin' the sidewalk. They crossed their arms and thrust out a hip, the pair of 'em gussied up like the new Malibu Barbie. Heather's hair geysered into a flaming ponytail that spilled down her shoulders, on her lips a screaming shade of purple lipstick right off Pedro's parrot. Trish flaunted a bleached-blond pageboy. They both wore tie-dye halter tops tight across their chests and hip-huggers adorned with rhinestones.

"What's the hurry?" The voice I'd heard over the rush of Diablo Creek carried no trace of a quaver.

"No hurry." *Y'all ever thought of doublin' as mannequins?* I pictured their jutted hips flanking the bikini-clad torso in the shop window.

"Going to the carnival tonight?" Pursing her fuchsia lips,

Heather regarded my windblown hair, baggy sweater, and mud-streaked jeans.

"What's it to you?"

"Just being friendly, that's all."

Pulling a fistful of lollipops from her purse, Trish held them out to me. Heather selected a Tootsie Pop, cherry like her nails. Trish unwrapped a grape one. "Sorry, no more Tootsie Pops. Want a Dum Dum?"

"No thanks."

"You don't like lime? How 'bout lemon?"

"I like lime just fine, but I don't want it."

"Save it for later." She pressed a green lollipop into my hand, smiled.

"We're headed to the carnival." Heather's lips had turned a sticky magenta. "Wanna come?"

"Yeah, yar shard jorn ursh!" Trish burbled, uncorking the Tootsie Pop from her mouth.

"Uh . . ." *First lollipops and now the carnival? What gives?* "No thanks."

Heather sighed, dropped her gaze. "I know we've never clicked, but only 'cause we don't really know you." She looked up. "Right, Trish?"

Trish gave a vigorous nod, her side-swept bangs falling across her face. "We wanna make it up to you," she chimed, reclipping them. "It'll be fun!"

"What about your boyfriends?"

"Whart barfronds?"

Heather met Trish's giggle with a frown. "All the guys are surfing tonight. Wanna watch the fireworks from the water. Fine by us. We could use a break from those bozos."

"Vince, anyway," Trish blurted with an eye roll. "On and off, those two."

"We're gonna hang with the girls tonight. Jules, Alison, Tiffany—"

"And you," Trish finished, twisting her lollipop in her mouth. "If you come."

Me, hang with the girls?

"Uhh, no. But thanks."

"Aw, c'mon, don't be a fuddy-duddy," Heather ribbed as I brushed past Trish. "You don't know what you're missing."

Missing? A lump formed in my throat, and jamming the lollipop into my pocket, I trudged up the hill. That was exactly the trouble. I knew only too well what I was missing. Our shoddy rental in sight, I broke into a jog, returning far later than I'd meant to. Mama would be fryin' up chicken, running the bathwater, shoving her stocking feet into white oxfords, all while beseeching heaven to bring her delinquent child home. Nothing had gone right today.

I heard her heels first.

"Eden, wait!" Heather snatched my elbow, spinning me to a stop under the streetlight. A glance down Front Street showed Trish chatting with the shopkeeper as she locked up.

"I'm not going, okay?"

"There's something you should know." Her breath washed warm and cherry sweet across my face. "About the bird girl."

"What is it?"

"Not here." She ducked her head as a car rolled by, her words rushed. "I can't be seen talking to you."

"Why not?"

"Look, I'm sorry the guys cornered you. Ben is a ret— dunce. And Vince can be a real jerk. But he's spooked." Heather lowered her voice, the surge and break of waves muffling her words. "It's twisted enough, trashing the church and shooting a seal, but she straight-up threatened him. He's convinced you know something."

"Well, I don't."

"I believe you. That's why I want to help."

"You wanna help *me*?"

"Not just you, but Vince too. He's gonna get himself killed trying to protect our town."

"Sounds like a discussion for your boyfriend."

"Vince won't listen to me. Hothead's already taken matters into his own hands." She scanned the shore, the street, leaned in. "I can help. But I gotta be sure I can trust you."

"I'm all ears." Like as not, Heather was blowin' smoke, but if anyone knew Vince's next move, she did.

"Not here." She hugged herself, shifted her stance. "At the carnival."

"Never mind then. I call a bluff." I started up my yard.

"Sure you wanna risk juvie?"

I halted mid-step.

"Meet me at the Ferris wheel tonight, nine o'clock." The hiss in her voice sent a shiver down my spine. "Unless you'd rather take the fall."

Heather didn't wait for a reply, darting into the shadows that lined the street, her suede platforms a quick tap toward the shops. I stood rooted in my yard, a queasy feeling risin' in my stomach, same as when I walked the pier alone. I watched her link arms with Trish, thought I heard shrill giggles, kept watching as they faded into the evening, on the breeze the faint scent of citrus hairspray. She'd played a card I knew I needed.

Meeting Heather at the Ferris wheel was impossible. Duty called.

THIRTY-ONE

STEPPING INTO THE house was like stepping into a promise of fleece slippers, the misted chill of the dark street and all the night's uncertainty falling away at the smell of fried chicken an' biscuits, the chatter of a radio host, the warm glow of the hall light. But it was a promise gone back on, same as Hollis had done me, whisked away by a familiar sense of misery as I laid eyes on a kitchen cluttered with pans, heard water splashin' in the bathtub, spotted a laundry basket teeming with wrinkled clothes, and knew the shabby rental for the imposter it was.

Tailing my shadow—a barefoot silhouette against the hallway wall—I padded toward the bathroom, drawn by the scent of lavender soap, by Mama's coaxes, Dex's gurgles and grunts. And also repelled. Mama didn't bother waiting any-more. She'd fed and bathed Dex without me. His coos told me she hadn't yet washed his hair.

"Praise be, Eden, do miracles never cease?" Mama poured water over a wriggling Dex, no reproach in her voice, though I would have felt a whole lot better for it. A harness secured him in his tub chair, his ribs straining beneath papery skin. The chair wobbled as he slapped at a rubber duck floatin' on the fizz of bubbles 'round his waist.

"He's too big for that chair." At my voice, Dex raised his head and searched the room, his maple eyes unfocused.

"Heya, Dexie. Having fun?" I gave him a gentle noogie.

Throwing back his head, he let loose a roof-raisin' hoot, smacking the water into tidal waves.

"Works all right when there's two of us." Mama squeezed the washcloth and handed it to me. "He liked his mashed 'tatoes so much he decided to wear them. Steady him for me, please."

My knees pressed into the tile floor, I held his legs as Mama tipped a pitcher over his head. Though she shielded his eyes from the trickle, he gasped, his squeals giving way to splutters, his splutters to wails.

"Dex, darlin', Mama's got to wash you." She stroked his sticky tangles under the tepid stream. "It's not becomin' for a gentleman to have potato in his hair." The gentleman shrieked more loudly. "That soap smells like a dream, doesn't it, honey?"

"Lawdy, you're gonna bust Sissy's eardrums!" I dabbed his eyes with the washcloth as Mama drizzled baby shampoo over his curls.

"Eden Mae, did I just hear you take the Lord's name in vain?"

"No, Mama, I was implorin' him, same as the Good Book instructs."

She had no choice but to let the matter go. Dex howled bloody murder, his small body convulsing under my grip, fat tears welling beneath the washcloth, squalling the fury of the double-crossed as Mama lathered his hair with one hand and tipped the pitcher with the other, water drenching my shirt.

"My, my, such a fuss." Mama rinsed the last of the suds from his shoulders, patted his blotchy face dry. "Hush now, darlin'. All done."

Lifting him from the tub, we cocooned him in a fluffy towel. While I blotted his *no more tears*–scented locks, Mama buttered his skin with lotion, planting soft kisses on his quivering cheeks. His wrenching sobs simmered into sporadic gulps as she dusted cornstarch under his arms, inside his thighs, between his toes. He'd be plumb tuckered out by the time we clipped his toenails, swabbed his ears, and snapped on his Big Bird pajamas—as would we.

Then as he slept, Mama's whispered prayers could finally be for herself, for the grace of a second wind to carry her through the evening shift at the clinic. Bathing Dex had become a Saturday affair, with nightly sponging the rest of the week, but a midweek purgation wasn't unusual given the spills and messes and calamities that beset our lives.

It took some doing to pry Dex's arms off my neck, his legs from around my waist, and settle him onto his mattress, the floral fragrance of him filling my nostrils. Before Mama could tuck a blanket over him, his head jerked up, dewy eyes searching for us, pained.

"Looks like he's holdin' a grudge." Mama tucked Aslan into the crook of his elbow. "When you change his diaper, use the ointment. Powder's too dryin'."

"Mm-hmm."

"And brush his teeth."

"I know."

"And there's laundry to fold. I didn't have time." She said it like an apology.

"Yes, okay." I trailed her into the hallway, feeling I ought to say something, explain my whereabouts, offer up some remorse, confess with the apostle Paul that the spirit was willing but the flesh was weak—but my transgressions plagued me plenty without adding flat-out lying.

"I'll be home by midnight, 'less we're short-staffed again." She switched off the radio and grabbed her coat. "There's pudding settin' in the fridge." Her hand on the doorknob, she paused and tilted her head "Music?"

"From the carnival. Starts tonight."

"Uhngung gung!" Dex sang from the playbed.

"Don't forget his cough syrup, one tablespoon. And check—"

"Mama!"

Slamming the front door against the sputter of her leaky Corvair, I stomped into the kitchen, tinkly melodies breezing through the open window, dumped the fried chicken and mashed 'tatoes into Tupperware, telling myself I didn't deserve even a lick, shoved them beside the chocolate pudding in the fridge, sprayed down the counters, rammed the chairs under the table, and filled the sink with soapy water, dunkin' pots and pans into the bubbles, dishes and cups, forks and spoons, scrubbing them one by one, rinsing them, flicking them dry, stacking them, and letting Dex wail himself into prostration, into quiet, into that sleep Mama promised would come.

He'd wearied me good, and I wasn't 'bout to jump every time he hollered.

Fishing my sketchbook from the laundry basket, somehow tossed in with my dirty clothes and rescued by Mama from a watery end, I curled up on the couch and turned to a fresh page. With the flat edge of my pencil, I shaded the grainy paper, working fast but gentle, line blending into line, the charcoal gliding 'cross the paper, aimless. Dex breathed noisily, on the air an odor like spoiled milk, the telltale sign of soiled diapers.

Beneath my pencil, the shadows took on dimension,

fashioned a tapered arc, the sweeps dipping into smudges in mirror image, arch reflected under arch, a lake of white between them. Lifting my pencil, I waded into the lake, rippling it with unbroken swirls like the rings of Saturn, then left the galaxy to sweep bold strokes out from the arches, velvety, mascara-black lashes above, a smoky fringe of curves below, and an eye emerged—the cool, haughty eye of Heather.

Meet me at the Ferris wheel tonight, nine o'clock.

Dex's chirps told me his battery had recharged, enough to keep me up till midnight. I'd need a stiff chew of Bazooka to get me through. Rootin' in my pocket, my fingers bumped against the lollipop Trish had forced on me. I ferreted it out, along with two quarters, three pieces of gum, my lipstick, and a barrette, and dumped the lot on the couch. One by one I replaced my pocketful of whatnots—all but the lollipop. *That* I stashed behind a pillow.

"Uhng uhng!" Dex had hauled himself to his knees and was swatting the marble beads, spinning 'em into blue whirls. One lucky smack landed his fingers on the top rail, where holding fast, he hoisted himself to his feet. *One Mississippi, two Mississippi, three Mississippi*—thud! Over he toppled, his fall cushioned by a menagerie of stuffed animals. Without his braces, his legs were those of a marionette.

"S'pose you want out, Dexie." I wrinkled my nose at the yellow goo seeping into his pajama bottoms. "Law-aw-dee, how do you manage to stink so much?"

Using a tore-up dishrag and mountain of cotton balls, I cleaned him best I could, restraining him with one hand and yanking on a fresh Pampers, all while bellowing umpteen verses of "The Wheels on the Bus," minus the motions.

"A person only has so many hands," I scolded Dex, who'd latched onto a fistful of my hair.

The carnival spilled through the kitchen window—brass bands blaring, rides whizzing, kids whooping—swept down the hallway, surged into the front room, and with them, the woodsy aroma of barbecued ribs, the burnt sweetness of caramel corn. Headlights flickered through the slanted blinds, a rumbling parade of cars seekin' somewhere to park. Folks roamed the sidewalk, snatches of chatter and laughter ebbing and flowing with the sea. But no scent was stronger than that of citrus, and no sound louder than the echo of Heather's words. *There's something you should know.*

Leaving Dex splayed on the floor, I marched into the kitchen and banged the window shut. Above the stove, the clock hands crept toward eight.

Meet me at the Ferris wheel tonight, nine o'clock.

But I couldn't. I wouldn't.

For the next hour, I amused Dex, building towers just to knock down all the blocks, singing along with his Golden records, playing peekaboo. Whatever card Heather had could wait. Fact was, my hand wasn't half-bad. And luck had dealt me an ace with that hoopla of a carnival workin' the sheriff overtime. Once I got to the cave, I'd throw down my cards for the win. And get to the cave I would, come hell or high water, and sooner rather than later. Tonight, I'd stick to the business of entertaining Dex and shake Heather out of my head.

Without Mama to furrow her brow, I sat Dex on the couch and spooned pudding into his mouth, letting it dribble down his shirt but catching it before it splattered onto the cushions. Near starved from renouncin' dinner, I helped myself to a double portion, one small bite for Dex, two large bites for Sissy, and a splotch or two for the armrest.

Full up, I slung him onto my hip, carted him to the bathroom, wiped his drool, brushed his teeth—ditching the toothpaste, which he would only eat anyway—dug out a Superman pajama bottom from the laundry basket, and trekked back to the living room.

"There's gonna be fireworks tonight, Dexie. Just like on the Fourth, 'member? You 'bout rattled my molars loose with all your squawkin'." I strapped his glasses to his head.

His diaper only soggy this time, it was an easy change. With Superman zooming toward Big Bird, I switched off the table lamp, shucked him onto the couch, and knelt beside him. Leaning against the back cushions, I raised the blinds. No light streamed from the streetlight—or any of the streetlights along Front Street, the shore a ribbon of black. Fixin' for the fireworks, I reckoned. Stars dotted the inky sky, glimmering like a thousand shards of glass.

"Ooh, Dexie! Look!"

Dex bounced and flung his arms, knocking his glasses sideways.

"Hold still. There. Okay, now look at the water." I pointed but couldn't be sure of Dex's roaming eyes. "See the pretty lights?" Two barges floated between the near buoy and the pier, twinkling like Christmas trees. "Lucked out tonight—clear skies!"

Casting the pillows aside to prop Dex higher, I felt something bump against my shin—the lollipop. I snatched it before it could sink between the seat cushions, cocked my arm to try Hollis's *swish!* into the trash, then paused. So what if Trish had given it to me? So what if I didn't much like her? I liked lollipops. Unwrapping the candy, I stuck it in my mouth, puckering at the sour lime. It was just a stupid Dum Dum.

"Ooh, a flare! The boats are gettin' ready to shoot the fireworks!"

Dex squealed, pitching so sudden that I had to grab his pajama bottoms.

"You an' me, Dexie Day"—I snugged his glasses again, his eyes wide as ginger snaps behind the thick lenses—"we're gonna watch the whole show."

Unhitching the arms 'bout to choke me out, I laid him flat on the cushions, pinning him with an elbow while I groped under the couch. "Front row seats on the sea wall, Dexie. What you say to that, heh?" I worked fast, strapping his braces over his pajamas, buckling his orthopedic shoes, hefted him into his wheelchair, his tumbleweed body near twice its weight.

"Uhngung gung!"

"Doggone right! A walk with Sissy *and* fireworks! Just as soon as I'm back."

I squinted at the clock as I wedged his wheelchair between the couch and the bookcase, his hands slapping at the window but missin' by a mile. Fishing for his seat buckle, I caught sight of an upside-down Aslan in the playbed and, grabbing the knotted tail, nestled the lion into his lap.

"Here ya go, wiggle worm." I cupped his face and trained it out to sea. "Till I get back, you and Aslan are gonna watch all the pretty lights. Just got some business first, quick as a hiccup. I won't be long, Dexie. I promise. Only long enough."

Not bothering to grab my jacket, I bolted out the front door and down the porch steps, pausing at the sidewalk to glance at the house.

Dex sat framed in the window, a cameo against the dark, and for one heartbeat, I hesitated. A sportscar hummed past, its headlights washin' over him, painting his face ivory, tinging his hair gold, and though I could not hear him, I could see that he was laughing and whooping at the glittery night.

Five minutes, ten at the most. Front row seats. But I would be back before the fireworks started.

I'd promised.

THIRTY-TWO

A HURRIED LOOK at Front Street told me all I needed to know, folks clogging the sidewalks thick as molasses, swarming the shore and crowding the pier, tussling for spots to watch the fireworks. I spun 'round to run the back streets instead. Chasing the hill past the Sea Crest Motel, I veered left and sprinted down three dimly lit blocks of shuttered shops and shadowed houses, dodgin' cars snaking off the highway, skirting a construction site and cutting through an alley. At the corner, two men having a smoke sounded an awful lot like Pedro and Ernesto. Hobbled by a side ache, I trotted the last stretch, panting under the archway of colorful balloons that marked the carnival entrance. My stomach seethed with lime and chocolate pudding.

Where had sprawled the town's only public parking lot rose a vast playground of revelry, an unfolding cornucopia of rides, game booths, and concession stands. Lights sparkled and pulsed, molten reds and burnished yellows, currents of electric green. Roller coasters howled in whiplash loops, streaked 'cross the charcoal sky, thundered with screams at the click-clack that meant *plunge*, plummeted to earth.

For three Mississippi counts, I teetered on second thoughts, half a mind to beat a hasty retreat, to fend off the neon tendrils jolting the machinery alive and reachin' for me, to slink home in a narrow escape from temptation, from the curiosity that had lured me here and the guilt that would follow me back. Just three Mississippi counts.

Meet me at the Ferris wheel tonight, nine o'clock. Unless you'd rather take the fall.

I won't be long, Dexie. I promise. Only long enough.

A cacophony smothered my thoughts, carnies calling out winning scores, riders bellowing from bumper cars, parents cheering on jittery children. A stone's throw away, cackles and snorts erupted from a gaggle of teens, the girls licking ice cream cones, the boys flickin' each other's heads. Kids from the valley, I figured, scouring their faces, finding no Heather.

Above them, ablaze with incandescent bulbs, towered a ring of fire—the Ferris wheel.

Without my pearl-faced Seiko, I couldn't be sure of the time. A gift from my father for my thirteenth birthday, the watch hadn't left my wrist for a year. Now it lay buried in an unpacked box, along with the other remnants of a life reduced to memories, a scrapbook of newspaper clippings and faded photographs.

Meet me . . . at the . . . Ferris wheel . . . meet me . . . at the . . . Ferris wheel.

The words clanged in the whir of the Octopus ride, its steel tentacles hoisting cars up, droppin' 'em down, a cold mechanical grind. My hands over my ears, I pushed through the crowd.

Churning the night sky, the Ferris wheel glinted metallic jade, hulked over me as I approached the ticket booth. Marquee lights flashed a swim of words to a shimmery Beach Boys song. Gondolas swayed, rose, a circular stairway, hitched and hung, suspended for the better part of forever— then plunged, caught, plunged. I stared, woozy, as the Jolly

Green Giant touched the sky, spokes cracklin', rainbows ricocheting off a white-hot core.

If I had to choose my druthers, I'd rather topple off the pier than plummet from the Ferris wheel, rather splash into murky waters than splat onto hard gravel. Fact was, I'd rather *heights* were off-limits to humans, meant only for birds. Hadn't height been the ruination of the Tower of Babel? Even the word made me queasy. Whatever Heather was fixin' to say, she'd better say it on the ground.

Heather. Where was she? I scanned the crowds, the corkscrew ticket queue, the gondolas. For a second, I wondered if Raven might be nearby, lurking in a dark corner, flitting among the shadows, crouching beneath the far trees, stirring a cauldron of vengeful hexes. Some kids from school huddled 'round a coin toss—Wes and Oran, Gloria and Monique. Slim to none they knew my name.

"Eden?" Someone grabbed my wrist.

My stomach, already in revolt, launched into my throat. "Lord a'mighty, Hollis! Don't sneak up on me like that."

"What are you doing here? Thought you couldn't come." Hollis spoke through a mouthful of corn dog, under his arm a stuffed giraffe.

"I'm meetin' someone, not that it's any of your business."

"Well, that's a fine howdya-do." He narrowed his eyes. "What's going on? And don't say 'nothing.'"

"Nothing." I tried to swallow my stomach back down. "You followin' me?"

"You need following?" An edge crept into his voice, the same edge I'd heard when he told me to keep away from Vince. Then, more softly, he added, "You okay?"

"I'm fine." A plume of red hair caught my eye, the gleam of hoop earrings. "Gotta go." Leaving him dazed, I pelted toward the Ferris wheel, toward Heather.

"I'm here." I grasped the rope separating us.

Heather stood a frog leap from the front, the other ticket holders jostling her forward, a letterman jacket over her halter top. "It's about time." She flapped two tickets in my face. "And you owe me."

"I'm not getting on." The line shortened as a mother boosted her children into a gondola and climbed in after them. "What do you wanna tell me?"

"I'll clue you in once we're on the wheel."

"I told you, I'm not getting on."

The carnie motioned us forward, hollered at the people behind us. "Move along, folks! Move along!"

We watched an elderly couple embark.

"Do you wanna hear what I have to say or not?"

"You can tell me right here."

"Move up!" someone yelled.

An empty gondola swayed before us, the buffer of bodies having thinned to none. Heather handed the tickets to the carnie, and he swung open the safety bar.

"Get in," she hissed, climbing onto the seat.

"I . . . I can't." The words stuck in my throat, my stomach roiling.

"C'mon, toots, move it." The carnie, a pimply twenty-something sproutin' chin fuzz, spat a wad of sunflower seed shells to the ground. "We don't got all day."

"Holy smokes, Eden!"

I whirled to see Hollis plowing through the crowd, waving his giraffe.

"You're not getting on that, are you?"

I was asking myself the same thing. But I had to. I'd come this far. "Why shouldn't I?"

He was within feet of me now. "You're scared stiff of heights, for one. And aren't you supposed to be watch—"

"Let's go already!" Heather glared at Hollis.

"I'm conquering my fear." I forced a laugh, tossing my ponytail. "'Bout time, right?"

"If you say so." He chucked his corn dog wrapper at a trash can, missed.

"Girlie!" The carnie flicked his inked wrist at me. "Move! You're holdin' up the line!"

"Okay, sorry." Ducking under the rope, I clambered onto the seat beside Heather, closed my eyes, and leaned against her. She shoved me into the corner. Before I could change my mind, the carnie was lowering the safety bar across us, locking me in, and there was only a hard bench beneath me, cold steel behind me, and the abyss of night around me. As the wheel lurched into motion, I gripped the bar, my gumption nowhere to be found, and tried not to puke.

"Don't be afraid to open your eyes!" I heard Hollis call from somewhere below.

"Your charity boyfriend's cute."

If only the wasp had landed on her nose.

"Guess he's not sticking around," she sneered, her laugh cutting.

"So what is it?"

"What is what?"

"What should I know 'bout Raven?"

"Oh, nothing."

"N-nothing?" I could barely say the word. *Nothing?* A gale swept in from nowhere, shook the gondola. "Then why'd you bring me here?"

"Wasn't my idea, that's for sure. You think I wanna be seen with you?" Disdain dripped from her voice. "But

I did my job. I got you to the carnival."

"What?"

"You're such a sucker." I imagined her rolling her raccoon eyes. "Did you like the lime?"

"I don't under—"

The gondola wrenched to a stop, dangled recklessly, buoyed on the swell of shuddering machinery, inched higher. In the distance, the perky tune of the carousel looped like a child's music box, and though I tried not to, I pictured Dex, all wriggles an' shrieks in his wheelchair, starlit face to the window, clapping and waiting for the fireworks. Waiting for me.

"You're lucky the guys feel sorry for you, enough to let you off the hook for helping that commie freak."

My stomach knotted.

"Don't bother denying it. You heard us at the creek, spying like you do." The gondola pitched upward along with my gut. "You knew we'd find the gun, turn her in. So you helped her hide it."

"Why would I do that?"

"Gee, I wonder. Maybe 'cause she's your only friend?"

"She's not my friend."

"Uh-huh, right. You could double as her shadow." A frigid updraft rocked us, the gondola twisting. "Not to mention how you're always at the wrong place at the wrong time."

"What are you even talkin' about?"

"Hmm, let's see. Catholic church ring any bells?" Heather giggled.

"I just wanted to—"

"What about the swings? The pier? Her shed?"

"How do you know—"

"Speaking of which, why *were* you snooping around her house of horrors? *I* figured you two losers had a slumber party, but Vince thinks you were getting rid of evidence. Maybe plotting how to torch the place?"

"You're both wrong!"

"Prove it."

"I . . . I can't. But I didn't start the fire." I swallowed hard, my eyes shut tight, my fingers clenched 'round the safety bar. "And I didn't take any gun."

Her disembodied voice pierced the night. "Soon as the sheriff has the gun, you're going down. Course, you could still do the right thing. Better late than never."

Right thing? What right thing?

"I mean, we get why you cozied up to her, being the odd girl out, especially with a spaz brother." She sighed and let her words fall like a comforting pat. "But we'll cover for you. Hand over the gun, and we won't snitch."

"I . . . I don't understand," I finally stammered, choking on a miasma of citrus, cinder-dusted leather, and soapy flowers.

"Gosh, you're thick." Her voice hardened. "We're giving you a way out. The gun for our silence. Take it or leave it."

My mind turned in slow motion, like the wretched crawl of the Ferris wheel.

"Suit yourself, pinko. The guys will find it anyway."

"They can't find what I don't have."

"We'll see." She shifted on the bench. "You're missing quite the view, ya know. Always the chicken. And too stupid to save your own skin."

"Always? When have you ever seen me scared?"

"Ah, and there's the stupid."

"Are you done?" I needed her and the ride to stop. I was going to be sick.

"Not yet. Your own skin is one thing. But if you care about your comrade, you might wanna save hers. Tell her and her creepy uncle to beat it before the cops come. No one wants them here, not even in jail."

The wind wailed 'cross the carnival tents, buffeted our gondola.

"I can't . . ."

"Your choice. But if you cover for her"—she laughed, a shrill cackle I'd heard somewhere else but couldn't place—"well, two birds in the same cage."

If Heather had more to say, I didn't hear it, losing her drone to a mounting panic. Our gondola swayed with a pendulum force, the carnival jangle faint, distorted. We had reached the top. Heather's *oohs* told me that hundreds of miles below spun a globe with continents and oceans and polar caps, that thousands of miles to the east and west, galaxies swirled like fireflies, that were I to stretch out my hand, my fingers would graze a star. Rocked by cold updrafts, by sea winds raking the stratosphere, we dangled, waitin' for the lurch that would plunge us back to earth.

"Hey, looks like your brother's out for a spin."

"What?"

The Ferris wheel heaved, dropped, resumed its slow rotation.

"Down there." I could feel her pointing. "By the beach."

"The bea—my br—" My thoughts skittered, slammed into my chest. "*What?*"

Hot wax seemed to seal my eyes shut. If I couldn't see anything, it couldn't be happening. The Ferris wheel rumbled to a halt.

"I could swear that's him. But what's *she* doi—" Her voice cracked. "Oh my go—"

My eyes shot open. Fightin' like the devil not to retch, I gripped the safety bar and leaned forward. The ground rushed toward me, a vortex of color and speed. Heart a gallop, I scoured the blur of feverish rides, the warp of honeycombed streets. The slate-black sea bled into a curved horizon, flickered with glass shards. Spectators packed the pier, the beach, Front Street.

Front Street! A wink of metal. A wheelchair in a zigzag. And a boy—head bobbing, arms flailing—his small frame sickeningly familiar, my heart seeing what my eyes could not. Then he vanished, swallowed by the crowd, emerged, his wheelchair hurtling toward the pier, and behind it, flying like a thief in the night, a slender girl in billowing skirts.

"Let me off! Let me off!"

The safety bar refused to budge. I tried to wriggle under it, climb over it, ignored the carnie's shouts to *Sit down!*, Heather's cries that she didn't know, she didn't know. The descent seemed an eternity—lurch, halt, lurch—the earth finally within reach, Hollis lunging for me, hoistin', dragging me, and I was stumbling onto the ground and running, Hollis running too, strides ahead, somehow knowing, racing to stop Raven as I screamed into the wind, "Dex!"

THIRTY-THREE

As we spilled onto Front Street, bolts of lightning shot from the barges into the tarry sky, streaking golden arcs over the sea before bursting in a blaze of glory. A second volley rang out, the crowd erupting with more cheers and clapping. Hollis had long outpaced me, leaving me caught in a swell of tourists. The harder I fought to get through, the more they closed in on me, dads with toddlers on their shoulders, teens snapping Polaroids, old folks clinging to walkers, beboppin' to the rhythm of a stand-up bass.

The stink of skunk tinged with Christmas washed over me as a pack of long-haired hippies ambled past, bell-bottoms swishing, arms linked. Even the sea wall crawled with people, some standing and blocking the view, some sitting and hollering at 'em. Another *boom!* sent arrows skyward, winged flames exploding and splintering into a dozen colors. My frantic sprint became a patchy jog and then a hobble.

Pushing past a street magician twirling his hat, I climbed the sea wall, shooing off a hissing cat, and scanned the shore for Dex, for the glint of a wheelchair, the dim pier flashing alive only when the heavens lit up. Revelers thronged the planks, hugged the railings, bees swarmin' a log. Beyond the barricades, the pier dissolved, the lampposts' usual halos snuffed out beneath an upturned bowl of stars.

"Pick a card, any card!" The magician fanned a deck between his fingers.

Spotting a bucket hat in the crowd, I waded back into the street, eyes fixed on the tattered brim, shouting myself hoarse. Then, like a riptide, the crowd washed backward, sucking me with them to the shriek of a whistle. A traffic cop stood in the intersection, waving like a madman at a stalled delivery truck. With a roar, the truck jerked to life and bucked in reverse, wheels squealing as it hopped the curb, almost takin' out a trash can. His whistle a staccato of sharp blasts, the cop gestured wildly as the driver crept into a U-turn.

"Oh, sorry!" An elderly woman shouldered me, her panting German shepherd winning their tug-of-war.

Of all the con*demned* times.

"Move! *Move!*" I butted against the clog of bodies, fighting to wedge between sweaty limbs. "I've got to get through! For the love of—*move!*"

Above the crowd, impossibly small, floated the Corona parrot, as trapped as I was.

I'm coming, Dex. I'm coming, I mouthed. *Sissy is coming.*

But I wasn't coming. I wasn't moving at all, hemmed in by a wall of people, the delivery truck stalled again, above us a crack of fireworks, a shower of electric rain. I squeezed forward only to be thrust back, ensnared in the slow-motion sequence of a horror film, anchored to the ground by the weight of my own shame.

Wait for me, Dexie. Please wait for me.

He *had* waited, a little boy in his wheelchair, wriggly as a hooked worm, aimless eyes seeing everything out the window, seeing nothing, had waited for his promised walk, waited to reach for the fireworks. And then *she'd* taken him. Raven. But why? She'd nearly drawn me in with the mystery of her scrapbook, the silken spin of her dance. If not for the gun clatterin' at my feet, I'd have believed her innocent. Now I'd become the loose thread that could unravel her web. *Just a matter of time till she comes for you too*, Vince had said.

But why take Dex? I wanted to find Hollis, to ask him. He'd know. He would say . . . what would he say? As though he'd heard my question and I his answer, I knew. *Isn't that the wrong question, Eden? Isn't the right question, why did you leave Dex?*

No! This was Raven's doing, not mine. She took him. I only left—

There are many ways we leave each other. And many reasons.

Angry tears stung my eyes at the echo of Rev. Travers's voice. There's no reason to leave a child. I should know. Was there any difference between us, then, my father and me?

That's another thing we have in common, Eden—the need to forgive.

"Move, oh please, *move!*" A creeping dread choked my shouts, and unable to cry any louder, to reach Hollis, I felt the molten fury that had hurled me off the Ferris wheel seep from my body, cool and harden 'round my ankles, cement me to the ground, render me limp, chilled. "Lord, help me," I whispered.

"What's the holdup?" Voices coursed over me, bounced off each other.

"Truck stalled in the intersection."

A wheezy man, beer belly flapped over his belt, dropped into a folding chair and lit a cigarette. I let the acrid smoke settle over me, too numb to fan it away.

"Learn to drive!" someone else yelled. "Moron!"

The truck coughed and sputtered, exhaust belching from the tailpipe, until finally catchin' with a *vroom*, it shuddered to life and trundled across the intersection. With a thumbs-up at the driver, the traffic cop waved us forward, his whistle blasts echoed by the rapid *pop-pop-pop!* of side-street fire-crackers. People shoved and elbowed their way forward, the bottleneck loosening, then jamming abruptly, sending the paunchy man slamming into me, and me stumbling.

"Ow!" Before I could hit the ground, someone snatched my arm. Rallying, I turned heel, expecting—hoping—to see Hollis.

The eyes I met were ice.

"*You?*" I flung her off, all my spent fury surging back. "Where's Dex? What did you do with him!" I knew I was shouting, that a dozen people now stared, but I didn't care.

"Take." She grabbed me again, doubled down on her grip, her nails diggin' into my skin, and pointed toward the pier.

"They were right about you, you crazy commie—no!"

With a startling strength, she pulled me the opposite direction, away from the pier, away from Dex.

"Officer! Officer!" I strained to keep my footing, plowed backward into the crowd, dragging her with me toward the traffic cop. "She's taken my brother!"

In an instant, Raven let go, but now *I* held *her*, seizing her wrists in a sudden reversal as she tried to twist free. Slight as she was, she had towed me several yards, and now tusslin' shoulder to shoulder, I could feel the arctic chill of her gaze, the keen exhale of her breath, smell her musty clothes, wild violets and pungent camellias, hear the urgent tumble of incanted words.

"Hey, settle down!" someone barked.

"She's the one you're lookin' for!" I bellowed, mustering all the voice I had left, the cop no longer in sight. "She's be-hind everything!"

My reckless plow turned heads, the German shepherd growling.

"Hold up!" A man steadied me as I tripped over his cane. "What's the problem?"

The distraction was enough. Raven jerked free and, like the sorceress she was, vanished into the crowd.

"Condem—" The unholy utterance stuck in my throat, and I went stiff, uncertain whether to chase after Raven, catch up to Hollis, call out for Dex, or track down the cop, tell him 'bout the cave, 'bout the gun, set him on Raven's heels, right at least one wrong, like I should have done after Raven took me to her hideout. If I had, none of this would be happening. Dex would never have sat wedged against the picture window, Aslan in his lap, waitin' for Sissy to walk him to the sea wall, to brush fingertips along an exploding heaven, front row seats.

No, not now. My civic duty could wait.

Now, I needed to find my brother. Where had Raven taken him?

Whoosh, crackle, boom! A volley of fireworks emblazed the sky, a sparkle of fly lines by the dozens, casting, unspooling, splintering into ripples of silver and gold, on their tails a whistling rocket, then the *CRACK!* of a pool cue on a cosmic billiard table. With a yelp, the German shepherd tore free of his mistress and made a break for it, thwackin' my legs as he bolted past. Quicker than quick, I stamped on the chinking metal leash and scooped it up, the chain gritty, cold.

"Oh dear—I'm so sorry!" the flushed woman stammered, coiling the leash 'round her wrist. "Are you all right?"

"Sure." But I was feeling another chain, one coated in sand, Raven trying to urge it on me at the swings, Joe whisking it across the store counter, Rev. Travers puzzling it between his fingers, and my thumb catch—no, not the same chain. My thumb had snagged on a different chain as it spilled free of Ben's shirt, one that held a cross.

Or had it?

Though I watched the woman tug her skittish dog to the sidewalk, another scene was unfolding behind my eyes, Raven pressing the chain to her neck, my feet draggin' the swing to a stop, my hand nudging hers away, her finger pointing to where the seal had lain, the chain falling to the sand.

No cross? Mind if I take it?

Ben's chain? Ben who wished he'd been there to prevent it, who wasn't with his buddies at the seal's removal? Voices clamored, echoed, mocked against my now closed eyelids.

What if you're too late? Or Ben does something stupid again?

Again?

Just give us the gun. It's evidence.

Evidence against who?

Ben got a tad too fired up, patriot that he is.

Patriot or vigilante?

I'm just not sure you're reading the cards right.

Had every ace become a joker?

I did my job. I got you to the carnival.

My eyes flew open.

"Liliya! Wait!"

And I was elbowing folks left and right, bumbling over their shoes, hollerin' my fool head off, shouting loud as all get-out, *Liliya! Liliya!*, until she heard, until she pivoted with hand outstretched, and we were pushing against the swells, weaving between night revelers, she forging a path unseen, couples parting, parents yanking toddlers close, and then a breeze slapped my face, cool, salty, and we broke free, swerved onto the pier, and ran, dodgin' women with strollers, rounding thickets of teens, racing, Raven swift and strong, flying ahead of me, gripping my hand, her scarves unraveling, billowing, dried petals scattering, carpeting the planks beneath our feet.

THIRTY-FOUR

WE WERE ALMOST to the barricades when she veered left, skirting two men raisin' Cain, shoving and cussing, only to pull up short beneath an unlit lamppost. Slogging to a stop beside her, I clutched my side and gulped the chilled air, sharp with sulfur and sea rot. People buzzed the railings, clapping at the rapid-fire launch of rockets, the comets and whirligigs.

Where are you, Dexie? Sissy's here now!

"Fool kids," someone near me sniped. The brawl had grown louder, drawing a circle of bystanders. "Someone break those hooligans up!"

Teetering on my toes, I could just make 'em out, two scruffy men trading licks and hurling curses. One man barreled into his rival, unleashing a flurry of wild strikes, blood streaming from his nose. With a start I recognized Vince.

"*You?* T-tellin' *me* wha' tuh do!" Even from a distance, I could hear the slur in his words. "You're nothin' but a path . . . pathetic preacher's kid . . . ch-chicken-livered, ssssonuva—"

Ben, slighter but quick, ducked the hammering fists. "Better that than a poor little rich kid!" he spat, letting fly his own better-aimed punches. "Why'd ya have to go so damn far?"

"Knock it off!" A third man busted into the fray, shoulders squared, hands raised, bucket hat askew. Shoving Ben clear of Vince's swing, Hollis took the blow himself and, catching the next haymaker, sent Vince reeling with a crack to the jaw. "Where is he!" Before Ben could seize the moment, Hollis hooked him 'round the waist and hauled him to the ground, pinning him in a headlock. But Vince had regained his wind, was charging them both, kickin' like a mad mule, Hollis unable to fend off the raging boots.

"That's enough!" Peeling from the ringside gawkers, several husky men pounced on Vince, held him back—a knock-down, drag-out I had no more time to watch. Raven was carting me away from the mob, pulling me not forward but up, up the four-tiered railing.

"Are you insane? No!"

Wrenching free, I shrank back, rootin' my feet to the planks, certain she'd lost her mind. Scaling the rails like a ladder, Raven crouched on the topmost board, an acrobat on a highwire, and then, her body unfolding, she rose, her skirts rustling to an upsurge of wind, lissome, one hand anchored to the darkened lamppost, the other beckoning me, pointing to something beyond the barricades, something I couldn't see, would never be able to see, unless I stood beside her.

Bracing against a whitecap gust, I forced a foot on the bottom rail and reached for Raven, letting her hoist me up, one rail, two rails, untethered but for her grip, my heart crashing against my ribs like the sea against the pilings, my stomach churning for a second time that night, but now with no safety bar 'cross my lap, only fervent prayers between me and a freefall into the frothing abyss below. To think *this* had been my chosen druther. Though icy spray pricked my eyes, the hot wax that had sealed them atop the Ferris wheel refused to come. My knees buckled, the rails warped and wavered, my hand began to slip.

"I . . . I c-can't!"

"See!" Raven's fingers were a vice as she stayed me on the third rail and pointed again.

Folks packed both shoulders of the pier, givin' the barricades wide berth, faces upturned, riveted by the hissing rise of fireworks. Beyond them, beyond the barricades, nothing, the pier vanishing into a murky void. Gasps and cheers greeted a thunderclap that rent the sky, and for an instant a dozen bursting suns ignited the night, scuttled the shadows. In that moment, as day conquered night, I saw.

Near the storm-mangled brink, a barricade lay toppled, breached, the orange cones scattered—and mere feet from the splintered rails, tangled in caution tape, glinted a wheelchair.

"Dex!" I tried to yell, yearning to snag him with my voice, hook and reel him to me, but all that came out was a strangled rasp. Glued to the third rail, with Raven hovering above me like some mythical creature, I watched time unfold in slow motion as Dex bounced and squirmed in his chair, his arms batting at the silvery catapult of rockets, his squeals in delighted discord with a chorus of whizzes and bangs, watched with each exuberant motion his wheelchair roll closer to the shattered rail, to the rippling tinseled heavens mirrored in the sea.

Before the cascading glitter could fade from the sky, I dropped to the deck, scraping my knee as I tumbled, and was bulldozing through the knots of people, some shouting at me to slow down, others oohing at another launch of fireworks, a few still bustin' up the fracas. Reaching the fallen barricade, I froze. Dex sat spitting distance from the splintered ledge. Terrified of startling him into sudden movement, of sending the wheelchair plunging, I eased into the shadows, barely daring to breathe, my eyes fixed on the golden-haired boy showered in dying embers.

If anyone had gathered at the barricades, stock-still with indecision and stammered prayers, I wouldn't have known it. If Hollis had turned Vince and Ben over to the sheriff and was now runnin' for Dex, I wouldn't have heard his footsteps. If Raven had flung wide her bangled arms and donned the white wings of the caladrius, swooped over the town to gaze into Dex's face, and flown to the sun, I wouldn't have seen it. There was no past. No future. Only time suspended, erased. No one. Nothing. Just me and Dex.

"Dex!" I called softly, choking on the panic that seared my throat. "It's Sissy."

A cannon blast drowned my voice, strewed a galaxy of confetti stars above us, sending Dex into peals of whooping *uhngs*, his writhing body fit to bust, throwing him forward, off the chair and into a stagger, his heavy shoes catching, forcing him upright, his legs a stiff wobble, the braces holding. Though he stood so near me, he might have been a universe away.

"Dex!" One false move—his or mine—would send him plummeting. "Dexie, I came back, just like I promised."

Where there are promises, they will fail. Where there are dreams, they will die. But love never fails.

Though he faced the sea, the barges, I held out my hand. "How 'bout a walk with Sissy? What you say, heh?"

Fireworks like gunfire ignited the sky, one, two, three, four. Dex crowed, stumbled into a step, halted, listing as though drunk. The caution tape that spanned the gaping hole glistened like a spiderweb.

"Dexie, do you hear me? Dex!" I was shouting now. "Dexie!"

From behind, where seconds before had been cheers and whistles, came an uneasy silence, then an urgent murmur, and I knew a crowd had formed at the barricades.

"Move aside!" someone yelled.

Footsteps pounded in our direction.

"No! Stay back!" I flung my arms into a barricade of my own. "He's mine!" Hot tears sprang from my eyes. I tried to shout again, but my voice broke, fell, crumpled petals at my feet. "Dex is mine."

He heard the whisper, I told Hollis later—despite the blare of barge horns, the sizzle an' crack of rockets, the whoops of children, despite the howl of wind, the creak and moan of the pier, the rumbling sea, despite the shattering of promises, the splintering of a family beyond repair. It was impossible. Yet he wavered, head tilted, eyes roaming from behind lopsided glasses.

And then the moment was gone.

Five, six, seven fireworks blazed across the sky, a finale of bursts, of sparklers and spoolin' rainbows, Dex a whirling dervish of jubilant arms and delirious hoots, his legs thudding, one spastic step, then another, drawn to the rim of heaven— *with God, all things are possible*—and the breath I hadn't dared breathe ripped from my chest.

He was falling.

No!

He was turning.

I caught him as he doddered, tripped, knocked an orange cone toppling to sea, let him crash onto me, fell with him, my shins bangin' against his braces. Tucking him beneath me like a rag doll, I inhaled his sour-curd breath, his *no more tears*-scented curls, rapid-fire hoots pelting my ears deaf, the glisten of a wondrous night in his maple eyes.

"Hey, Dexie Day, *mi tesoro*," I murmured, rolling him from the ledge and coming to rest beneath a dome of celestial sequins, the Creator's own connect-the-dots. "Lord a'mighty, you stink!"

And then Hollis was leaning over us, helping me to my feet, warding off onlookers. People jostled us, dozens talking at once, someone commanding folks to stand back, someone else lifting Dex into his wheelchair, Hollis scooping him out again with a wince, saying through gritted teeth, "I think you've had enough wheelin' for one night, matey," and plopping his hat on Dex's head.

"Helluva show, missy!" a man barked from the rabble. "No-good kids causing trouble." Joe shoved apart the barricades like they were Legos, his voice booming above the ruckus. "Clear a path! Out of the way! Let the lady through! I said *git!*"

Hollis steered me past the barricades, slowing his stride to match mine, Dex cradled against his chest, one arm floppy like Cappy's bum arm, the other yankin' his tongue. As the barges went dark, a lamppost flickered on, then another, until the pier emerged dappled in halos.

"What? What is it?" Hollis pulled up short beside me, gasping sharply as he hitched Dex higher. "I'm fine," he added quickly. His bottom lip sagged, swollen and split, a trickle of blood staining his chin. "What's wrong?"

I'd paused in the soft spill of lamplight, families milling 'round us. "Where's Raven? She was right here."

But where she'd braved wind and sea only minutes before, a gossamer silhouette of whipping hair and scarves on the topmost rail, not even a seagull roosted. And though I searched the bevy of merrymakers ambling toward town, I knew she was gone.

THIRTY-FIVE

Popeye kept vigil at the water's edge, one ear perked. His good eye fixed on the noddin' buoy, the waves a gentle slosh over his front paws. We'd arrived before sunrise that last July Saturday, Hollis and I, taken up watch behind the briny mutt, had somehow missed Jake's wade into the froth, and now admired a crescent sun afloat a turquoise sea. A glossy bird, slender-necked and long-beaked, sailed overhead, landed, and pecked at a chip bag.

"Cormorant," Hollis announced.

Striding past the reach of a brisk wave, it fixed greenish eyes on the still dog, flapped its strong wings twice, then soared up to the pier and settled on the damaged railing. Two fishermen strolled the empty stretch, spooking the bird into flight, rods slung 'cross their shoulders.

"Fine morning for a catch."

Shivering, I hugged my knees to my chest.

"Might even be the best fishing of the summer." Hollis broke into a whistle that sounded like a rockabilly twist on "When the Saints Go Marching In."

"Yeah? Howdya figure?" His fish smarts were a marvel to me, though I wagered the key lay in the tide tables. I picked up a broken shell and shoveled the sand.

"July fog's gone. You won't be so cold up on the pier. Might actually last long enough to hook a shiner perch.

Perfect for baitin' real fish."

I made to knock off his hat, but he dodged my swing with an impish grin.

"Plumb lousy," I muttered, "summer and school startin' near the same week."

The tug-of-war between coastal fog and golden sun would linger till September, when the fog loosed its hold but for sleepy wisps. Though only my second summer in Harford Beach, I'd heard the rumors, and this one I knew to be true.

"Aren't you done with school yet?"

I looked him full on. "Got three years left, or can't you count?"

His mouth fell open in feigned surprise. "Who'da thought? As learnt as you already are?"

I gave him my best Anna snort.

"Guess time's got a lotta Septembers in her yet," he added by way of comfort. "At least if you don't up and move."

"No place I'd wanna go." Though it was my own mouth saying it, the words blind-sided me. For most of forever, I'd wanted to trade our rattletrap rental for my ranch house in the San Sebastian. "And there's no tellin' about time. Ain't no tide tables for it." Now I sounded as wise as Hollis, and I wasn't sure it suited me. "Still, there oughta be a law 'bout school starting in August."

By way of agreement, Hollis resumed whistling.

At my frown, he broke off his funky tune, eyes bugging. "What? No 'hot fun in the summertime' for Scoot?"

Though I socked him in the shoulder, it was all I could do not to bust up. "Like you'd know anything about it, gettin' schooled at home." My bit of shell packed smooth, I trickled sand down his neck. "Reckon you've got no use for school, 'less they're schools of fish."

Snatching my wrist, he flicked loose the shell but chuckled. "Might be right." He swatted his neck and tugged at his shirt. "But might be wrong too. Signed up for a class at Mission Hills College."

Now I was the one with a raised eyebrow. "What for?"

Picturin' Hollis in a classroom with his rangy legs stretched into the aisle and his slouchy canvas hat tipped low over his eyes, well, it could hardly be done. "You already know most everything. Everything that matters leastways."

"Nah, not by a long shot." He shrugged, but a smile tugged at his mouth. "Wanna learn bookkeeping and take some shop classes. Then I can help my dad open a hardware store. Besides, I lost a bet with my mom."

"What b—*pfft*—bet?" Popeye's tail smacked me in the face.

"Said I could fix up Anna's dinghy so it'd actually float."

"Did ya use bubble gum?" I unwrapped a piece and stuck it in my mouth.

"Probably woulda had better luck. Good thing Anna can swim."

"Ha! Wouldn't be *Patches* without all those holes." I squinted at him despite my Jane Jetsons. "Just like you wouldn't be Hollis without a toppled signpost an' the stench of manure."

"About that—"

"Fancy yourself real slick, huh? Well, your mom set me straight."

"I heard."

"Hollis Percival, named after your great-grandfather." I peered at him through a pink bubble.

"How 'bout we keep that between you and me?"

"If only your mom *had* named you after a town in Kern

County." I peeled bits of popped gum off my chin. "Button-willow Sweet woulda made for some mighty fittin' initials!"

Hollis let out a scandalized gasp, shoved me sideways, and was fixin' to tickle me when Jake strode out of the waves, Popeye leaping and woofing in relieved welcome.

Felt like a month of Sundays since we'd bantered like this, though it hadn't been two weeks since the fireworks, three days since the carnival had packed up and left town. The vendors' hasty exodus saw the parking lot littered with spent balloons and candy wrappers, the tree branches dusted with confetti and fading echoes.

ℝ

DECLARED A "RAGING success" by the *Harford Herald*, so Mama had read at the kitchen table after duty called me home, "'the traveling fair drew a record number of tourists, most hailing from the central valley—'"

"I'll say."

"'—transforming the once fishing town into a sun-and-surf mecca.' Eden, is the toaster on the right setting?"

I nodded, blew at the smoke driftin' from the slots.

"'The night festivities kicked off with a bang as fire-works exploded from twinkling barges and—' Well, never mind." Pulling out the ad insert, she smoothed the crinkly paper beneath the feet of Dex's high chair. "No choice but to tolerate it."

I wasn't sure if she was referring to the unwanted pub-licity or the flying grits.

"Well, the toast is toast."

"Here, have yourself an apple." Mama slid a bowl toward me. "Rosa brought 'em by, says they're your favorite."

That was a misery of my own doing.

"'Cause they're sour like me, I guess." I unwrapped a piece of Bazooka.

"Oh sugar, there ain't nobody sweeter than you."

My gum hitched mid-way into my mouth. Seemed Mama needed a loan of my Jane Jetsons. Or maybe—and I suppose I had Mar Vista Chapel to thank for the truth of things—maybe, sometimes, there are reasons for not wantin' to see too clearly.

"The tourists always come in summer," Hollis said when I grumped after church the next day, trading me a Slim Jim for a green apple on the sea wall. "But when they go, we stay. They don't know the real Harford Beach."

Maybe I didn't either, not yet. But I caught glimpses of it, smells and sounds, tastes and textures, capturing it in sketches, my charcoal pencil workin' rapidly, driven by a mind of its own. Here, a lazy ribbon of unremarkable coast-line, of fog-fringed beaches and slate sea, of fishing lore and ghost-ridden swings. There, the stalwart pier a rose-hued avenue on misty mornings, weathered anglers hoisting rods over the railing, days unburdened by hurry.

Here, the distant bells of St. Francis stirring the town awake, shopkeepers rolling out canvas awnings, students sighing their way to school, trapped inside dreary corridors plastered in rumors and grime, biding their boredom until they couldn't, ditching to skateboard, to surf, to cruise the Front in souped-up glory. There, streets studded with shabby shops and funky bungalows, backed by purling hills dotted with vineyards and rambling estates, the afternoon train snaking the ridge in tandem with the slushy creek markin' the shantytown. Into the sketches I stippled the stench of kelp and sand flies, of stagnant eddies and pelican droppings, of town drunks slumped in happy stupors, blended the scent of churros and caramel corn, of Corona and Marlboro.

Often, the single-spire Mar Vista Chapel with its single-minded fervor, zealous to beckon the lost, baptize the saved, preach the fear of God and—provided a body could stop trembling long enough to hear it—the mercy of Jesus.

Never, the lashed eyes that were wings.

The real Harford Beach, emerging from moments and memories, yes. But not the same Harford Beach we'd moved to almost a year ago. Not after the carnival. Not after Raven.

I had found Dex, but I had lost her. Somehow I knew—even before searching the lamplit railing, scouring the departing faces, Hollis enfolding Dex in strong arms, Dex clenching my hand, or perhaps I clenching his—somehow I knew she'd be gone.

80

I MIGHT HAVE looked harder for her, combed the lower dock, the swings, the sea wall, but Dex had started to whimper at the street entrance, and by the time we reached Cappy's, his whimpers were wails, his body racked with sobs. It was then, as I went to comfort him with Aslan, that I saw the wheelchair empty. I whipped 'round to scan the sidewalk, the street, the intersection. Candy wrappers littered the pavement, popcorn bags, ticket stubs and cigarette butts, confetti—but no stuffed lion. He'd likely tumbled from Dex's arms in the mad careen to the pier and now lay buried in a dumpster or at the bottom of the sea or in the hugs of another child.

"Oh no, Hollis" was all I could manage, and though he met my groan with quizzical eyes, he did not press.

And then someone had lumbered into the neon glow of the Corona parrot and lifted Dex from Hollis's arms, gathered him and his wretched shrieks into his own arms, against a chest that rattled and heaved, and carried him the two blocks to my porch, a hula girl dancin' beneath his sleeve. Hollis had taken over the wheelchair, both of us behind Jake, and I remembered a time my father cradled a small girl in his arms and wondered if all fathers outgrew their children. Not till Jake had laid Dex on the living room couch did the old man burst into a fit of coughs that doubled him over, Anna materializing out of nowhere to hand him a flask and steer him into her station wagon.

Next thing I knew, Mama was tapping on my bedroom door, cracking it just enough to peek in, and announcing softly that my young gentleman stood on the porch. "Harris, I think." But I must have slipped back into sleep, because then she was stroking my tangled hair and lamentin' poor Harris, telling me he had waited forty minutes and perhaps she should fix him a po' boy, bending so close I could count the bluish veins along her temples.

I remembered the flicker of alarm in her eyes as she'd stepped through the front door, the wall clock ticking half past ten, her mouth slack, face drained of color but for the blue veins. She'd returned from her shift to a houseful of muffled chaos, folks makin' short work of the disarray, straightening the couch cushions, righting my bedroom drawers, repacking my father's boxes, slipping from room to room, exchanging whispers and agitated glances. From the kitchen came the honeyed scent of brewing chamomile tea, from the porch the reek of a cigar. Father Miguel ushered windswept witnesses to the cluttered table, while Sheriff Moretti took statements and bagged a crushed beer can.

Dex lay asleep on the couch, my worn teddy bear snugged under his arm, and soon forgotten in the bustle, I curled up beside him, drifting into uneasy sleep. Mama had asked no questions, had instead whispered me awake and guided me upstairs, nudged me into bed, drawing my rumpled blanket over me and gasping faintly as I pressed her cheek to mine. From the din below erupted a burst of heated Spanish, and knew I had what-for comin', but it didn't bother me a bit, warmed me right over, and sleep came sweet.

I yanked a sweatshirt over my pajamas and ran downstairs.

"Hollis?"

He rose from the top stair as I stepped onto the porch, moving gingerly, his lip fat, a strip of gauze 'round his knuckles.

"Don't you look a sight. What's up?" I rasped, letting the door slam behind me.

"They left. I didn't want you to hear it from anyone else."

"Left? Who?" I stared blankly at him. "You mean her uncle?" That would make sense. As a long-haul trucker—carrying intel if not freight—he'd be on the road for weeks on end.

"Both of them. Packed up in the night."

I didn't bother asking how he found out. Of course Hollis would know. He always knew.

"But she can't. She can't just up an' leave. I need to tell her I was wr— I need to than— She took me to Dex."

"Went to Gulch Run myself. The house is boarded up. Smoke damage is pretty bad."

I tried to force my sluggish brain to think. "She could be at the cave."

I expected Hollis to frown, to furrow one brow, arch the

other. Instead his eyes widened, and with a groan, he bounded down the steps, spinning as he reached the sidewalk. "Meet me at the dock in an hour."

Clambering through the hatch forty-five minutes later, I spotted him shinin' up the seats of a dinghy I'd never seen before, the name *Sweet Stuff* painted on the side.

"That your dad's dinghy?"

"Nope." He tossed the rag on the dock. "It's mine."

"Yours? Wha—how come you never told me you had a dinghy?"

He cracked a wry smile as I took his hand and scrambled in. "Don't recall you ever askin'."

Anyway, he hadn't had it long, he continued, bought used and kept moored at the farthest pier, but I was only half listening, remembering the last time I'd traveled by dinghy, lured by my own curiosity but afraid of what I might find, and now again lured by curiosity, afraid of what I might not find.

Hollis fastened his life jacket, tossed his hat under the seat, and untethered the dinghy. "Ready?"

My nod reflecting in his dark aviator lenses, I fixed my gaze on the eastern shoreline, the contrary motor finally hurlin' *Sweet Stuff* across the sea. In a shiver of déjà vu, I traced the shift of pebbled beaches to craggy rises to sheared cliffs, scanned the fleeting coves for arched caverns, the caverns for her cave, our cave.

"There!" I yelled over the lashing wind, nearly missing the cleft between the rugged bluffs, my hair blinding me, spray coating my face. As Hollis steered the dinghy inland, a narrow strip of sand appeared, flecked with driftwood and kelp, desolate, the beach strewn with broken shells.

Cutting the motor, Hollis vaulted into the shallows and dragged the dinghy to shore, steadying me as I hopped out, the foamy waves soaking my shoes.

"Helloo!" I splashed past the boulder, the tide suckin' at its base, and darted for the cave. "Anybody here?"

Hearing nothing but the moaning sea, I plunged inside just to stop cold, squinting. From the murky dark, hulkish shapes crept toward me—ghostly fingers, jagged teeth— then faded, shifting shadows of imagined dreads. For a Mississippi moment, I wondered if we'd moored in the wrong cove, stumbled into the wrong cave.

It was as though she'd never been.

"Any luck?" Hollis trailed close, ducking where I had passed easily.

"I'd see better in a bucket." Creeping farther in, I clung to the damp wall, probing the gloom.

"A high tide could trap you in here." He'd hardly gotten the words out when I heard a *drip, drip*. "And it wouldn't take but a clap of thunder to collapse the roof. Drowned or buried alive, all a matter of druthers."

"Good heavens, Hollis. And I have the gothic imagination? Ow!" My toe banged against a pile of stones I didn't remember. "Where's your flashli—up there!" The cave shouted back at me. "That's the shelf."

Skirtin' the pile, Hollis brushed past me, scaled the boulder in quick bounds—though not without a pained wheeze—and bracing himself against the cave ceiling, groped the deep ruts. Shafts of filtered sun dusted his hunched shoulders as I watched him find the shelf and reach inside, just as I had watched Raven do, my breaths just as ragged. But where she had wrested free a keepsake box, he withdrew only grimy fingers.

"Nothing." He dropped to the ground with a grunt, wiped his hands on his jeans. "Anywhere else to look?"

I shook my head, dismay and vexation and a churning stomach driving me from the cave. Blinking beneath the rock arch, I scanned the shore, a tinseled sash in the rising tide. She had lifted bangled arms, danced to the music of the sea, woven a ballet from a scrapbook past, poetry in motion, shedding the raven's *shadow that lies floating on the floor*, emerging a swan on a nightly shore. And somehow, for reasons I didn't understand, I had become part of her story.

And now she had vanished. Just like that, she was gone.

"Not a trace, Scoot. Not even a footprint." Catchin' up to me, Hollis flexed the knuckles of his right hand, the gauze loose, and foraged in his pocket.

She had wings.

"Oh, hey—meant to give you this." In his palm, beside the fresh bandage, lay a wilted white flower.

"Her camellia," I whispered.

"No, yours." Hollis tucked it into my ponytail. "A gardenia."

"But—" The faintest of scents wafted from my hair, sweet and creamy. "All along?"

"All along."

My eyes stinging white-hot, I shut them, saw muted colors exploding like fireworks, unfurling, spiraling, fading into fallen roses, and I let the darkness take her, curtains closing on a stage. When I opened my eyes again, there appeared only sand and sky and breaking waves, silver fringes lapping a half-moon shore, and something else, something that caused my breath to catch, that sent me racing toward the frothy waters—but it was gone.

No, wait!

As the waves slid back, I saw it, a letter etched in the

sand, washing out to sea but not yet erased, and then another. I dropped to my knees and traced the eroding word, water slappin' my hands.

"What does it say?" Hollis leaned over my shoulder. "L-i-i—no, L—"

"*Liliya.*" The sand crumbled between my fingers, swirled, dissolved. I watched the letters slip into the sea. "Her name."

THIRTY-SIX

JUST AS RUMORED, August ushered in summer's sweetest sun, like Turkish delight on Edmund's tongue, left a lingering that begged for more. Hollis and I staked out the pier early mornings, hooking anchovies and squid and reelin' in mackerel and croakers. Of a pokey afternoon, we'd putter *Sweet Stuff* to the raft of barking sea lions, cutting the motor near the otters. Long evenings saw us gallivanting between the swings and firepits, chasing moonlit breakers, the water cold between our toes.

Mama didn't seem to mind my late-night saunters home, "Harris" in tow, the doff of his bucket hat under the streetlight met with a flush he couldn't see, a smile at my first glimpse of Dex inside, sprawled in his playbed, breath a steam engine, face smashed against Aslan. The frayed lion had shown up one day, rather the worse for wear, its mane sporting a bicycle tread, its tail held aloft by the gumption of one strand of Gramma Kay's yarn. He'd scoured the town, Mama said . . . my father.

Anna doled out the details that first August game night, as we burned and mucked cards 'cross Cappy's storeroom table, having uncovered the facts, she said, in ways she wasn't at liberty to share, but swearing to their veracity on a Bible she didn't have. Seeing as Anna alone could converse without soap-latherin' words—that was, if she had a mind to—I reckoned she'd gotten a few civilized folk to give her the rundown, and not a little gossip, courtesy of the LUV hospital visitations. We grumbled our way through a few rounds first, Jake hackin' to bust between swears at Ernesto, who thumped him on the back, spilling elixir on Popeye's sneak paw. Joe seemed particularly subdued, dealing the flop—three cards up—without his usual snarl.

"Jake, you needa *vete* home," Pedro finally ventured. "You no sound good."

"Don't sound any different at home." Jake stared hard at his cards.

Cappy slid a canteen of water at him and reached for an apple.

I sat real quiet, didn't feel much like talking, didn't even feel much like sorting through my cards, instead nuzzled Popeye and worried myself over Jake's cough. Now my attention was fixed on Anna, who'd pulled up a chair next to Jake.

"Her name was Galina Zhuravlyova." Anna looked around the table. "Any ya heard of her? Russian ballerina."

We met the question with shrugs, mumbles.

"Ain't none of us cultured," Jake offered between hacks.

"Except maybe Ernesto here." Cappy slapped at Ernesto with his schooner's cap. "He can play a mean harmonica."

Ernesto gave a thumbs-up and continued stackin' his poker chips.

Galina Zhuravlyova, the Soviet newspapers reported—and Sheriff Moretti had the archived clippings to prove it—was set to become the next principal ballerina with the Bolshoi Ballet. "Anyone heard of that?"

The mumbles swelled, someone said "Nope."

"Told ya none of us was cultured."

"Bah! Speak for yourself." Cappy flipped open his pocket-knife and carved a circle 'round his apple stem. "Saw 'em when I was stationed at Hunters Point, near a decade ago."

Stunned silence met this revelation. We knew Captain Thomas O'Malley had been stationed near San Francisco, knew he'd commanded a destroyer, though he kept mum if asked about it, knew he'd been hit by torpedo shrapnel, but no one knew he'd been to a ballet.

"*You* saw a ballet?" Jake raised a Hollis eyebrow.

"Well, saw the sign on the opera house stairs. 'Bolshoi Ballet, SOLD OUT.' Sum'n 'bout a gazelle."

"Bolshoi, eh? More like Bullsh—" Popeye barked, thumped a paw next to Jake's elbow. "Aw, yer 'bout as cultured as a boil on my butt."

"Quit yappin'." Joe looked ready to fold, then showed his cards. "Gonna make yourself sick."

"I'm already sick."

What the newspapers didn't report—because they didn't know it, and they didn't know it because it was a scandal— was that Galina Zhuravlyova had gotten pregnant.

"That'll happen sometimes."

"But it can't happen. Not to a prima ballerina." No one could know, Anna continued, confiscating the elixir from Jake, so Galina left Moscow on pretense.

"On what?"

"The claim that her brother was deathly ill. He forged the documents."

"Blasted risky, if yeh ask me."

"Risk was worth it. Church ladies say Sergey's no friend to the KGB. Anyway, Galina got her emergency leave and retreated to her brother's house in the countryside. A few months later, she had her baby."

The fact that Anna could speak so proper-like played second fiddle to the fact that she now lapsed into a heavy pause, settin' me on pins an' needles. But still she waited, content to watch a series of folds, raises, and draws, allowed the men to sort the particulars.

Cappy dealt us the neatly sliced apple along with the next hand of cards, rocking his stool forward. "You mean that girl who wears all those gypsy rags? What's her name, Rav—"

"Liliya." I twisted Popeye's bandana around my fingers, saw again the faint letters fading with the tide. She knew I'd come back. "Her name is Liliya."

"Thought her name was Blackbird."

I might've popped off on Joe, tryin' to bait me at a time like this, only he was right.

"Go on." Jake nodded at Anna but cast a troubled glance my way.

Galina had no choice but to leave the baby with Sergey and his wife. But then Vera went missing. A few weeks later, her car was spotted crumpled in a gully off an icy ridge, her body nearby.

"I no like this story." Pedro threw down the deck he'd shuffled.

"Newspapers reported she'd been drinking. Only Sergey says she didn't drink."

"*Asesinato!*"

Even Popeye stared at Ernesto.

"Then what happened?" I'd found my voice too.

"He went on the run. Defected."

"And *bebé*?" Pedro asked.

"Took her with him."

"Away from 'er mother?" Cappy wasn't liking this story either.

"Galina made him swear to it. She meant to follow, not right away, but soon."

"*Qué bien.*" Pedro nodded.

"Sergey and the baby made it to Austria."

"Ah, *canguros.*"

Two months there, three months here, traveling Europe, never in one place long, always on the run, lying low, waiting. The girl was four, maybe five, when Soviet newspapers announced that the great Bolshoi ballerina Galina Zhuravlyova had contracted tuberculosis and would be replaced.

Anna rose and, grabbin' the broom, swept under Joe's feet. "Rest of it ain't pretty."

"Ha! Pretty good KGB cover, if you ask me." Joe kicked at the rabid broom.

"Any yeh ask Joe here?" Cappy growled. "Didn't think so. Now shutcher trap."

Truth was, Galina had been arrested at the border trying to escape and exiled to northern Siberia. The settlement had no fuel and less bread. She lasted only a few months.

You could have heard a card float to the floor.

"Fine story for a poker night. She died. The end." Joe stuck a cigarette in his mouth, lit it, saw Ernesto fan a menu in Jake's face, and snuffed his Lucky Strike on the table.

"Not the end."

The KGB had tracked them down, were closing in, but Sergey and the girl gave them the slip, escaped to New York just before Christmas. Although the US government granted them asylum, the KGB would never stop searching.

"They're still running."

"*Qué tragedia.*" Pedro shook his head. "Belong no place, is no life." Then as though to cheer himself, he raised his Corona. "*El que es perico, donde quiera es verde.*"

"The damn parrot is purple. When you gonna figure that out?"

Twiddling the tufted hair on his chin, Pedro bowed to Joe. "*Sí.*"

"You're so fool colorblind, you can't even see that Ernesto is black."

"He's my brother." Pedro blew Ernesto a kiss.

Before Joe could fire off a retort, Cappy thwacked his bum arm on the table, sending two beer cans rolling. "Ain't either o' yeh heard Anna? There's a kid run outta town 'cause she was different. Now stow it before I run *you* out of my diner!"

No one felt much like playing after that. Oh, there were some half-hearted calls, raises, and checks, a few spats. Ernesto brandished his harmonica, Joe barking that if he blew one infernal note, he'd set the Cuban's hair on fire, which wasn't much of a threat considering Ernesto had no hair, 'less Joe meant the handlebar mustache swallowing most of Ernesto's face. Uncapping the canteen, I poured some water into my empty coffee cup and lowered it to the floor for Popeye. He lifted his head, sniffed, and lay back down.

"Think I'll head home now." I slid my glasses off my nose. I'd gone back to wearing 'em, and whether it was my sharpened eyesight or the bookish effect of my pinched nose, my bluffs had been a heap more convincing. "I'd say it's the distraction," Hollis had offered. Whatever the reason, my Jane Jetsons, cat-eye an' all, found me some sorely needed good luck.

"How's your li'l bub?" Anna tossed my empty Dr Pepper can into the trash. "Doin' okay?"

"Sure is. Why, he's a right celebrity at church."

Joe humphed but allowed a faint smile.

"Yes sirree," I continued. "Smartest dresser there, polka-dot bow tie and black patent shoes."

"And me Dixie cup sittin' on 'is noggin'." Cappy beamed.

"Like it was made for him!" I gave Cappy a salute. "Dex sends a big ol' thanks. Y'all oughta come see for yourselves."

"Well, there's an idea." Anna swiped the top of Jake's head. "When's the last time we seen the inside of a church, eh?"

"Every time I step outside and look up, that's when," Jake said through a spate of dry, braying coughs.

"The reverend would be awful proud of you, Jake." I scraped back my chair and rooted in my pocket for some gum. "He says every star has a name, and God doesn't forget a one of 'em. Not a one! I suppose they're kinda God's congregation."

"You done preaching yet?" Joe eased Jake to his feet.

"You done sinning yet?" I met Joe's scowl with my sweetest Southern lilt. "Y'all take care now. See ya 'round."

Jake walked me to the door, Popeye loping behind, his checked bandana so knotted from my twisting that I had to refasten it.

Cloaked in mist, we lingered beneath the violet glow of the Corona parrot, watching the quiet creep of fog over the sea, saying nothing, Jake's every breath labored. And then seized by some unknown need, I stood on my tiptoes and kissed Jake's bristly cheek.

"What's that for?" He mustered his gruffest voice.

"Don't go anywhere, Jake."

His worn face softened. "Now where would I go?" A fit of hacking leaned him against the diner door. "Sea walk at dawn, Joe's bench for a smoke, this ol' dive for grub and poker. The extent of my travels."

"Gonna miss our morning smoke. School starts next month."

He snorted. "Sounds like yer the one goin' someplace."

I scraped gum off the bottom of my shoe.

"They gonna learn you to be a lady?"

"Might. But I'd rather you learn me to be a card shark."

Jake smiled, his pale eyes embedded in crinkles. "There's hope in Mudville yet. Friday nights we'll learn you all we know—me and this cheatin' hound. Now go on."

I scooped Popeye into my arms and planted a kiss on his head.

Jake gave me a noogie. "Night, Swee'Pea."

By the time I reached my yard and turned to wave, the fog had swallowed them up. Only the neon parrot rose luminous in the cottoned street. In the distance, I heard the whistle of a train.

Jake was as good as his word too, leastways for the next month, imparting some mean card skills to me, "less Swee'Pea and more Alfalfa," he ribbed, a little rascal with no shortage of gumption—and still not much of a lady. School days hadn't kept me from squeezing 'round the poker table Friday nights, Mama turning a blind eye, or keeping watch by the surf on a Saturday dawn. Though a little worse for wear— the wear being *Where did Anna hide the elixir now?*—Jake still rose like a sea god, on occasion gruff but ever the gent, and regular as rain.

℘

TWO WEEKS INTO September, after a tense poker night that saw the best showdown yet—Ernesto sweeping the pot with a royal flush to *huzzahs* and a jaunty harmonica riff for himself, Joe toleratin' the ruckus without even a smirk—I woke to discover Saturday had started without me, a sunlit butterfly tapping at my window, and dashed to the shore. Popeye sat at the water's edge, one ear perked, a paw on Jake's towel, nose twitching slightly. Hollis sat beside him, knees bent, chin resting on folded arms.

"No Jake yet?" I called, running up to them.

The sun had breached the horizon, baking the pair into stone, boy and dog, sculptures chiseled by wind and a gnawing ache. Neither moved to greet me as I dropped to the warm sand, scooting close to Popeye.

I shielded my eyes to survey the sea. "Hollis?"

No answer.

I tugged on his sleeve. "Hollis?"

Grabbing Jake's salt-crusted duffel bag, I did what I'd never dared—dumped out its contents: yesterday's *LA Times*, a pack of Marlboros, the tin flask, a half-eaten bologna sandwich, and a tatty leather wallet, inside an expired driver's license and a twenty-dollar bill. If I expected to find Jake himself, all I got was the ID photo, a younger Jake I might not have known 'cept for the roguery in his deep-set eyes.

"He has to finish his sandwich." My voice quavered.

In the silence that followed, all sound magnified, the slap of foamy waves, the cry of seagulls, the dull roar of surf, and my heart, a mounting *not yet, not yet* in my ears.

I buried myself in Popeye's matted fur. "He'll come, boy. He always does."

We waited, payin' scant notice to the sunbathers tramping past us and spreading striped towels, our gaze fixed on the horizon, straining to see, to see.

When it seemed we'd crack from the sun's smolder, crumble beneath the wait, Hollis kicked off his shoes, peeled off his T-shirt and jeans, and sprinted toward the sea, clad only in his shorts, his tattered hat sailing. I watched him dive into the cresting waves, his strokes taking him farther and farther out until he vanished, re-emerging small beside the buoy, bobbing and tossing alongside it, bell clanging, and then there was just the buoy, and Hollis was swimming back, stroke after stroke bringing him closer, and he was on his feet, ascending from the ocean depths, striding through the surf, walking toward us.

Popeye's floppy ear shot up, and letting out a yelp, he lunged, knocking Hollis down, the crazy hound a mess of wriggle, tail wagging, Hollis tusslin' with him, panting and rolling, a boy and his dog in embrace.

"That dog isn't too bright." My throat burned.

"Oh, I think he is," Hollis replied from beneath the licking mop, his voice muffled, his drenched curls caked with sand. "He knows he just has to wait long enough."

"That's ridiculous," I said, but even as I did, I felt a rush of tears course down my cheeks.

And then Hollis was pulling me to him, plunging me into the warm tangle of smelly fur and gritty paws and wet noses, wrapping his damp arms around us, cocooning me in a collision of bodies. And in this way, held together even as we fell apart, we bid Jake a last goodbye.

THIRTY-SEVEN

IN EXCHANGE FOR the hound's loyalty, Hollis had promised Popeye a seaside vigil every day for the duration of his old life, and Popeye had held him to it. That's how we found ourselves larkin' about my A− in US History and his C+ in English Comp that crisp October dawn, side by side on a beach towel, sucking donut crumbs off our fingers. Without fog to soften the glare, Hollis and I had to shield our eyes as morning rose over Harford Beach, the sun glancing off the sapphire sea, scattering flecks of light 'cross the horizon, amber rays warming us despite the chilly breeze.

From our sprawl near the waterline, we could see the arc of fishing rods over the pier railing, trace the cascading lines, the waves a steady slosh against the pilings. The storm-ravaged section had been replaced with new posts and an amber, fresh-cut wood that lay tiered in stark contrast to the ashen gray of the weathered rails, work yet to be done to buttress the weakened pilings. Kickin' up puffs of dry sand, Popeye barreled past us, hot on the trail of a menacing yellow-tailed kite, swerving with its low-flying zigzags and barking furiously.

"That dog has no sense."

"Oh, I think he does," I said, as the ferocious guard dog moseyed over, panting with victory, red gingham bandana wonky. Helping himself to most of the towel, he set a paw on my arm. "Well, blow me down! Hollis is bluffin'?"

"What have I got to bluff about?"

"Seems to me you said something 'bout catching us a big ol' halibut, like Smitty did last week."

Hollis chuckled. "Nearly pulled him over the rail."

"Well, is you or ain't you telling fibs?"

"Guess there's only one way to find out." He stood, brushed off his pants, and picked up his fishing rod. "You comin'?"

"I dunno." I squinted up at him. "You comin' to church tomorrow?"

"Thought you said your priest stepped down."

"Pastor, and just for now. He said it was about time the right things mattered." I ladled sand over Hollis's navy Chucks. "I reckon he meant Ben."

"Reckon so."

Hollis talkin' like me made me squint at him again.

℘

TO HEAR BEN tell it, they'd only meant to scare the commies away, stir up the town's suspicions—a score of swag here, a reversed street sign there, front doors pennied, mailboxes smashed. Then Vince had to pull the parking-lot stunt in the Old Clunker, forcing Ben to take the rap for nearly mowing Raven down. That's when things turned ugly, escalated to tagging the church with anti-American slurs and planting both spray paint and crowbar in her shed. Ben had only *borrowed* the gun—and, well, stolen a box of ammo—that fourth backbreaking Saturday, stashed inside a kindling bin, figurin' to return it after a little target practice at the off-trail dunes, no one the wiser—not even Vince. Plug a few kelp clumps, y'know?

But then that lousy morning, they'd barely made it into the waves before a cotton-mouthed Vince doubled back to the Old Clunker for Ben's canteen. Moments later, he came tearing down the beach, brandishing the gun he'd found wrapped in a towel behind the seat, demanding answers, accusing Ben of keeping secrets. When Vince aimed the gun at the seal, snickering about how *that'd* send the commies up the river, Ben had tried to wrestle it away, shoved Vince, took an elbow to the ribs, the scuffle spiraling fast. The gun went off—a friggin' fluke, Vince insisted, didn't even know it was loaded—got knocked to the sand and kicked far, Vince slingin' curses as Ben bolted with his board into the waves—minus his gold chain.

Ten yards out, he'd heard a yelp and looked back. Vince was running for the gun, but she'd gotten there first, the bird girl, scooping it up in her skirts. Shouting something in Russian, she pointed the barrel at Vince. He slammed to a halt, hands raised. She spun, wild eyes locking on Ben, and streaked toward the rocks. They couldn'ta planned it any better. Helluva lucky break. By then nearby surfers had reached the shallows, but Ben had already split, paddling around the bluff to the other side of the cove, scaling the cliffside unseen. Of course Vince would pin it all on him. But no matter what Vince swore, Ben would swear the opposite, and on a stack of Bibles too. Fact was that girl had the gun, with their prints all over it.

And the fire, well, musta started after they swiped the Russki vodka from the shed. No surprise, what with Vince always tossin' his cigs so careless. Had to be an accident, right? They'd hit the ravine for a little harmless fun, Vince, the rest of the gang, close enough to book it to the blaze. Another lucky break.

Things got outta hand that night at the carnival. Vince wanted the gun, said no matter which way you looked at it, it pointed to him, to them. They waited till the house was all clear, started with the bedrooms, working fast despite the stiff motorcycle gloves. Struck out twice, so Vince combed the living room while Ben braved the sticker patch to the Clampett shack. No way he'd get wasted enough to take Dex on a joyride, pull a stupid, mean-spirited stunt, claim the crippled kid as some sorta warped consolation prize. Hell no, that was all Vince, who'd chugged a beer from the fridge and lit down the street before Ben had escaped the weeds. Course Vince said he felt bad for the kid, hangin' solo in a dark house, just wanted to show him a good time, five minutes max, no one the wiser. Though Ben caught up quick, he hadn't the guts to stop Vince, not at first, not till the idiot busted through the barricades, laughing and popping wheelies, skidding dangerously close to the mangled edge. But Vince had gone too far. And this time Ben was gonna stop him. Damn right he'd jumped him, scared as all get-out for the both of 'em, him and that kid. Thank God no one went for a swim. Or maybe it was just a third lucky break. Then Vince came swinging.

It'd taken Hollis a ripped shirt and bloodied lip to separate them—and ribs so sore he refused to sneeze for a week.

"Woulda gotten there faster if I hadn't run the beach after Raven," he'd rued, nursing his bruised knuckles.

"Then the lot of you mighta joined Davy Jones. We thought she had Dex." He'd kicked at the sand, same as he was kicking himself. "The sheriff said you did mighty fine, clockin' Vince and collaring Ben." He'd seemed only slightly comforted.

Word had it that Rev. Travers had watched from the street as Ben got hauled down the pier, limping, eyes low, handcuffed alongside Vince, and rammed into the back of a squad car. Hadn't stepped in. Hadn't pressed upon the sheriff. No pleading his boy's innocence. Just stood in the shadows, still as a tombstone, Vince cussin' up a storm about commies, swearing he wasn't drunk, just patriotic as—well. A Smirnoff bottle wedged under the seat of the Old Clunker debunked that, thanks to the Honorable Mayor Mac, who, not wanting to be derelict in his mayoral duties, conducted a thorough investigation of the getaway vehicle abandoned by *his* firepits, the window conveniently cracked open, and submitted the evidence to the sheriff upon finding it sadly empty.

The reverend hadn't posted bail right away either, letting his prodigal sweat it out in juvie, a bleak concrete barracks on the outskirts of the city, while Vince stewed in the county jail, two blocks from Mama's clinic. There was no end to the charges—vandalism, animal cruelty, arson, child endangerment, public intoxication, conspiracy, obstruction of justice. And those were just for starters. No longer a minor, Vince druthered a plea deal, knowing a jury wouldn't do 'im no favors, his parents nowhere to be seen. Rumor had them sailing the Aegean Sea, but more like they'd washed their hands of him, a man now and responsible for his own undoing, nothin' but a blight on their reputation. He'd broken down at his hearing, a momentary lapse rectified with a defiant silence, and not a few LUV ladies made it their mission to rehabilitate the boy.

At seventeen, Ben dodged the worst of it, the charges reduced considerably but doing nothing to lift his spirits, standing before the judge more hangdog than a basset hound. Still, his father didn't do diddly-squat on his behalf. Just showed up to court, staid in his three-piece suit and horn-rimmed glasses, hands folded as if in prayer, the missus dabbing a hankie to her eyes, still offered not two words of imploration nor condemnation. Hadn't said bad company corrupts. Hadn't argued for leniency. Just let the chips fall: three months in juvenile hall, counseling, a year of probation, community service.

And if that wasn't surprise enough, when all was said and done, the reverend broke his silence, read a statement to the judge, saying his son deserved what was comin', but so did he, pastor or not, which wasn't a thing most folks expected—any more than the penny loafers sighted on his feet—the Mar Vista Chapel faithful crammed in the four-bench courtroom like a congregation on Easter, gathered to weave prayers, a basket for a Moses adrift. Nor did they approve of his faulting himself, if the murmurings were any indication, noble as it might be, contending that the father shouldn't have to pay for the sins of the son, but then I reckoned the reverend had his reasons.

℘

"Doesn't mean there's no church." I poured more sand over his shoe, shifting on the towel so that his lanky frame blocked the sun. "Last Sunday, a missionary from the Ecuadorean jungles gave a slideshow. Baptized an entire village in the Tena River, he did."

Hollis's whistling came to an abrupt stop. "You already baptized me, Scoot."

"That took care of your old sins. Now we gotta account

for your new ones. It's called subscribing to the faith." I stood and, though more than a head shorter than Hollis, looked him square in the eye. "Man does not live by fish alone."

His brows arched, then furrowed, his mouth workin' out a reply.

"Glory be, Hollis Sweet, you'd think I just asked you on a date."

"Well, between the two, s'pose I'll suffer church."

Quick as a wink, I snagged his bucket hat and raced for the water, waving it like a checkered Daytona flag, twisting and ducking as he grabbed for me. Popeye bounded ahead, his clumsy paws sending a flock of sandpipers skitterin' to shore, his barks mingled with my whoops. Overhead, seagulls squabbled with pigeons, jockeyed for space on the pier railing, the wooden beams crimson in the rising sun. Apart from the fracas, perched on rails wounded by wind and waves, a lone egret watched as we tumbled into the cascading foam. With a parting glance back, I saw her turn her gaze to sea, spread her white wings, and take flight.

ACKNOWLEDGMENTS

A WISE TEACHER has written that "of making many books there is no end" (Ecclesiastes 12:12), yet this foolish writer has persisted anyway. That you are here reading mine is indeed an honor and delight.

To quote another wise teacher, "It is not often that someone comes along who is a true friend and a good writer" (E. B. White). Charlotte did, after all, save Wilbur's life.

I hope that I'm a good writer, but I hope more that I'm a true friend. And if I am a good writer, or at least a writer of good, then it is largely in heartfelt thanks to the many who've supported me along the way.

To remember and credit all who have worked, in one way or another, behind the scenes is an impossible task, like naming the many stars that form a constellation. But I will touch on some of the brightest that helped lead the way and gave of themselves to make this novel happen.

Mrs. Phyllis Manley, my second-grade teacher who tesseracted me into realms unknown during the sacred hour after lunch when she read to us. Little did she know the miracle she wrought in the young girl who loved to live the lives of others: Meg Murry, Taran the wanderer, Lucy Pevensie, Karana, the Waterbury children, Wilbur the pig. Three years later, when I was placed in Mrs. Manley's combined fifth- and sixth-grade class, I felt like I'd hit the jackpot. To her I owe my love of story and the desire to likewise tesseract others to wondrous worlds.

M. S., a high school classmate as elusive, mysterious, and shunned as Raven, and who was also known by a curious nickname. Where my courage failed me in being the true friend I might have been, my imagination resolved to right my failings in the someday telling of a redemptive tale.

Daniel, my half brother, who entered this life in a body and mind severely disabled, but with a sweetness and goodness almost too beautiful to bear.

My writing tribe of lovely colleagues who have encouraged and inspired me, far too many to list here, but most faithfully Kelly Fernlake, Paige Reed, and Jeremiah Friedli.

My long-ago first readers who endured my early drafts, in particular those brave enough to look horrified and redirect my efforts. You know who you are, and I'm sorry to have put you through it. (Sarah L., Dawn D., Cheryl D., Helen R., Katie H., Kelly F.)

Those readers who helped refine the final story, most especially my sister Linda, whose answer to my never-ending requests for help was "Sure, I'll take a look" (bless you!), and her husband, Steve, who read an early draft and assisted with historical accuracy. Couldn't have done it without you, Steve.

The authors, agents, and editors who loved the story and advocated for me, specifically Sarah Sundin, Rachel McRae, and Karen Neumair. Despite the rigors of the industry, that you championed the novel gave me the strength to forge ahead. You are so very appreciated.

A special shout-out to those who gave me a helping hand at critical junctures: Jane Daly, Karen Grunst, Ginny Yttrup, Robin Sanny, Tia Jacinto, Dori Harrell, Katie Isaacs, Jayna Baas, and the inimitable Zena Dell Lowe. My heartfelt thanks to Cynthia Hickey and Winged Publications for giving this book a chance.

Enormous gratitude and love to my husband, Tom, for the simple kindness of tending to me in small and large ways so that I can write and who never bemoans attention for himself, content to do what he does best: see to the bills, weed the garden, buy the groceries, make my breakfasts and our dinners (granted, he wouldn't eat otherwise), wash the dishes, and drop everything the moment a voice hollers from upstairs, "Dear, I need to ask you something!" In this doing of the seemingly menial tasks year after year, the quiet acts of service, he has made my writing life possible, and in making my writing life possible, he has loved me. And if I didn't love him already, I'd love him for that.

I could go on—so many have contributed to this work. But for those who've shared this journey, please know that the debt of gratitude for my beloved parents (if I were to write about them, I would soak the paper in grateful tears), my immediate family, my closest friends is deep. Again, you know who you are and how much your love means to me.

I've left the last for the one person to whom I am most indebted, to whom I credit all that is polished in this book, from the plot to the voice to the writing to the "Think of a new word, Mom!" scoldings. I'd like to say that Ambria Florence, as my editor, has been my right-hand woman. But the truth is that she's been my right hand, period. She has loved this story from the start, immersed herself in its world, and given the characters life.

If not for her gumption, I may have allowed the manuscript to languish. And if not for her occasional "Don't cut that line—it's *so* funny!" pleas, *I* might have languished. We've had many a laugh ("Better luck next time, Mr. Chang!") and many a meltdown ("Fix it? *How?*"), but as we've come out the other side of this miracle-slash-debacle, there is one thing we can both say: We'll always have Eden.

Back to that first wise teacher: Solomon also writes that the words of the wise prod us toward right action and turn us toward the holy, for they are "given from one shepherd." It is that shepherd I write for and because of, in gratitude and in worship. There is no distance so far that should we turn, we will not find him waiting. For, as Meg Murry discovers, the ultimate tesseract is love.

S D G

A NOTE FROM CATE

Dear Reader,

Thank you for reading! Harford Beach wouldn't be the same without you.

If you enjoyed this book, please visit **www.catetouryan.com** and join my crew. As a subscriber to my quarterly newsletter, you'll be the first to receive my free short stories, publishing updates, and cover reveals. I also do fun giveaways throughout the year.

As a thank-you for hopping aboard, I'll send you a link to download my short story "The Gulch Run Gangster," a prequel to *Turning Toward Eden*. Read the print copy or listen to the audiobook as we travel back in time for a rollicking adventure with Jake and Anna.

Reviews: I'd be grateful if you could leave a review on your bookseller's website. Your thoughts mean the world to me and help other readers discover my work.

Connect: Did you love this book? Do you want a sequel? Let me know if you'd like to spend more time with Eden and Hollis in Harford Beach. You can find me under "Cate Touryan" on Facebook, Instagram, and X. You can also message me through my website.

ABOUT THE AUTHOR

"I COULD TELL you my adventures—beginning from this morning," says Alice.

And so could I, in adventures both true and almost true. But like Alice, if you aren't very careful, you might begin my stories as one person and end them as another, discovering stories beyond the story, endings never imagined but always wanted.

And that might be more than you bargained for—but everything I hoped for.

Is Harford Beach a real place? Yes, in a once-upon-a-memory way, and I live not too far from it on California's foggy but beautiful central coast with my husband, a flower garden, a charm of hummingbirds, a lounge of lizards, and a rafter of turkeys—as in a whole bunch of them *and* in the rafters.

DISCUSSION GUIDE

Turning Toward Eden explores family, friendship, and faith—as well as the quiet, powerful ways we come of age in the midst of loss and hope. Set against a richly drawn small-town backdrop, this novel invites readers to reflect not only on the lives of its characters but also on their own journeys.

The following questions are designed to spark conversation, deepen understanding, and connect readers with the themes of the story—whether in a classroom or a cozy book club circle.

For more discussion questions, visit www.catetouryan.com.

∽

1. THE CHICKEN AND THE BARNYARD CAT
Why does Anna tell the story of the chicken and the barnyard cat? What is this story a metaphor for, and how does it relate to Eden's life?

2. POE'S "THE RAVEN"
How does Edgar Allan Poe's poem "The Raven" mirror or contrast with Eden's experience—especially in her relationships with her father, Dex, and Liliya?

3. WAYS OF LEAVING
Reverend Travers says, "There are many ways we leave each other. And many reasons." What are some of those ways and

reasons in the novel? Can you relate this observation to your own life or people you know or once knew?

4. POPEYE'S PATIENCE

Hollis argues that Popeye "knows he just has to wait long enough." How might this principle help characters like Eden cope with disappointment or change? What are some things we, too, may just have to wait long enough for?

5. WHAT DEX KNOWS

Eden says Dex "doesn't know anything," but Rosa insists, "He know *mucho*. He know the heart." Who do you think is right— and what does it mean to "know the heart"?

6. UNDERSTANDING EDEN'S FATHER

What's really going on with Eden's father? Is he merely selfish, or does more lie beneath the surface? How do his feelings about Dex complicate his behavior?

7. BEN AND THE CRIMES

Ben's version of events points to Vince as the driving force. Do you believe he's telling the truth? Why or why not? What does his version—or his perception—of events reveal about guilt, influence, or denial?

8. LOVING THE UNLOVELY

Reverend Travers has told his congregation, "Nothing is more unlovely than a person who won't love the unlovely." When Eden's mother repeats this to her, the words begin to echo through her journey. Who in the story might be considered "unlovely," and who seems "lovely"? How does Eden's understanding of this saying evolve over time, and what does her increased awareness reveal about her growth?

9. What Eden Gets Wrong

Eden is wrong about many things throughout the story—some insignificant, some consequential. Hollis is one of the few people who challenge her. What are some things Eden misunderstands, and how do her mistaken notions shape her growth?

10. What Eden Comes to Understand

By the final chapter, what has Eden come to understand about herself, her family, love, loss, faith—and perhaps even God?

11. Camellias or Gardenias?

What's the significance of Eden realizing at the end that Liliya's camellias were actually gardenias? What might this moment symbolize in terms of perception, memory, or healing?

12. Turning Toward Eden—the Title

What are the layers of meaning embedded in the title *Turning Toward Eden*? Who else in the novel makes a "turn"? What are they turning from—and what are they turning toward?